Should a noble rogue choose
an acceptable bride...or pursue
true love to possible ruin?

D1013550

## "You'll decide whether to marry *me* on the basis of *his* kiss?"

*H*is words were a low growl, and hung on the air.

Eleanor let her head fall back and examined the hyacinth-colored sky. Villiers made a small movement next to her, and she felt a surge of power. She knew exactly what to do. She turned her head, just slightly. She didn't even smile at him; she just allowed the invitation to be in her eyes.

"Are you playing the siren with me?" he asked, his voice low, almost incredulous.

"Only for the space of the moon."

"You surprise me," he said, bending toward her. His lips tasted of anisette, like spice and like a man. She opened her mouth, remembering instantly how delicious a kiss could be. How the touch of lips could change the whole feeling of her body. She leaned toward him and gave him everything he wanted.

And he took it.

**By Eloisa James**

# Eloisa James

## A Duke of Her Own

**AVON**

*An Imprint of HarperCollinsPublishers*

AVON BOOKS
*An Imprint of* HarperCollins*Publishers*
10 East 53rd Street
New York, New York 10022-5299

First Avon Books paperback printing: August 2009

Avon Trademark Reg. U.S. Pat. Off. and in Other Countries, Marca Registrada, Hecho en U.S.A.
HarperCollins® is a registered trademark of HarperCollins Publishers.

Printed in the U.S.A.

10 9 8 7 6 5 4 3 2 1

This book is dedicated to all the readers who fell in love with the Desperate Duchesses series and begged me to write Extra Chapters for my website . . . When you finish reading *A Duke of Her Own*, stop by *eloisajames.com* and you'll find a final Extra Chapter that will catch up on every duchess and her beloved. I hope you enjoy it!

# Acknowledgments

My books are like small children; they take a whole village to get them to a literate state. I want to offer my heartfelt thanks to my personal village: my editor, Carrie Feron; my agent, Kim Witherspoon; my website designers, Wax Creative; and last, but not least, my personal team: Kim Castillo, Franzeca Drouin, and Anne Connell. A particular thanks for this book goes to Sylvie Clemot for her French translations. I am so grateful to each of you!

# Chapter One

*London's Roman Baths*
*Duchess of Beaumont's ball to benefit the Baths*
*June 14, 1784*

"The duke must be here somewhere," said Mrs. Bouchon, née Lady Anne Lindel, tugging her older sister along like a child with a wheeled toy.

"And therefore we have to act like hunting dogs?" Lady Eleanor replied through clenched teeth.

"I'm worried that Villiers will leave before we find him. I can't let you waste another evening chatting with dowagers."

"Lord Killigrew would dislike being identified as a dowager," Eleanor protested. "Slow down, Anne!"

"Killigrew's not eligible either, is he? His daughter is at least your age." Her sister turned a corner and peered at a group of noblemen. "Villiers won't be in that nest of Whigs. He doesn't seem the type." She set off in the opposite direction.

Lord Thrush called after them, but Anne didn't even pause. Eleanor waved helplessly.

"Everyone knows that Villiers came to this benefit specifically to meet you," Anne said. "I heard it from at least three people in the last half hour, so he might have been civil enough to remain in the open where he could be easily found."

"That would deny most of London the pleasure of realizing just how desperate I am to meet him," Eleanor snapped.

"No one will think that, not given what you're wearing," her sister said over her shoulder. "Rest assured: I would be surprised if you attained the label *interested,* let alone *desperate.*"

Eleanor jerked her hand from her sister's. "If you don't like my gown, just say so. There's no need to be so rude."

Anne swung around, hands on her hips. "I consider myself blunt, rather than rude. It would be rude if I pointed out that at first glance any reasonable gentleman would characterize you as a bacon-faced beldam, rather than a marriageable lady."

Eleanor clenched her hands so that she didn't inadvertently engage in violence. "Whereas you," she retorted, "look as close to a courtesan as Mother would allow."

"May I point out that my recent marriage suggests that a more tempting style might be in order? Your sleeves are elbow-length—with *flounces,*" Anne added in disgust. "No one has worn that style for at least four years. Not to mention that togas are *de rigueur,* since your hostess requested the costume."

"I am not wearing a toga because I am not a trained spaniel," Eleanor said. "And if you think that one-shoulder style is any more flattering to you than my flounces are to me, you are sadly mistaken."

"This isn't about me. It's about *you*. You. You and the question of whether you're going to spend the rest of your time in dowdy clothing simply because you were spurned in love. And if that sentence sounds like a cliché, Eleanor, it's because your life is turning into one."

"My life is a cliché?" Despite herself, Eleanor felt a tightness in the back of her throat that signaled tears. She and Anne had amused themselves for years with blistering fights, but she must be out of practice. Anne had been married for a whole two weeks, after all. With their youngest sister still in the nursery, there was no one to torment her on a daily basis.

Anne's face softened. "Just look at yourself, Eleanor. You're beautiful. Or at least you used to be beautiful, before—"

"Don't," Eleanor interrupted. "Just don't."

"Did you take a good look at your hair this evening?"

Of course she had. True, she had been reading while her maid worked, but she certainly glanced in the mirror before she left her chamber. "Rackfort worked very hard on these curls," Eleanor said, gingerly patting the plump curls suspended before her ears.

"Those curls make your cheeks round, Eleanor. Round, as in fat."

"I'm not fat," Eleanor said, taking a calming breath. "A moment ago you were insisting that I'm out of fashion, but these curls are the very newest mode."

"They might be among the older set," Anne said, poking at them. "But Rackfort's inadequate use of powder makes them anything but. For goodness sake, didn't you notice that she was using light brown curls, even though your hair is chestnut? It's oddly patchy where the powder has worn off. One might even say mangy. No one would think that you are the more beautiful of the two of us. Or that you're more beautiful than Mother ever was, for that matter."

"Not true!"

"True," her sister said indomitably. "I've begun to wonder why our mother, so very proud of her glorious past, allows you to dress like a dowager."

"Is this sourness the effect of marriage?" Eleanor said, staring at her sister. "You wed barely a fortnight ago. If this is the consequence of wedded bliss, I might do best to avoid it."

"Marriage gives me time to think." Anne smirked. "In bed."

"I feel truly sorry for you if your bedtime activities involve consideration of my wardrobe, not to mention Rackfort's lackluster hairdressing," Eleanor said tartly.

Anne broke into laughter. "I just don't understand why you dress like a prissy dowd when underneath you are quite the opposite."

"I am not—" Eleanor flashed, and caught herself. "And I don't understand why you are wasting time fussing over me when you have the very handsome Mr. Jeremy Bouchon claiming your attention."

"In fact, Jeremy and I discussed you. In a slow moment, as it were."

"You didn't!"

"We both agree that men don't look past your dowdy clothing. Jeremy says he never even considered the possibility of courting you. He thought you an eccentric, too pious and haughty even to take notice of him. You, Eleanor! He thought that of *you*. How ridiculous!"

Eleanor managed to bite back her opinion of her brother-in-law. "We're in the middle of a ball," she pointed out. "Wouldn't you be more comfortable sharing Jeremy's charming commentary later, in private?"

"No woman here has eyes like yours, Eleanor," her sister said, ignoring her comment entirely. "That dark blue is most unusual. I wish I had it. And they turn up at the corners. Don't you remember all those absurd poems Gideon wrote comparing your eyes to stormy seas and buttercups?"

"Not buttercups," Eleanor said. "Bluebells, though I don't see how this is relevant."

"Your mouth is just as lovely as it was years ago. Back before the buttercup king himself left for greener pastures."

"I don't like to talk about Gideon."

"I've obeyed you for three, almost four, years, but I'm tired of it," Anne replied, raising her voice again. "I'm a married woman now and you can't tell me what to do. Granted, you fell in love—"

*"Please,"* Eleanor implored. "Keep your voice down, Anne!"

"You fell in love with a man who turned out to be a bad hat," her sister said, albeit a bit more quietly. "But what I don't understand is why Gideon's rejection has resulted in your becoming a squabby old maid. Do you really intend to wither into your grave mourning that man? Will you have no children, no marriage, no household of your own, *nothing*, all because Gideon left you?"

Eleanor felt as if the air actually burned her lungs. "I shall probably—"

"Just when *are* you planning to marry? At age twenty-five, or thirty? Who will marry you when you're that old, Eleanor? You may be beautiful, but if you don't make an effort, no one will notice. In my experience, men are not terribly perceptive." She leaned forward, peering. "You aren't wearing even a touch of face paint, are you?"

"No," Eleanor said. "None." Of course she wanted children. And a husband. It was just that she wanted Gideon's children. She was a *fool*. Seven times a fool. Gideon was not hers, and that meant his children wouldn't be either. How on earth had the years passed so quickly?

"I am not finished," her sister added. "There's not a bit of your bosom to be seen, and your skirts are so long they're practically dragging in the mud. But it's your attitude that really matters. You look like a prude, and you jest and poke at men. They don't like it, Eleanor. They flee in the other direction, and why shouldn't they?"

"No reason." Eleanor resorted to praying that Anne would run out of words, though she saw no sign of it.

"Everyone thinks you're a snob," her sister said flatly. "All of London knows that you swore not to marry anyone below the rank of a duke—and they don't think well of you for it. At least the men don't. In one fell swoop you made almost every eligible man in London think you are a condescending prig."

"I merely intended—"

"But now there's a duke on the market," Anne said, overriding her. "The Duke of Villiers, no less. Rich as Croesus and apparently just as snobbish as you are, since everyone says he's intent on marrying a duke's daughter. That's you, Eleanor. You. I'm married, Elizabeth is still in the nursery, and there isn't another eligible lady of our rank in London."

"I realize that fact."

"You're the one who announced that you'd marry no one below the order of a duke," Anne continued, scarcely pausing for breath. "You said there were no eligible dukes and then one appeared like magic, and everyone says that he's thinking of marrying you—"

"I don't see anything particular to celebrate in that," Eleanor retorted. "Those same people describe Villiers as quite unpleasant."

"You said you'd marry no one but a duke," her sister repeated stubbornly, "and now there's one fallen into your hand like a ripe plum. It wouldn't matter if the duke were as broken down as a cart horse, or so you always said."

Eleanor opened her mouth and then realized with some horror that the Duke of Villiers was standing just behind her sister's shoulder.

"Remember dinner last Twelfth Night? You told Aunt Petunia that you'd marry a man who smelled of urine and dog hair if he had the right title, but no one below a duke."

Eleanor had never met the Duke of Villiers; nay, she had never even seen Villiers, but she had no doubt but that she was facing him now. He was precisely as described, with the kind of jaw and cheekbones that wavered between brutish and beautiful. By all accounts, Villiers never wore a wig, and this man didn't even wear powder. His black hair was shot with two or three brilliant streaks of white and tied back at the neck. It couldn't be anyone else.

Her sister just kept going, with the relentless quality of a bad dream. "You said that you would marry a duke over another man, even if he were as stupid as Oyster and as fat as Mr. Hendicker's sow."

The Duke of Villiers's eyes were a chilly blackish-gray, the color of the evening sky when it threatened snow. He didn't look like a man with a sense of humor.

"Eleanor," Anne said. "Are you listening to me? Aren't you—" She turned. "Oh!"

# Chapter Two

The Duchess of Beaumont was standing beside Villiers, obviously fighting to suppress her laughter. "Good evening, Lady Eleanor. And Lady Anne, though I really must call you Mrs. Bouchon now, mustn't I? I have been looking everywhere for the two of you. May I present to you His Grace, the Duke of Villiers."

"Your Grace," Eleanor said, sinking into a deep curtsy before the duchess. Anne gave something of a bob, since she was hampered by her toga. "And Your Grace." Eleanor curtsied again, this time before the Duke of Villiers.

Like herself, the duke had eschewed the compulsory toga, presumably with the same insouciance with which he refused to wear a wig. Instead he was wearing a coat of heavy, brandy-colored silk. The cut was simple, but the embroidered vine in coppery silk that danced among his buttons and around the hem turned simplicity to magnificence.

"Lady Eleanor," Villiers said. He looked at her from head to foot, his eyes pausing for a moment on the curls next to her ears. A blaze of humiliation went down her spine, but she raised her chin. If the duke wanted nobility, she had it. Elegance, no. Blood, yes.

When Eleanor had fixed on the idea of insisting that she marry a duke or no one, she wasted no time imagining a potential suitor. She had intended her proclamation to reach the ears of one duke—a *married* duke—so he would realize that even though he had been untrue to her, she would hold true to him. It was a stupid strategy that had hurt no one but herself, obviously.

The Duke of Villiers was altogether a different order of duke from Gideon. She had not known, would never have been able to imagine, such a potent mix of elegance and carelessness. It wasn't the silk embroidery, or the sword stick, or the careless power about him. She hadn't imagined the pure raw masculinity of him: the brooding look in his eyes, the jaded lines around his mouth, the width of his chest.

If Gideon looked like a prince in a fairy tale, Villiers was the tired, cynical villain who would try to usurp the throne.

"I gather that you heard my sister teasing me about my childhood wish to marry a duke," she said. "I do apologize if you felt your consequence reduced by comparison to Mr. Hendicker's sow."

"Oh, Villiers never experiences such awkward emotions, do you?" the Duchess of Beaumont said, laughing.

"I was more intrigued by the idea of being stupider than an oyster," Villiers said. He had a deep voice, the kind that made Eleanor instinctively wary. It wasn't the voice of a man who could be led; he would always lead. "How does one determine the intelligence of such a silent creature?"

"Oyster is Eleanor's puppy," Anne put in.

"In that case, it would depend on Oyster's breed," Villiers said. "Unless you have a pet poodle, I am fairly sure that I exceed expectations on both counts."

"I can also assure Lady Eleanor that you never smell like urine, although I gather she is gracious enough to overlook that in a spouse," the duchess said with a giggle. "Now if you'll forgive me, I must introduce Mrs. Bouchon to my second cousin's daughter; the poor dear hardly knows a soul in London. And you must tell me all about your marriage and the wonderfully successful season you've had . . ." She drew Anne's arm through hers and began leading her away without further farewell.

"It appears that we are both looking for the same thing," Villiers observed.

"A spouse?" Eleanor still felt so shaken by her conversation with her sister that she could hardly formulate a coherent thought. She had thought of herself as presenting a modest appearance. Demure. Virginal. But Anne made her feel like a balding old maid.

"A spouse of a certain rank," Villiers qualified.

Eleanor felt a stomach-churning qualm of embarrassment and took recourse in sarcasm. "Now all that is left is to assess each other against such criteria as the weight of a sow, or the brains of a poodle."

"In truth, I would rather not marry someone with less intelligence than the aforementioned Oyster."

"I never pee on the floor when irritated," Eleanor told him.

"You can have no idea how pleased I am to hear that," Villiers said. Perhaps his eyes weren't quite as frosty as they first appeared. "In that case, I have no cause to query the intelligence of our future offspring."

Her sister was wrong. She could talk to men without

sniping at them. Absolutely she could. "You play chess, don't you?" she ventured. It was one of the few things she knew about Villiers: that he was ranked number one in the London Chess Club.

"Yes. Do you?"

"I used to play with my brother when we were young."

"Viscount Gosset? He's a decent player."

Eleanor personally thought that her brother was a terrible player, but she smiled anyway.

"I am more curious about why you set your cap for a duke, to use the vulgar phrase," Villiers said. "When I first heard of your requirement, I assumed you were driven by pride. But you don't appear to be quite as high in the instep as a young woman with such stringent ambitions ought to be."

Anne was right. Her foolish comment had given her the reputation of a turkey cock. She managed a smile. "Ducal marriages are a matter of precedence and fiscal responsibility. Since I am uninterested in forging an alliance based on anything less practical, I decided quite early that I would like to marry a duke."

"Admirably succinct."

If quite untrue. Eleanor raised an eyebrow. "And you? Why do you care for the status of your wife, given that you will make her a duchess by marriage?"

He looked her directly in the face. "I have six illegitimate children."

Eleanor felt her mouth slip open, and snapped her teeth together. Was she supposed to congratulate him? "Oh," she ventured.

"I wish to marry someone who will not only mother my bastards, but launch them into proper society when the appropriate time comes. The Beaumonts have assured me that no woman below your rank will be able to cow the *ton* to the extent that I demand. You needn't look so surprised. I assure you that many men at this ball have a bastard or two being raised in the country."

There was something extraordinarily annoying about the way he paused after that, as if expecting her to scream and faint. "One or two . . . versus *six*," she said musingly. "I gather you have led a life of rather extraordinary dissipation."

"I'm not as young as I look."

"You don't look very young," she observed.

"I see you're not expecting to charm your way into a title."

"Given your family situation, I think most people would agree that the burden of charm falls on you. Are you planning to legitimize your children?"

"I couldn't do that without marrying one of their mothers."

"More than *one* mother is involved?"

"Dear, dear," Villiers said. "That was almost a yelp, Lady Eleanor. We seem to be attracting some attention; perhaps we might stroll down a path."

She glanced to one side, only to meet the avid eyes of Lady Fibblesworth standing with the Earl of Bisselbate. Of course, their meeting would be extraordinarily interesting to most of London, given the rumors about Villiers's hunt for a wife. She threw the couple a stiff smile and tucked her hand into the duke's arm.

"I had assumed that the children were the offspring of your mistress," she said a moment later, when they were far enough away to be out of earshot.

"Oh, they are," he said. "Four mistresses. Have you examined the baths yet?"

"The baths are not open to the public until after restoration," Eleanor said. "I understand that the tiles are in delicate condition."

"Surely you know that marriage to a duke allows one to flagrantly ignore rules of this sort?" he asked, turning toward the ruined baths at the entrance to the gardens.

"My father is quite punctilious."

"No breaking the rules constructed for ordinary mortals?" He sounded bored.

"And no illegitimate children," she said, allowing her voice just a touch of frost.

"Touché!"

The Roman baths were guarded by a phalanx of footmen, but apparently they knew the duke. At any rate, they moved silently to the side as Villiers approached. Eleanor looked about her with some curiosity. The baths had been fully enclosed at some point in the past, of course. But now a wall had fallen in and was replaced by a thick hedge of what seemed to be lilac, though it wasn't blooming.

The duke led her across cracked tiles scattered higgledy-piggledy on the ground. Eleanor slipped her hand from his arm and stooped to pick one up. It was indigo blue and painted with a silver arabesque.

"How lovely!"

"That deep blue color seems to be rare," Villiers said. He looked around on the ground. "Pity; I don't see more of the same."

Eleanor sighed and bent to put it carefully in its place.

"Don't you like it?"

"Of course."

"Take it."

Eleanor raised an eyebrow. "We're at a ball to benefit the baths' restoration. As I recall, the king just described it as one of the nation's greatest unknown monuments. And you're telling me to steal part of the floor?" She began walking forward again.

There were fewer torches here, and the sound of a

minuet being played by the orchestra grew fainter as they walked among the pillars. Some were broken, but many remained, the starry sky seeming to offer a fanciful roof.

"The actual bath is down here," the duke said, taking her arm again to steer her down a shallow flight of stairs.

"It's delightfully warm." Moist air was rising from below. Eleanor walked down the last step and stopped. "And beautiful. Like a purple sea."

The bath was a large square basin, surrounded by soft cushions. Its entire surface, every square inch of water, was covered with violets. Their scent rose gently from the warm water.

"I gather that Elijah plans a private celebration this evening," Villiers said behind her.

She turned her head. "Elijah?"

"The Duke of Beaumont."

"Of course."

"I expect you don't know his personal name since he married years ago and thus wasn't eligible as a husband." His voice was silky but annoying.

She cast him a glance. "I don't know your name either."

"That seems remarkably careless," he remarked. "Narrowing your choices to dukes, and then not bothering to investigate their personal details."

"There aren't so very many of you," she observed.

"But I would have expected that fact might make your research on the subject more passionate. After all, you are no debutante, Lady Eleanor."

Apparently he also shared Anne's opinion of her advanced age. "I am two-and-twenty. I will be three-and-twenty in a matter of a month or so."

"And you reached this age without investigating

the limited group of men into which you had vowed to marry?"

"Yes." She walked down the last few steps. Pulling back her skirts, she scooped up a few violets in her hand.

He followed her. "You're not really interested in marrying a duke, are you, Lady Eleanor?"

"Not particularly." She pretended to smell the wet blossoms in her hand.

"Why not?"

The words hung in the damp air. She instinctively looked about the baths to see if there was anyone who might be able to hear them.

Villiers descended another step and stopped beside her. "Are you already married?"

She smiled faintly. "No." She met his eyes. "Quite the opposite."

"The opposite?" He knit his brow. "Am I to understand that you have announced your intention to marry a duke so as to lower expectations regarding your availability for marriage?"

"Exactly."

"And yet you are willing to consider matrimony with me? After all, you didn't turn on your heel, not even after my alarming revelation."

She let one of the flowers drift from her fingers, watching it rather than meeting his eyes. "I was young and impetuous when I announced my ambition to marry a duke."

"Surely you knew that the chance of a nobleman of the correct rank declaring himself was slim."

"Of course."

"You declared that you would marry a duke or no one, knowing full well that no one was likely to propose, since there are so few of us. I see."

"You *do*?"

"As you reminded me, I'm not young. I have seen a great deal and I certainly understand desire."

"Oh." Eleanor was a bit uncertain about what had happened to the subject of their conversation. "Are you saying that you understand *my* desire?"

"You should not throw your life away, Lady Eleanor, simply because you love elsewhere."

"How did you know that?" She looked up at him.

"You just told me."

"I did?" He had remarkably heavy-lidded eyes, lazy and seemingly uninterested, and yet apparently they saw everything.

"I am not a conventional man," Villiers stated.

With a start, Eleanor realized that if she did decide to marry the duke, she'd have to discuss the question of virginity or, specifically, her lack thereof. "Given your promiscuous progeny, I agree that you have no claim to conventionality."

One corner of his mouth quirked up. It had a remarkably beautiful shape, actually. "Oh, you'd be surprised. Men do the most interesting things in their private time and yet disparage women who commit even a tenth of the follies they enjoy."

"That's true." Gideon was the only man she knew who was punctilious as a Puritan when it came to virtue, as passionate about his honor as he had been about her.

"My point is that I am not a prude when it comes to human desire. I know how inconvenient it can be."

Inconvenient was an odd word for the way love for Gideon had shaped her life, but she saw his point.

Villiers tipped up her chin. "If you help me with my children, rear them, be kind to them, and fight society's belief that they are unworthy of the huge settlements I intend to give them, I will be lenient with regard to your personal life."

"You mean—"

"I would ask you to tolerate me only long enough to produce an heir."

"In fact, I want children," she said. She did want children. And for all Villiers's tolerance, she had no intention of straying from her marital vows, once she made them. After all, Gideon showed no interest. He had barely met her eyes these last three years. She knew he was at the ball tonight only because Anne told her. He hadn't searched her out, and of course she hadn't looked for him.

And more to the point, if she took vows, she would keep to them. Just as she had tried to keep to the vows she and Gideon had said to each other, private though they were.

Villiers smiled and the shape of his mouth caught her eye again. "I appreciate your saying so."

"You *appreciate* it?"

He nodded. "Like any other duke, I need an heir. But other than that, I must say that I have no deep desire for children."

"And yet you have so many," she observed.

"Carelessness," he said.

"Stupidity," she said, before she could bite her tongue.

"That too," he agreed. "I need an heir, but I would be perfectly happy to live an amicable existence with a wife who had no interest in my charms, such as they are. Although I would ask that you be discreet."

Without question this was the most shocking conversation she had ever had. Her mother would have fainted a good five minutes ago. "Will you do the same?"

"Will I add even more miscellaneous children to the household?" And, when she nodded, "Absolutely not. I am keenly aware of the idiocy of my imprudent attitude toward conception." He paused. "You might not be aware of this, but there are ways to prevent conception;

as a young man, I simply didn't care to employ those methods."

She nodded again. She knew them.

His eyes narrowed. "What an interesting young lady you are, Lady Eleanor."

"Why have you decided to house your own children?"

"I nearly died last year of a wound sustained in a duel." His voice was flat, uncommunicative. "I fought that duel for the honor of my fiancée, and lost."

"Apparently, you lost the fiancée as well," she put in dryly, trying to avoid any sort of melodramatic revelation.

Sure enough, his mouth eased. "True. The Duchess of Beaumont's brother, the Earl of Gryffyn, won the girl and the duel, leaving me with a wound that nearly carried me off."

"Whereupon you made a deathbed vow to marry?"

His eyelashes flickered. They were very long eyelashes.

"No," she guessed. "You made a deathbed vow to rear your own children."

"That was it," he confirmed. "The damnable thing about it was that I turned out to be not entirely sure where those children were."

"Beyond carelessness," she said. "That's disgraceful."

"I had been paying for them." He abruptly stooped down and snatched up a handful of flowers, sending a small wave across the pool. "When I demanded their addresses, my solicitor handed me a partial list and disappeared, along with many hundreds of pounds, I might add."

"How very odd."

"It seems that he had gradually removed the children from their lodgings and placed them elsewhere, pocketing the money I provided for their upkeep." Villiers threw the blossoms back toward the pool. They rained down into the blanket of violets.

"Not the workhouse!"

"Less scrupulous places," he said evenly. "A workhouse might have explored parentage, after all. To this point I have located my son Tobias, who was working as a mudlark, gathering valuables from the bottom of the River Thames."

"Damn," she said. Quietly, but she said it.

"A lady who swears?" He had that mocking tone in his voice again.

She ignored him. "How old is Tobias?"

"Thirteen. I recently found Violet, who is six, living in a brothel. I believe she is too young to know what lay in wait for her. She is untouched."

Eleanor shuddered. "Horrible."

"Colin is eleven years old, and had been apprenticed to a weaver."

"That's three . . . where are the others? And where are their mothers?"

"Well, you see," he said grimly, "I offered to take the children away from their mothers at birth. I thought that they would be better off under my care than they might be under the care of a courtesan."

"The irony is rather distressing."

"One of those mothers refused; Genevieve lives with her mother in Surrey."

"So Genevieve is well."

"Yes. My solicitor had ceased to pay support for the child, but her mother managed to scrape by."

"In her former employment?"

He shook his head. "Taking in washing."

There was something quite hard about his voice, the

kind of hardness that concealed deep shame, she guessed. Since he deserved every ounce of that shame, she didn't bother with soothing pleasantries.

"So that's Tobias, Genevieve, Colin, and Violet. What fanciful names. There are two more? Why haven't you fetched them?" Which was a tactful way of asking why he was at the ball at all, under the circumstances.

"They are twin girls. And I've been looking."

"You can't find them?"

"I have Bow Street Runners searching for them. They did find the woman who originally cared for them, but she has no idea where they were taken. She was merely told they were being sent to an orphanage. It turns out there are a great many orphanages in England, and a surprising number of twins."

"Surely . . . their surnames, their parentage?"

"My solicitor, Templeton, never shared information as to their parentage. Apparently that is common practice, as it does not allow the nurse to appeal directly to the father, who prefers to ignore the child's existence."

She sighed and walked back up the stairs. The air was too moist, and the last thing she needed was for her inadequately powdered hair to start curling in all directions.

Villiers kept pace with her, his long legs sending him effortlessly upward. "I heard just this morning that twins of approximately the right age are living in an orphanage in the village of Sevenoaks, in Kent."

"Lady Lisette Elys, daughter of the Duke of Gilner, lives nearby and might be able to help you. She does a great deal of work with the poor."

"How . . ." He paused. "How odd. I had considered paying a visit to the duke."

She said the obvious. "Lisette is the only other eligible duke's daughter of whom I'm aware, given that my sister

Elizabeth is only fourteen. Ducal progeny is quite rare, and when one is shopping for a wife, one ought to inspect all the available merchandise."

"Are you encouraging me to pay a visit to the Gilner estate?" he asked curiously.

She looked up at him. He wasn't beautiful. He was the opposite of Gideon, the man whom she loved with all her heart. Gideon had golden ringlets that curled at his neck like angel kisses. In fact, Gideon wasn't like any other man she knew, more like a true angel, with his ethical heart and his serious blue eyes.

This duke . . . this one was no angel. Villiers was all human, in his flaws, in the deep lines by the side of his mouth, the crinkles at his eyes that didn't look as if they came from smiling. He talked without shame of his illegitimate children. He was a man. No angel, a man.

And not even a very good man.

"I am fond of Lisette. Perhaps she would be a better duchess than I." She couldn't make herself care very much what Villiers decided. Though Anne's prickly comments were in the back of her mind, poking her, reminding her that she ought to make an effort to marry. Why not marry this duke?

"I would be a very comfortable type of husband," he said, clearly trying to be persuasive, though he sounded merely repetitive. It was a typically foolish male comment, because no one could look twice at the Duke of Villiers and imagine that living with him would be comfortable.

"I begin to think that you protest too much," she said, smiling. "I suspect you're a tyrant in private life."

"Never having had anyone to tyrannize, I can hardly defend myself. Did you know that your eyes are the exact color of wet violets? You must trail a string of broken hearts, given your provocative declaration as regards marriage."

Eleanor discovered that she had accidentally crushed the few blossoms she had carried away with her, and dropped them. "Not provocative as much as overly proud. And I have never found that men experienced a great deal of sorrow at the idea of not marrying me." She had been stupid to think that modest clothing would attract the right man, an honorable man. Perhaps just the right man had been in London, but had rejected her, based on her starchy reputation.

She could flaunt her bosom and chase men up and down shady alleys. Or she could just marry the duke in front of her, since he was there. At hand. Women had married for worse reasons.

"Are yours nice children?" she asked.

He blinked. "I haven't the faintest idea."

"Didn't you say that three of them are now in your nursery?"

"Yes."

"Surely you have visited them? I would imagine that moving from brothel to ducal town house would be rather shocking."

"Did your father pay visits to the nursery?"

"Yes, he did. Though more often we were summoned to the drawing room."

"I haven't got around to summoning them yet," Villiers said, an uneasy look in his eye. "My housekeeper found some nannies and I assume everyone is comfortable."

Eleanor didn't like the sound of that. She thought it unlikely that the duke's household had simply absorbed the presence of three bastard children without significant upheaval. Servants tended to be far more conservative than their masters. The *ton* would surely look askance at the presence of such children under the duke's roof once they learned of it, which meant that his servants were probably mutinying belowstairs. Not that it was her business. Still . . .

"I have meant to visit Lisette these past two years," she said, surprising herself.

He bowed. "Perhaps I might meet you in Sevenoaks."

Eleanor put her fingers on his outstretched arm. "I shall have to ask my mother, Your Grace. She may not be free to accompany me to Kent."

He smiled down at her. He knew as well as she did that her mother would throw all her engagements to the wind in order to further a marriage between the Duke of Villiers and her daughter, but he was polite enough not to point it out. "Of course."

"She will not be happy to learn of your family," she observed, in a coda to the unspoken question of her mother's approval of any prospective betrothal.

"Which makes it all the more surprising to discover that you are so calmly accepting of their existence. It seems you resemble neither your father nor your mother, Lady Eleanor."

"I am certainly temperamentally different from my parents. And you, do you resemble your parents?"

"They are both dead. I hardly knew my father, and had very little to say to my mother." There was something in his voice that did not welcome further enquiry on that front.

"Where is your country seat?" she asked.

He looked down at her and said, "You really don't know anything about me, do you?"

"Why should I?"

"There are so few dukes that I know quite a lot about them without even trying. I believe your brother is great friends with young Duke of Astley, for example."

"Indeed." She climbed the stairs.

"I haven't seen Astley in a few years," Villiers said. "I suppose you know him well."

"As you say, he is friends with my brother. He spent a great deal of time with us while we were all growing up," Eleanor said steadily. "Of course now that he's married, we see him much less frequently. I believe we shall find my mother in the refreshments tent."

"You should probably remove this curl," he said. With a start, she realized that one of the fat curls Rackfort had pinned into her hair was dangling by one pin alone. Villiers's fingers brushed her cheek; he twisted and the curl lay in his palm.

"It looks like a country slug," Eleanor said. She pulled off the other one as well.

"As opposed to a city slug?"

"A city slug would be wearing powder," she said, smiling at him. She tossed the slugs into a nearby hedge.

He almost smiled back. She could see it in his eyes.

"Would you like me to escort you to your mother?"

If the duke arrived at her mother's side, with Eleanor on his arm, rumors of a betrothal would flare through London. "I believe not," she said. "I shall consider the matter, Your Grace. Perhaps, if I decide to continue our acquaintance, I shall pay a visit to Kent."

"You are truly a very interesting woman," he said slowly.

"I assure you that you are quite mistaken. I am positively tedious in almost every respect."

"Not so. Do you know how unusual it is for a duke— myself—to speak to an eligible young lady without the woman in question making an overt expression of fierce interest?"

"I do apologize if I insulted you again," she said. "First I compared you to an incontinent canine, and now I have apparently not marshaled the proper enthusiasm."

His eyes *did* smile, even though his mouth didn't curl. "Does that apology mean you are mustering enthusiasm for my charms?"

"I expect we feel precisely the same way about each other," she said. "Cautiously interested. It appears that I suit your criteria, and you seem to suit mine, such as they are."

"A group of people is coming our way," he said, moving back slightly into the shadow of a pillar. "If you wish to retreat to your mother's side without being observed with me, you ought to leave."

She turned to go and his deep voice stopped her. "I set out for Sevenoaks in two or three days, Lady Eleanor. I would be—"

She looked back at him. "Yes?"

"I would be quite sorry not to meet you there."

She curtsied. "Good evening, Your Grace."

"Leopold," he said.

"What?"

"My name. It's Leopold." And with a quick glance at the group wandering toward them, he melted backward between the pillars and was gone.

# Chapter Three

*L*ady Eleanor might not have caught the connotations of that pool full of violets, but the Duke of Villiers certainly did. Once this party was over, his friend Elijah planned to lure his wife, Jemma, down into that fragrant bathtub and seduce her.

Villiers found himself smiling into the dark. He didn't give a damn what Elijah and Jemma got up to. After spending months mooning over Jemma like a sick calf, it was a pleasure to think of her without a surge of desire and jealousy.

Lady Eleanor Lindel, daughter of the Duke of Montague, might well complete his cure. She was certainly Jemma's opposite. Jemma was tall, slender, and duchesslike. Her every move signaled patrician blood enhanced by beauty, intelligence, and exquisite taste in clothing.

But Eleanor? She wasn't proud, as he had assumed when he heard of her express desire to marry a duke. Her clothing was abominable. And she clearly didn't give a damn about her appearance, considering the way she had tossed those curls into the bushes.

If Jemma was slender, Eleanor was curvy, with lush lips that resembled those of a naughty opera dancer. He could have sworn she wasn't wearing lip color, although her mouth was a deep rose that hardly seemed possible in nature.

People's faces tended to match their attire: a woman with a severe profile generally adorns herself with equally stern clothing, even though he himself chose to emphasize the rough character of his nose and chin by wearing outrageously luxurious garments. But Eleanor's mouth didn't match her prim attire and absurd curls. She was as mismatched as he was, albeit in a different key.

She looked acerbic. Peppery. Delectable. As if she'd get bored with chess, toss the board to the side, and climb into a man's lap.

Though presumably she'd be unlikely to climb into *his* lap, since she was pining for another man. In truth, he had given up hope of that sort of adoration. And certainly he had never wanted it from a wife.

He pushed himself away from the wall. He ought to go home and plan his trip to Sevenoaks. He was itching to be on the road, but the Bow Street Runner had sent the name of the orphanage only that morning. After the third disappointment, he'd learned to wait until the presence of twins was confirmed before haring off to check their lineage.

"Villiers!"

He turned to find Louise, Lady Nevill, waving at him. She was standing with his former fiancée, Roberta, now the Countess of Gryffyn. That betrothal had been a profound mistake, but, thank God, one from which he'd escaped. And now that Roberta was happily married, they exchanged civil conversation on occasion.

"Villiers," Roberta cried, holding out her hand. "I am so happy to see you looking so well. You were still terribly thin last time we met."

Lady Nevill gave him a lazy smile, accompanied by an appreciative survey from head to foot. "Roberta, darling," she drawled, "the man certainly isn't looking thin. Though I wouldn't call him precisely *padded* either." Her gaze lingered for just a second at his crotch.

Louise was wearing what he thought must be the only low-cut toga in existence. Her lush breasts threatened to spill free at any moment. "Roberta and I are amusing ourselves by comparing men to types of food," she announced.

"Louise says that Albertus Vesey resembles a stick of asparagus," Roberta said with a gurgle of laughter.

Villiers raised an eyebrow. "Given his girth, I would suggest a melon."

"Believe me," Louise said, "you should be thinking about asparagus. That rather exotic white kind." Her eyes twinkled wickedly. "Pale, slim . . . overcooked. Limp."

"Hush, Louise," Roberta said. "You'll make Villiers blush. Now what kind of food would the duke be?" They both looked him over.

"Neither of you has sufficient knowledge to assess my vegetable," he told them.

"Then you describe it for us," Louise suggested with a twinkle.

Roberta laughed and changed the subject. But it made him think just how long it had been since any woman—at least an available woman—had greeted him with Eleanor's profound lack of interest. In truth, it had been years since he encountered indifference.

He did not have pretentions when it came to his appearance. His face was ugly, to put it bluntly. But his title was beautiful, and the shine of his gold even more attractive, and the combination had delivered to him woman after woman.

"Your Grace," Lady Nevill said, tapping him on the arm with her fan. The lazy, sweet tone of her voice put her in the interested category, though in this case it was not for his gold or his title. Louise was married, after all, although her husband was incapacitated. "I have been told that you are looking for a wife."

"I never cease to be amazed at the triviality of conversation amongst the *ton*," Villiers said, by way of reply.

"I'm grateful for the early warning; it gives me time to rehearse my condolences once you find an appropriate lady," his former fiancée said with a smirk.

"Well, I would admit to being surprised," Louise put in. "After Roberta threw you over, I thought you would never succumb to the parson's mousetrap."

"Villiers is a *man*," Roberta said to her friend. "By definition he is in need of someone to look after him." She turned back to him. "I heard a rumor that you are considering no one below a duke's daughter. Should I be complimented, since I was apparently eligible last year, even given my lowly birth?"

"I just had a conversation with Lady Eleanor, the Duke of Montague's daughter," he admitted, ignoring her question. "And I'm traveling to Kent later this week."

"Lady Eleanor would be an admirable choice. But Lady Lisette . . ." Louise's tone cooled. Apparently, she didn't care for Gilner's daughter.

"And I intend to retrieve two of my six children and bring them back to be reared under my own roof." He knew he shouldn't enjoy Louise's dropped jaw quite as much as he did. But there it was: he had learned to enjoy the petty pleasures of astonishing the *ton*.

"Good for you!" Roberta said, without turning an eyelash. Since she was raising her husband's illegitimate son, he would expect no less. "It seems you are combining business with . . . business while in Kent. While I am all in favor of your rearing your own children, Villiers, I'm not quite as sanguine about your method of courting. You are as deliberate as Damon when he surveys mares he thinks to buy. Did you choose me with equally rigorous logic?"

"You were an impulse. And a lovely one."

She liked that. "I haven't met Lady Lisette. Of course, I've heard—" She broke off.

Louise shook open her fan so it hid her mouth. "One has to imagine that the rumors regarding Lady Lisette's witlessness are exaggerated. After all, so many people in London fall under that description."

A finely nuanced statement, Villiers thought. Guaranteed to make the point that the lady's mental state had been called into question. "Is that why she hasn't been presented at court?" he asked with some interest. "As far as I know, she's never been presented, nor yet appeared in London at all."

"Not everyone wishes to meet the queen," Roberta said. "And certainly there are many who consider occasions of this nature to be a waste of time."

From what he was hearing, meeting Lisette would be a waste of *his* time. He wanted a wife who would wield sufficient social clout to introduce his illegitimate children to society. Choosing a woman who hadn't bothered even to introduce herself to society could hardly fit the bill, especially if she were deranged.

Roberta's husband, the Earl of Gryffyn, strolled up and gave Villiers an insouciant grin. "Ah, my favorite dueling partner."

"Only because you managed to trounce me," Villiers replied. "And don't think it will ever happen again."

Gryffyn laughed and dropped a kiss on his wife's ear.

"Just think, darling," Roberta said. "Villiers has *six* illegitimate children and he's going to Kent to bring them all home to live with him. Are you quite certain about that decision, Villiers? We have only one, and even with two nannies, I have a strong belief that another child would give me hives. This morning Teddy trimmed the stable cat's whiskers. I would advise stowing your children in a French monastery and picking them up ten years hence."

"I doubt it was his illicit birth that gave the lad criminal tendencies," Villiers murmured, cutting his eyes to the earl. "Inheritance takes so many forms."

"Six?" Gryffyn asked, looking rather more shocked than a man raising his own bastard had a right to be. "And they're all in Kent? Why Kent?"

"Only two children live in Kent," Villiers said.

"Are you sure you will be able to persuade their mother to give them up?" Roberta asked. "I've been Teddy's mother for only something over a year, and I would take after you with a dagger if you tried to separate us."

Louise had apparently recovered from her shock, since she jumped into the conversation. "*Mothers* are such an intriguing question. Lord Gryffyn, you do realize how much passionate interest we all have in discovering the identity of your son's mother, don't you?"

"I fail to see why," Gryffyn said. "Why don't you contemplate Villiers instead? Teddy has but one mother, whereas Villiers's children will afford six times the pleasure."

"Ah, but there's a difference," Louise said. "We all know about Lady Caroline's unfortunate situation . . . Villiers, you *are* raising her child, aren't you?"

"I find this conversation most objectionable," he said flatly.

Louise fluttered her fan as if he hadn't spoken. "Not that all of us believe that Lady Caroline told the truth about the parentage of her child . . ." She paused. Villiers didn't deign to answer, so Louise rattled on. "As to the parentage of the duke's other five children . . ." She shrugged. "One has to believe that the mothers are not one's next door neighbors. Yet everyone is quite convinced, Lord Gryffyn, that your child's mother is well-born. There is nothing more fierce than an English lady with a nose for scandal and a mystery that involves her peers."

"Teddy shows no interest in the question, and he's the only person with the right to know."

"Even I don't know," Roberta said, giving her husband a mock scowl. "Damon promised to tell me on our wedding night, and then he reneged."

The earl tightened his arm around his wife and dropped another kiss on her head. "I remembered that it wasn't my secret to tell."

"But you two are supposed to be one body and soul now," Lady Nevill put in, just the faintest edge to her voice implying the impoverished nature of her own marriage.

"I don't want to know her identity," Roberta said, leaning against her husband. "That way I needn't think of her as a real person. Teddy is mine now."

Damon was smiling down at Roberta with such a foolishly loving look that Villiers felt nauseated.

Louise caught his eye and laughed. "I gather you plan to indulge in marriage, but not for love, Your Grace."

"Marriage is for the courageous, but love is for the foolish," Villiers said. "I have doubts regarding my own bravery, but I have long been convinced that I have at least a modicum of intelligence."

"In that case you will fall in love quite soon," Roberta

announced. "Such monumental arrogance must necessarily be answered by the gods."

Villiers walked away thinking of marriage. He could imagine nothing more repellent than the idea that his wife might fall in love with him. Or worse, far worse: that he might lower himself to worship a woman the way Gryffyn apparently did his wife.

A civil, practical union was far preferable to a messy pairing involving adoration.

That was an obvious point in favor of Lady Eleanor. She was in love with someone else. There was a courteous indifference about her that was remarkably peaceful.

It could be that he'd found his perfect match . . . as long as she decided to pay a visit to Kent, of course.

If not, he'd be stuck with the lady rather indelicately referred to as witless.

# Chapter Four

Eleanor found her mother in the refreshment tent, surrounded by her friends. The moment the duchess caught sight of her eldest daughter, she rose with the air of a mother cat shaking off a litter of nursing kittens and bustled Eleanor to the corner.

"Well?" she demanded.

"It seems quite possible that Villiers will offer for me," Eleanor admitted. "He implied as much."

"I am astonished," her mother cried, releasing her grip on Eleanor's arm. "Astonished!" She dropped into a chair in a dramatic flourish of her hands. "This will surprise you. I thought you were a fool."

The response that sprang to her mind seemed rather abrasive, so Eleanor said nothing.

"All these years, I thought you were a *fool*," her mother continued. "And yet here you are, marrying a duke, just as you always insisted you would. I suppose one is never too old to correct one's mistakes."

"I suppose not," Eleanor murmured.

"I made a mistake!" the duchess announced, patently dumbfounded at the very idea. "It never occurred to me, not even once, that you would have a chance at Villiers. For goodness sake, child, he is among the richest men in the kingdom."

At least until he endows all those illegitimate children, Eleanor thought to herself.

"He must be very high in the instep, given his search for a woman of equal rank. Everyone has been predicting that he will have to widen his focus to include the daughters of marquesses. But I always insisted that you should be the one, even given your age. Oh Eleanor, I am so very grateful to you!"

"For what, Mother?" Eleanor sat down.

"For not putting him off, of course. When I think of all the matches you could have made over the past four seasons! Here you are, past your first blush, and still dodging gentlemen. I was fearful, Eleanor. I know I kept my fears from you, as a mother should, but I was frightened for your future."

Eleanor smiled, as much from the idea that her mother kept any emotions to herself as anything else.

"I just couldn't *bear* the idea that I, the most beautiful woman of my year, would produce an ape leader for a daughter!"

Eleanor's smile withered.

"Thank goodness, you are the only eligible duke's daughter this season. I must write to your father and brother immediately and order them to return from Russia for the wedding. And we must order a new gown tomorrow morning. In fact, we should probably—"

"Villiers plans to pay a visit to Sevenoaks," Eleanor said.

Her mother frowned. "Sevenoaks, in Kent? Why? What— *No!*"

"Lisette." Eleanor nodded.

"But Lisette is mad. Poor girl," she added, but then returned to her main point: "The girl is mad as a March hare. Cracked. Moonstruck. And I say that not merely because I know the girl. Everyone knows it!"

"She's not precisely mad," Eleanor protested. "She's merely—"

"She's mad," the duchess repeated flatly. "That will come to nothing." A frown crinkled her brow. "Of course she is quite pretty."

"Lovely," Eleanor supplied helpfully. "Her eyes are a lovely blue, if you remember."

Her mother's eyes narrowed even further. "By now she must be fit for Bedlam. People never get better, only worse. Look at your uncle Harry. We used to think it rather charming that he believed he was a general. But now that he's taken to thinking that he's a Russian prince, your aunt Margaret has *such* an uncomfortable time. He's always insisting she wear furs and trundle about in a sleigh."

"Lisette has improved. She sends me quite cheerful letters."

"Villiers plans to visit Knole House, you said?"

"I told him that I had been planning to pay Lisette a visit."

Her mother's head snapped up. "Eleanor! That's the first intelligent thing I've seen you do in years!"

Eleanor involuntarily twitched but didn't reply.

"We'll leave tomorrow. Well, at the latest by the following day. I wonder if Gilner himself is home, though it hardly matters. I've lost touch with Lady Marguerite over the past few years, ever since Lisette's mama died. What an unfortunate life dear Beatrice had! Only one daughter, and the child deranged."

"Lisette has improved," Eleanor repeated.

"Nonsense! Pretty is as pretty does, and your Lisette is not fit to be a duchess. I trust the duke will realize that himself, but just in case, we'll be there as well."

Eleanor hated the times when the world gathered itself up and began hurtling toward a goal that she hadn't envisioned a mere five minutes before. She'd had the same feeling back on Gideon's eighteenth birthday, when he paid a sudden visit, his face as white as a sheet of paper. She remembered being surprised that he had sent in his card and requested a formal visit. Gideon had never been formal . . .

Gideon was always formal now that he was married to another woman.

Which was fine, because she, Eleanor, was going to be married to the Duke of Villiers. Just then her mother squealed with delight. "Duke!" she caroled, springing to her feet with a huge smile.

Eleanor jerked her head up, expecting to see Villiers—but it was Gideon. Gideon, the Duke of Astley, who never approached her if he could possibly avoid it.

A combination of kindness and genuine affection on the part of Eleanor's mother had caused her to insist that her son's closest friend, a poor motherless boy, spend his school holidays with them. Which was why Eleanor felt as if Gideon had grown up with them, scrabbling and squabbling around the estate as if he were another brother—until the day they looked at each other and he wasn't. He just wasn't.

Now he walked toward them, as lean and beautiful as ever. When he was just a boy, he had been rail thin. Later, muscles started to conceal his ribs. Her memory gave her an unbidden and unwelcome recollection of how soft to the touch the first dusting of hair covering his chest had been.

It was practically a sacrilegious thought. The man was married.

"Where is your lovely wife?" her mother was demanding. "Do tell me that she's *indisposed* due to an interesting event?"

"I'm afraid the duchess was too tired to leave her chambers tonight," Gideon replied in his calm voice. He nodded to Eleanor and bent to give her mother a kiss that made the duchess beam. It was the sort of kindness that marked his ways.

Eleanor held out her hand to be kissed. He bowed, touching his lips lightly to her glove. She considered whether he gave it a special pressure, but she couldn't delude herself.

Since the very moment that Gideon had discovered his father's will included a marriage contract wrought between the late duke and Ada's father, he had never touched her in any sort of intimate way. Never.

"We have such exciting news for you!" her mother burst out.

"Mother!" Eleanor protested. "It isn't—"

"Oh tush, Eleanor, the duke is part of our family." And, turning again to Gideon, "Our own Eleanor is finally going to take a husband." She caught herself. "Not that I mean *finally* as it sounds. Of course, Eleanor could have married any time in the last few years, but she'd never chosen to do so. And now she has agreed to a husband."

A courteous smile shaped Gideon's lips, but Eleanor thought she saw pain in the depths of his eyes. It made her feel better.

"It seems I owe you felicitations, Lady Eleanor," he said.

An uncertain smile wavered around her own lips. She could hardly say, *I would have waited forever.* "I am grateful for them, Your Grace." There. That was dignified.

"Surely you heard that the Duke of Villiers is looking for a wife?" her mother burst out.

"I had heard that rumor, but I could not believe that Lady Eleanor would consider such a spouse."

Eleanor was starting to feel quite cheerful. After years of trying not to watch Gideon with longing eyes, of trying to erase him from her dreams, it was satisfying to see that flash of fire in his eyes.

Let him experience what she had endured, watching him wait at the altar to marry Ada.

"Yes, the Duke of Villiers," she confirmed, giving him a lavish smile. "I am persuaded the two of us will be remarkably suited. You do remember how I used to beat you at chess, don't you?"

"You know how foolish my Eleanor has always been," her mother put in, laughing. "She announced years ago that she would marry a duke or no one. I was beginning to worry, I don't mind telling you."

"There was never any reason to worry," Gideon said. "I'm sure Lady Eleanor has her pick of eligible men."

"I wanted only a duke," Eleanor said. "And that meant so many men were ineligible. I suppose it was a foolish restriction to set for myself."

"Life does not always give us the choices that we might wish."

He was growing furious, and she rejoiced in every involuntary signal, in the rigid way he held his shoulders, in the firmness of his jaw.

"Luckily for me," she said cheerfully, "a duke came along just at the moment when I had decided to put away my childish feelings."

"Childish," he repeated.

"Yes. You know what it's like when one is very young. One believes in such foolishness . . . in men who will throw away the world to be at one's side. Fairy tales. I had just decided to discard all those romantic notions when, to my great surprise, a duke appeared who seems as charming as I could possibly wish."

"What does your childhood have to do with anything?" her mother said. "You two were always talking in riddles, but you're far too old for that sort of thing now."

"Far too old," Eleanor said, with a rueful smile just for Gideon. "Those riddles are nothing more than nursery rhymes, to be put away as one matures, along with childish emotions."

His jaw was clenched. "I was under the impression that the Duke of Villiers suffered a grievous injury last year after losing a duel."

Gideon didn't approve of duels, which was no wonder, since he'd lost his father as a result of one. When he and Eleanor were young, they had talked for hours about how unlawful and dangerous these confrontations were. And, since ascending to his seat, he had made it his life's work to convince society to see the duel as an indefensible and horrific act. She was always reading about speeches he'd given on the subject.

The duel alone would make him despise Villiers. Which was just as well, she thought, because once she married that dark-eyed fallen angel, she didn't want to think about Gideon ever again.

"So is dear Ada increasing?" her mother was asking. "I do hope you don't mind my inquiring. I adore her, of course, but she's so fragile. I must have my cook make up a good strengthening lettuce soup for her."

Gideon started to reply, but Eleanor's mother wasn't to be stopped.

"I expect that she is quite nauseated. When I had my first, I was so sick that I could barely stir out of the bedchamber for days. I drank lettuce soup morning and night. I shall send some over tomorrow. Nay, I shall send over my cook tomorrow to train your—"

"Your Grace." Gideon's quiet voice cut across her mother's rush of speech. "I'm afraid that Ada is not increasing. She's merely suffering a lung complaint."

"Oh."

Eleanor knew she should feel sorry for fragile little Ada, who always seemed to be in her bed or on a settee, coughing delicately. But try though she might, she still resented her. Ada's father had paid for Gideon, had sewed him up in a marriage contract when Gideon was only eight years old.

Which meant that Ada had the one thing that Eleanor had ever wanted in the world.

"Please sit down and tell me all about it," her mother said, patting Gideon on the hand. "That poor angel. Did she take a chill?"

The worst of it was that Ada didn't even care for Gideon, as far as Eleanor could tell. She had paid Ada dutiful visits over the past three years and seen the polite, uninterested manner with which Ada greeted her husband.

If *she* had been Gideon's wife, she would have leaped from the settee to greet him when he walked into the drawing room. In the first year or so after he married Ada, it was all Eleanor could do to keep herself frozen in a chair when he entered a room, and to stop a besotted smile from spreading across her face.

But Ada just held out her hand to be kissed and then turned away.

And Gideon . . . Gideon had gone from being Eleanor's closest friend, the confidant of her heart and the lover of her body, to bowing as if she were nothing more than a remote acquaintance.

"The duchess's cough has taken a turn for the worse in the last few weeks," he was saying now. He was endlessly solicitous of his sickly wife.

It was admirable. Really.

Perhaps it was just as well that they hadn't married. She could never be as punctilious as Gideon, not even if a dead father's will required it of her. She would have fought bitterly to marry him. She would have climbed a balcony in the middle of the night and lured her beloved into a clandestine elopement, and be damned with the consequences.

She would have . . . she would have gone anywhere with that lovely, golden boy. In fact, now that she thought on it, she came perilously close to giving up her whole life, remaining unmarried, and never having children merely because he wasn't free.

What's the good of being Juliet when Romeo shows no sign of killing himself for love, but instead prances off with Rosalind?

She felt as stupid as Oyster.

There was an audible hum of interest in the room, just as she sensed someone at her shoulder. "Astley," came the drawling voice of the Duke of Villiers. "Your Grace." He was bowing before her mother.

The duchess held out her hand to be kissed, doing a magnificent job of pretending that Villiers's appearance meant little, and that every pair of eyes in the tent wasn't focused on their little group. "I understand that we might well see each other in the country," she said, dimpling. "I'm not certain that I can spare the time for such frolicking, but I always try to please my daughters."

"London is so tiresome at the tail end of the season," Villiers said. "And you are so much in demand, Duchess. You must long to escape the throngs of your friends and admirers."

Since her mother loved nothing more than an admiring horde, Eleanor thought he was overdoing his praise. But her mother giggled, and might even be blushing underneath the permanent blush she had painted on earlier in the day. "That is so true," she agreed, fluttering her fan madly.

"You're planning a trip to the country, Duke?" Gideon said in his measured, formal tones.

"I have some business in Kent." Eleanor held her breath. She was hoping to break the news about his motley family to her mother at some later date. Preferably after the duchess had drunk two brandies. But Villiers said nothing further.

She caught sight of Gideon's still-clenched jaw out of the corner of her eye. "We are meeting at a house party," she said, favoring the three of them with a huge smile.

"I expect you'll be busy in the House of Lords," Villiers said to Gideon. "Such a pity; the countryside is beautiful at this time of year. But there you are . . . we grasshoppers will frolic, and the ants must needs keep slaving." There was a trace of scorn in his voice. Just a trace.

A second stretched to twenty before Gideon said, "Exactly so."

"What a pity you've never taken up your seat, Duke," Eleanor's mother said to Villiers, showcasing her profound deafness to conversational undercurrents.

"I can't imagine why I would," Villiers said lazily. "I don't see myself in a room full of bantam roosters strutting and squawking at the dawn."

"One could describe them as caring for the business of the country," Gideon snapped.

"Nonsense. The business of the country is shaped by two forces: the king and the market. As it happens, I know a great deal about the market. I can assure you, Astley, that quite frequently the market trumps the king."

Gideon's jaw worked. "The market can do nothing when it comes to serious problems. In the House of Lords we fight ethical lapses such as the slave trade."

"The slave trade is entirely governed by money: those with it, and those who wish they had more. And it has long been my opinion that the only way to end it is to cut it off at the root. You can make all the proclamations you wish, but it's only by cutting profit that that damnable practice will end."

"Wonderful!" Eleanor's mother said brightly. "I can see that you're both working toward the same goal."

"So to speak," Villiers said. His eyes slid to Eleanor, and suddenly she knew that he had guessed her most private secret. He knew.

"I doubt we have ever had similar goals," Gideon said.

"Given that my intentions are entirely honorable, I believe you," Villiers said with a faint smile.

Gideon drew in his breath sharply. The insult flashed by like a poison dart, so sleek and so pointed that Eleanor almost missed it. Her mother just smiled.

"That must be a novel sensation for you," Gideon said, making something of a rejoinder.

Apparently he had heard rumors of Villiers's illegitimate children. Both men were tall, but Villiers's physique was so much broader that Gideon looked willowy in comparison. Villiers didn't say a word, but all of a sudden he looked . . . dangerous.

Eleanor's mother apparently decided the same thing, since she suddenly shrieked, "Goodness me, just look at Mrs. Bardsley's absurd wig. It's tilting to the side!"

Villiers paid her no attention at all. He turned from Gideon as if the duke were no more than an impudent servant, bowed before Eleanor, and smiled at her.

That smile . . .

It could have seduced Cleopatra out of her golden boat.

It would have lured Bathsheba from her bath. It was the smile of a wicked man, a man who didn't bother much with honor, but promised to bother a lot about . . . other things.

"I know that you prefer I spare you a storm of gossip." His voice caressed her like a touch of his hand, just loud enough to be heard by Gideon. "I fully meant to stay away from you, but when I glanced across the room and saw you, I could not resist."

He took her hand. Then, without smiling at her, without saying a word, without doing anything other than meeting her eyes, he slowly peeled off her glove. It was utterly surprising—and scandalous. She heard her mother make a small huff of disapproval as he drew it off.

But Villiers didn't look away from her eyes, just lifted her bare fingers to his lips as if they were entirely alone. His gesture was the antithesis of Gideon's polite greeting. Villiers's kiss was slow and deliberate, giving everyone in the tent more than enough time to enjoy the spectacle.

For Eleanor, the world tilted—and changed. She suddenly saw the man before her in focus: his thick lashes, his deep bottom lip, the hard line of his chin, the thick hair tied back and defiantly unpowdered. The maleness of his shoulders. The coiled strength of his body.

A sultry warmth spread from her cheeks and flooded down her body. Yet it wasn't the kiss that did it. It was something in those black eyes that made heat rise in her cheeks . . . and in her body.

The Duke of Villiers was notorious for his chilly, indifferent eyes, famed for surveying the world from a height defined by his disdain and his title. What she discovered at that moment was a rather terrifying truth: when the duke's cold eyes turned voluptuous, it would be a rare woman who could resist him.

She was not one of them.

It was the first time in years that she'd felt a melting sensation course through her body, the very kind that had persuaded her to throw her chastity to the wind and seduce Gideon—but she knew it. She recognized it. And some treacherous part of her body welcomed it joyously.

Villiers saw; he knew. There was laughter in his eyes now, competing with a dissolute, and altogether enthusiastic, invitation to pleasure.

In one swift gesture he turned her hand over and pressed a burning kiss on her palm, a touch so fast that she didn't see it, though her hand curled instinctively, as if to protect the kiss itself.

She didn't have to see it to understand it.

It was the kiss of a man who was staking a claim.

There wasn't a man or woman in the tent who could possibly have misunderstood that.

# Chapter Five

To the boy's mind, the duke looked almost sleepy, despite the fact that he was holding a rapier with a dagger-keen edge. He padded in a slow circle, holding that blade as casually as another man might an enameled snuffbox.

But there was something about the way Villiers lazily watched his opponent . . . The silent boy slipped through the door, keeping his eyes fixed on his father.

Even so, he almost missed the opening foray. The duke's blade slashed forward with such quick force that the boy expected blood to splatter the floor. The ballroom rang with the clear, high notes of clashing steel.

"Sharpen the angle of your arm, Your Grace!" Tobias

had heard that kind of accent before. French, he thought. A Frenchman had hired him to hold his horse once, but afterwards he rode off without giving him a penny.

This particular Frenchman had a chiseled nose and an excitable look to his wide-set eyes. He wore no wig, and his short hair stood around his head like the needles of a pine tree. He was perspiring so heavily that Tobias could see the wet on his upper lip, even from the side of the room.

Tobias looked back at the duke. Villiers had raised his right elbow, but even so, the Frenchman seemed to be beating him back, step by step. Tobias slid quietly down the wall onto his heels. His heart was pounding, which was stupid, because he knew it was only practice. It looked violent, but that was nothing more than pretense.

"I would advise—" The Frenchman's voice broke off.

In one lightning quick motion, the duke slipped through his opponent's guard. His right arm was poised high in the air; his rapier just touched the Frenchman's throat.

The only sound to be heard in the ballroom was the panting of the two men.

Then the Frenchman fell back a step. "Your *cavazione* is still too easily countered." He sounded peevish. He turned to the large glass on one side of the ballroom and readjusted the hang of his waistcoat.

"Damn it, I'm covered in sweat!" Villiers complained. He put his sword down, hauled his shirt over his head and threw it to the side.

Tobias's eyes widened. The duke was all taut muscle in his middle, and above his waist those muscles widened to a broad chest. He had never seen anything akin to the duke's stomach. It was covered with ridges formed of muscle.

He couldn't help a glance at his own skinny limbs. He looked better than he had a month or two ago, remarkably well, considering he'd spent the last few years in a "highly undesirable situation," as Ashmole the butler had described it. Tobias didn't quite see how "undesirable" covered wading through sewers filled with muck, fishing for silver spoons and lost teeth, but he got the idea.

The men started circling each other again. He had never seen his father without a shirt before now. In fact, he'd never seen him in less than formal attire, clothed from head to foot in silk or velvet adorned with fantastical embroidery.

Just this morning the duke had paid a visit to the nursery, and the children had all sat about, staring at his coat. It was made of red velvet with a pattern of small flowers, the whole of it covered with twining vines made from gilt thread with pearls sewn here and there.

Even one of those pearls could keep a family in meat pies for weeks. Months, maybe. He was getting used to Villiers's extravagant clothing, but his little sister, the one whom the duke had fetched a fortnight ago, and his brother Colin, who had arrived a mere week before, had been struck dumb.

Suddenly, Tobias realized that the duke was staring straight at him. He quickly came to his feet, back against the wall. The duke opened his mouth as if to say something, and then pivoted to parry a thrust from the Frenchman.

Tobias felt his heart beating in his throat again. Their swords clashed until his ears rang. Then the duke twisted his wrist sharply and his blade darted forward. His opponent's blade flew down and to the side, skidding to a halt a foot or two away.

The Frenchman broke into a string of incomprehensible curses, but the duke walked away as if nothing were being said. He plucked up a linen cloth from the bench and walked toward Tobias.

Tobias pulled his shoulders back. It was hard to imagine that someday he too might have a body like that, all gleaming muscle. Like that of a wild animal, really, he thought, remembering the body of his former employer. Grindel was flabby and soft, even though he had terrible strength in the swing of his arm. But Villiers was stronger.

"Your Grace," he said, barely inclining his head. The butler, Ashmole, had instructed him to bow whenever he met the duke, but he couldn't make himself do it. Bowing was for—for people who bowed. He had a strong feeling that if he started bowing to people, he might just find his head down all the time.

That was what life was like for bastards, he reckoned.

Villiers answered in that dusky voice that Tobias knew well enough was an older version of his own. "That was bloody hellish in the nursery this morning," he said, pulling the ribbon from his hair and rubbing his head all over with the linen cloth.

Tobias quelled an impulse to grin. You weren't supposed to smile around a duke. Ashmole had made that clear too.

"Are those children always so quiet?"

Given that Tobias had fled the nursery an hour ago because Violet's happy, high-pitched screaming was threatening to drive him out of his mind, he could answer that. "No."

The duke pulled his shirt over his head again. "I have met a lady whom I'll probably marry. Clearly, we need a woman in the house. And since I'm going in a few days to look at an orphanage in Kent, and there's another appropriate candidate living close by, I'll meet her as well. I can choose between them." His head reappeared through a billow of white linen.

"A—A *wife*?" Tobias stammered.

"You and I could probably just rub along together, but I'm no good with girls. They need a mother."

Tobias just stared at him.

"All right," Villiers snapped. "I'm no good with boys either."

He strode off before Tobias could say another word, but he paused next to the Frenchman on his way out the door. "Naffi, I have a feeling my son might have a talent for the rapier. I think he would benefit from some lessons. See Ashmole about arranging it." And he was gone.

Tobias had learned a lot about the natural order in the months since Villiers plucked him out of a back street in Wapping and brought him to the mansion. Dukes were gods, and servants were rubbish; gentlemen were somewhere in between. Bastards were at the very bottom of the heap.

But as far as Tobias could tell, Villiers treated everyone as if they were rubbish. He had walked straight past Naffi without waiting for an answer, even though the Frenchman had lost two bouts in row. The man was quivering with annoyance, and Villiers's abrupt command could only have made things worse.

Tobias watched warily as the Frenchman walked over to him, rapier in hand. His lower lip was curled so savagely that Tobias could see the pink flesh inside. "So I'm to teach the by-blow to fence," he said in a low, dangerous tone, picking up his wig and jamming it onto his sweaty hair. "I, the great Naffi, lauded in three courts, am to waste my time teaching a trollop's bit of rubbish. As if *you* would ever have cause to defend your honor. What honor?" He threw his head back, laughter erupting from his mouth like a horse's whinny. "Honor! I hardly think so. Bastard begot, bastard in mind, bastard in valor, I say!"

Tobias had learned that watching people silently made

them uneasy: it was only after he moved into the duke's house and observed his father's chilly eyes that he realized it was a family talent. So he said nothing, just let his eyes rest on the sweaty hair sticking out from under Naffi's wig, the red patches high in his cheeks.

"I don't care even to cross my sword with a whoreson like yourself," the Frenchman said. "To contaminate my blade jousting with a bastard. I, who jousted with His Grace the Duke of Rutland only last week? *You* don't need to learn proper conduct. Blood tells, and your sort will always end in the gutter."

Tobias didn't give a fig about insults to himself, but "whoreson" was different. Naffi was saying something about his mother. He never thought all that much about his mother until he met the gilded, glittering duke. Then he realized that it wasn't her fault, what had happened to him. It was the duke's fault.

"If blood is a reliable guide to conduct, it would explain your father's horns," he said, spacing the words so that Naffi would understand.

It took a moment for his insult to sink in. Then the Frenchman's voice rose. "You impudent little goat! You dare imply my *maman*—" His voice broke off as he unexpectedly shot forward, like a cork from a bottle.

Tobias jumped to the side just in time as Naffi bashed against the wall and rebounded, his nose gushing startlingly red blood.

Ashmole, Villiers's ancient butler, grinned at Tobias. In his right hand he held a large golden staff with a huge knob, with which he had apparently jabbed Naffi in the back. The Frenchman lurched around, clutching his nose with one hand and screaming incoherently.

"That'll teach you to insult the young master," Ashmole said, his voice cracking only once.

Blood was splattered down Naffi's white shirt. "How dare you lay a hand on me, you disgusting *imbécile*!" he shrieked.

Tobias began to laugh, when he suddenly realized that Naffi still had a rapier in his right hand, and that if the man would hesitate to assault a son of the house—even a bastard—he would feel no such compunction about a servant.

"I'll teach you to touch your betters!" Naffi snarled, bringing his blade up.

"Stop!" Tobias cried.

But the Frenchman was already poking the old butler hard in the chest, prodding him with the button-covered tip of the rapier. His lips curled happily, and Tobias could see that he was enjoying Ashmole's squawking protests and the way the old man stumbled back each time he was struck.

Villiers had left his rapier on the bench, and Tobias picked it up.

Naffi swung to face him, uttering his horsey laugh. "*You* dare to face me with a sword? *Moi*, the great Naffi? The man whom even the Duke of Villiers begs to train him?"

"That duke beat you twice this morning," Tobias observed.

"I could slash you," Naffi hissed. "Such a regrettable accident. Yes, I think that's what I'll do. A little slash to the face that will mark you as the gutter rat you really are."

Naffi had spittle around his lips, which made Tobias feel faintly nauseated. He tossed the rapier to the ground between them. The man broke into that donkeylike laughter again, throwing his head back so his chin pointed to the ceiling. "So you're not so stupid but that you—"

Tobias snatched the staff from Ashmole's hand and slammed its large knob under Naffi's chin. The man fell straight backward without a word.

The thump echoed in the empty ballroom. "I doubt you kilt him," Ashmole said. He prodded the man with his toe. Naffi made a snorting noise but his eyes stayed shut.

"Unlikely," Tobias agreed. He picked up the duke's rapier and twisted the button off its tip. It was sharp as a needle's point.

"Are you going to kill him now?" Ashmole inquired. He didn't sound terribly scandalized. "It'll make a terrible mess."

Tobias put the rapier in position and brought it carefully straight down. "Absolutely not."

Ashmole cursed and jumped back. "You're set to ruin the polish on my floor."

"No." Tobias was concentrating. The rapier was heavy, and employing it as precisely as a knife took all his attention.

Ashmole peered over his shoulder. "No blood."

"Of course not."

"You're putting a cut in his coat? What's the good of that?"

Tobias looked at him incredulously. "Have you been wearing the duke's getup your whole life? This fool is wearing all his money on his body."

Ashmole cackled. "Not anymore."

They both looked down at the floor. Naffi's mouth hung open; he was breathing heavily through it. His brocaded waistcoat was now vented like an apple pie.

Ashmole raised an eyebrow. "Yer leaving him with his breeches, lad?"

Tobias raised the rapier again.

"Careful around them jewels of his," the butler commanded. "Wouldn't want to be responsible for changing him from a rooster to a hen."

Tobias cut a slice down the right leg of Naffi's pantaloons.

"I'll get one of the footmen in here to drag off the riff-raff," Ashmole said with palpable satisfaction. "He won't wake up for a while, from the look of him."

"A blow beneath the chin can put a man out for hours," Tobias said. He was wiping the duke's rapier carefully. "This blade might have been slightly dulled by slicing that brocade. Perhaps you should have it sharpened."

"Frosty, that's what you are," Ashmole said. "You're yer father's son all right."

"The duke is leaving in a few days for Kent," Tobias said.

"He's got to follow up on them twins," Ashmole said. "Not that we need more brats around this house." He started rubbing his chest. "I'll have bruises tonight, so I will, thanks to that French varmint. The duke'll never take you with him. You stay at home with the little girl. It's sweet the way she's taken to you."

"What time of day does he usually call for his carriage?"

Ashmole peered at him. "Think you'll beg him to take you?"

"I never beg," Tobias stated.

"Father's son," Ashmole cackled. "Father's son. He's prone to leaving early, for him. He's not one to see the sun rise. Likely around ten of the clock. So you can make your case, but I wouldn't hold your breath. He's like you, if you see what I mean. Not going to take you up just out of the goodness of his heart."

# Chapter Six

*London residence of the Duke of Montague*
*Same day*

"We'll pack all your best gowns," the duchess announced at luncheon. "And your riding habit. It *is* the country, and one must make the effort, I suppose. But not that trimmed habit you were wearing in the park last week. Trimming suddenly looks rather tawdry."

"Plain *is* best," Anne agreed. "Lady Festle wore such a cunning riding habit the other day. It had a waistcoat of ribbed white dimity . . ."

Eleanor wasn't listening, which didn't matter, as her mother didn't consider conversation to be an occasion for interaction. Her sister Anne had appeared that morning in a costume that Eleanor would never have dreamed of ordering: a close-fitting coat of sky-blue taffety with a low neckline. It flared into folds at her hips, with a short petticoat of white linen underneath. In short, Madam Bouchon looked like the dashing and delectable young matron she was.

Whereas her own gown was a perfectly good stone-colored muslin. It was definitely serviceable. In fact, she thought it had served her for at least two or three seasons. The petticoat had a deep flounce, which was all one could say for its claim to fashion, especially since it also had the dreaded ruffled sleeves.

"I do not wish to pack my best gowns," Eleanor interrupted, putting her fork down.

Anne raised an eyebrow.

Her mother just kept talking. "I shall send a message to Madame Gasquet and beg her to deliver the costume we ordered a few weeks ago."

"I no longer want that particular gown," Eleanor said, thinking of its long sleeves and longer petticoat.

"You simply must make an effort," her mother scolded, finally looking up from the head of the table. "Anne took me to task this morning for allowing you to look so passé, and she's right. You have shown so little interest in your appearance that I had lost heart for the battle. But now you are to be a duchess. You *must* dress *à la mode*."

"I intend to," Eleanor said. "The problem is that I own very few gowns that are akin to what Anne is wearing this morning. I would like to be as fashionable as she is at this moment."

"The only thing that could make my jacket more modish would be tassels on the collar," Anne said, with a complete lack of modesty. "I am considering the alteration. Did Villiers effect this miraculous change in your attitude? His coat *was* rather magnificent."

"He has little to do with it. Your assessment brought me to my senses."

"Brought you to your senses?" their mother intervened. "You've always been comfortingly sensible, Eleanor. Unlike Lisette."

"What Eleanor means," Anne said, "is that she's agreed to stop hiding her beauty. She intends to dress like a desirable lady instead of a frump."

"No daughter of mine could be a frump," the duchess said. "I wouldn't allow it." Still, Eleanor could see that the idea was sinking into her mother's head. She picked up her lorgnette and frowned through it at her. "I wouldn't want you to dress like trollopy slattern. I find some current styles unacceptable."

"Certainly not," said Anne, who prided herself on wearing the most risqué fashions in all London. "You needn't worry, Mother. I'll send the footman for an armful of my gowns. Another footman must go to Madame Gasquet because I have three gowns on order, and I'll donate them to the cause. Perhaps she will even have time to adjust for Eleanor's bosom. If not, the necklines are quite low, and I doubt it will matter much."

Eleanor bit her lip. She was apparently going from modest to decadent overnight.

"What we must consider," the duchess announced, "is that your sister made a splendid match in her very first year. She turned down a marquis for Mr. Bouchon; he may not have an illustrious title—"

"But darling Jeremy has that lovely land in the dells," Anne pointed out. "Acres and acres and acres, all filled with sheep. I am *very* expensive."

"That is certainly true," her mother agreed. "I do believe that your wardrobe this year cost double mine and Eleanor's put together. Your father complained bitterly."

Eleanor had never been expensive. If her mother indicated that a new gown was in order, she got through the fitting without fuss and with only one dictate: that she didn't resemble a hussy.

"You and I are not so dissimilar," her sister said now, apparently guessing exactly what was going through Eleanor's mind.

"There I disagree," the duchess said. "From the moment you debuted, Anne, I lived in fear that you would be compromised, whereas I've never had a moment of worry about Eleanor."

"Eleanor is certainly prudent," Anne said with a little snort that her mother didn't hear.

"You must try to look more like your sister," their mother said, nodding at Eleanor. "Now I think on it, Anne, you'll have to accompany us."

"Oh, I couldn't leave Jeremy!"

"Of course you can. There's nothing better for marriage than farewells. Your father and I rarely quarrel, a fact I attribute entirely to our lengthy separations."

Since their father was prone to travel and spent most of his time in foreign climes, it was true that the opportunities for marital strife were limited.

"You needn't come with me," Eleanor said to Anne. "I'll just inform Rackfort that I wish to pay more attention to my attire." There was a moment of silence as her female relatives examined her. Eleanor raised a self-conscious hand to her hair. "I thought it looked quite nice, given that Rackfort was complaining of a toothache."

"You're right, Mother," Anne said decisively. "I shall come, and I shall bring my maid. No, I shall do even better. I'll give you Willa for the trip, Eleanor. It will be a true sacrifice and I expect I'll gain a halo just for it. Let no one say that I don't love my sister!"

Eleanor rolled her eyes. "Couldn't Willa just give Rackfort a lesson or two?"

"Rackfort is worse than no maid at all," Anne stated. "You shall have Willa, and I will make do with my second maid, Marie. I've been training her, and she's quite good with hair."

"I suspect you want to travel with us just for the sake of gathering gossip."

"*Someone* has to make sure that you look your best," Anne said virtuously.

"I can lend you one of my gowns, if need be," their mother said. "Luckily, I have retained my figure."

"Eleanor is not going to wear your gowns," Anne stated, "though I know you meant it kindly. She already has the knack of dressing like a dowager; now she needs to learn a different style."

By nine in the morning two days later, the redoubtable Madame Gasquet had sent the gowns ordered for Anne, as well as a deep blue brocade designed for some soon-to-be disappointed lady who happened to have appropriate measurements.

"It's utterly perfect," Anne said with satisfaction. "I happened to wander into the back room, and the moment I saw the girls stitching I knew that the color was just right for your eyes."

"You snatched it away from whomever had ordered the gown?" Eleanor asked, eyeing her sister.

"Snatched has such unpleasant connotations," Anne said. "I offered Madame Gasquet three times the price. Of course, she was lavishly grateful and practically threw the gown at me. You do know how much your patronage will mean once you are the Duchess of Villiers, don't you?"

"Because the duke is so fashionable?" Eleanor asked, with a pang of misgiving.

"Precisely," Anne said with a nod.

Eleanor opened her mouth to say that she couldn't imagine herself achieving Villiers's splendor when their mother called from the entrance hall. "I just need to say good-bye to Oyster," she said, looking about for him. "He was here a moment ago."

"Oh no, Oyster will come with us," Anne said. "I'll tie a bit of white lace on his collar so that he's more fashionable."

"Don't be a fool," their mother said, appearing in the doorway. "Of course Eleanor is not bringing her potbellied little horror of a dog."

"She must," Anne explained. "She and Villiers had a laugh about Oyster at the benefit the other night. He's a joke between them, you see. An intimacy."

"Nothing could make Oyster look fashionable," Eleanor said flatly.

"I'll pin one of my ostrich feathers into his collar. Queen Charlotte herself adorned her dog with ostrich feathers. Or was it peacock feathers? This will show Villiers that you are truly *à la mode*. Everyone has a pug these days."

"But I am not *à la mode*," Eleanor began. "And more to the point, Oyster is not a pug."

"Part of him is a pug," Anne said, patting the dog. "Wait until you see how wonderful he looks with an ostrich feather." She was wearing a wildly fashionable chip hat lined with sarcenet, with a cluster of white feathers on one side. Without pausing for breath, she plucked one of her plumes and knelt beside Oyster.

"He *is* a pug," her mother announced. "Mr. Pesnickle said so, and although he might have been more tidy in his dog's domestic arrangements, we must take him at his word."

"No pug has those ears," Eleanor said. "And more to the point, Oyster will not add to the occasion."

"Your sister, young though she is, is much better at understanding men," her mother ruled. "You have never shown the faintest interest in attracting a man's attention, Eleanor; now you must accept advice from a younger sister."

*"Voilà!"* Anne cried. "He's wearing his feather *à la conseilleur.* See how it tilts sideways?"

"Who could miss it?" Eleanor asked, leaning down to give Oyster a pat. He panted enthusiastically, looking up at her with adoring eyes. She was very fond of Oyster. But he was one of those odd dogs who just missed being attractive. His body was cream, and his nose and muzzle were black, and then he was pop-eyed. The feather didn't help.

"The point is," Anne told her, "Oyster gives you something to talk about."

Oyster's incontinent habits certainly did generate conversation. "I don't think he likes that feather, Anne." It curled over his back and brushed his tail. Not the brightest of dogs, Oyster was convinced a fly was trying to bite him and so he began twisting around to snap at his own tail.

Though he was far too fat to actually reach his tail.

"It's fashionable," Anne said stubbornly. "Mother, don't let her take the feather off. Oyster will get used to it, and the queen's dog wears one precisely the same. Though I seem to remember hers does wear a peacock feather."

A pug wearing a peacock feather. That would be a conversation piece, all right.

"When we arrive, you must go down for a nap immediately, Eleanor," the duchess stated. "I want you to look your best by the time Villiers appears. *Certainly* better than Lisette!"

"Mother," Eleanor said, "Lisette is a friend of mine. There's no reason to use that tone."

Her mother narrowed her eyes. "Eleanor, you are such

a fool that it's a miracle they're calling Lisette cracked instead of yourself."

Eleanor said nothing.

Her mother gave a faint shriek. "I'll be blessed if I haven't forgotten to take your grandmother's silver combs! I want to arrange them on your bedside table." She trotted from the room.

"Does she think that I'll invite the duke into my bedchamber to examine my combs?" Eleanor said.

Anne gave her hand a squeeze. "Mother is accustomed to overstating her opinions."

"I know."

"She didn't mean to call you stupid."

But she did mean it. Eleanor had always been a puzzle to her mother, and not a pleasant one. Part of the problem was that the duchess had never known about Gideon, never known about the glorious year in which they grew closer and closer, fell in love, told each other everything, and finally, in that last delirious month before his birthday, made love.

Because her mother never knew that, she knew nothing about her.

The greater problem was that Eleanor simply didn't fit in. She said the wrong things. She was too sarcastic.

Eleanor had figured out long ago that her mother was oblivious to her feelings and didn't mean most of her insults. But the knowledge didn't help. Every time her mother called her stupid, she felt more bitter, like a knife sharpened in the cold.

Then she would say something sarcastic again, exasperating her mother with her stupidity.

"Mother and I saw Gideon at the Duchess of Beaumont's benefit ball," Eleanor said, needing to tell someone. "He was in the refreshment tent and he came up to speak to us."

"Was he with Ada?"

"She is ill again."

Anne wrinkled her nose.

"Don't! It's not her fault."

"I think she likes to lie about on a sofa and court attention," Anne said with the relentless lack of sympathy that only a young healthy person could feel.

"I was there once when she had a coughing attack," Eleanor said. "It sounded terribly painful. She couldn't straighten up."

"I don't like her."

"Don't, don't say that! It's not her fault."

"You're right about that. It's not her fault," Anne said.

Eleanor blinked.

"I don't mean her illness: I mean the rest of it. It's Gideon's fault, Eleanor, and now that you're finally considering another man, I'm going to say it. He shouldn't have left you like that. He should have broken that will. He never, ever should have behaved with such dishonor."

"Dishonor!" Eleanor cried. "Why, that's the opposite of what he did. He——"

"He dishonored you," Anne said, steadily, holding her eyes. "Didn't he, Eleanor?"

Eleanor had never been quite sure whether her sister knew the extent of that summer's folly. "It wasn't dishonor," she said haltingly. "We are—we *were* in love."

"If a man falls in love to that tune," Anne said, "then he incurs some responsibility in the matter. Gideon is a cad, Eleanor. A louse. I've thought so forever, but I couldn't say it because you made him into a saint, and yourself nothing more than a worshipper at his worthless shrine."

"Not a louse," Eleanor protested. "He's honorable, and good. But once he learned of that will, it all became so complicated——"

"He's a hoity-toity prig," Anne interrupted. "Do you think he would have broken that will if you hadn't—" She paused. "You might hate me for this, Eleanor, but I'm going to say it anyway. If you hadn't given your virginity to Gideon, don't you think he would have broken that will?"

"That's a wretched thing to say!" Eleanor snapped. "We were in *love*! You may not know what that is like, but—"

"I agree with our nanny," Anne said, overriding her. "Why buy the cow when you can get the milk for free?"

"That's—you can't—" Eleanor felt rage rising in her chest and she tightened her grip on Oyster's leash so suddenly that he gave a sharp yelp. The thought that Anne might be right was heartbreaking, literally.

"All I'm saying is that if you want to marry Villiers, you shouldn't let him in your bedchamber to look at your combs—or anything else. That's all I'm saying."

"We were in *love*," Eleanor repeated.

"He sneaked about, and did secret things with you," Anne retorted. "How would you feel about him if you heard that he had been tupping one of the second footman's daughters? You were a young girl, not old enough to know better."

"You just don't understand. We were both young. I was lucky to have loved like that for a time." She said it stoutly, even though she didn't really believe it.

Anne snorted. "I hope I'm never so lucky."

Eleanor managed to summon up a crooked smile. "I won't invite anyone into my chamber to examine my silver combs, I promise you that." It was an easy enough promise to make.

She and Villiers had an utterly different sort of relationship in mind. If she and Gideon had married, they would have been like twigs caught in a forest fire. They had made love barely ten times, and she remembered every single time. Every single moment.

"Stop smiling like that," Anne commanded. "Gideon is married, remember? Think about Villiers."

"I was, actually," Eleanor said.

"No, you weren't," Anne said sourly. "I've been your sister for eighteen years. I know what that daffy look means, and it has got nothing to do with the Duke of Villiers."

"Do you really think that I've been worshipping at Gideon's shrine?" Eleanor wrinkled her nose. "How wet I sound."

"You were unlucky. He is a debaucher who took the first chance he could to leave you in the dust and marry the oh-so-pretty Ada."

Eleanor bit her lip.

"I didn't mean it like that!" Anne said hastily. "You're pretty too, Eleanor."

"In my own way."

"It's just that Ada has that heart-shaped face and seems so fragile. She's like a fairy princess. Irresistible, for a man who loves to think of himself as a knight in shining armor."

"She truly is fragile—*and* sweet," Eleanor said. "I'm not, and I can't pretend that I am."

"Of course you're not. And Gideon knows it now," Anne said with unmistakable satisfaction.

"What do you mean?"

"I mean that he's tired of Ada and her fainting and coughing and carrying on. I saw it last time Mother took me there for tea and he stayed with us for barely a moment or two. I think he probably fell in love with the idea of saving her, poor fragile little darling that she was, but now he—"

"Don't go on," Eleanor said. "You're making everything in my life, everything I care for, seem shabby and nasty. I know you don't mean it, but I want you to stop now."

The door bounced open again. "Girls! Don't keep me waiting, *if* you please!" Their mother stood in the doorway, ringed by three maids. "Hobson, gather that lace shawl, if you please. Eleanor, hand the dog to Hobson; he can travel with the maids. Oyster may be a source for conversation, but I'd rather arrive without urine on my skirts."

"We'll be there in a moment, Mother," Eleanor said. Her mother swept back into the entryway, demanding her gloves.

"I'm sorry," she said to Anne. "I didn't mean to be unkind. It's—"

"No, you were right," her sister said, darting over to give her a hug. "That's the problem with me. I see everything in the darkest possible light."

"Don't you think I'd know it if Gideon had showed the slightest interest in me after marrying Ada? He has rarely spoken to me since hearing his father's will read."

"But you would never consider adultery, would you?" Anne asked, sounding truly scandalized.

"Of course not! I would never do anything so depraved."

Anne kissed her. "I want you to be married, Eleanor. You'll be a wonderful mother."

"I shall. That is, I already like Villiers, and that's all that's necessary for a sound marriage."

Their mother's voice shrieked from the entry. "Oyster has peed on the marble again, Eleanor!" There was a smacking noise and a yelp. "You bad dog! Hobson, make him sit down."

"I have to rescue poor Oyster," Eleanor said, hastily

straightening her bonnet and snatching up her gloves. "Poor thing. I'm afraid that when Mother is excited it all gets worse, and smacking does *not* help."

"We have to make sure he doesn't get nervous on Lisette's carpet. Or on Villiers's boots. It might be enough to ruin your chances of being a duchess. Men are absurdly attached to the shine on their boots."

"You think you know everything about men, don't you, little sister?"

"I consider myself a naturalist of the male species," Anne said loftily. "I have made a study of their habits."

"I shall wear your clothing," Eleanor said. "Because the truth is that I don't want to appear like a frump, and I didn't really understand that I was. But I can tell you this: a new gown won't make Villiers burst into my bedroom and assess my silver accoutrements. We plan to have a quite different kind of relationship."

"After I transform you, you can choose whatever sort of relationship you wish—but Villiers won't have the same freedom of mind. I'll guarantee you that."

"You're no naturalist," Eleanor said.

"Then what am I?"

"A hunter. Poor Villiers."

Their mother appeared. "Eleanor, I'll thank you to use what intelligence you have and follow me to the carriage. At this rate, Villiers will appear before you, and Lisette will snap him up without a moment's remorse."

Anne leaned over and ripped the lace fichu straight out of Eleanor's bodice.

"What on earth are you doing!" Eleanor looked down. Without its lace kerchief, her neckline was shockingly low.

"Preparing you for the trip," Anne said, standing back and nodding with satisfaction. "I must say, it doesn't seem fair to me that you inherited those eyes *and* that bosom."

"I don't see why I must display every inch of my inheritance," Eleanor retorted.

"Because you wish to present a delicious contrast to Lisette," her sister said. "Unless Lisette's shape has changed a great deal, she is less fortunate than you are. Think of it as a generous toss of corn."

"What?"

"The corn will draw the pheasants," Anne said with a wicked grin. "And then the hunters can take them down."

# Chapter Seven

*London residence of the Duke of Villiers*
*15 Piccadilly*
*June 17, 1784*

Tobias had made up his mind to go to Kent with Villiers by hook or by crook. In the beginning, he had been happy simply to eat whatever he wished. But that paled quickly, and now he was bored. The other children were babies. Colin was obsessed with learning how to read, and Violet had found an old doll that she talked to all the time.

The only dilemma was how to stow away on Villiers's coach without being caught. If he could just sneak inside, one of the seat cushions concealed a large box meant for storing blankets. He knew because he'd been cold on the way from Wapping, and the duke had thrown one at him.

But he would have to time his escape perfectly, before the duke's four grooms emerged from the stables.

After breakfast he strolled casually out the door. Likely, Ashmole would have seen through him, but he had taken care of that by asking Violet to create a diversion. The fire she had started on the nursery floor ought to keep Ashmole busy. She needn't have thrown Colin's book onto the blaze, however. He could still hear Colin's howls from the front doorstep.

None of the footmen knew how to treat him—as a child of the house, or as a by-blow? Their dilemma just made Tobias grin: he didn't give a rat's ass how they treated him, as long as they danced to his tune. A solitary groom standing at the horses' heads gave him a bored glance but said nothing until Tobias pulled open the door to the carriage.

"Here, you!" the man bellowed. Tobias stuck his head back out of the carriage and gave him a cheerful smile. "Just doing an errand for Mr. Ashmole," he said. "Getting a blanket he asked for."

"An errand for Mr. Ashmole?" He could see the concept slowly trickling into the groom's mind. An errand put Tobias into the category of servant. And that meant he could kick Tobias into shape if he wanted to. It was obviously a comforting thought.

"I like to help Mr. Ashmole whenever I can," Tobias said, ladling it on. "Perhaps someday I can be a butler just like him." He tried for a soulful look, which probably made him look like a sick calf.

The groom thought this over. Tobias could almost see him relaxing: if Tobias wanted to be a butler, well then he wasn't getting above his place in life. Much.

"Like to see *you* a butler!" the groom said, guffawing as he would at any beggar who expressed the same wish.

"I'll make it someday," Tobias said, putting on the

brave and cheerful face of an orphan. "I don't mind hard work. That's why I'm trying to help today."

"You'd best get on with it, then," the groom said, waving him on.

"Could I do something for you, next?" Tobias asked. "Hold the horses for a moment, maybe? I do love horses."

"I could take a piss," the man said. "Bring that there blanket to Ashmole and come back here, smart-like."

"Yes, sir," Tobias said, pulling the blanket out of its place and trotting up the steps back to the house. 'Course, it wasn't a normal blanket. It was soft as a baby's backside, and trimmed in some sort of fur. Ermine or suchlike. He handed the blanket to the footman stationed in the hallway and told him that it was to be sent to the laundry.

"You shouldn't be using the front steps like that," the groom told him a moment later, as he handed over the reins. "Ashmole will whup you if he sees you at it."

"I think he said something about that," Tobias said vaguely, stroking one of the horses' noses.

"I'll be back in a minute," the man said, heading around the side of the building. "Mr. Seffle will be coming to drive the coach around the block again. Doesn't like the horses to get antsy."

The moment he disappeared around the side of the building, Tobias called to the footman just inside the door. When he appeared, Tobias shouted, "Tell Mr. Seffle I took the horses around the block."

By the time the duke's coachman, Seffle, rushed around the side of the house, Tobias was already hidden in the coach. The horses hadn't even had time to realize that they were free to trot off. From inside the blanket box, Tobias could faintly hear Seffle swearing, followed by a shouting match between Seffle and the groom and the ensuing search for himself, but after a few minutes it all settled down and Seffle jumped on the coach to drive it around the block.

Tobias wasn't overly uncomfortable. He could sit with his arms clasped around his legs. They trundled around the final corner and pulled to a halt again. He heard the duke's drawling voice. "Are you saying that Ashmole asked my son to run errands for him?"

Tobias couldn't help grinning. He hadn't made up his mind about his father. Villiers was like some sort of weird exotic bird with nasty eyes and a strange way of talking. He wasn't friendly. Or warm.

But Tobias still thought about the way Villiers had knocked over Grindel, the man who forced him to root around in the mud to pick up things like human teeth. Grindel had hit the ground with an enormous crash. And now there was a tone in Villiers's voice that said Ashmole was in danger of losing his job if he confused Tobias with a footman.

Villiers seemed to think he could make everyone forget that his son was a bastard. Which was idiotic, though Tobias appreciated the thought.

Finally the coach lurched to a start. Tobias planned to wait until they were on the outskirts of London before he announced his presence. But they couldn't have gone more than a block when the wooden roof over his head suddenly flew open.

He raised his head slowly, and met his father's eyes. He had learned long ago to stay silent in awkward situations, so he said nothing.

Unfortunately, it seemed his father adhered to the same lesson, and after an uncomfortable moment Tobias couldn't take it any longer. "Ashmole didn't ask me to do an errand for him. How did you know I was in here?"

The duke arched an eyebrow. "A blanket carried into the house followed by a missing boy hardly posed much of a conundrum. And there was the fire in the nursery as well."

Tobias climbed out of the blanket box, pushing the flap back down. Surely the duke would shout to the coachman, stop the carriage, and send him back in the care of the furious groom, who would likely give him a clip on the ear, if not worse.

But his father said nothing at all, simply turning his eyes to a small book he held in his hands.

After a while Tobias asked, "Aren't you going to send me back?"

The duke looked up. "I assume that you have some desire to accompany me."

Tobias opened his mouth, but Villiers raised a hand. "You needn't embellish. I gather that after a few years chasing through a muddy riverbed in danger of life and limb, you find the nursery tedious. I suspect," he added, "that the addition of a six-year-old girl to that nursery has not improved matters."

"She was quite good this morning," Tobias said fairly.

"Ah, the fire. I do wish that you had told her that the embroidery samplers from the west wall were not for burning. Ashmole seems quite distressed by their demise. They were over one hundred years old."

"Probably moldy, then," Tobias pointed out. "I didn't specify the sort of fuss she should make. I would have told her not to burn Colin's book."

"She burned *all* the books in the nursery," Villiers remarked.

Tobias didn't believe in apologizing, as a matter of course. But somehow he found his mouth opening and something along those lines emerging.

Villiers merely shrugged. "We'll have to watch her on Guy Fawkes Night."

Tobias began to feel more comfortable. "Are we really going to Kent to meet your wife?"

"She's not my wife yet. I'll choose whichever of the two women seems likely to be the better mother to the lot of you."

"I don't need a mother," Tobias said.

"Violet does." His father turned a page. "And so do the twins. They are much younger than you."

"Boys or girls?"

"Girls."

"Did you know that I was a boy?"

"Yes."

"What was my mother like?"

"Extremely pretty."

Tobias froze, hoping that he would continue. But Villiers turned another page.

"You're being an ass," Tobias said, dropping the words into the silence of the carriage with great precision.

At first his father didn't move. Then he looked up again. "Am I to gather you believe this is an unusual occurrence, or merely that I should be concerned by your assessment?"

"Why didn't you marry my mother?" But he knew. He knew even as he asked it.

"I didn't marry your mother because she was an opera singer, and my mistress. She was also Italian, and quite beautiful, and rather mad. She was not a lady in the strict sense of the word."

Tobias hated him, from the tip of his polished boots to the sheen of his heavy silk coat.

"She didn't care to rear you," Villiers said, putting his book down. "She was not a motherly type. But she thought you were beautiful."

"How do you know?"

"Unlike the other children, you were born on my estate. She was on tour through England, and when her confinement interrupted that tour, she and the rest of the troupe stayed with me."

"In the house? With Ashmole?"

"With Ashmole, but at one of my country estates."

Tobias couldn't imagine that. "Did you ever see her again?"

Villiers looked at him straight in the eyes. "She was a very famous opera singer, Tobias."

Tobias felt his blood running cold. But it was no more than he already knew, had known for years. There was no one for him in the world.

"She died in Venice of an ague. She had stayed out too late after singing a special concert for the doge."

Tobias shrugged. "She means nothing to me. Just a doxy who was too pretty to wed."

His father met his eyes until Tobias dropped his. "She thought I would keep you safe. You should be angry at me, if anyone."

"If it's all right with you, I shall take a nap," Tobias said, closing his eyes.

He thought he heard his father say, "Toushay." What did that mean, Toushay?

# Chapter Eight

*Knole House, country residence of the Duke of Gilner*
*Late afternoon*
*June 17, 1784*

The Duke of Gilner's estate lay deep in the green hills of Kent. It was a square house with aggressively symmetrical wings, the whole of it arranged with every bit of mathematical rigor that could be summoned to the task. Windows marched around the wings like soldiers on parade.

And yet . . .

If everything about the house celebrated the ideals of reason and rationality, the rest of the estate seemed to express the opposite. The gardens and the avenue had undoubtedly been calculated with algebraic excellence. Years ago, trees probably marched down that avenue at precisely calibrated intervals. Moreover, those trees had been chosen for their melancholy regularity, like the tall skinny mourning trees that surrounded Italian cemeteries.

But now the geometric skill of the architect was defeated by chaos. The avenue had begun with a series of oaks, now grown to stately proportions. A few had been lost to wind or were cut down. Missing oaks had been replaced with a beech here and an apple tree there. A short squat tree that looked like nothing so much as a claret bottle tipped gently to the right between two dignified trunks.

And the grounds! Worse and worse. Someone had apparently planned a hedge maze to the right of the house. Eleanor could see the vestiges of its lanes and alleys, but the hedges had withered and been cut down in places. A ramshackle cottage off to the left might have been called a folly, but only by those who were truly charitable. The untidiness of it all was exacerbated by several faded archery targets. They were stuck around the lawn with a permanent look to them; one had a rambler growing up its post.

"The estate looks even more disreputable than I remember," she said, stepping down from the carriage with the help of a groom. "Why did we stop visiting? I remember when we used to pay a visit every year. Did you and Lisette's mother quarrel?"

"Of course not! As if I would ever be so ill-bred as to quarrel with someone," her mother replied, magnificently ignoring the many squabbles that enlivened her days. "And certainly not with poor Beatrice. I was one of her dearest friends; we were presented in the same year. And then when we both became duchesses, well . . ."

"What happened?" Anne prompted, hopping out of the carriage. "Goodness me, I'm happy to be out of that vehicle."

"Lisette is a few years older than Eleanor," her mother said, gesturing to one of the grooms, who trotted off to bang the knocker. The household appeared not to have noticed the arrival of a coach-and-four on the drive, let alone the second coach carrying three maids and a quantity of trunks. "There was a catastrophe. Beatrice quite lost heart, and when she was carried off with pneumonia a mere year later, I knew the real cause."

"What catastrophe?" Eleanor asked patiently. The footman was thumping the knocker but apparently having no success.

The duchess hesitated. "It's all very well for Anne to know, since she's married. Though I suppose you're a woman now."

"I have been reconciled to that status for several years," Eleanor said.

"How queer you are," the duchess snapped. "Well, I'll make it blunt, then. Lisette formed an unfortunate attachment to a gentleman."

"She never seemed very interested when we were girls," Anne observed.

"That could be due to the fact that she is unable to hold an interest in any subject for more than a day or two," Eleanor pointed out. "It's hard to imagine a man holding sway. She certainly never mentioned anything in her letters. Although to be fair, she has developed what seems to be a long-term interest in helping orphaned children."

"I blame Beatrice," their mother said darkly. "I have done my duty by you girls. Neither of you would ever shame me by an illicit liaison." She shuddered.

"Was the gentleman ineligible?" Eleanor asked, thinking it best to draw her mother's attention quickly away from the putative chastity of her own daughters.

"I shall never reveal that," the duchess announced,

taking on the tone of a martyr facing a hostile crowd. "I promised Beatrice that I would take the truth to my grave. But—" She relented suddenly, lowering her voice, "I will tell you that the child—"

"Child!" Eleanor exclaimed. "You didn't say there'd been a child!"

"I said a catastrophe," her mother replied. "And believe me, in cases such as these, the words are one and the same. We shall speak no more of it. Look at this house! Beatrice would be horrified by the muddle. But I am not one to criticize; I understand the difficulty of keeping household help." It was certainly true that the duchess's acerbic comments had a tendency to drive said household help straight out of said household.

Finally the groom's repeated bangs on the door produced a response. A butler was trotting down the main steps, bowing slightly from the waist as he came, as if he wanted to get a head start on his salutations.

"Your Grace," he said, swinging into a deep bow like a marionette. "This is such a pleasure, such a pleasure. I'm afraid that the Duke of Gilner is not at home, but I shall send him a message."

"Absolutely not," Eleanor's mother declared with a wave of the hand. "I didn't come to see Gilner, but his daughter. This is nothing more than a pleasant little visit, a matter of a few days at the most. Between friends."

Because the butler was still blinking at her rather than escorting them directly into the house, she said, "Lady Lisette is in residence, is she not?"

"Of course," he said, "but I'm afraid that Lady Marguerite is paying a visit to a relative. She'll be back tomorrow afternoon."

"Well, then, bring us to our chambers so that we can refresh ourselves after this journey," the duchess commanded. "It may be only a few hours from London, but you would not countenance the dust. At one point I thought I was sure to suffocate."

Eleanor was interested to see how distressed the butler appeared to be. He was literally wringing his hands. "Perhaps there are no free chambers?" she inquired.

He rushed into speech. Apparently, there were more than enough chambers, but in Lady Marguerite's absence—

Her mother lost her patience immediately and waved him quiet. "Eleanor, did I not instruct you to write a note announcing our visit?"

"I did, Mother. Perhaps Lady Lisette neglected to inform you?" Eleanor said, giving the butler a smile.

"Be kind enough to escort us to some chambers, my good man," the duchess said before he could answer. "I am not used to parrying words with a butler in the open air!"

The man tore back up the stairs as if the devil were behind him. Eleanor, Anne, and their mother followed, trailing a phalanx of groomsmen carrying their trunks, the sheer number of which belied the question of a visit of a mere day or two.

The moment they entered the house the source of the butler's distress became obvious. If the estate's grounds were somewhat disorganized, the entrance hall was a jumble.

The hall was designed in a graceful circle stretching to the second floor, which was encircled by a banister. But at the moment that banister was apparently serving as an impromptu place for dirty laundry. It was hung with sheets that swayed in the breeze of the open door.

"An odd way to manage your linens," the duchess said, turning in a stately circle and craning her neck. "I can't say I recommend it. And these sheets are disgracefully unclean. What *is* your name?"

"Popper, Your Grace," the butler said, looking miserable. "They're not laundry, Your Grace, but backdrops for the play."

"Those appear to be trees," Eleanor said, pointing to a sheet marked with blotches that might have represented a forest in a high wind.

Her mother narrowed her eyes. "More likely a field of carrot tops."

A peal of laughter answered her, and they all looked up and saw Lisette lightly running down the stairs. For a moment they just stared up at her, and then Eleanor gave a little wave. She hadn't seen Lisette in seven or eight years, but if anything, she had grown only more exquisite. Eleanor had always envied her hair; it was pale, pale blond, and naturally formed beautiful ringlets. Her face was the peaceful oval of a medieval madonna. Most of the time.

"Ellie!" Lisette dashed down the stairs and gave Eleanor a hug, and another hug. She turned with a similar cry to Anne.

The duchess stiffened at the first hug, and became rigid by the third. When Lisette finally dropped her arms from Anne, Eleanor said hastily, "My mother, the Duchess of Montague."

"It's been years, hasn't it?" Lisette said, smiling at the duchess with sunny charm as she dropped a shallow curtsy. "But I couldn't forget such a beautiful chin as you have, Your Grace. Your skin has loosened slightly, around the jowls, but really, hardly at all."

Her mother appeared stunned into silence, so Eleanor put in, "Surely you remember that Lady Lisette is an enthusiastic painter, Mother."

"Oh, please, no *ladies* here," Lisette said. She waved her fingers in the air and they saw that they were splotched with red, blue, and purple. "I have been painting backdrops for a village play. I can find you a role, if you'd like."

Eleanor couldn't help smiling. That was just like Lisette. She would hop out of a seven-hour carriage ride and throw herself into painting backdrops, and it wouldn't occur to her that others might not be so eager.

"I must return to the back garden," Lisette said. "I'll look forward to dining together. Popper, do put our guests somewhere, won't you?" Without further ado, she turned and left.

Her mother's face contorted in such a manner that Eleanor knew precisely what she thought of Lisette's manners.

Popper wrung his hands again. "If I'd known you were coming, Your Grace, I would have made sure that the house was decent."

"If you would be so good as to allow me to retire," the duchess stated with a quiet ferocity. "I have a powerful headache coming on. I expect it has something to do with the reek of paint in this house. And I'll thank you to take those sheets down, Popper. I hardly think Lady Marguerite would approve."

"Yes, Your Grace," Popper said. "Of course, Your Grace. Please, follow me."

A few minutes later Eleanor, Anne, and Popper tiptoed out of the duchess's bedchamber, leaving her in the tender care of two maids, who were busy fanning her forehead and mixing various restorative powders.

"I'm afraid I shall have to put you in the other wing," Popper said anxiously, as he and Eleanor walked down the corridor, having deposited Anne in a room next to their mother. "We don't often have visitors, and many of the rooms are draped in Holland cloths. I shall remove the sheets immediately, of course. The look on the Duchess of Montague's face!" He shuddered. "I arrived here from the household of the Marquess of Pestle. I am not ignorant of a well-ordered household."

"Of course not," Eleanor said soothingly. She had a sudden thought. "I do believe that the Duke of Villiers may pay Lady Lisette a visit today or tomorrow, Mr. Popper, so you might want to prepare another chamber."

He turned even paler, if that were possible. "And her aunt's gone visiting! Perhaps I'll send a note to Lady Marguerite and beg her to return this very evening."

"Likely a good idea," Eleanor agreed. "Would you mind having my dog brought to my chamber, Mr. Popper?"

He starting wringing his hands again. "A dog? There is a dog?"

"Yes," she said. "My dog. He's a small pug, cream-colored with a black muzzle. One of our groomsmen has him, no doubt."

The butler took a step closer. "If you don't mind my saying so, Lady Eleanor . . ."

Eleanor put on her mother's best quelling expression, and Mr. Popper shifted back immediately. "Yes?"

"Lady Lisette is frightened by dogs."

"She won't be afraid of Oyster. He's a pug, the kind that doesn't grow very big. He'll be far more afraid of Lisette than she will be of him. Everyone loves Oyster." She waved him off toward the stairs.

That was true, too. Except for the people he peed on, of course. But there hadn't been all that many.

By the time Eleanor bathed and Oyster had arrived, she was feeling better. She put on a dressing gown and scooped Oyster into her lap to sit by the fire. He was really too fat to sit comfortably in anyone's lap, but he loved it, and she loved it. So they sat together while he squirmed and wriggled, and got short bristly hairs all over her lap.

"You need to grow up and stop this indiscriminate peeing," she told him.

He wasn't much of a talker, more of a nuzzler, so he nuzzled and begged for more scratching until Eleanor decided that she ought to dress. It would be a disaster if Villiers arrived before she was downstairs to blunt her mother's ambitions.

"What if I wear the cherry cotton with the gauze overlay?" she asked Willa. It was one of her old gowns, rather than Anne's, but she felt too tired to achieve decadence.

Willa had spent the last two hours emptying the trunks that Eleanor had brought with her for this short, casual trip to the country. "There's no cherry cotton here, my lady," she said, adding, "My mistress selected your gowns herself and she had to remove some garments in order to accommodate those she brought for you to wear."

Eleanor sighed. "I have nothing to wear that wasn't handpicked by my sister?"

Willa shook her head.

She might as well be hanged for a sheep as a lamb. "In that case, why don't you choose something for me?"

"The figured silk," Willa suggested. "You can wear it with small side panniers." She held it up.

"It is beautiful, but there isn't much of it," Eleanor pointed out. "If I lean over, the bodice might open almost to my waist."

"If you're not comfortable, we can pin some lace at the neckline," Willa said reassuringly. "I'll put lace in your hair as well. We needn't put a touch of powder in your hair; did you see Lady Lisette?"

"Lisette never wears powder," Eleanor said. "Nor wigs."

"Then we shan't either," Willa said, snapping her small

white teeth together. Obviously Anne had filled her in on the matrimonial sweepstakes, so to speak.

An hour or so later Eleanor wandered down the stairs. It was some comfort to know that she truly was looking her best. Her hair would never be the spun gold color of Lisette's. But she liked the way it glowed, with a kind of brandy burnish. It was thick too, thicker than Lisette's, and would hold a curl, or fall sleek and straight, whatever she wished.

Willa had piled it on top of her head, with gorgeous little silk twists among the curls. And even though she still felt that the gown would look better in a candlelit drawing room, it was exquisite. The lace had looked foolish, so there she was with her breasts on view, which was clearly what Anne had in mind.

She brought Oyster down with her too. He had been very good the last few hours, but he was just a puppy. He couldn't stay in the room all day. Willa had treated him like an accessory and tied little knots of silk on his collar so that he matched her dress.

The sheets had disappeared and the house was as silent and ordinary looking as any gentleman's country house, barring a complete lack of servants. She poked her head into the sitting room, and then wandered into the library. The shelves were crammed with books reaching the ceiling, though on close inspection most of them turned out to be books about music, which was disappointing.

At length, Oyster gave a little yelp, and she realized that it would be an unfortunate way to begin her visit if he were to anoint the library rug.

The library opened to the garden, so she tugged open the tall doors and walked out onto the terrace. To her surprise, the entire household was clustered on a grassy slope at the bottom of the garden, maids in white aprons and footmen in livery, all seated on what appeared to be the backdrops that had formerly hung in the entryway. There even seemed to be some children tucked in front.

At that moment the door at her back opened and a deep voice drawled, "Perhaps they've all been taken by the fairies."

"Villiers!" she exclaimed, turning. And there was Anne as well, smiling with gleeful pleasure.

The duke bowed and kissed her hand. Eleanor found herself sorry that she'd left her gloves upstairs, if only so he could strip one off again. Then she met his eyes and colored. He was damnably good at guessing her thoughts.

"Where is everyone?" Anne asked.

"They're out there, in the gardens. Do come onto the terrace. There is a very pleasant arrangement of chairs and— Oh, no, I dropped Oyster's leash!"

Sure enough, a plump little figure was tearing across the lawn, yipping madly.

"The famous Oyster," Villiers said.

"He can be a trifle overenthusiastic," Eleanor said.

"He sheds," Anne said disloyally. "And he seems to think he's irresistible. Let's not even mention the fact that he sprinkles constantly."

"He's just a puppy!"

"Now, now, no squabbling," Villiers said.

There was a piercing shriek from the lawn, followed by another. The little group seemed to explode, children running and wheeling.

"What the devil?" Villiers said, starting forward.

Anne laughed. "He's already peed on someone, Ellie."

Eleanor began running after Villiers. As she grew closer she saw with a sinking heart that Oyster did appear to be the center of the fracas. He was dashing madly in a circle, yapping with the sort of strained excitement she associated with household accidents.

There were a great many children, at least seven or eight, milling about in blue pinafores. And still the screaming: she just couldn't see who was doing it. Oyster ran toward her, barking hysterically, his ears flopping. He was trying to tell her something . . .

The butler was dashing after Oyster. "Popper," she called, "what on earth—"

But then the screaming stopped, the knot of people separated, and Eleanor saw the heart of the matter. Lisette was nestled in Villiers's arms, one arm around his neck, head against his shoulder.

"I'm very much afraid that Lady Lisette was surprised by your canine," Popper said, breathing hard. "As I mentioned, she is afraid of dogs."

Long ago Eleanor had decided that what made Lisette truly beautiful was that she rarely showed emotion. There was nothing to prevent appreciation of her blue eyes, her perfectly straight nose, her pale rosebud lips.

Even now, when she was apparently terrified by Oyster, her face was expressionless: no anxiously squeezed eyes or pursed mouth, or ungraceful pant. Instead she was curled in Villiers arms, looking like a portrait come to quiet life.

Eleanor reached down and picked up her squat little dog, which at least made him stop yapping. "Scared?" she said. "She is frightened by *Oyster*? He must have startled her."

Brushing past Popper, she walked over to Villiers. "Hello, Lisette."

Lisette didn't answer. Her eyes were now closed. "Surely she didn't faint?" Eleanor said to Villiers, not believing it for a moment.

He looked down at Lisette with a rather queer expression on his face. "I think she's recovering from the shock. When I came up, she was utterly beside herself with terror. Of course, I swept her up and out of harm's way, but it took a moment to sink in."

"Out of harm's way," Eleanor said, looking down at Oyster. He lay along her arm like a particularly warm, heavy baby, which, in fact, he was. Barring the fact that he had all four paws in the air and was panting, he could have been taken for a fat and hairy newborn.

Well, perhaps that wasn't true. Eleanor had to admit that her preference for pugs was not shared by all.

"I can see you're listening, Lisette, so please open your eyes," she said sharply. "I'd like to introduce you to my puppy."

Lisette opened her eyes, but the moment she caught sight of Oyster, she screamed again and shuddered closer to Villiers. "He's so *ugly*!"

"He's not—" Eleanor began. But there was no getting around the fact that even a creamy white coat and a midnight black muzzle couldn't make a pug precisely beautiful. "He's not ugly," she stated firmly. "He is a fine dog."

"I am afraid of dogs," Lisette said, shuddering visibly. "And that one is monstrously shaped. There is something *wrong* with its eyes! They look like—like disgusting fish eggs!"

Eleanor looked around at the circle of rapt children. "You're not setting a good example, Lisette. This is Oyster," she said to the children. "He's a very sweet puppy who wouldn't dream of hurting anyone. And his features are completely appropriate for the kind of dog he is."

Naturally, given Lisette's revulsion, the children were eyeing Oyster as if he had three heads.

"He's grotesque," Lisette said breathily.

"Our hostess is afraid of dogs," Villiers pointed out, rather unnecessarily to Eleanor's mind. "Perhaps you might keep the animal in your bedchamber during your visit."

Eleanor blinked down at Oyster. He certainly wasn't beautiful. But he was no bulldog either. "Lisette," she said incredulously, coming a step nearer. "Are you really saying that you're afraid of a dog who weighs less than a stone? He still has his milk teeth, for God's sake!"

"I am," Lisette said, a gasp breaking her voice. "I know I'm an idiot. I'm so stupid. I know it. Just please—please—will you take him away? Please?"

"Of course," Eleanor said, stepping backwards again. Oyster snorted and reached up to lick her chin. She turned around and marched back to the house, feeling her ears burning red with rage.

It wasn't just the way Lisette had shuddered. Or even the way her eyes had started to bulge so that she actually resembled Oyster. It was the way that Villiers had looked down at her, as if he were protecting her from a man-eating crocodile.

Ridiculous. They were both utterly ridiculous.

Anne was comfortably seated on a small settee, powdering her nose. "Let me guess," she said as Eleanor came up the steps to the terrace, clutching Oyster. "Lisette turned into the trembling maiden, but luckily a big, strong duke was there to rescue her? Wait—haven't we heard this story before?"

Eleanor plumped down beside her and turned Oyster free to scrabble about. "Are you implying that Lisette is akin to Ada?" she demanded, still furious. "Because I can assure you that Ada would never behave in such an unreasonable manner."

"What on earth are all those children doing out there?" Anne asked. "Do you suppose one of them is the child to whom Mother referred so darkly? Perhaps Lisette didn't stop with one." She giggled madly. "Perhaps she is a female match to Villiers!"

"Don't be foolish. They're wearing pinafores. I assume

they're from the orphanage," Eleanor said, shrugging. "I know that Lisette—" She sat upright. "The orphanage!"

Anne raised an eyebrow.

"Two of those children may be Villiers's."

"What a naughty boy," Anne said, without showing the faintest bit of shock.

"For having two?"

"I already heard that he had some illicit offspring. No, rather, for stowing them in an orphanage. That's not acceptable."

"He lost them," Eleanor said, finding it very queer to defend the duke, even as she did so. "He had a crooked solicitor, and the man ran off with his funds. It turned out he'd been defrauding the children of their support."

"So the duke's offspring were plunked in an orphanage. It sounds like a bad play."

Eleanor narrowed her eyes. Across the lawn, Villiers had placed Lisette back on her feet, but she was still clinging to him. "Maybe he has decided to marry her so he can defend her from wild animal attacks."

"She could do much worse. After all, she's already met his children."

"Not all of them," Eleanor said. "Apparently he has six."

"Trust Villiers to double the common allotment of iniquity," Anne said placidly. "The poor man must be desperate to prove his virility. I wonder why?"

"I think it was just carelessness," Eleanor said.

"Oh, look. Popper has lined up all the orphans and is marching them off somewhere. If I'd known Lisette had turned her estate into an orphanage, I wouldn't have come, even for you, darling. I am not fond of children."

"I think they live in the village, not on the grounds."

"Do you see how she is leaning on Villiers as she gracefully limps back to the house?" Anne inquired. "We could all take lessons there, I think." She gave Eleanor a meaningful look.

"Perhaps she hurt her toe running away from nasty Oyster."

"That would explain why I can tell from here that the supposedly chilly Duke of Villiers is tying his heart in knots over the defenseless girl he just rescued from certain death."

"Is he really?" Eleanor refused to look. "Too bad. He seemed halfway sensible. If you think that I might transform into a trembling maiden to catch a husband, Anne, you're wrong."

"For one thing, you'd have trouble with the maiden part," her sister said, chortling.

Eleanor threw her a quick frown as Villiers and Lisette neared the terrace. She looked around for Oyster, and realized to her relief that he'd collapsed into his favorite position and was engaged in his favorite activity: sleeping. Thankfully, well-hidden under the sofa.

Lisette perched on the arm of the sofa and bent to give Eleanor a little kiss. Her slipper was a hairbreadth away from Oyster's chubby paw.

"That was such a turmoil that I never got to say how wonderfully happy I am that the two of you are paying me a visit," she exclaimed, as if the whole event had never happened. Eleanor suddenly remembered how hard it was to stay angry at Lisette. Since she forgot her own emotions so quickly, it felt churlish to say a cross word to her. And that, of course, was how she got away with such outrageous behavior.

"I should have visited you before this," Eleanor said, feeling a mild pang of guilt. "I can't believe so many years have passed."

"Popper tells me that we must all prepare for dinner.

But I just wanted to say . . ." Her voice trailed off and she twisted her hands together.

"It's all right," Eleanor said. "I know some people loathe dogs. If I'd known, I wouldn't have brought him with me, Lisette."

"It's just that I was attacked by a dog once," she said in a rush. "I was just telling Leopold all about it."

*Leopold?* She was already calling the duke by his first name?

"I was younger than I am now, and even less brave," she said with a charming catch to her voice. "I was knocked over, you see, and—" She thrust out her arm.

Eleanor saw to her horror that the skin was puckered by fang-shaped scars. "Oh, Lisette, that's awful!"

"I think the fear is worse than the actual bite," Lisette said, sounding almost practical.

Anne murmured something that sounded like encouragement.

"Because fear doesn't go away, and bites do," Lisette added.

At that moment Oyster made a woofing sound in his sleep and moved his bristly little paw closer to Lisette's slipper. Eleanor hastily coughed.

"I must take a bath," Lisette said, rising with all her usual grace. "It was such an exciting afternoon—oh, not because of your dog, Eleanor. We were discussing the play the children were to put on, and then I had the sudden realization that what we really ought to do is a treasure hunt, rather than a play. It's so much more interesting for the children, and they're the ones who matter, after all. I simply insisted that the whole household hear my new idea, though Popper did protest. After all, you had your maids if you needed something." She gave a charming shrug.

"Of course," Eleanor said, not getting up. If she rose, Oyster would realize his nap was over and likely offer up his squeaky bark to remind her of his presence.

"I do believe I'll just sit here and enjoy the last bit of sunlight," Anne said. "Eleanor, stay with me."

Lisette danced off with a wave of her hand.

"Villiers," Eleanor said, "what did you think of the children?"

He frowned. "Children?"

"Small creatures, wearing blue pinafores," Anne prompted helpfully. "I didn't stir from the portico because of them. At least Oyster has the good manners to occasionally silence himself. Children never do."

"Children," Villiers repeated. "You mean the village children?"

"The *orphan* children," Eleanor prompted.

His eyes narrowed. "Those were *orphans*?"

"I gather your attention was elsewhere," she said sweetly. "I can certainly understand that. Poor Lisette was so afraid of the big bad wolf named Oyster."

"Now, now," Anne said. "I don't see you with a disfiguring scar on your arm, Eleanor, so don't mock it until you have it. Have you never been afraid of anything?"

Eleanor didn't need to think hard about that. She was afraid of important things, like people being ripped away from her without warning. Never of spiders or puppy dogs or thunderstorms. "Of course I'm not mocking Lisette. I was merely sympathizing with the duke. Lisette's alarm engaged him so deeply that he didn't notice he was surrounded by orphans, two of whom might well have been his own children."

Villiers was likely trying to frighten her with that scowl. She smiled right back at him.

"How do you know they were orphans?" he demanded.

"What else did you think they were?"

Anne interjected. "I suggested that Lisette had started a family, but that was too scandalous even for Eleanor to consider. I don't know if you realize this about my sister, Villiers, but she's very hard to shock."

"I have learned that already," Villiers said. He had a white line around his mouth that almost made Eleanor feel sorry for him. But not quite.

"Do you have any idea of the age of the children you're looking for?" she asked, needling him and enjoying it.

"Of course I do. If you'll excuse me . . ." And he left without another word. And without a parting bow either.

"Dear me, Eleanor. I don't think you've made your future spouse very happy," Anne said meditatively. "Remember how I suggested you might try to be a wee bit more conciliatory toward the male sex?"

"He may be my future spouse, and he may not," Eleanor said. "My chest is quite chilly at the moment, I might add. You'll have to be satisfied with my sartorial transformation and leave my personality alone."

"I'd like you to marry him. He's terribly rich. And I do like those shoulders."

"That's not a good enough reason to marry someone."

"Well, what would you say is a better reason? Not, I hope, the sort of frantic passion you and dear Gideon shared. Besides, you know perfectly well that his choirboy looks played a part in that."

"One doesn't marry a man for his shoulders," Eleanor said. "Brains ought to rank high on the list, and anyone who looks at Lisette with such a look in his eye is stupider than Oyster. I have standards."

Oyster grunted at the sound of his name and inched out from under the chair so he could put his chin on Eleanor's slipper.

"Don't underestimate Villiers," Anne said.

"More importantly, I shan't underestimate Lisette!" Eleanor retorted. "She's perfected her trembling maiden act since I saw her last."

"It's not an act," Anne said. "That's why it's so successful. Goodness me, Eleanor, you sound as if you care."

"I'm not sure whether Lisette should marry him either. After all, he does have a thoroughly disreputable number of children."

"Not just children—bastards," Anne said with her usual bluntness. "Wait until Mother hears that little detail. Lisette may have a brain as empty as a washhouse on Sundays, but I agree with you. She doesn't deserve the kind of scandal broth that will follow those children. She has her own to cope with."

"You know Lisette. She changes her mind every five minutes. She may be smiling at him now, but wait until tomorrow."

"What an interesting visit this shall be," Anne said, coming to her feet. "Wake up that dog, Eleanor. Did you know there's a puddle under our settee?"

Eleanor shrugged. "I should have taken him for a walk on the lawn, but I was so rattled by all the screaming that I forgot."

"Bastard children or not," Anne announced, "Villiers really does have beautiful shoulders. I married Jeremy in large part because he has such a beautiful nose."

"Nose?" Eleanor had never noticed her brother's-in-law nose one way or the other.

"Beautiful other things too," her sister said impudently.

Eleanor sighed.

# Chapter Nine

Villiers walked up the stairs to his chambers, exasperation pulsing through his body. He couldn't believe that he was considering marriage to Eleanor. She had actually laughed at him for not realizing that those children were orphans. Laughed at him about something as sensitive as his children.

A moment after she taunted him, he had realized that none of the orphans could possibly be his. The twins were only five years old, and every child he'd seen was at least seven. But did he really know the difference between the sizes of five-year-olds and seven-year-olds?

Something in his gut twisted. It was absurd, humiliating and absurd. He hadn't given a damn about the existence of his children for the whole of his thirty-five years. And now, all of a sudden, he was consumed by them?

It made him feel as if he should just cut off his own head and be done with it.

Tobias was curled in a chair in his chambers. "The nursery is useless," the boy said, staring at him unblinkingly. "There's an old nanny up there who used to care for Lady Lisette. She tried to feed me gruel, so I left."

"Did you tell her where you were going?"

"No," Tobias said with a patent lack of interest.

Really, Villiers thought, wasn't that precisely what he himself would do? He never informed servants or anyone else about where he was going or why.

Though he'd always taken that as the prerogative of being a duke. Tobias was no duke.

"What are you reading?"

"It's a book about this Cosmo Gordon, see? He killed someone."

"In a duel. I know. He killed Frederick Thomas in Hyde Park last year. How did you learn to read?"

"Mrs. Jobber taught us. I can write too."

"I meant to get you a tutor but I forgot," Villiers said, frustration licking at him again. So far fatherhood felt like an exercise in failure. "Where's my valet?"

"Popper is so cross about Lady Eleanor's dog that Finchley went off to try to calm him down."

"Ridiculous. That animal is so small that it can hardly be called a dog. It's more like a stuffed cat."

"I wish I'd seen it frighten Lady Lisette," Tobias said wistfully. "Look at this." He held up a small bronze horse with a tail that whisked in the air.

Villiers hauled on the bell cord, wishing that Finchley would drop the errands of mercy and stay where he was supposed to be. "Where'd you get it?"

"It was sitting around in the nursery," Tobias said. "They haven't had any children there in a long time. Everyone knows that Lisette won't have any."

"She is Lady Lisette to you," Villiers pointed out. "Why won't she?"

"She loves babies. But her father says she needn't marry until he dies. You aren't thinking of marrying *her*, are you? Is she the one?"

"Yes," Villiers said decisively, putting Eleanor out of his mind. "She is."

"She's potty," Tobias said. "Cracked. They all say so."

"Who says so?"

"Her old nanny. The maid said the same. And Popper said that once she starts that screaming, there isn't anyone who can stop her. Except you, I guess. He said you picked her up and she settled down just like a baby with a bottle of gin."

"Babies don't drink gin," Villiers said, pretty sure that he was right about that.

Tobias shrugged. He obviously had about as much interest in baby care as Villiers did.

Lisette had been surrounded by children from the orphanage. She clearly adored children, and even more importantly, his children's illegitimacy wouldn't disturb her. It was unlikely that any of those orphans had parents whose domestic arrangements could be termed regular.

By now Finchley had reappeared. "Would you like the young master to return to the nursery now?" he asked as he pulled off Villiers's boots.

Villiers glanced over at Tobias. The boy was listening, of course, though he was pretending to read. "He doesn't look as if he'll be shocked by the sight of my pump handle."

Tobias's face didn't even twitch. Passed on my poker face, Villiers thought with some satisfaction. And without further ado he dropped his breeches and stepped into the bath.

"I don't think you ought to marry someone who's cracked," Tobias offered a few minutes later.

"Lisette is not mad," Villiers said impatiently. "She

was just afraid of that ugly little pug belonging to Lady Eleanor. She was terrorized by a dog as a young child."

"The maid told me all about it," Tobias said. "It wasn't so long ago."

"That explains it, then," Villiers said. "The fear is still fresh."

"The maid said that Lisette insisted on jerking a puppy away from its mother, and the puppy was nursing. So the mother dog bit her. Then her maid—not the one who was telling me, but another one—tried to drag Lisette away, and she got bitten as well. And she—the maid—lost her finger. Or maybe two fingers. The nanny said that her hand is just disgusting looking now," Tobias said with relish. "She has to work in the kitchens because it turns Lisette's stomach just to look at her."

"Come back in ten minutes," Villiers told Finchley. Normally he never spared a thought for conversation in front of his servants. In fact, he'd once boasted that his servants were so well trained that he could tup a woman on the dining room table and they wouldn't turn a hair.

But chatter about the future duchess was another matter.

The moment Finchley closed the door, he said, "Get over here, you turnip, so I can see you while we talk."

Tobias came around. "I'm not a turnip," he said. "My name is Juby."

"Juby, juicy, that sounds like a garden vegetable. Your name is Tobias."

"I've been Juby since I can remember. It's too late to change over now."

"It's never too late for anything," Villiers said. "More to the point, I think I'm going to marry Lisette, so you need to stop telling stories about her, particularly ones that are obviously untrue." He raised a hand as Tobias opened his mouth. "And if it wasn't untrue, it was definitely unkind. I'm sure that Lisette had no idea that the mother dog might attack her."

"Even the most buffle-headed fool knows that," Tobias said scornfully.

"Welcome to the world of well-bred ladies," Villiers said, sinking a little farther down in the bath. "What they know and don't know will never cease to amaze you."

"I don't like ladies," Tobias said.

"Neither do I," Villiers agreed.

"It's too bad you have to marry one, then."

"It's part of being a duke."

"Getting married?"

"Yes."

"Good thing I'm not a duke." Villiers was queerly glad to see that Tobias's eyes looked clear as he said that. "I'll never get married, not if it means you have to marry a cracked lady who doesn't know beans about anything," Tobias continued.

"Lisette is beautiful."

Tobias curled his lip. Villiers was startled: over the years he'd caught sight of that precise gesture on his own face a time or two.

"You don't like beautiful ladies?"

"You should marry the one with the dog," Tobias said firmly.

"Why?"

"Because she's got a dog. And she's not *too* pretty."

"Actually, she is beautiful, in her own way."

"Lady Lisette looks like one of those missionary ladies. All clean and gold-spun. You'd never know where you are with her because nobody is really like that. Not inside."

"I wouldn't?" Villiers was suffering from a terrible fascination. Even though his water was cooling and he knew he should cut off the flow of unsolicited advice, he couldn't bring himself to. "Why not?"

"Likely no better than she should be," Tobias concluded. "Aren't you tired of sitting in all that dirty water?"

The truth was that he was used to Finchley handing him a towel. He stood up and plucked it off the back of a chair. "It's not dirty water. It's clean bathwater."

"Once you're in it, it's dirty. Better get in and out quick." He said it with the tone of a boy who had never bathed more than once a month before coming to Villiers's house and had taken to the practice only reluctantly.

Finchley slipped back through the door with the wounded look of someone barred from the family home on Christmas morning. "It is time to dress, Your Grace. The pale rose or the black velvet?"

"The rose," Villiers said at the same moment Tobias said, "The black."

"Why the black?" Villiers asked.

"Because you look a proper fright in those fancy coats," Tobias said. "Even if you decided on Lisette—and I'm not saying you should—she'd never take you looking like that."

"Like what?"

"A posy. You look like a blooming posy. Like you don't care for your bag."

"My *what*?"

"Your potato-finger. Your holy thistle!"

Villiers was aware that Finchley had stopped feeling insulted and was trying to suppress a smile. Finchley never smiled. "If I understand you, you're saying that my pizzle doesn't show to best advantage in the rose coat."

"Not if you're talking about that pink one, no." Tobias pointed at the offending garment. "Only a man who had a withered pear would wear that."

Finchley snorted, and Villiers cast him a glance. "There's nothing withered about me," he said, pulling on the rose-colored coat over his sleek, skintight breeches.

"I'm not the one you need to convince of that," Tobias said, plopping down into his chair again. "It's your wife who's going to wonder if you're a molly or not." He turned back to his book.

Villiers felt his lips twitch. No one had ever called him a molly. Or implied he had a limp potato-finger.

Finchley looked at him sympathetically and, quite wisely, kept his mouth shut.

# Chapter Ten

"You look exquisite," Anne said, popping into Eleanor's bedchamber. "The color suits you better than it does me. The woven silk is beautiful. And the lace accents . . ." She kissed her fingers. "Exquisite!"

Eleanor looked down at her skirts. The fabric was rose-red silk, with trails of white flowers woven throughout. The bodice and sleeves were edged with a splash of rose lace sewn with tiny spangles. "The bodice doesn't fit properly." She gave it an irritable pull.

"Don't touch it," Anne gasped. "You'll tear the lace. Look, there are gold threads among the silk. Father swore I bankrupted him with that one gown alone. You shouldn't do more than breathe on it."

"My breasts are almost entirely exposed. Maybe you haven't noticed, but the only thing between the open air and my nipple is a mere inch of lace!"

"I did notice," Anne said happily, "and more to the point, so will every man in the room."

"I'm thinking about Mother."

"She ordered you to wear my clothing."

"Yes, but what looks merely saucy on you looks utterly debauched on me," Eleanor pointed out.

"Are you implying that's a disadvantage? Believe me, you should thank God for every inch you have. Where's the dog?" Anne said, cautiously dusting off a chair before she sat in it.

"Willa took him to the kitchen for the evening. She'll bring him up the back stairs later."

Anne wrinkled her nose. "He sleeps with you?"

"Yes." Eleanor was unapologetic about that. "He's a puppy. He's lonely at night."

"Are you planning to wear some lip color? You look like the ghost of Lady Macbeth."

"I never wear face paint," Eleanor said. "I—"

"You are so lucky that I'm your sister," Anne said. She placed her net bag on the dressing table.

"What is that?" Eleanor asked.

"Kohl black, for your eyes," Anne said. "Hold still or I'll blind you."

Eleanor froze.

"You can open your eyes now." She stepped back. "You have lovely eyelashes, Eleanor. Who knew?"

"They're the color of my hair," Eleanor said. "Nondescript."

"Now some rouge, and then a little lip color. And I'm going to put just a touch of black at the outside corner of your eyes. Your eyes are already large, but this will make them mysterious."

"Mysterious?" Eleanor snorted. "No one with my name could possibly be mysterious."

"Every woman is mysterious to men," Anne said, dabbing more color on Eleanor's lips. "Villiers is the kind of man who takes appearances very seriously. You do him dishonor by just throwing yourself together."

"I don't throw myself together," Eleanor said indignantly. "I give the process a reasonable amount of time."

"But you never try to make yourself attractive to a man," Anne said.

Eleanor was silent.

"I was shaken by the bastard children, I don't mind admitting. But now I've decided that Villiers is definitely the one for you. You don't mind a dog in your bed, so I assume a bastard or two in the wings of your household will be equally acceptable."

"Children are not dogs," Eleanor pointed out.

"Of course not. They're a good deal easier to take care of. One never sees children when they're at the stage of peeing on the floor, for instance. Whereas everyone seems to think that dogs can't be hidden in a nursery and trained by servants, the way offspring are." She started tweaking Eleanor's curls.

"What are you doing now?"

"Making you look more rumpled."

"Rumpled? I don't want to look rumpled!"

"Yes, you do. If Lisette's appeal is that of the fragile young maiden, yours is going to be pure sensuality. And the lovely thing about that, Eleanor, is that you actually have an appetite for the bed. Many women don't, you know."

"All this advice assumes that I want to be a duchess," Eleanor noted.

"I'm assuming that you'd like the choice," Anne retorted. "There! Let's go."

Eleanor started to turn toward the glass but her sister grabbed her shoulder. "No, don't look."

"What have you done to me?" Eleanor asked with a wave of misgiving.

"You are absolutely beautiful," Anne said. "But if you

see yourself, you'll want to pin your hair back like a shep-
herdess in a bad play."

"Are you saying that I normally look as if I'm tending
sheep? With straw in my hair? As if I might yodel?"

"You spend a lot of time looking like a virgin," Anne
said. "And may I point out that you haven't had claim to
that title since you were, what . . . fifteen?"

"Sixteen. And in fact I stopped dressing like a debutante long ago. You're being unfair. I don't believe I even
own a white gown."

"And yet you cling to clean-scrubbed modesty, as if
you were going to fall in love with the evil landlord and
end up throwing yourself off a cliff."

Eleanor thought about the implications of Anne's description. "I have not been wandering around in a melancholy daze," she stated.

"It's as if Gideon stole all the life out of you, those
years ago." Anne reached in her net bag and brought out
a thin silver box, flicked it open and displayed a row of
cigarillos.

"I can't think that tobacco is good for you," Eleanor
observed.

"This isn't for me, but for you."

*"Me?"*

"You. You're going to offset Lisette's pallid brand of
perfect Englishwoman by appearing absolutely wicked.
Lusciously licentious."

"Wicked? Me?"

"The only way to stay young is to try new things,"
Anne said. "God knows virtue never shaved off anyone's
years. On second thought, I'll wait to give you a cigarillo
until after supper. But then *you*, Lady Eleanor, are going
to have a glass of wine and smoke tobacco. I shall tutor
you myself."

"Pah!"

"You don't have to smoke it. I've found that merely holding a cigarillo catapults one from tedious virgin to something far more interesting. Here's my point, Eleanor. Gideon the Godless stole more than your virginity when he turned his back and married Ada instead. Now could we please go downstairs? I need something to drink, and so do you."

"Mother believes drinking spirits before meals causes mental instability," Eleanor said, following her.

"Ratafia promotes mental instability: that's why there are so many silly women in the *ton*. Rum is what you need," Anne said. She breezed into the drawing room, paused for a moment on the threshold so as to draw all eyes, and then moved to the side, pulling Eleanor forward.

Lisette beamed at them, of course. Lisette was always happy to see her friends. Their mother opened her mouth and snapped it shut, for all the world like a beached fish. Villiers said nothing, nor did his face change.

Anne tucked her arm through Eleanor's. "Good evening, everyone." She turned to Popper, who was proffering a silver tray. "Is that ratafia, Popper? And orgeat? Absolutely not. We know exactly what we'd like. Rum punch, if you please."

Lisette came to her feet as if she had just remembered she was their hostess. She was wearing a charming gown of cream silk, embroidered with tiny forget-me-nots. Her bosom was chastely covered, and her panniers equally modest. Eleanor felt like the Whore of Babylon by comparison, dressed in crimson and painted to match.

Her mother appeared at her side. "Why?" the duchess whispered, horror in her voice. "Why?"

"I am wearing Anne's gown, precisely as you bade me," Eleanor said to her, sacrificing her sister without guilt. "You instructed me to listen to her advice as regards men, Mother. You said that I must learn from her experience."

"But—But—"

"Doesn't Eleanor look absolutely ravishing?" Anne put in.

"She does!" Lisette crowed, joining them. Lisette had never expressed a stick of jealousy, as far as Eleanor knew. "I wish that we had more visitors to admire you." The smile fell from her face. "We never seem to have visitors anymore. My aunt, Lady Marguerite, tends to discourage our neighbors from joining us for dinner. Oh, I know!" She waved madly at Popper.

He was mixing rum punch at the sideboard.

"Popper! *Popper!*"

The butler turned around. "Yes, my lady?"

"Send a footman to Squire Thestle immediately, if you please. Do beg him the courtesy of joining us for supper, he and his lovely wife. And Roland, if he's at home." She turned back to Eleanor, smiling. "Sir Roland would be perfect for you, dearest. He has a Roman nose. Yes, and a Grecian chin."

"Perhaps you could turn him to currency and trade him on the Exchange," Anne remarked. "Villiers, how kind of you to finally decide to greet us. You appeared frozen in your place, as if you had turned into a Roman statue yourself."

"I was struck dumb by your beauty," Villiers said, bowing.

Eleanor just stopped herself from rolling her eyes.

"My lady," Popper was saying in some distress. "I am not sure . . . in Lady Marguerite's absence—"

"For goodness sake," the duchess burst out. "You'll forgive me, dear Lisette, if I observe that a strong hand is needed in training this household." She rounded on Popper without pausing for breath. "I do hope that you are not questioning Lady Lisette's direct order? We will, naturally, wait for supper until the squire and his family arrive. I am not hungry, although I trust your cook can bring us something to nibble on."

Eleanor was hungry, but she took a sip of her rum punch instead. It was surprisingly good, rather sweet and fruity. She had always thought men drank fiery drinks, meant to straighten the backbone.

Popper had a noticeably wild-eyed look, but he trotted into the hallway. "That looks very good," Lisette said, noticing Eleanor's glass. "What is it?"

"Rum punch," Anne said. "It's utterly delicious, which is why gentlemen tend to gulp it all themselves. Here, darling, you may have mine. I haven't even touched it. Villiers, you know none of us can match you at chess, and besides, it's such a deadly boring game that we would fall over with fatigue if you started a match with one of us. Do you know any other games, perhaps something all of us might play?"

"No," Villiers said. He wasn't the sort of man who could be easily flirted with, Eleanor noted.

Anne didn't seem to notice. "I expect we have at least an hour before the squire arrives," she observed. "We could have an interval of improving conversation." Her tone made it clear that she'd rather jump into a lake.

"I know exactly what we should do to amuse ourselves," Lisette said.

"What do you propose?" Villiers asked, bending solicitously toward her.

Eleanor drank some more of her rum punch.

"We'll play knucklebones!" Lisette said, smiling at him.

There was a moment's silence. "*Knuckle*bones?" the duchess asked. Her tone was not friendly, but Lisette was oblivious.

"You might know it better as dibs," she said happily. "It's no end of fun." She waved at a footman and a moment later was holding a pile of knobby bones and a small wooden ball.

Eleanor peered at the bones with some interest. It went without saying that her mother had never allowed a game so unsanitary and altogether common in the ducal nursery.

"Now," Lisette said, "we must make ourselves comfortable. Of course we need to be able to toss the bones properly, and that means a wood floor. Perhaps I should have that big rug taken up." She looked over at the remaining footman as if about to order him to get to work on the spot.

"Not tonight," Anne said. She looked distinctly amused. "There's plenty of bare floor; we are standing on some at this moment. But where do we sit, Lisette?"

"On the floor, of course," Lisette said.

"On the floor," Anne repeated. "Of course." Without hesitation, she gracefully sank to the ground, and beamed up at them from the wide circle of her skirts. "Do join me."

The duchess cleared her throat with a sound of utter disbelief.

Eleanor didn't want to sit on the floor. Her side panniers were likely to spring into the air and throw her skirts over her head. On the other hand, she didn't want to align herself with her mother, especially given that Villiers was apparently finding the whole idea charming.

At least, that was what she gleaned from the laughter in his eyes. Naturally, he said nothing. Lisette, meanwhile, had dropped to the floor, scattered the bones, and was now practicing throwing the ball in the air and catching it.

"Knucklebones is a game for children," the duchess pointed out.

Lisette's mouth drooped. "I know. I do wish we had children in the house."

"But we do have a child in the house," Villiers said.

Lisette blinked up at him. "They all went home."

"My son is here."

Being Lisette, she didn't wonder how Villiers had a son, given as he had no wife. "Leopold, how wonderful you are," she crowed, as if he had produced that son solely for her pleasure.

Eleanor's mother had been occupying herself by glaring at Anne's bent head, but now she jerked around to stare at Villiers instead. She, if not Lisette, knew perfectly well that Villiers had never married.

"A ward perhaps?" she asked, her tone just this side of glacial. "Surely the word *son* was a slip of the tongue, Duke?"

"In fact, Tobias is my son," Villiers said. He turned to the footman. "Summon my son from the nursery, if you please."

"How lucky you are!" Lisette said wistfully. "I do wish I had children."

"Be still!" the duchess snapped.

*"Mother,"* Eleanor said, feeling a pulse of sympathy. She had realized long ago that her mother found situations even slightly out of the ordinary to be frightfully upsetting. It wasn't that the duchess had a puritanical attitude toward sin, precisely—but she had a positive loathing for irregularities of any sort.

"Hush," her mother said, rounding on her. "You are far too innocent to understand the implications of this— this—of—" She ground to a halt, and then said, "Your son should not be in the vicinity of decent gentlewomen, Villiers. I should not have to emphasize such a common point of decency. You have offered your hostess a monstrous insult."

Villiers's gray eyes rested thoughtfully on the duchess and then moved on to Lisette. "I have an illegitimate son," he explained. "I apologize for insulting you by bringing him under your roof."

Eleanor felt like applauding. Villiers's voice was so composed that not even a tinge of irony leaked into his words.

Since Lisette cared nothing for irregularities and indeed created them on a regular basis, she smiled up at Villiers. "You're very lucky."

"You see what you are doing?" the duchess hissed at Villiers. "Contaminating the ears of the innocent. She doesn't even *understand* your effrontery." If Villiers had himself under such tight control that he appeared emotionless, her mother was on the verge of losing her temper altogether.

Eleanor glimpsed the bleak look in Villiers's eyes, and the unmindful—though not innocent—smile playing around Lisette's lips. She hated the choking sense of inferiority she felt whenever her mother was about to call someone stupid. It didn't even matter that she herself was not the subject of the diatribe.

What she hated, and had hated since childhood, was the moment when her mother lost control of her temper and flayed all those in her path.

"I have half a mind to leave this house immediately," Her Grace said now, her voice rising. "Villiers, you are a fool if you believe that—"

Something snapped inside Eleanor: that same frail thread of patience that had carried her through twenty-two years of her mother's bouts of irritability. She was tired of hearing people called stupid. She was tired of agreeing with her mother's pronouncements simply because opposition took effort.

"Mother," she said, stepping forward to put a hand on Villiers's arm. "The duke has done me the inestimable honor of asking me to marry him."

There was a moment of frozen silence. Even the gentle rattle of Anne's tossing the knucklebones ceased. The only sound Eleanor heard was the muttering of two footmen stationed in the hallway.

"I have accepted," she added, just to make everything clear.

Villiers's eyelashes flickered as he glanced around the group. Really, his eyelashes were too thick for a man. "I was overcome by joy," he said solemnly. "I shall never forget the moment that she accepted my hand."

He drew Eleanor's hand under the crook of his arm and gave her a smile. She retaliated by giving him a little pinch.

Lisette looked between them. "Are you saying that you're going to be a duchess, Ellie?"

Since her mother was still paralyzed, trapped between outrage and ambition, Eleanor smiled down at Lisette. "Yes."

Anne leaped to her feet and gave Eleanor a kiss. "What a surprise!" she cried, throwing a soulful look at Villiers. "Ah, Duke, you'll never know what a treasure you're stealing from those of us who love Eleanor best."

Eleanor wished she had her hand free so she could pinch Anne as well.

"Isn't that lovely," Lisette breathed, rising as well. "I adore weddings. So pretty. So festive." She waved at the footman who had just entered the room. "Champagne, James!"

James obediently trotted back out.

Apparently, that was the extent of Lisette's interest in Villiers's announcement. "Why don't we start our game?" she asked, dropping back to the floor. Anne immediately sat back down, skirts spreading in an elegant circle around her.

Eleanor's mother cleared her throat and turned to Villiers. "I will be blunt. I am not particularly pleased, given the circumstances."

"I have six illegitimate children," Villiers informed her, not kindly.

She visibly paled.

"Mother," Eleanor said, "I know this has been a terrific shock."

"My daughter is marrying a duke," the duchess said between clenched teeth. "True, he apparently has the morals of a squirrel, but that's my cross to bear."

"Actually, the children will be Eleanor's cross to bear," Villiers said all too cheerfully.

"I gather you have this particular boy with you for a purpose," the duchess said. "I must suppose you are conveying him to an appropriate household in the country. Surely you need not have effected this errand in person?"

Eleanor intervened before Villiers could deliver a death blow by informing the duchess that he intended to raise the children under his own roof. "There's no reason to discuss such particulars now."

Her mother's eyes snapped to her. "Eleanor, you must forget that you ever heard this discussion. If your father were here, he would talk to the duke himself. But since he is ungrateful enough to be in Russia with your brother, I shall undertake that task myself. Duke, we shall discuss this tomorrow. In private!"

"I live in anticipation," Villiers drawled.

His future mother-in-law gave him a look of extreme dislike, but she held her tongue.

"Do join us!" Lisette called from the floor.

"Are you suggesting that I sprawl about on the floor?" the duchess demanded.

At that moment the door opened and a thin boy in a brown velvet suit entered. He was dressed like any boy of the aristocracy, Eleanor thought, though he clearly wasn't one of them. There was something wild and proud in his face, as if he were more duke than the duke.

He walked forward and bent his head.

"Bow," his father said, though not sharply.

He bowed.

Anne and Lisette both looked up. "Sit next to me!" Lisette caroled, patting the floor. "I am having a terrible time catching this little ball."

The boy was like a miniature version of Villiers, from his cool gray eyes to his extreme self-possession. "May I present my son," Villiers said. "His name is Tobias."

The boy turned his head and looked at his father.

"He prefers to be called Juby," Villiers added.

It was the first time she had ever seen Villiers bested, and by someone less than half his weight. Eleanor stepped forward and smiled.

"Lady Eleanor," Villiers said. "My future wife." There was just the slightest edge of irony in his tone.

Eleanor dropped a curtsy. The boy bowed his head again. He was fiercely beautiful in the way some young males are, as if their whole life were being lived through their eyes, and their large noses, and their ungainly limbs.

"Bow," his father said unemotionally.

He bowed.

"Lady Eleanor's mother, the Duchess of Montague."

This time Tobias bowed without being told, which made Eleanor feel better. If this wild boy interpreted her mother's murderous gaze properly, then perhaps she herself wasn't such an incompetent coward for having given in to her so many times in the last twenty-two years.

"On the floor are Lady Lisette and Mrs. Bouchon," Villiers continued. "Bow."

Tobias bowed. Lisette looked up again and patted the ground. Naturally, Tobias dropped instantly into the place she indicated.

"I shall retire until supper to compose myself," the

duchess announced, her voice indicating that she was on the very edge of a swoon. She paused, clearly to allow Villiers and Eleanor to chorus their protests. Their eyes met.

"You must be exhausted by the long trip, Mother," Eleanor said.

"Though one certainly couldn't tell," Villiers put in. "You look as exquisite as ever, Duchess."

She automatically raised one shoulder in a coquettish gesture. "Oh, how can you say so!" she said, though without her usual vigor. "The dust! The dryness. We were easily half a day in the carriage."

"Only a woman of remarkable fortitude could look as fresh as you do after a journey," Villiers said.

"I'll walk you to the stairs, Mother," Eleanor said. "A footman will inform you the moment that the squire and his family arrive."

As they walked into the entrance hall they came face-to-face with an enormous gilded mirror. Eleanor saw herself and stopped short.

"Just look at yourself!" her mother snapped. "What you've done to your eyes makes you look shameless." She clutched Eleanor's arm a little tighter. "I never thought I'd say such a thing, but I'm not certain you should marry Villiers, Eleanor."

She kept talking, but Eleanor wasn't listening. The kohl black that Anne had put on her lashes and smudged around her eyes made them look twice as large as they normally did. She looked . . .

Beautiful. Mysterious. Sensual. Anything but a virgin.

"Your curls are in terrible disarray," her mother said. "You shall come upstairs with me, Eleanor, and I shall have a word with Willa. That sort of tawdry effect she's created simply won't do. If we do decide that you should accept Villiers's proposal, you'll have to find someone who understands the consequence of your position."

"No," Eleanor stated. She couldn't pull her eyes away from her own face. Her small, ordinary face was transformed. Her lips looked naughty, like a woman who kissed in corners and laughed inordinately, rather than with the kind of constrained emotion that befit a duke's daughter.

She didn't look like the kind of woman who stood around, moping after her former lover. She looked like the kind of woman whose former lover pined for *her*.

"What on earth do you mean?" her mother demanded.

She turned to her mother, chin high. "I like the way I look, Mother."

"You don't look like a duchess."

Eleanor knew perfectly well that her mother loved her, and that she only wanted the best for her daughters. But she was finished with the pretense that she was a perfect daughter.

"I don't want to look like a duchess," she stated.

"Villiers pays more attention to his appearance than the queen herself does. You wouldn't catch him going about with his hair falling out of its ribbon. I've never even seen his neck cloth in less than pristine condition. He must assign a footman to follow him with spare cloths."

"Quite likely," Eleanor said. "But if he wants to waste his time being perfect in dress, he'll have to do it alone."

"Eleanor!"

It was harder to withstand her mother when she was pleading rather than browbeating. But Eleanor didn't want to dress like a wilting virgin any longer. "You've often criticized me for not being appealing enough to gentlemen," she pointed out.

"I never criticize," her mother said stoutly. And the worst of it was that she believed it.

"You have called me foolish," Eleanor replied. "And you were right. I simply wasn't interested in getting married. I couldn't picture myself doing it."

"Until Villiers changed your mind. I suppose every gentleman has peccadilloes. I'll just have to impress upon him that he may never mention those children in your presence or mine again."

"It wasn't Villiers who changed my mind."

"Whatever it was, I don't see why that change entails dressing like a shameless wagtail," her mother said, reverting to her former theme.

"Wagtail, Mother?"

"You know precisely what I mean!"

Eleanor smiled at her reflection. "I like that word." She gave an experimental wag of her hips. "And more to the point, Villiers likes the way I look."

"It is true that he proposed to you immediately."

"There's the evidence, Mother," Eleanor said, cheerfully ignoring the truth of the matter. Unfortunately, Villiers hadn't turned a hair when he saw her transformation. He must have noticed her face paint, but it certainly hadn't warmed his heart, given the way he had been hovering over Lisette.

As if her mother read her mind, she gave her a little shove. "You'd better go back in the sitting room, now that I think of it. Lisette is the same as she ever was, but she's so pretty that one hardly notices at first."

"Poor Lisette," Eleanor said.

Her mother snorted and headed up the stairs.

# Chapter Eleven

Villiers looked down at his son's head. Tobias—he'd be damned if he'd ever call him Juby—was sitting on the floor throwing the knucklebones. The boy had inky black hair that was just like his own. He'd have to warn him about the white streaks; they'd showed up just past his eighteenth birthday.

At first, as a boy, he'd been afraid that he would turn as white as an ostrich. Then he realized that the ducal picture gallery held a portrait of an ancestor from years back, who had the same hair. The same face too. Nasty cold-eyed bastard, he looked, and so Villiers didn't have any illusions about his own visage.

The whole idea that Tobias had his hair and eyes gave him a queer feeling.

Lisette looked up and gave him the lavish smile with which she seemed to greet everyone. He'd seen many beautiful women—his former fiancée, Roberta, was exquisite—but Lisette was extraordinary. She was like some sort of chaste and joyful goddess.

"Join us," she cried, gesturing toward the floor. She was seated in the middle of a puddle of shimmering silk, looking like a flower. It was refreshing to see someone with no regard for convention, as opposed to the Duchess of Montague, a woman whom he would personally nominate as the person one most doesn't want to welcome into the family.

"I'll wait for Lady Eleanor to return from escorting her mother," he said.

Lisette gave her charming little shrug. It seemed she'd forgotten about Eleanor.

Whom he was apparently marrying. From all appearances, Eleanor had decided to kick over the traces, but he didn't have any real belief that she had actually decided to marry him. She had announced that merely to silence her mother.

He couldn't think of another woman in all of England who would dare to announce their engagement without waiting for him to propose.

Eleanor walked back into the room. If Lisette glowed with a kind of concentrated gold, Eleanor had the crimson lips and sultry look of an English harem dancer, if such a thing existed.

Without a word to him she dropped on the floor next to Anne. Her side panniers were too large for the indignity of sitting on the floor. One of them bounced into the air and he caught a glimpse of a deliciously slim ankle before she slapped it back down.

"I was about to ask if I might offer you a chair," he said, just for the pleasure of having her scowl at him.

Her eyes were as sooty as a fashionable strumpet's. But she was trained to be a duchess, and so she sat straight upright, even though seated on the floor. A ducal doxy, that's what she was. A dissipated duchess. Whatever she was, his body responded to her signals as if he really were in a brothel—not that he ever entered those establishments.

He should probably join the group on the floor, but he loathed that sort of informality. And he didn't trust Popper's housekeeping skills, either.

"What do you do besides throw the bones and try to catch the ball?" Eleanor was asking. She had the ball in hand and seemed to be catching it easily enough.

"Juby says he and other boys make up their own rules," Lisette put in. "I don't see any reason why *we* should have to be precise. I want to try riding the elephant."

Riding the elephant? Villiers realized he had clearly missed an important part of the conversation. It was a pity that his blood was at a slow boil, all due to Eleanor's pouty lips. It made him think of bedding her.

She was a fierce, sharp-tongued little thing who would probably turn into her mother. And if that wasn't enough to frighten a man into flaccidity, nothing would.

"Juby?" Eleanor said to Tobias. "That name makes you sound like a boiled sweet."

Villiers had to stop himself from grinning. She might be sharp-tongued, but she was echoing his opinion. He pulled over a chair and sat down behind his son.

Eleanor cast him one of her bird-quick looks. "Why do you get to sit in a chair while we're on the floor?"

"You chose to sit there," he said pleasantly. "I choose not to join you."

"What a stick-in-the-mud you are, Leopold!" Lisette laughed. She put her arm around Tobias. "We like being on the floor, don't we?"

Tobias edged away. He wasn't old enough, or young enough, to want to be hugged. But it was pleasant to see how charming she was with him. Obviously, Lisette was completely unaffected by the circumstances of Tobias's birth. She was treating him as she would any child: with that artless joy she brought to her daily life.

She was laughing now, and clapping at the way Tobias was catching knucklebones on the back of his hand.

After five or six minutes Lisette was out of the game and so was Anne, who in fact had taken herself out. She had lit a cigarillo and was leaning against one of Villiers's chair legs and blowing smoke rings at the ceiling.

"This is boring," Lisette said, looking up at him with a pretty pout.

"Villiers," Eleanor said, without even bothering to glance at him, "Lisette wishes to do something else."

She really would turn into her mother if she didn't watch out. Still, he helped Lisette to her feet, noticing that she was as lithe as she appeared. "You have a vast array of musical instruments on the far wall," he noted.

Her eyes brightened immediately. "I've learned to play all of them; I adore music!"

His own mother had loved music as well, and used to spend hours playing a harpsichord in the drawing room. He smiled down at Lisette, imagining for a moment what their children might look like. All that gold delicacy would offset his dark, brutish looks.

Not that Tobias looked terrible, but he had to admit that his daughter Violet was no— Well, she was no violet. She had an oddly lumpy look, and a huge chin. He didn't know how he'd ever marry her off, but he figured that enough money would do it.

And maybe being around Lisette would teach Violet to be charming and happy. Lisette was doubly beautiful because she was so cheerful.

He glanced back at Eleanor, who was scowling at Tobias. She could use the same lesson. Still, common sense told him that Tobias didn't care about a scowl or two. Not after the abuse he had suffered at Grindel's hands.

Villiers's hands involuntarily curled into fists. He'd knocked the man out, taken all the boys away, and then spoken to a Bow Street magistrate he knew. Grindel was now in prison for life, but still he lay awake at night thinking about ripping the man's head from his body.

"Leopold!" Lisette called prettily. "Will you help me take down this lute?"

Normally he would have frozen out any person with the temerity to call him by name. Yet somehow Lisette disarmed his every criticism. It was an interesting realization that warranted further thought.

Out of the corner of her eye Eleanor saw Villiers trot after Lisette, but she didn't spare him a withering glance. Not that he'd be looking; the pathetic awe in his eyes when he looked at Lisette told its own story.

Instead, she hunched over and watched like a hawk to make sure that Tobias didn't try to palm any of the bones. She'd already caught him with one under his leg and another up his sleeve.

Across the room Lisette began tuning the lute. She had an angelic voice, and never seemed more the perfect lady than when she was singing. That was the sad thing about Lisette: it was no act. She was a lady . . . *when* she was a lady.

With an effort, Eleanor banished Villiers and Lisette from her mind. For the moment she just wanted to trounce this ill-tempered, ill-mannered, miniature Villiers. There was something about him that she liked. For one thing, he had been completely uncowed by her mother's glare.

They were tied going into the final game. He threw a perfect round. She countered. They switched to left-handed throws. Luckily, she was actually left-handed. He threw another perfect round, and again she countered. He returned to his right hand, but with a handicap of a bent little finger. Finally he missed. It was her turn.

She threw the ball, scooped—and the sixth knuckle-bone slid, smooth as butter, under her spreading skirts. She closed her fingers around the bones.

"You won!" Tobias cried, looking utterly shocked. "But I never lose."

She took a second to savor her victory. "That's likely because you've never played a woman before."

"You think girls are better at knucklebones than boys?" She'd seen that jutting jaw before. Villiers had it. Well, every boy had it when they were confronted with an unpleasant reality.

"I'm better than you are," she pointed out. "Why shouldn't the two of us stand as emblems for our sexes?"

He thought his way through that language. "I've played lots of girls before," he reported. "And I always win."

"Pride goeth before a fall," she said. And then she relented, grinning at him. "I cheated."

*"What?"* His voice suddenly dropped a register, taking on, in its disbelief, his father's low voice.

She whisked aside her skirt and showed him the hidden jack. "You should always count the bones when someone claims victory."

"I do always count the bones!" he cried. "Well, normally. But you're a lady!" His voice swooped from high to low. He would have his father's deep velvet tones someday.

"Your mistake," she said cheerfully. "I cheated—but I still won. You tried to cheat and you lost. When I decided to cheat, I won because you didn't see it."

Tobias narrowed his eyes. "You're a strange lady."

"Very strange," Villiers said from above her shoulder.

"I have thought Eleanor strange since our nursery days," Anne laughed. She sounded a little drunk.

"Tobias," Eleanor said, ignoring them, "do you suppose that you're strong enough to haul me into a standing position?"

He jumped to his feet. "You're not so large." He had decided to like her, she guessed. Now that she had cheated. Men were strange, no matter the age. "I'll be taller than you in a month or so."

"You're as boastful as my dog," she told him. Sure enough, he managed to get her to her feet. She twitched her skirts so they flowed over her panniers.

He was longing to tell her that she was crazy and that dogs didn't boast, so she put him out of his misery. "My dog Oyster is a terrible braggart."

"What does he boast about?" Tobias asked.

"His tail, for one thing. He loves his tail. The problem is that he can't see it because he's too fat. So he goes around and around, barking so that I realize how important and beautiful and special that tail is."

Tobias had clearly learned not to laugh, because he just watched her with those curious, intent eyes that reminded her of his father. It made her itch to comfort him, which was absurd.

"Second, Oyster is ridiculously proud of his ability to defend me."

"*Defend* you? The nursemaid told me that he was the size of a piglet."

"I have to admit that there may be a certain resemblance. But my point is that he thinks he's very fierce. Extremely so. He likes to pretend that the fire andirons are about to attack me. He creeps up, attacks them savagely, and manages to save my life."

Tobias hesitated.

"I know . . . you wish to inform me that Oyster is not the brightest canine," Eleanor said, sighing.

Tobias almost smiled.

"The third thing he's very proud of is his pizzle," she said.

He grinned outright at that. "I thought ladies never mentioned such things."

Actually they didn't, generally speaking. "You also thought you could beat any woman simply because you *have* a pizzle," she pointed out. "Not to mention the fact that you thought a lady wouldn't cheat, so you didn't count the bones."

"I'm horrified," Villiers said with a drawl. "Horrified." He turned to his son, his eyes so serious that Eleanor wondered if Tobias would get the joke. "She's no lady, son. I'll have to find another duchess."

"Oyster has the smallest pizzle you can imagine," Eleanor said, glancing at Villiers just to make it clear that she *might* be able to imagine one smaller. "More like a radish than anything to be proud of."

Tobias giggled, sounding like any other child.

"But when he starts waving it around," she said, taking another sip of her rum punch, "you'd think that it was a royal pizzle."

"What does he do with it?" Tobias asked. He sounded about five years younger than he had on entering the room.

"Well, I hate to tell you this, because it's going to reduce your opinion of him," Eleanor said, "but he is uncommonly fond of Peter, one of our footmen. Or perhaps it is more accurate to admit that his object of passion is Peter's leg."

Who would have thought it? Father and son laughed in exactly the same way.

Eleanor finished up her drink, thinking about how utterly predictable the male sense of humor was. Tobias reacted precisely as her own brother would have, at the same age. It seemed that men never really got past that age, in fact.

The Duke of Villiers. Age thirteen, going on . . . forty.

Typical.

# Chapter Twelve

*B*y the time Squire Thestle and his family finally appeared, Tobias had been dispatched to the nursery, and the entire company had consumed three glasses of rum punch each. Villiers showed no signs of intoxication, but Anne was weaving a little as she walked.

Eleanor prided herself on being able to manage several glasses of wine, but she was slowly coming to realize that rum punch was not like wine. Her head was swimming and she had to curb the impulse to beam.

Luckily, her mother had reappeared and taken over the role of hostess, since Lisette didn't even bother to rise to greet the squire. Lisette, seated on a couch beside Eleanor, had been talking, almost without breathing, for twenty minutes. Really, Eleanor thought sentimentally, Lisette was greatly misunderstood by the *ton*. She almost always made sense.

"Lisette," she said, interrupting, "Don't you wish to marry someday?"

"Of course I plan to do so. I'm engaged; did you know that?"

Eleanor sat up. "You're betrothed? To whom?"

"Roland's older brother," Lisette said, waving her hand at the squire and his son. "My father and his arranged it eons ago. His name is Lancelot."

It must have been arranged when the betrothed couple were in their respective cradles, given the edgy politeness with which the squire nodded in the direction of Lisette. "Roland and Lancelot . . . No wonder Roland became a poet. Where is Lancelot?"

"He went on a tour some years ago," Lisette said with complete unconcern. "When he comes back, I suppose we'll marry. I'm quite comfortable as I am. Or if I meet someone I like better than Lancelot, I'll just marry him instead. The squire wouldn't mind."

"What would you think of marrying Villiers, for example?"

"Villiers?" Lisette seemed to have forgotten who he was, so Eleanor waved her hand toward the duke. He was standing with his back to them, talking to Anne. She didn't know why Anne was so taken by his shoulders. She preferred his thighs. His muscles were positively immoral, the way they strained the silk of his pantaloons.

"Oh, *Leopold*," Lisette said. "I thought you had decided to marry him, Eleanor. I'm sure you told him so earlier."

"He did ask me," Eleanor said defensively.

"Really? He looked so surprised." There wasn't an ounce of condemnation in Lisette's tone. Clearly, if she wanted to marry someone, she would simply go ahead and announce the impending nuptials. "No, I don't wish to marry Leopold."

Eleanor felt quite relieved. Well, of course she was relieved, because she had lost her head and announced her intention to marry Villiers, though she would have backed down if Lisette had strong feelings for the duke. Possibly.

"He does have lovely hair," Lisette said. "I never really thought of him as a husband." She bent her head to the side and peered at him.

"Why are you bending your neck?"

"People are so interesting viewed sideways," she said. "Just look at Leopold, for example. His nose is even bigger from the side."

Eleanor bent her neck but began to sag to the side so she straightened quickly. It must be the Champagne on top of rum punch.

"I wouldn't mind marrying Leopold," Lisette continued. "Leopold and Lisette sound quite nice together. Almost as nice as Lancelot and Lisette. What's more, he saved me from a quite savage dog this afternoon." She looked at Eleanor. "Did you hear about what happened to me?"

Eleanor managed a smile. "It was my puppy, remember, darling?"

Lisette blinked. "Oh, of course it was!" Her smile was a little forced. "I've been fearful of dogs since I was attacked by a mongrel in the village square. It was nearly the size of a wolf, starving to death, I expect. The villagers had to shoot it."

"That must have been awful," Eleanor said flatly.

"But that's not what we were talking about. We were talking of marrying Villiers. You know, I am going to think about that very seriously. Thank you for suggesting it. My aunt Marguerite can be so annoying sometimes. Do you know that we almost never have visitors? I expect that people come to your house all the time, don't they?"

"At times."

"I feel as if my spirit is trapped here." She flung open her arms and knocked Eleanor's glass to the floor. "Oh, well, it must be time for supper," she said, glancing at the spilled drink. "I'll tell Popper that he should ring the bell this minute. Dinner!" she called, waving to the room at large.

They all looked up. Eleanor's mother was obviously enjoying a comfortable coze with the squire's wife.

"Time to eat," Lisette said cheerfully. "Eleanor is getting tipsy and dropped her glass."

Eleanor quickly straightened her back again and tried to look sober.

"Since Popper isn't here, I'll inform a footman," Lisette said. She darted out the door and a moment later they heard the dinner gong.

"Lady Lisette is remarkably spontaneous," Villiers said, appearing at Eleanor's side. His voice was far more admiring than she appreciated.

"She has always had that quality," Eleanor said.

"We spend a great deal of our time hemmed in by customs and manners," he said thoughtfully.

Manners were certainly not Lisette's strong suit, but Eleanor kept her mouth shut.

Squire Thestle was a tall, thin man who had powdered his hair so heavily that little snowfalls kept drifting to his shoulders and then sliding, as if down a mountain slope, to the floor. He had melancholy eyes that reminded Eleanor of Oyster after a bout of incontinence and a scolding. His wife was even taller than he, and certainly broader in the shoulders.

Strangely enough, these homely parents had produced a remarkably beautiful son. With a brilliant smile, Lisette introduced Eleanor to Sir Roland. "Lady Eleanor, I know that you will be *so* pleased to meet Roland. Or Roly-Poly, as we used to call him. Roly, will you escort Lady Eleanor to her seat, please?"

Sir Roland clearly didn't care to be reminded of this nickname; he looked at Lisette with the respectful dislike one reserves for a venomous viper. Eleanor certainly understood that feeling. She was starting to remember just how much she used to dread her annual summer visits to Knole House, before Lisette's mother died and their families drifted apart.

By five minutes later she was feeling much better. Roland didn't look at her with cool eyes that made her feel as if he was secretly laughing at her. Lisette had been right about his Roman nose, but she forgot to add how handsome a nose like that could be when it was paired with a deep lower lip and a strong chin. A Grecian chin, didn't she say?

Whatever kind of chin it was, she liked it. And Roland apparently liked her as well. They found so many agreeable subjects of conversation that she had to remind herself to turn now and then and ask the squire a few more questions about the birds nesting in the church steeple.

The admiration in Roland's eyes was very soothing. "I'm so surprised that I've never met you before," he was saying now.

"I find Almack's boring," Eleanor said, ignoring the fact that she was there every Wednesday last season. No one who'd seen her in April would recognize her now. "So tedious . . . All the same people, and everyone on his best behavior."

"I know just what you mean," Roland said, looking at her a little shyly. He had nice eyelashes. Not as thick as Villiers's, she noticed, but long and curling. "How do you like to entertain yourself, Lady Eleanor?" He caught himself and actually turned a little pink. "I certainly didn't mean that in an improper manner."

Anne answered him from across the table, which was a breach of etiquette, but it was that sort of dinner party. "Eleanor does what every woman does for entertainment."

Villiers cut a glance at Eleanor and she could see laughter in his eyes. Anne was definitely the worse for all that rum punch, not to mention the Champagne. Popper seemed to have decided that the best way to survive the evening was to float all the unwanted guests in a sea of bubbles.

"And what is that?" Roland asked, looking adorably interested.

Eleanor smiled at him. He was as fresh and sweet as an early peach. For all he must be older than she was, he seemed younger. He looked like someone who was ready to fall in love.

"We watch men, of course," Anne said with a tiny, ladylike hiccup. "Men are endlessly amusing."

Eleanor had discovered that if she leaned toward Roland, his eyes slid down to her breasts as if he couldn't stop himself. And when he looked back up at her face, there was something in the depths of his eyes that made her shift in her chair.

"I can't imagine why you aren't married," he said, pitching his voice below the hum of conversation.

She was boggled for a moment. If she admitted to her own ruling about dukes, she sounded like a snobbish fool. On the other hand, if she admitted to being tenuously engaged to Villiers, she would have to stop flirting. Rather than decide, or dissemble, she turned the topic back to Roland. "What do you do for recreation, sir?"

"I write. Day and night, I write poetry." He met her

eyes again, steadily. "I feel as if we shall definitely meet many times in our lives, Lady Eleanor."

Her heart skipped a beat at the pure intensity in his gaze. "Ah—I hope so."

"I write poetry," he said again. A lock of dark hair fell over his eyes and he threw it back. "Have you ever read the verse of Richard Barnfield?"

"I haven't read much poetry," she confessed. "I'm half-way through Shakespeare's sonnets at the moment, but I'm finding them slow going."

Roland picked up Eleanor's Champagne glass and leaned toward her. "Shakespeare is all very well, but of course his work is terribly out of fashion. I prefer a line that's more evocative. *Her lips like red-rose leaves floated on this cup . . . and left its vintage sweeter.*"

"That's lovely," she breathed. "Did you just write it this moment?"

He grinned at her, and his smile was even more enticing than his intent gaze. "I would lie to you about that, but I don't want to lie to you, *ever.*" He handed her the glass. "Taste. *Honey from Hyblean bees, matched with this liquor, would be bitter.*"

"Where *is* Hyblea?" It was Villiers, speaking across the table as rudely as had Anne.

Eleanor blinked at him. She was caught in the web of Roland's words. The last thing she wanted was a geographical discussion. She frowned and turned back to the poet. "Do tell me the rest of the poem?"

"I'm afraid that the rest of the poem isn't fit for the supper table," he said with a glance from under his lashes. He put one finger on the inside of her wrist. "This blue vein touches your heart, Lady Eleanor."

"I would love to know the remainder of the poem," she said, her voice dropping to a near whisper.

"So would I," Villiers put in.

She glared at him. Couldn't he tell a private conversation when he overheard one? But now everyone was looking down the table, and Roland withdrew his finger as if she had burned him. She twitched with annoyance.

"It is part of my own version of *Romeo and Juliet*," Roland said. "I won't share more; people find poetry tedious. Certainly my family tells me that mine is tiresome."

"Too flowery, in my opinion," his father said. "Of course, he's had quite a bit printed. He's not just some ne'er-do-well with nothing better to do."

"Printed?" the duchess said, her tone dripping with disdain.

"Likely you aren't knowledgeable about the literary world," the squire told her. "The very best have their poems printed, and no shame in that. The shame is in *not* printing."

"Humph," was Her Grace's response to that.

"In fact, my son was knighted last year for his poetry writing," the squire said, puffing up his thin chest.

"A veritable troubadour," Villiers said. His comment was perfectly pitched to make it unclear whether he meant it as a compliment or an insult.

"When we tragically lost Prince Octavius last year," the squire continued, "Roland wrote an exquisite verse in his memory. Truly beautiful, and the king himself thought so. He felt it succored him in his time of suffering, and he summoned the lad to Buckingham Palace and knighted him on the spot."

Roland's lowered eyes were, perhaps, a bit more humble than Eleanor would have liked, but that was her ungracious, sarcastic nature coming out, and as Anne had told her, she needed to curb that trait. Luckily, Champagne had a mellowing effect.

"Well, let's hear a bit of this poetry, then," Eleanor's mother allowed, in a considerably warmer voice. "Not the piece for Princess Amelia. I can't abide feeling sad. Something more entertaining, if you please."

"Here's a bit from when Romeo promises to climb to Juliet's window," Roland said. He put his right hand at his side and it just touched Eleanor's. "Juliet tells him to *come before the lark with its shrill song has waked a world of dreamers.* And Romeo promises to climb to her balcony in a ladder wrought out of scarlet silk and sewn with pearls."

His finger barely stroked Eleanor's wrist.

"Is that it?" Her Grace said after a moment.

"That's all I can remember," Roland said.

"Well, I like the idea of a ladder sewn with pearls," the duchess allowed. "I have a red bonnet sewn with pearls that may be something of the same idea." She turned to the squire. "Aren't you a little worried that all this talk of red silk and pearls makes your son sound like a milliner?"

"He's a clever lad," the squire said, pride evident in his voice. "He's never caused me a moment's worry."

"Well, that's more than I can say for my daughters," she said, glancing down the table. "Eleanor, you are too pink in the face. How much Champagne have you drunk?"

"Not as much as I have," Anne said cheerfully. She looked at Lisette. "Darling, don't you think you could rise now, so that we could leave the table before I slip under it?"

"Oh! Are you waiting for me?" Lisette said. "Goodness, and I'm such a slow eater. I eat like a bird." She took another bite.

Villiers smiled down at her. "A very graceful bird, my lady."

Eleanor turned back to Roland. "That poem is beautiful."

"It's actually not that good," he told her with a twinkle. "I wouldn't even try to publish that in its current state. Too flowery, as my father said."

"Perhaps the ladder could be just silk with no pearls," Eleanor suggested. "One has to think that pearls are not only ruinously expensive, but uncomfortable underfoot."

"Depending on the weight of the climber, they might even be crushed," Villiers said, interjecting himself into their conversation again. "Is Romeo the one who's fat and short of breath? Or is that Hamlet?"

Roland threw him an unfriendly look. "That sort of verisimilitude has no place in the land of poesy."

"I'm just trying to point out a logical problem," Villiers said innocently. "Cleopatra used to pulverize pearls and put them in her wine, after all. While I've never stamped on one, I'm certain that they would shatter easily."

"Oh, I don't think so," Lisette put in. "I have any number of pearls and they aren't crushed."

"But have you stamped on any of them?" Eleanor asked.

Lisette stared at her for a moment, clearly searching her mind for the shards of crushed pearls. "No," she said, jumping to her feet. "Let's try it!"

Villiers actually laughed, looking up at her. "You are a true original, Lady Lisette."

Eleanor felt her lips tightening. Glancing at Roland, she saw an expression in his eyes that she guessed mirrored her own.

"Sorry," he whispered to her, "I've lived next to Lady Lisette my whole life. Do you know that my brother is betrothed to her?" And, when she nodded, "It all happened in the cradle, naturally, and it would bankrupt my father to repay her dowry. So Lancelot never comes home. We haven't seen him in six years. He does write now and then, hoping that she's run off with someone."

He held back her chair. "We're about to watch the demolishment of some pearls."

A short time later they were all in the sitting room, holding cups of tea, when Lisette's maid appeared with a string of pearls and a most disapproving look on her face. The poor woman even tried to remonstrate with her mistress.

Roland had come to sit next to Eleanor, as naturally as if they'd always known each other. He put his mouth near her ear and she could feel his breath tickle her neck. "If someone takes the pearls away she'll turn into a whirling dervish."

"What's a whirling dervish?" she said, giggling.

"A monster who terrorizes the populations of India, as I understand. Or perhaps it was Turkey. Honestly, I hardly know, but I'm sure you can imagine."

"We *must* stop her," Eleanor said. "It's absurd to crush a pearl on such a pretext."

"Just look how she's making the Duke of Villiers laugh," Roland said. "I believe he's quite taken with her. If you take the pearls away, you'll ruin her chance of making a match that would free my brother from his bondage."

"Villiers wouldn't," Eleanor said.

"Oh yes, I expect he would. She's quite beautiful, you know. And the odd thing about her is that she's not a bad person. He won't know what she's really like until it's too late. She has enormous charm."

"I know," Eleanor said, feeling guilty. "And she can be so joyful."

"Pity she'd be such a horror to live with."

The duchess had apparently just realized what was about to happen. She put down her tea cup with a little click, rose from her chair and snatched the pearls before Lisette could react. "Am I to understand that you are planning to *crush* these pearls?" she said in an awful voice.

"Exactly," Lisette said, as blissfully unaware as ever. "You see, Your Grace, we are wondering how hard it is to crush a pearl. The Duke of Villiers thinks that Roland would smash a pearl under his feet. But I don't agree. He used to be roly-poly, but he's not at all plump any longer."

Eleanor turned to Roland with a grin, but his brows were drawn together and his face looked black with fury. Villiers, on the other hand, was laughing openly. That's the first time I've heard him laughing, she thought sourly. I should have assumed it would be at someone else's expense.

Lisette held out her hand for the pearls, her pretty smile not even slipping. It was a quality that Eleanor envied. Because Lisette never envisioned opposition to one of her plans, she didn't flinch until the moment was upon her.

"Absolutely not," the duchess announced in a dreadful voice. "I have seen your mother in these pearls a hundred times."

Lisette blinked. "Mother is dead. She doesn't care what I do to them now."

"Her memory is not dead."

"They're *my* pearls," Lisette said, her lower lip starting to tremble.

"Here we go," Roland murmured.

Eleanor couldn't bear to see it happen. She jumped to her feet and hurried to Lisette's side. "We just want to make sure that your pearls remain intact," she said as persuasively as she could.

But Lisette's eyes were taking on that wild spark that Eleanor remembered. "You are crossing me!" she cried, rounding on the duchess.

"Of course I am!" she snapped back. "Your mother was one of my dearest friends."

Eleanor braced herself.

Villiers stepped forward and put a hand on Lisette's arm. She froze. "Her Grace doesn't understand." His voice was dark and cool and mesmerizing. "When my mother died I wanted to burn her clothing. Her jewelry. Her scarves."

Lisette stood still. Even as Eleanor watched, Lisette shed her anger and her eyes turned grief-stricken.

"I know how you feel," he finished.

Lisette's lip trembled. "I miss my mother," she whispered.

Eleanor retreated back to her seat.

"For God's sake," Roland said in her ear, "an innocent bystander might think that Lisette's mother died a year or two ago."

But Eleanor was watching Villiers. "I'm not sure you get over the death of your mother all that easily." Though she wasn't actually sure that Villiers meant to express grief when he talked of burning his mother's clothing. There was a shade of something darker in his voice.

"Would you like to hear a song?" Roland asked.

"What?" Eleanor said, noticing that Lisette's white-blond curls just reached Villiers's shoulder; they looked quite striking together.

Roland looked down at her, his dark poet's eyes flaring. "It's the one thing Lisette and I have in common. We both love music. If I borrow a lute"—he nodded at the far wall—"at least it will halt the tender scene. Though in my opinion Villiers's days as a bachelor are numbered. And his days of peace as well, but there's no need for us to play witnesses to that tragedy."

Eleanor thought about confessing her own semi-betrothed state and decided not to. Besides, Roland was already striding over to the wall and pulling down a lute.

He plucked a string and then called, "Lisette, you've let this go out of tune again!"

She leaped away from Villiers the moment the note sounded in the air, sadness falling from her like a discarded cloak. "I played that one earlier this evening," she said, running to his side.

"I suppose it's not too bad," Roland allowed, sitting down, the better to tune the instrument.

Lisette's face brimmed with happiness. "Let's all sing."

"I am fatigued," the duchess announced.

She retired with little more than brief goodbyes to the squire and his wife. She didn't care for music any more than she appreciated poetry. It turned out that the squire's lady shared her lack of appreciation, and so the elder couple left, promising to send the coach back for their son.

It occurred to Eleanor as she curtsied goodbye that Squire Thestle's smile seemed to indicate hope that his son would make an advantageous match. With herself. She felt a bit more sober at the thought.

"A lute, for God's sake," Anne said, falling into the seat next to Eleanor that Roland had deserted. "Your medieval lover is far too passionate for me. I feel as if I'm caught in some sort of Shakespearean nightmare."

"A glass of anisette?" Popper said, offering a tray of small glasses.

"If I drink that I'll fall asleep in public," Anne said, pulling herself upright. "No, I'm for bed." She looked down at Eleanor, a wry smile on her lips. "How complicated is the game of love, wouldn't you say?"

"Shakespeare?" Eleanor inquired.

"I haven't the faintest," Anne said, taking herself off to bed.

# Chapter Thirteen

"Oh lovely, all the old people are gone," Lisette said gaily. "Let's sing outside, on the terrace."

"Won't we keep people awake?" Eleanor asked, sipping her anisette. It tasted like distilled licorice root, strong and sweet, with a sensual promise.

There was no gainsaying Lisette, of course. A moment later the four of them were outside. Light streamed from the library, but the terrace itself was in shadow. The air was warm and fragrant, like evening primroses.

Lisette had brought out another lute and she and Roland were seated together, so Eleanor made for the settee where she and Anne had sat that afternoon.

Villiers had been leaning against the stone railing, but when Lisette and Roland began to sing, he joined her.

For a few moments they just listened. The lutes had a tremulous sound, as if notes were barely shaped before they slipped away. *"Who spoke to death?"* Lisette sang, high and clear and beautiful. *"Let no one speak of death,"* Roland answered her. His voice was a silky honey-smooth tenor that wove around hers. *"What should death do in such a merry house?"* they sang together.

Eleanor took another sip of her anisette and leaned her head back. Far above their heads the stars shone like silver buttons on a dandy's waistcoat.

"Beautiful, aren't they?" she said to Villiers.

"Pearls," he said laconically. "Crushed to make stardust."

She turned to meet his eyes and choked back a laugh.

*"Let death go elsewhere—"* Lisette sang, and broke off at Roland's impatient gesture.

"You have the fingering wrong again. Listen." He played the refrain again. And again.

"You look extremely beautiful tonight," Villiers said suddenly.

"Me?" Then she remembered that Anne had painted her beautiful and smiled. "Thank you."

"You are driving the poor poet mad with desire."

Villiers was looking at her so coolly that she didn't know what he thought of Roland's admiration. Perhaps he was suggesting that she might like to marry Roland instead of himself? She took another drink and the liqueur burned down her throat. It sang to her of confidence and passion, of men who would never leave her.

"I'd like to kiss Roland," she said, "before I make a final decision."

It was only when he made a small incredulous noise in the back of his throat that she realized she had been less than clear. "Before I decide whether to marry him instead of you," she clarified.

"You'll decide on the basis of a kiss? *His* kiss?" A strand or two of Villiers's hair had fallen from its ribbon and swung near the curve of his jaw. It wasn't a poet's jaw. It was a harsh, male jaw, the kind belonging to a man likely to issue decrees. And feel that women should pay attention to his proclamations.

Roland and Lisette had started singing again, something about love this time. *"I made the prince my slave,"* they sang together. *"He was my lord for the space of a moon."*

"The space of a moon, my arse," Villiers said into her ear.

Eleanor started. She hadn't realized he'd moved close to her.

"Why don't they just sing what they mean: *I tupped him for a month?"*

She gave him a frown.

"You'll decide whether to marry *me* on the basis of *his* kiss?" His words were a low growl, and hung on the air.

*"I put a ring on his finger and brought him to my house,"* Lisette sang, and Roland joined in: *"I clothed him in hyacinth and fed him honey-berries."*

Eleanor let her head fall back and examined the hyacinth-colored sky. Villiers made a small movement next to her, and she felt a surge of power. She knew exactly what to do. She turned her head, just slightly. She didn't even smile at him; she just allowed the invitation to be in her eyes.

"Are you playing the siren with me?" he asked, his voice low, almost incredulous.

"Only for the space of the moon."

"You surprise me," he said, bending toward her. His lips tasted of anisette, like spice and like a man. She opened her mouth, remembering instantly how delicious a kiss could be. How the touch of lips could change the whole feeling of her body. She leaned toward him and gave him everything he wanted.

And he took it.

She realized, in the first second after their kiss began, that Villiers would always take what he wanted. He crushed her mouth, cupping her face in his hands and pulling her toward him.

Dimly, she thought how different this first kiss was from the one she had shared with Gideon, years ago. They were young and unpracticed. Gideon fumbled; she giggled; he apologized. It soon became clear that she enjoyed kissing far more than he did.

Probably all young men were the same: eager, driven by lust. He longed to touch; she longed to kiss.

She remembered chasing him around the barn once, trying to catch and kiss him, until he suddenly turned around and snatched her up, his hands falling on her—

"What?" a dark voice said in her ear.

"Yes?" she asked, startled.

"I'm kissing you, damn it."

She looked up at him, confused. In the light falling through the windows behind them, Villiers's eyes looked black. Eyelashes shaded his cheekbone, putting it into high relief. "I was thinking of something else," she said honestly.

He stared at her for a second and then let out a howl of laughter that punctuated the singing she barely heard. "Between you and Tobias, I'm achieving a modicum of humility, for the first time in my life."

"That I doubt," she observed.

His eyes narrowed. "I suppose you were thinking of Astley."

She felt a little dazed, as if the liqueur had gone to her head, and she couldn't follow what he was talking about so she just shook her head. "I'm sorry if I punctured your vanity," she said honestly. "It was a nice kiss."

"Nice?"

He sounded incredulous. Apparently the Duke of Villiers was accustomed to women falling at his feet after one touch of his lips. "You taste like anise," she said, settling back into her position. "I'm very fond of licorice. Did you ever find the plants and chew them when you were little?"

"No."

She turned her head slightly, just enough so she could meet his eyes again. Of course he hadn't wandered about fields grazing on wild plants. He was likely swathed in velvet from his toes to his collarbone from age five. No, four.

"Of whom were you thinking?" he asked. "Was it Astley?" There was something dangerous in his tone.

She took another sip of anisette. It slid sweet and hot down her throat, adding to the heat in her insides that had jumped to life with his lips. And that was making her nervous. She had now kissed two men in her life, Gideon and Villiers. Both of them made her feel slightly delirious, wild with pleasure, wanting nothing more than to kiss again and again.

She had the uncomfortable feeling that she was a wagtail by nature. Her mother would not approve. "In truth, it was the Duke of Astley," she admitted.

Villiers's expression didn't change. "He *is* pretty. A maiden's dream, in fact."

"He was my dream," she confessed. In the background, Lisette and Roland were quarreling over a musical notation of some sort or other. "After his father died, he started coming home with my brother during holidays."

"From Eton."

"Yes, exactly. I never really paid much attention to him, but then one day . . . well, there he was."

It was embarrassing the way that Villiers's lips made her want to lean over and—and nip him. Lick him.

"What then?" he inquired.

"Oh, it took us months to kiss," Eleanor said lightly. "Though I spent a great deal of time dreaming about it. It's quite common to fall in love at that age."

He nodded, rather unexpectedly. Eleanor couldn't imagine the Duke of Villiers in love with anyone. *"You?"* she asked.

"Why the surprise?"

"Oh, the dukeness of you," she said with a wave of her hand, wondering if she might have drunk a bit too much. Just to prove to herself that she hadn't, she finished her glass.

"My dukeness," Villiers repeated.

"Swathed in velvet, from the moment you left the crib." She looked away because the very sight of his lips made her feel like squirming, as if her soft parts became softer at the sight of him.

"I was in love with a woman named Bess. She was a barmaid."

Eleanor giggled. "Buxom and beautiful?"

"I actually don't remember whether she was buxom," Villiers said. "Certainly she wasn't as fortunate in that regard as you." His eyes didn't drop below her face. "I would remember that."

"My bodice is a bit small," Eleanor confessed. "This gown belongs to my sister. My preference is for less revealing clothing."

He nodded.

"Did Bess return your affection?"

"How could she not?" he asked. There was something hard in his voice. "I was already a duke."

"That needn't have—"

He interrupted. "Believe me, the barmaid who turns down a duke should be cast in bronze."

"Nonsense," Eleanor said tartly. "You have a distorted

idea of your own consequence." A thought occurred to her. "Is Bess the mother of one of your children?"

The edge of his mouth quirked, sending a blaze of heat down Eleanor's legs.

"My children really don't bother you, do they?"

She considered that. "Should they, on moral grounds? Religious? Ethical?"

"Any of the above."

"I myself would prefer to have tidier domestic relations," she said. "But I don't see that it's any of my business if you don't agree with me."

"Well, you are marrying me," he pointed out. "Or so you said."

Eleanor reached out and took his glass of anisette. He had barely tasted it, after all. "Perhaps. An announcement before my mother is hardly a commitment. Either of us may decide that we would rather marry another."

"You would consider our betrothal a tentative one?"

She glanced deliberately at Roland. He looked like the embodiment of a medieval troubadour, dark and dreamy, singing of love. She listened for a moment. He was actually singing about a widow marrying her sixth husband, but the principle was the same. He *sang.* "I don't suppose you sing?" she suggested.

"Never."

"I don't either," she sighed.

"Bess is not the mother of any of my children," Villiers said.

"All right," Eleanor said agreeably.

"She fell in love with a much prettier fellow."

She considered his face. He was not pretty, not by any stretch of the imagination. Everything about him was just slightly rough-hewn, aggressive, male. Too male. He made embarrassing ideas float through her head. As if the Duke of Villiers would suddenly swoop on her, push her down on the settee, and throw himself on top of her.

"I thought a duke's precedence was all-important," she said hastily.

"The Duke of Beaumont stole her from me."

"Goodness," Eleanor said, smiling. "Lucky Bess! Chased by two dukes. Do tell me that you fought a romantic duel?"

"There's nothing romantic about duels," Villiers said. "But no. I had no claim over her, you see. I had completely lost my head. But a young man's adoration was no match for Beaumont's Adonis-like profile."

"I suppose Beaumont is handsome," she agreed. Not as handsome as Gideon, in her opinion, but good-looking enough. Still, he always looked so tired that it was hard to imagine him young.

"You are practically the first woman I've spoken to who doesn't rhapsodize over Beaumont's face," Villiers said.

She glanced at his nose and looked away again. She could hardly admit that Gideon had soured her interest in beautiful men. To the point to which she felt far more attracted to Villiers's sort of rough-hewn looks.

"And yet I suppose that Astley is even more beautiful than Beaumont, to your eyes?" Villiers asked, uncannily echoing her thoughts.

She nodded.

"More golden, more sleek, more attractive in every way?"

"Yes," Eleanor agreed. She took another drink of Villiers's anisette.

"I'm sorry," he said, and the sharp edge dropped from his voice. He actually sounded sympathetic.

"It was years ago," she said.

"If you still think of him while kissing another man, then it hasn't been long enough."

She couldn't think how to refute that, but at that moment she looked up to see Lisette sling her lute at Roland's head. Roland threw himself sideways and at the same time managed to put up a hand and catch the lute.

"You wretched little—" he hollered.

Lisette opened her mouth to scream back, cast a look toward Eleanor and Villiers, and ran into the library.

It all happened so quickly that she was gone by the time Villiers looked around.

"I apologize," Roland said, walking toward them. "When two musicians come together, we lose sense of time. Even worse, we sometimes lose our heads."

Eleanor felt her cheeks growing pink. She certainly had forgotten their presence during Villiers's kiss.

"Your music played so sweetly on the night air that we all lost track of time," Villiers said at her shoulder.

Roland glanced at him. "Shakespeare on music. I gather that's part of *If music be the food of love, play on*, etcetera? Is that from *A Midsummer Night's Dream*?"

"Actually no," Villiers said. "The beginning of *Twelfth Night*."

"I hate those old plays," Roland said to Eleanor with a comical grin. "So stuffy and antiquated. You have no idea how hard it can be to make older people realize that fresh material can be so much better."

He didn't glance at Villiers, but she felt an irresistible urge to smile. Obviously he had seen them kiss.

"We old people generally go to bed with the chickens," Villiers said, without a trace of resentment in his voice.

"Ah well, I certainly didn't mean that comparison," Roland said, leaving in doubt exactly what comparison he had meant. "Lady Eleanor, may I call for you tomorrow? I would love to show you the countryside."

"Of course," Villiers said genially, taking on the demeanor of a kindly uncle. "You young people ought to trot about on horses while the rest of us are taking our morning constitutional."

"I would be happy to see you again, Sir Roland," Eleanor said, holding out her hand.

He fell back into a flourishing bow, raising her hand to his lips and holding it there for a long moment. "Tomorrow," he said, meeting her eyes.

"Don't leave those lutes," Villiers said.

Roland's bow to the duke was extremely brief, barely more than the kind of bob Eleanor had seen irate footmen give to a butler.

Villiers leaned back on the settee as if there was no question about the fact that they would stay there, unchaperoned. "I didn't see what happened to Lisette, did you?"

Eleanor thought of the jerky violence with which Lisette had swung the lute. "I believe she was irritated by something Roland said."

"I can certainly understand that. I would suggest that Sir Roland's manner could be considered a far more reliable guide to matrimony than might his kisses."

"What do you mean?" Suddenly the stars seemed much closer, now that there were only the two of them outside together. The night air was velvety and warm on her skin.

"If I were married to him, it would be about a week before I pushed one of his pompous, artistic poems down his throat," Villiers said with a perfect lack of expression, which made his comment hilarious.

Eleanor burst into laughter. "You hurt his feelings with that twaddle about Shakespeare. It could be that he'll be a great writer someday, you know."

Villiers leaned a little closer. "Dropping the tiresome

poet from the conversation, I don't think I want my marriage decided by a kiss that includes the Duke of Astley as an unknowing partner."

"I thought of Gideon for only a moment." Her treacherous heart sped up a bit.

"Why don't you kiss me this time? Perhaps that will help to focus your attention on the man before you."

Of course she could kiss him. She was good at kissing, and those dalliances with Gideon weren't all that many years ago. So she leaned forward and kissed him with all the persuasive power that she'd polished with Gideon. Her lips slipped along his, begged him for entrance.

His lips didn't move.

She swallowed a little humiliation, leaned farther forward so he could see her bosom if he wished.

Gideon always closed his eyes when she kissed him, but Villiers kept his open. And to her dismay, he seemed to be looking at her with amusement rather than raw desire.

"What?" she demanded.

"I don't think I like being kissed. That was as boring as *my* kiss, the one that drove you to start dreaming about Astley."

Gideon hadn't liked her kisses all that much either. "Very well," she said, moving back and feeling around for her wrap. "I really should go to—"

"I didn't say I didn't like kissing you," he interrupted.

"Yes, you—"

"I don't like *being* kissed." And with that rather cryptic statement he reached across and pulled her against his chest.

Eleanor's arms went instinctively around his neck. But she didn't have time to think before his hands laced into her hair and his mouth took hers. He didn't beg or seduce. He invaded. He took her mouth hard, with a kind of concentrated lust and fever, and she knew exactly why all those women had never said no to him.

It didn't have anything to do with his ducal crest, as he seemed to think. It was the moment when the immaculately dressed, starched and beruffled duke suddenly turned wild, his mouth hot on hers, his hands gripping her hard.

This kiss was unlike any she'd shared with Gideon. There was nothing sweet about Villiers's kiss. And *Villiers* didn't feel like the right way to think about him.

She broke free and his lips slid, hot, across her cheek. "What's your name?" she whispered, knowing it perfectly well. Leopold was too accustomed to women's avid attempts to claim intimacy with him. He was spoiled by too much adoration.

He said it against her lips. "You do remember my title?"

"I don't care about your title any more than—" But she didn't want to talk, so she turned toward his mouth again, starving as a new-born chick. He made a growling sound in his throat, and their tongues tangled. She was shaking, she thought dimly, pushing her fingers into his hair and pulling it free of its ribbon so that it slid like rough silk across her skin.

"Leopold," he said.

She wasn't listening because she was burning, breathless.

"Leopold," he growled.

She turned her mouth, wanting more of *him*, not words.

"You are a surprise," he said a moment later, pulling back again.

Men never wanted to kiss as long as she did, she thought, and then pulled herself together. "A surprise?"

Instinctively she knew instantly that she had to—*must*—cover up the extent to which she was unable to think because of this craving. For him. For this man who was looking at her with absolute self-possession, pulling his hair back and swiftly retying its ribbon. Apparently the duke didn't tolerate being unkempt for long.

She managed a shrug. "Because I enjoy your kisses? Since you imply that every woman falls prey to the ducal title, how do you know that I'm not belatedly captivated simply by your crest?"

"Are you? After all . . . I am the second duke with whom you've cavorted, if we count Astley. And I think we must count Astley, mustn't we?"

There was just the subtlest insinuation to his voice. "I was in love with Gideon," she said, not bothering to try to fix her own hair. It was probably a mess, but she refused to care. Instead she picked up the anisette, but it tasted sickly sweet now, and she put it down after it had barely touched her tongue. "I suspect that I loved him more than you loved Bess."

"I can't imagine how we would determine such a thing," Villiers—no, *Leopold*—said.

"I wanted to marry him," she confessed. "I thought we would marry."

"So I surmised. Since I can't imagine that Astley chose his languid wife over you, I gather that fate intervened."

The pleasure of that compliment warmed her. "Fate in the form of his father's will."

"I expect you did love him more than I loved Bess, then," Leopold said. "For I never thought to marry her. I was infatuated with her laugh. She had a wonderful chuckle. I wanted all her laughter for myself."

Eleanor raised an eyebrow. "I would have thought that most young men felt possessive about other attributes of bonny Bess."

"Oh, I wanted those too," he said wryly.

"You mean you didn't—" She stopped.

"Elijah intervened before my adoration of Bess could

lead me to convince myself that I should offer her money," Leopold said. "I'm afraid that I merely stood about the inn adoring her, and never thought about money until it was too late."

"Oh."

"Elijah, of course, didn't need to offer money because he was so very pretty."

He would hate sympathy, but she felt a flash of it anyway, followed by a wave of rage at stupid Bess for following the luscious Duke of Beaumont wherever he willed her. Presumably to Beaumont's bed.

"I must take another look at Beaumont in the future. I'm afraid that I always dismissed him—he has that tiresome puritanical look—but now that I know he stole your barmaid's attentions . . ."

He laughed, and Eleanor liked the sound. "Your problem is not choosing between myself and Beaumont, but choosing between myself and young Roland."

"And yours," she countered, "has nothing to do with a barmaid. Instead you are faced by two nubile daughters of dukes."

"You think I should consider Lisette?"

She knew perfectly well that he was considering Lisette. She'd seen the way he watched her, with a kind of fascination, as if she were a fairy plaything.

"She's exquisite," she said. "I would marry her, too."

He raised an eyebrow at the detachment in her voice. With luck, that meant he hadn't guessed that she was lusting after him with embarrassing heat.

"I wouldn't marry a woman for her beauty," Villiers said. She caught just a trace, just the smallest trace, of the unlovely boy thrown over for his handsome friend. "I need a mother for my children."

"Lisette loves children," Eleanor said, meaning it. "She truly loves them."

"I can tell. And she does so much work with those orphans. I believe that she wouldn't be put off by illegitimacy."

"Absolutely not. Lisette would never think twice about a person's origins."

"She could teach them to care as little about society as she does," Leopold said. "I asked her why she was never presented, for example, and she just laughed. She didn't care."

"Lisette has never cared for convention. It's not in her nature to kow-tow to someone because he is of high rank."

"I've seen that in Quakers. But never in a woman of the aristocracy. It's unexpectedly alluring."

"Yes," Eleanor said, gathering her wrap. "Lisette is definitely alluring." She was *not* going to say anything about Lisette's inability to care for anything for very long. Or, for that matter, about her betrothal.

"Do you really mean it?" he said. Now he didn't look like a Leopold any longer: she was faced once more by the Duke of Villiers.

"Mean what?"

"That we might treat our betrothal as something of a . . . temporary state, perhaps to be dissolved by either of us."

"Of course," she said quickly. "I am certainly looking forward to Roland's visit tomorrow."

"So *he* is Roland. And I?"

"Villiers," she said.

He didn't like that. His gray eyes turned cold, and she was glad that Roland had made an appearance, glad that she didn't care too much.

"You *are* the Duke of Villiers," she told him.

That glare of his probably withered other people. Those who cared more.

But she was determined not to care—in fact, never to care that much about any man again, she reminded herself. "That's not to say that I'm not interested in marrying you."

"Then call me Leopold."

"Perhaps, if we decide to marry," she said, standing up. "But I think that you are far more Villiers than you are Leopold. My mother always calls my father by his title."

"And yet you refer to Roland by his first name."

She took her time winding her wrap around her breasts, even though Villiers had never given her the satisfaction of knowing that he was looking at them. "Roland is a Roland," she said finally.

"And I'm a Villiers?"

"Lisette is a Lisette," she pointed out. "It's a lovely, flirtatious name, perfect for someone with flyaway curls and a giggle."

He raised an eyebrow at that description. "Remind me not to cross you. Does your name suit you?"

"Oh, Eleanor," she said. "I'm certainly an Eleanor." Or at least she was from her mother's point of view.

"Eleanor, Duchess of Aquitaine, and Queen of England," he said, sounding amused again.

That didn't make her amused, so she said her goodnight and retired to her chamber.

# Chapter Fourteen

*Knole House, country residence of the Duke of Gilner*
*June 18, 1784*

*V*illiers never woke early in the morning. Finchley, his valet, knew better than to even appear at his door before eleven. His ideal day consisted of playing chess most of the afternoon and then making love most of the night. He never paid calls, and he had discovered as a youth that a gift for chess translated into a gift for numbers; he gave his estate manager an hour a week, and within a few years his net worth had grown to one of the greatest in England.

He pulled himself out of sleep thinking that someone was beating down the door, only to suppose groggily that rain was crashing against his window. A moment later he realized that mere rain couldn't be causing that amount of noise. The window seemed about to shatter.

It must be hail. The worst hailstorm to hit southern England in years.

Villiers threw back the covers, fought his way through the bed hangings, and staggered out of bed.

Another blast of hail hit the window, shaking it so hard that the drapes actually shuddered. He walked over to the waiting basin of water and thrust his face into it. Then he straightened up and shook himself, chilly droplets flying in all directions. Finally he pulled back the drapes, expecting a sour gray light.

But instead there was sunshine. He closed his eyes and raked his hands through his hair. No hail. That implied . . .

He grabbed his towel and wound it around his waist, unlatched the door, pushed it open and stepped onto the stone balcony that looked over the gardens.

A thirteen-year-old boy was standing on the grass below, eyes bright.

"For Christ's sake," Villiers snarled, squinting down at Tobias. "What hour is it?"

"Late," Tobias said cheerfully. "You don't have any clothing on."

He leaned against the balustrade and stared down at his progeny. "What in hell's name do you think you're doing?"

"Waking you up."

"How did you know which window was mine?"

"Lisette told me."

"Lisette? Lady Lisette told you which window to throw rocks at? You could have broken the glass."

"Actually, she threw quite a lot of them," Tobias allowed. "She just went around to the side of the house."

"What is happening out here?" came a smoky voice.

He actually started. Eleanor wandered from her window onto what he now understood was a shared balcony—her chamber, it appeared, was next to his. Unlike him, she was swathed in some sort of thick wrapper that went from her collarbone to her toes.

Yet her clothing didn't matter. There was something about her that made him want to nibble her all over. It had to be the dissolute appeal of her. Her hair tumbled down her back, not in pretty ringlets, but in the kind of wild disarray that a man wants to find falling around his face as he thrusts up and—

Villiers jerked his mind away, suddenly aware that his towel had tented in front.

Now Eleanor, too, had discovered that they shared a balcony. She didn't turn a hair at the idea that he was practically naked. No blushing. The corner of her mouth tipped up and she looked him over, so fast that he would have missed it if he hadn't been watching her at precisely that moment.

Villiers had no problem being surveyed. He had no illusions about the beauty of his face. His title and money brought women to his bed, but his body kept them there.

But Eleanor turned away as if he were no more interesting than a grasshopper and called down to Tobias. "You're cracked if you think someone like the duke is going to get up this early."

Tobias smiled, a bit shyly. "We thought—"

"We?" Eleanor asked, straightening up.

"Lady Lisette thought that the duke might like to go riding," Tobias said.

"Can you imagine the duke on a horse without being dressed head to foot in gold lace?" Eleanor said mockingly. She glanced at him for a split second, but he felt it like a caress. "Your father takes so long to get dressed that the sun would be going down by the time he emerged from his chamber."

She had said just the right thing. Villiers watched Tobias's grin get bigger. He was a fool to hope that it was the words *your father* that made the boy crack a smile. Tobias was too serious.

He leaned back against the balustrade again and deliberately crossed his arms, because it made his muscles look even larger and he had the feeling that Eleanor liked muscles. Thank God, there was no way that Tobias could see the tent in his towel from below.

He moved his legs apart a bit, just in case she wanted to take another look. Obviously nothing would shock the woman.

"Am I to understand that you think I couldn't be ready in less time than you?" he demanded.

She didn't look at him. "Where's Lisette?" she called down to Tobias.

Villiers moved away from the edge of the balcony. He didn't mind showing some skin to Eleanor. But Lisette was a gently bred lady, with a kind of innocence that made her eyes shine with a deep-down purity.

Eleanor was leaning over the balustrade now, bantering with Tobias. Her bottom was very round under her thick robe. She was the antithesis of innocent. She made a man long to wake her up early enough so they could step out on the balcony with the first dawn light—

He wrenched his mind away again and readjusted his towel. This was becoming painful. It was rather fascinating to imagine how Eleanor became the woman she was, given that her mother seemed altogether wedded to convention.

Whereas Lisette, who seemed to be living more or less without a chaperone, was clearly untouched by the baser passions of the body.

"Women take much more time to dress than do men,"

he told Eleanor, deciding that he ought to give her one more chance to look him over before he returned to his chamber.

"You're not most men," she said flatly. She did turn to face him, but her eyes stayed on his face rather than dropping lower. There was just a tinge of rosy color in her cheeks. Good.

He widened his stance again, daring her to look down. "You're right. I'm not like other men," he said.

Eleanor choked with laughter. "Because your sense of consequence is bigger."

"And the rest of me too," he said, wondering if he'd lost his mind. The Duke of Villiers never traded bawdy quips on a balcony. He never—ever—*flirted*.

"That remains to be seen," Eleanor said saucily.

He bit back a grin. The Duke of Villiers didn't smile in the morning. He squinted at the sky. "What time is it, anyway?"

"Don't look so afraid. I assure you that the sun isn't made out of green cheese," she said to him. "I suppose it's around eight o'clock."

"Eight!" He shuddered.

"Leopold!" came a clear voice from the lawn. "Would you like to join us on an excursion?"

Villiers looked cautiously over the balcony, trying to keep his body out of sight. Lisette was the very picture of an English lady. Curls crested on her head like a frothy wave; her eyes shone brightly; she was wearing an enchanting riding habit.

"Hello!" she called, waving her hand at him. "Time to rise and shine, Leopold!"

"Yes, *Leopold*," Eleanor said in a low, mocking voice. "Do start to shine, please. I think I saw the rising, but I definitely missed the shining."

"As you said, there is a great deal of me that remains to

be seen," he said silkily, loving their verbal jousting.

Even though he never engaged in anything as déclassé as a flirtation.

"I'm afraid I can't join you," he said, raising his voice as he replied to Lisette.

She pouted. "No! Why on earth not?"

"I plan to pay a visit to the orphanage in Sevenoaks as soon as I am dressed."

Her mouth formed a perfect rosebud. A confused rosebud. "Why on earth do you need to do that? The orphans will return this afternoon, I assure you. A group of them come every afternoon to work on the play, though now we've turned it to a treasure hunt."

One couldn't help but admire her devotion to those poor children. But the fact that two of them might be his own made him edgy. Still, he couldn't figure out exactly how to answer.

Eleanor broke in. "The duke is thinking of sponsoring the orphanage," she called down to Lisette. "He's quite charitable, you know. I've heard tell that he's peopled his very own orphanage."

Tobias snorted, but Lisette's smile didn't waver. "I am thinking of doing that as well," she said earnestly. "Occasionally I have thought that the orphans are too thin, and wondered if they were well cared for. But I am assured that they eat sufficiently. If I had my own orphanage, I would make certain that they were offered only the foods they preferred."

"So I shall tour the orphanage this morning," Villiers said.

"We shall come with you!" Lisette said, clapping her hands. "Do you know, I've never toured the building? The children simply come to me, whenever I request it. I should like to see their dear little beds."

"Excellent," Eleanor said. "We shall all go to the orphanage this morning. Lisette . . . Tobias." She walked back into her room without saying goodbye to Villiers, which didn't sit well with him.

He scowled and didn't even realize that Lisette was cheerily calling him to meet her in the breakfast room until Eleanor had already left. At least Lisette understood that one didn't simply turn away from a duke.

He turned to enter his chamber.

"Hey!"

*Hey?* Could it be that someone was addressing him such? He turned, reluctantly. After all, he knew the voice.

"Do you want me to go to the orphanage and poke around?"

"Poke?" he said, staring down at Tobias. "What on earth would you look around for?"

"I can see what it's like. I've heard stories about that sort of place."

"Stories about orphanages?" Villiers's jaw tightened but he pushed the thought away. Of course his children were fine. For one thing, Lisette saw to the orphans' welfare herself. But Tobias had an awkward eagerness to him, as if he were a setter on a leash. "All right," he said.

Tobias gave a sharp nod and set off.

"Wait!" Villiers bellowed. And then, feeling very queer to be saying it, he asked: "Have you broken your fast?"

Tobias cast him a look of absolute scorn. "I'm in the *nursery*," he said. "I was offered gruel at six this morning."

"Gruel? They made you eat gruel?"

He gave a sharp burst of laughter. "I don't eat that! The footman brought me a meat pasty."

"I hope you tipped him." Villiers paused. "Do you have any money?"

"No thanks to you," Tobias said, but without anger. "Ashmole gave me some. I'll be off now." And he was gone.

Villiers dressed meditatively, but with speed. In the last month he had gained some experience in dealing with the class of persons who cared for indigent children. With the intent of inspiring awe, if not fear, he chose a riding costume of a deep scarlet, with buttonholes picked out in gold thread. His breeches buttoned tightly to the side of his knee; his hussar buskin boots gleamed, and more importantly, each sported a tassel of French silk. He pulled back his hair and tied it with a scarlet ribbon. Finally he slid on his heavy signet ring and belted on his sword stick.

Some minutes later, Lisette sat beside him in the carriage, chattering like a magpie about the children, the treasure hunt, and about Mrs. Minchem, who ran the orphanage.

"Mrs. Minchem?" Eleanor inquired. "I don't like that name."

Villiers didn't like it much either.

Lisette was off in a peal of laughter. "You can't judge people by their names, silly Eleanor!" she said. "Why, think if we were to judge you by the name Eleanor."

"What of it?" Eleanor said, raising an eyebrow.

But Lisette galloped ahead. "You know what I mean," she cried. "It's a *heavy* name, isn't it? Don't you think so, Leopold?"

"It's a queen's name," he said. "A chaste name." He didn't look at Eleanor. "Yes, I think it sounds like the kind of queen who is locked in a tower and never allowed to fall in love."

"That's sad," Lisette said, her mouth drooping.

"Whereas your name is as pretty as you are," he said.

Eleanor's eyes narrowed and he realized too late that
he had inadvertently implied that Lisette was prettier than
Eleanor. Lisette *was* prettier than Eleanor, but since Eleanor had that sultry ladybird look, no red-blooded man in
the vicinity of the two of them would want Lisette over
Eleanor. Eleanor was bewitching.

He could hardly point that out, though, so he just leaned
forward as the carriage jolted to a halt and examined the
orphanage's façade. It was big enough, but it looked like
a mausoleum. He'd been in a number of orphanages and
children's workhouses in the last two months, and had yet
to see one that he'd want to live in.

Not that the question was really important. He was
a duke. He'd never even noticed the many places he
wouldn't want to live in before, so why was he giving a
second thought to the issue now?

He was still thinking about the many unpleasantries
that dukes never contemplate when his footman announced them to the orphanage's headmistress.

Mrs. Minchem, unfortunately, lived up to her evocative
name. She looked like a cheese-paring, bitter woman, the
kind of woman whose small mouth was more vertical
than horizontal. She looked like an irate rodent. But she
smiled, showing every single tooth.

"Your Grace," she said, dropping into a curtsy that made
all the keys on her chatelaine jangle. "And Lady Lisette,
what an honor it is to welcome you to Brocklehurst Hall.
Lady Eleanor, it is indeed an honor." The ribbons on top
of her cap trembled with her emphatic words.

But Villiers wondered, looking at her pinched
mouth. He decided to say nothing of his children for the
moment.

"We would much appreciate a tour of your establishment," he said with his most charming smile.

Mrs. Minchem wasn't stupid; she actually recoiled.

There must be something in his smile, he thought, that wasn't quite as benevolent as it could have been.

"Do you take both boys and girls?" Eleanor asked, intervening.

Mrs. Minchem snapped the answer out as if she were being interrogated by the Watch. "No, indeed, my lady! There are no male children. *Ever.* This orphanage is run by a ladies' committee, and we allow orphans of the female persuasion only."

Villiers instantly felt twice as male as he had a moment ago. Lisette was drifting around the room, humming a little tune, and examining some rather dreary watercolors depicting the dells. "What do your orphans become when they leave your establishment?" he inquired.

"Not *that*!" Mrs. Minchem said. "Good women is what they become."

Eleanor walked forward a step. "My dearest Mrs. Minchem, the Duke of Villiers is considering the foundation of an orphanage of his very own. He has heard such excellent things about Brocklehurst Hall from Lady Lisette that he insisted on coming here first thing this morning."

"It is rather early in the morning," Mrs. Minchem allowed, thawing slightly.

"Are the orphans not awake?" Villiers asked.

"Of course they are! They're up at four-thirty in the morning, Your Grace, with a full hour of improving prayers before they begin their day."

"Four-thirty. My goodness," Eleanor said. "And a full hour of prayers before breakfast?"

"Of course. Children learn better on an empty stomach," Mrs. Minchem said authoritatively. "After they're fed, they're good for nothing and fall asleep on their feet."

Likely because they were up at four-thirty in the morning, Villiers thought grimly. He was starting to have a very bad feeling. And Eleanor shared it, because their eyes met, and there was a frown in hers.

"We are interested in seeing *everything*," Eleanor said, turning to Mrs. Minchem and smiling like a madwoman. She seemed to think that lavish charm would win admittance.

Equally clearly, Mrs. Minchem wasn't charmed. "I wouldn't feel comfortable without the agreement of the ladies' committee," she said, jangling her huge circle of keys. "They never authorized me to allow sightseeing trips."

Lisette drifted over from the other side of the room. "There's no need to worry about that, Mrs. Minchem," she said. "I am *on* the committee. Don't you remember that you didn't wish the orphans to visit me until I joined the committee?"

She turned to Villiers. "Mrs. Minchem is an absolutely wonderful headmistress for the girls. She is fiercely protective of them, which is of course exactly what she should be."

"I would prefer to have warning before I give tours of this nature," Mrs. Minchem stated.

But Eleanor could have told her that no one gainsaid Lisette when she had made up her mind. "Dear, dear Mrs. Minchem," Lisette cried. "You know that I am tasked by the committee to make four visits a year. And because I do delight in having the orphans to my house, I haven't paid you a visit in . . . oh . . . three years."

"I thought you said you had never visited Brocklehurst Hall at all," Eleanor said.

"True," Lisette said. "And all the more reason that we absolutely *must* pay a visit today. Now."

Mrs. Minchem still looked ready to complain, so Villiers stepped in. "You certainly wouldn't want anyone to think that there was something untoward happening with your orphans," he said softly. "So annoying . . . the investigation . . ."

Mrs. Minchem's eyelashes flickered, and she protested with real-sounding distress, "But the beds won't be made yet! The house will be—"

"We know exactly how it will be," Lisette said, putting her hand on the woman's arm. "Now you just show us their cunning little beds, Mrs. Minchem. We don't mind if they're not made up. We know that the girls need to learn to care for themselves, and I'm sure that some of them are rather lazy!"

"They are that," Mrs. Minchem said grimly. She nodded to the servant standing by the far parlor door, opposite where they entered, and he opened it.

The door opened into a perfectly ordinary corridor, lined with doors. Mrs. Minchem seemed resigned now, and she opened the first on the right. "These girls are learning to sew," she said, standing to the side. "They begin with sheets and progress to sewing a man's shirt before they leave."

Villiers followed Eleanor and Lisette into the room. A group of girls in plain white frocks were seated on a half circle of stools before a window, industriously sewing. As the door opened they sprang to their feet and formed a line.

At a signal from the eldest, the entire line dropped into a curtsy at precisely the same time.

Lisette burst into a crow of laughter. "How perfectly adorable!" she cried, clapping. "Please, do it again."

With a nod from Mrs. Minchem, the girls dropped another curtsy. And another.

"They don't curtsy individually," Eleanor said after the

third round. "They dip to exactly the same distance from the floor, no matter their height. How on earth do they manage it?"

"They train with a ruler," Mrs. Minchem said briefly, turning to go.

"No, no," Lisette said. "They *must* do it one more time." She clapped. "Come, girls, curtsy!"

Villiers felt a bit ill. The girls ranged from age five to perhaps fourteen. Every single one of them kept her eyes fixed on Mrs. Minchem, as if there were no visitors in the room at all.

Mrs. Minchem nodded.

They all dipped to precisely the same distance and rose again.

"It's like a dog act I saw at Bartholomew Fair," Villiers heard Lisette say to Eleanor as they left the room. It wasn't the most politic thing to say.

He was the last to leave. There were no twins in the line; he was certain of it. Although of course the twins might have been separated.

He should just ask Mrs. Minchem. But Eleanor was marching ahead, her back stiff with a kind of outrage that showed she hadn't enjoyed the dog act.

Mrs. Minchem opened the next door. She appeared to think that everything was going very well, and she seemed more relaxed. "The next group is made up of my parlor boarders, so to speak."

She tittered, but when no one responded, she explained: "These girls aren't quite orphans. That is, they are orphans in that their family cannot care for them, but they arrived with some money for their support."

"How can they be orphans if they have family?" Lisette asked, knitting her brow prettily.

Mrs. Minchem glanced at her and then said, "I'd not

soil your ears with the telling, my lady. I'll just say that in many cases their fathers have handed them over with a bit of money to tide them by."

"Very nice!" Lisette said.

"The other girls pay for their own keep by making buttons and wigs," Mrs. Minchem said. "But these girls are training to become the very best ladies' maids, so they learn to be French."

"What?" Eleanor asked. "Did you say that they are learning to be French?"

"Exactly," Mrs. Minchem said.

"This was one of my ideas!" Lisette cried, clapping her hands again. Villiers realized that he would be quite happy if Lisette never clapped again. "All the best ladies' maids are French, aren't they? So I told Mrs. Minchem that she simply must turn some of the girls into *mademoiselles*."

"It took some doing," Mrs. Minchem said grimly. "But they've got the trick now, and I think they'll find good places. We had to give them fancy names, of course." She opened the door.

There were six girls, also wearing white gowns and seated in a circle, but instead of sewing, they were apparently having a tea party. As the door opened they rose to their feet, lined up, and dropped into a synchronized curtsy.

"Now girls," Mrs. Minchem said heavily, "demonstrate, if you please."

The tallest girl stepped forward and curtsied before Lisette. *"Bonjour, mademoiselle. Comment allez-vous? Votre coiffe est très élégante."*

"We concentrated on three things," Mrs. Minchem said. "A proper command of French, development of an appropriate accent while speaking English, and a French manner."

"A French manner?" Eleanor asked. "How does one quantify such a thing?"

"The national character of the French is frivolous," Mrs. Minchem announced. "It is their lack of practicality that explains why they do not thrive. Nevertheless, they are very good at hair and clothing. We teach the girls to be voluble, excitable, and easily swayed by passion. Demonstrate."

At a nod from the eldest pupil, two girls stood forward.

"*Je m'appelle Lisette-Aimée,*" one said.

"*Je m'appelle Lisette-Fleury,*" said the other.

"How adorable!" Lisette cried. "They both have my name!"

"They all respond to Lisette," Mrs. Minchem said in answer to Eleanor's questioning glance. "That makes it easier for the staff."

"*Madame! Vos souliers sont salis. Permettez-moi de les nettoyer pour vous,*" said the first in rapid French.

"*Madame! S'il vous plaît, attendez. Vous ne pouvez être vue ainsi! Votre tenue est en complet désordre!*" said the other, her voice rising.

"*Pardonnez-moi,*" cried the first, collapsing into the second's arms.

"Enough," Mrs. Minchem said.

The girls sprang apart and dropped into identical curtsies.

"The girls will be a credit to this establishment," Mrs. Minchem said, opening the door. "We will place them with gentlewomen in the next few months."

"There is something extremely bizarre about Mrs. Minchem," Eleanor said quietly to Villiers as they followed the other two down the corridor again.

"Did you think that the two Lisettes at the end of the line looked alike?" Villiers asked.

"They were not identical, and they were older than your children, no?"

"Apparently, my daughters are identical."

"Then they have not been turned into Frenchwomen."

"Thank God for small favors," Villiers said. He was starting to get an edgy, angry feeling.

Ahead of them Lisette apparently grew tired of listening to Mrs. Minchem prose on about the virtues of laundry. She abruptly turned to the side and put a hand on a doorknob.

"I must insist that you allow me to direct your visit!" Mrs. Minchem snapped.

Villiers eyed the two women. Mrs. Minchem had burning eyes and the voice of a circus barker. But he'd put his money on Lisette. The more he saw of her, the more she seemed like a force of nature.

Sure enough, with a charming smile that completely ignored Mrs. Minchem's purple cheeks, Lisette turned the doorknob and pranced inside.

"Ugh," Eleanor said, and hurried forward.

Villiers took the opportunity to open another door, the one closest to him, and walk through. Inside, a half circle of girls sat before the window, heads bent over their work. He stopped, feeling foolish. The girls sprang to their feet, but without Mrs. Minchem there, they obviously didn't know where to look, or whether to curtsy.

"Good morning," he said, closing the door behind him.

"Good morning," they chorused, after a nod from the tallest girl. Then they dropped one of those uncannily accurate curtsies.

"What are you working on?" he asked uneasily. As far as he could tell there were no twins in the group.

There was a silence. "Buttons, sir," the tallest girl said finally.

One had to suppose that buttons were made somewhere, but Villiers had never imagined that they came from orphanages.

"Are there any twins in the orphanage?" he asked abruptly.

Again, they all blinked at him, until the tallest girl said, "Jane-Lucinda and Jane-Phyllinda were born on the same day, sir."

"Did they have the same mother?"

They all nodded at that.

"Where are they?"

"Phyllinda was rude again and they're—" the youngest girl piped up, and abruptly went silent after a ferocious look from the tallest girl.

"I'm sure we wouldn't know, sir," she said calmly. "We're snails, and Jane-Lucinda and Jane-Phyllinda are gold twist."

"Snails!"

She didn't smile. "We are making snail buttons, trimmed with French knots. Sometimes known as death's-head buttons," she added.

Villiers looked down the row of perfectly solemn faces. "You refer to yourself as snails?"

"We make snail buttons."

He nodded. "And your names?"

"Mary-Alice, Mary-Bertha, Mary . . ." And so it went. There were six Marys.

Villiers bowed. "Where will I find the Janes?"

There was a moment of silence. "Two doors down on the left, sir," the girl said finally.

"But you won't—" said the little girl, and stopped again.

In the hallway everything was quiet. Two doors down on the left he found a circle of girls. The only difference was that these girls were wearing brown pinafores over their white dresses. "Are you the Janes?" he asked.

They sprang to their feet, lined up and dropped a curtsy. He looked them up and down but there wasn't a face there that resembled his own.

"Where are Jane-Lucinda and Jane-Phyllinda?" he asked.

The youngest girl in the row put her fingers in her mouth, but otherwise no one moved. "We really couldn't say, sir," the tallest girl finally said.

He looked down the row. Cowed, dull eyes stared back at him until he reached the youngest, the one sucking on her fingers. Her eyes were bright blue: cautious, but awake. He walked over to her.

"What is your name?"

"Jane-Melinda," she said around her fingers.

"Hands out of your mouth," the eldest girl snapped.

Jane-Melinda took her fingers out of her mouth, and Villiers grabbed her wrist before he was even aware of what he was doing. Her fingers were bleeding, four of them, and the fifth was deeply scored.

"What in the hell is this about?" he asked, putting her hand down gently and turning to the head of the line.

"Gold twist can be hard to manage in the beginning," the girl said.

He picked up the hands of the girl next in line. Her fingers were swollen, grotesque, and bleeding sluggishly in a few spots. The brown pinafores suddenly made sense.

In the middle of the circle was a basket full of buttons, glittering in the sunlight. Before each chair was a half-covered bobbin, a nub of a button in the process of being wound with the treacherously fine, cutting gold twist.

"It's wire," the tall girl said, ducking her head as though ashamed. "It does hurt now and then but you have to make it tight or the button falls apart."

"Christ," he said under his breath. And then: "Tell me where to find Lucinda and Phyllinda, *now*."

The eldest girl froze, trembling. "I daren't," she gasped. "Mrs. Minchem . . ."

Down to his left, the smallest spoke. She had her fingers back in her mouth so it was difficult to understand her.

"Jane-Lucinda was smart to Mrs. Minchem," she said, big blue eyes fixed on Villiers's face. "So she was sent to that place. And Jane-Phyllinda went with her, of course."

"Where is that place?" he asked. And then realized that his voice must be quite awful, as a few girls flinched.

"The sty," the eldest girl finally whispered.

"The pigsty?" He could see the confirmation in their eyes, so he stepped back and made an elegant bow. He didn't know what to do. He didn't have any boiled sweets. He had nothing to give children with bleeding fingers.

The basket of gold twist buttons twinkled up at him innocently from the floor. He couldn't leave them to twist more wire. "Come along, all of you," he said, turning to the door.

"Wh-What?" It was the tallest girl, Jane-something.

"Follow me," he said impatiently. "I can't leave you here." He looked back and held out his hand. "Melinda."

She trotted over to him and put a warm, wet hand in his. He tried not to think about blood and saliva, but simply pulled open the door and exited.

The corridor wasn't the quiet refuge he had rushed through on the way from the snails to the gold twists. He came out like a mother duck, trailing a limp line of girls in brown pinafores to find a group of screaming females milling around.

Mrs. Minchem was in the middle, looking like Lot's wife after the salt hit: stiff and bitter. Eleanor was in front of her, yelling something. Her whole body was so vibrant with fury that he was surprised that Mrs. Minchem didn't just dissolve. Lisette was off to the side, surrounded by a circle of girls in white dresses.

"Who are these girls?" he said, looking down at Melinda. She had edged closer to him at the first sight of Mrs. Minchem, and was sucking her right hand again.

"The Sarahs," she said, rather obscurely.

"What do they make?"

"Wigs," one of the other Janes said. "They make perukes for gentlemen."

That didn't sound as difficult as gold buttons. Villiers strode forward as if he always had a small girl in one hand and a train of others following.

Eleanor swung around. Her eyes were smoldering, but not in a sensual manner. Rather, she looked like a firework about to explode. "Villiers, you will not believe the manner in which these children are treated!"

She *had* exploded, obviously.

Unfortunately, Mrs. Minchem was also an exploding rocket. She gobbled in a voice so high and screechy that he could hardly understand it.

He dropped Melinda's hand, since he needed that hand to draw his sword stick. It slid free from its sheath with a swoosh.

Instant silence.

It was quite gratifying.

"Now that I have your attention," he said, "I have one question. Where is the punishment room, Mrs. Minchem? Or should I say, the pigsty?"

Eleanor drew in her breath, but what really interested him was the way Mrs. Minchem drew up her bosom. It was a formidable bosom. It jutted before her like the prow of a ship approaching a new land.

"You are interfering with my methods," she spat. "Why have the Janes left their work?" She rounded on the eldest Jane. "How dare you, Jane-Jolinda? You will not finish your quota!"

Melinda pressed against Villiers's leg.

"The Janes will never make a gold button again," he told her. He brought the tip of his sword gently down to the ground. Everyone's eyes followed its bright surface.

Mrs. Minchem didn't quail. Instead she took a step forward. "Do you dare to threaten me? Me, who cares for the neglected orphans of England? Me, who spends every waking moment of my day shaping these negligent bits of humanity into something that society might find useful? *Me?*" She wasn't shrieking anymore. Her voice had taken on the brawny tones of a dockworker.

"Yes, you," Villiers stated.

She laughed at him. "I do the work that no one else wants to do. My girls won't be prey to the likes of you. They'll know a trade when they leave me. You think you can come in here and lord about, but what do you really have in the way of morals?" She spat it.

He managed not to flinch.

"I see that you think you're coming in here like a knight in shining armor, coming to save the poor orphans. You fool, you fool! Do you have any idea how much work it takes me to give each of them a trade and a sense of purpose? And you—you're one of them!"

"Them?" he asked. Melinda was clinging to his pantaloons now, so he switched his sword to his left hand and put his right on the child's shoulder.

Mrs. Minchem's eyes were maddened now. "You're one of the men who incontinently fill the landscape with the offspring of your illicit, your disgusting, unions!"

Villiers resisted the impulse to cover Melinda's ears. It

was regrettable that Mrs. Minchem actually had a point.

Eleanor marched around to confront Mrs. Minchem. "The pedigree of these children does not excuse your treatment." Her voice was at once soft and terrible, and cut through the woman's strident tones like a knife. "You are wrong to treat them so, *wrong*."

"What do you know of these girls?" Mrs. Minchem said shrilly. "If I do not subdue them, keep them working, they will betray their origins. They will become night-walkers, like their mothers."

"I will not bandy words with you," Eleanor said, and there was a crushing finality to her tone. "Leopold, summon your footmen. Mrs. Minchem will be leaving the premises and she may need an escort."

Taking just a split second to savor the fact that she'd used his given name instead of his title, Villiers turned to the eldest Jane. "My coachman is waiting in the court-yard, fetch a footman." She scurried off after one look at Mrs. Minchem, who was shuddering, like the surface of a seething volcano.

"You—you—"

"Hush," Eleanor said, cutting through her words. "You can explain yourself to a judge. The children have heard enough, and so have I."

Villiers thought of agreeing, and decided that would be undignified.

"Lisette," Eleanor said, not raising her voice.

Lisette skipped up, children clinging to both hands.

"We need a good woman to make sure these children are warm and clothed, and that their injuries are attended to. Do you know of someone in the village, or in your household?"

"I've never treated these girls with aught less than loving kindness," Mrs. Minchem squealed.

Villiers met her eyes and she sputtered to a halt. "I gather that my children are in the pigsty, madam. Do you wish to point the way?"

"Your children—your—"

"*My* children," he confirmed. "Twins. Currently named Jane-Lucinda and Jane-Phyllinda. My daughters, who are apparently residing in the sty."

"You have children living here?" Lisette exclaimed.

"The sty!" Eleanor said. "As in a home for hogs?"

For the first time Mrs. Minchem looked a little frightened. She gulped like a snake trying to swallow a large bird. "Those girls had to be separated from the rest because they were a bad influence." Her jaw firmed and she put on a defiant air. "Wicked, they were, especially Jane-Lucinda, and anyone who knows them will agree with me."

"My children the fiends," Villiers said pleasantly. "Yes, that seems appropriate. Now you will do me the pleasure, madam, of telling me where to find the sty." He paused. "I hardly need add that I hope, for your sake, that the both girls are healthy."

She flashed a look that tried to act like a hammer blow but failed.

"It's behind the milking shed," a tall Sarah said suddenly, standing forward. "I've been there only once."

"And you see how healthy she is," Mrs. Minchem said defiantly.

"She always said—" Melinda piped up, then faltered to a stop after a glare from Mrs. Minchem.

"Yes, Melinda?" Villiers asked, peering down at the little girl attached to his leg.

"She said as how the hogs would eat us if we fell asleep," Melinda said, and pressed herself even harder against Villiers's thigh. "And she left Lucinda and Phyllinda in there all night long." She gulped. "Maybe they've been et up."

Villiers looked at Mrs. Minchem and she actually recoiled. "You might want to spend the next few minutes praying that your hogs haven't acquired a taste for little girls," he suggested.

He waited until he was out of earshot before assuring Melinda that pigs were vegetarians. But when he and Eleanor, trailed by various orphans, undid the huge rusty clasp shackling the door to the sty, and stuck their heads into the dark, odiferous place, he felt serious misgivings.

There was no one in the sty but three extraordinarily large pigs and a litter of piglets. The sow lumbered to her feet with a murderous look in her small eyes.

In the middle of the soiled straw was one small shoe.

"That's Jane-Lucinda's!" the eldest Jane said, bursting into noisy tears.

# Chapter Fifteen

"They must have escaped," Eleanor said, giving the girl a hug. "They are, after all, *your* children, Villiers. That is surely what happened."

He had picked his way through the filthy straw and was examining the window, set up high and caked with indescribable dirt. "They didn't go out this way." Of course the pigs couldn't have eaten two children. One of the animals was so fat that he couldn't imagine it on its feet. Though one had to suppose that there was room in that vast stomach for a small child—

No. Of course not. One could not imagine that.

"Someone let them out," Eleanor said. "*Someone* in this house had the Christian decency to look out for two small girls locked in this nauseating place overnight."

His blood was beating in his ears and he heard only part of what she said. Suddenly she was next to him, hand on his arm. "A servant rescued them," she repeated.

A servant . . . a servant. Of course a servant rescued

them. The red haze in his head miraculously cleared. He didn't even thank her, just pushed his sword back into its scabbard; he must have withdrawn it without realizing. "Whoever saved my children will be handsomely rewarded."

But after Mrs. Minchem had been led away by Villiers's grooms, cursing and protesting, and all the servants gathered around, it became clear that not one of them had dared to gainsay their mistress's commands.

"You frequently left children overnight," Villiers stated, looking from face to face.

"She weren't an easy woman," a servant said.

He was a craven fool who turned his face to the side rather than meet Villiers's eyes. "You're all dismissed," he said. "Lady Lisette will make certain that you are not hired within the county." He turned to Eleanor. "Where is Lisette?"

"She felt dizzy at the idea of the sty," Eleanor said. "I sent her home. She'll send the carriage back for us. Your twins are on the grounds somewhere. We must find them."

But two hours later the children had still not been found. Every room had been searched; the barns had been rifled; the sty was turned inside out.

There was no sign of two small girls.

"They must have run away," Villiers said. "That's what I would have done."

"There's nothing more we can do at the moment," Eleanor said. "We must go home. It's long past time for luncheon. You'll send your footmen out to search the surrounding countryside and they'll find the children in no time. They can't have gone far."

That was true. He could feel the logic of it like a balm to his soul. "You called me Leopold in the orphanage," he pointed out.

"A moment of weakness," she said, accepting a footman's hand to climb into the carriage.

Once in the carriage, he put his head back so he didn't have to meet her eyes and said, "You must think it's very odd that I . . ." He tried to figure out how to phrase exactly what happened to him.

"You were terrified," Eleanor said, pulling a little mirror from her net bag and rubbing a smudge on her cheek. "That sty! That grotesque woman! I was just as frightened, and the children aren't even mine."

"I can hardly claim them as my children, in that sense of the word. I didn't even know where they were living until a few days ago. I never gave them a second's thought until this year. They could have been spending every night in a sty, for all I knew."

"Nonsense. You paid for them to be well-housed, warm, fed, and educated. That's more than many fathers in the same situation do." She peered at herself in the small glass and then dropped it back into her bag. "Lord knows, you're rich enough to give them all settlements, and that will buy them a future."

"No man is rich enough to buy back his past," Villiers said.

She met his eyes and the regret in hers made him feel better. "True. But there's no point in wailing over it. I hope to goodness that Willa remembered to walk Oyster. If not, my chamber is going to be as malodorous as the sty itself." She started searching about in her bag again.

She is a good person, Villiers thought, watching her under half-closed eyes so that she didn't realize. He'd never noticed what a firm chin she had until she faced off with Mrs. Minchem.

There was something about Eleanor that made him want to bite her. He'd like to bite that firm little chin. And then do the same to her neck. Her neck was as strong as she was: a beautiful, fierce column.

Without thinking too much about it he rose and sat down beside her, crushing her skirts. She squeaked some sort of reproach, but he kissed her silent. She tasted like one of the first raspberries in spring, so sweet and tart that it bit the tongue. And she tasted angry somehow, which made him wonder about why he could taste what she was feeling.

But then she stopped being angry and her arms wound around his neck and she said "Leopold" into his mouth. He stopped thinking altogether and just focused on kissing her. After a while it dawned on him that there was something different about the way she was kissing him. Something he didn't recognize.

She was kissing him back. Really kissing him back.

She had one hand woven so hard into his hair that it almost hurt. And her tongue was playing with his, swooping and hiding and generally driving him mad with desire.

It wasn't as if he hadn't been kissed before. But when he let his mouth trail away over her cheek, thinking to bite her ear, she bade him return in a husky little command. And when he didn't, she grabbed his head and pulled him back.

*That* was new. No woman had ever . . .

He lost the train of thought again because she said his name, his given name, in sort of a purr, and every inch of his body blazed.

She was flushed and pink and utterly desirable. She looked at him that way she had, as if she were smoldering, as if she wanted only one thing in the world . . .

"You're no virgin," he said, surprising himself. Gentlemen didn't say that sort of thing to ladies, let alone the gently-bred daughters of dukes.

She let a finger run over his eyebrows, down his nose. He almost shuddered at her touch. Not even the highest paid courtesan in the world could manage the sultry look that Eleanor seemed to wield at a moment's notice. There was something about that . . . he needed to think it out, but he didn't have time.

"Tell me you're not a virgin," he said after a moment, assuring himself that he wasn't begging.

"I don't see how that is relevant to our particular activity."

She wasn't a virgin. He knew it. It would be extremely ungentlemanly to make her confirm it. The promise of illicit pleasure sang in his blood, so he had to kiss her again.

They stepped out of the carriage only to be greeted by frenzied barking. Oyster launched himself from the front steps, so ecstatic at the sight of his mistress that his squat little body actually twisted in the air. He literally catapulted into her arms. "Sweetheart," Eleanor said as he licked her face. "Were you afraid I'd gone away and left you forever?"

Villiers could help thinking that he had reached a new low in his life. Jealous of a dog. Wonderful.

"Now I'm going to put you down, Oyster," Eleanor said. "You must not start barking again, because Lisette is afraid of you."

Oyster gave her a last lick; she put him on the ground; he started barking again.

Villiers stepped forward. "Oyster."

Oyster sat back on his haunches and looked him over. Villiers had no pretensions about dogs. They were smart; they were self-centered; they were single-minded. Oyster opened his mouth.

*"Oyster,"* Villiers said, dropping his voice an octave or so.

Oyster shut his mouth, showing that he was as smart as the other dogs Villiers had encountered in life.

"What a good dog he is," Eleanor said, sounding utterly delighted with the plump little mongrel she had just been kissing all over his absurd-looking head.

"There's no such thing as a good dog," Villiers said, "any more than there are bad men."

"There certainly *are* bad men! And bad women too. Witness Mrs. Minchem."

"There are men who lose fear. Mrs. Minchem had no fear, and therefore she acted with impunity. She wanted to put a troublesome child in the pigs' dormitory, so she did. That's not necessarily bad—just opportunistic."

"I think it's bad. And Oyster is a *good* dog, because he obeys. Stay, Oyster. And don't bark. There, you see—"

Oyster suddenly leapt into the air with his strange twisting jump and began barking like a maddened rabbit with a voice box.

"Oyster!" Eleanor cried—but Oyster had leapt past both of them and through the open door of the carriage.

"No untrained animals in my carriage!" Villiers snapped.

He and Eleanor reached the door at the same moment.

Oyster was barking with the singular fixation that a beggar might give a steaming pudding.

One of the seat cushions was thrown to the side, the wooden lid was up, and two extraordinarily dirty and rather sleepy faces were staring back at Oyster. The faces were identical.

"Jane-Lucinda," Villiers said. One of the girls nodded.

"And Jane-Phyllinda," Eleanor breathed.

Having made his point, Oyster stopped barking.

"How do you know our names?" Lucinda demanded, putting her arm protectively around her sister.

"We've been looking for you," Eleanor said after a second's silence during which Villiers tried to figure out how to say *Because I'm your father.*

"Looking for us? Why?" The girl's chin jutted out. "You can tell Mrs. Minchem that we hope she falls over and the pigs eat her ankles, because we aren't going back."

"I agree," Villiers said.

"Ever."

"Would you like to get out of the blanket box now?" Eleanor inquired. "I can assure you that Oyster won't hurt you."

The bolder girl climbed from the box. She was wearing hardly any clothing, just a rough gown with no stockings and one shoe. Oyster started forward and began smelling her legs with an air of deep interest.

She certainly had an interesting odor; Villiers identified it immediately as Scent of Sty. In fact, now that he thought of it, all four of them were likely pungent.

"Oyster won't hurt you," Eleanor said encouragingly. "He's just a puppy."

Lucinda gave Oyster a pat. He had finished sniffing her legs, so he sat back down, looked up at her face and gave a brisk command.

"What does he want?" Lucinda asked.

"He wants you to give him a proper pat," Eleanor said. "And scratch his ears. He likes that. Would you care to come out of the box?" she asked Phyllinda.

Phyllinda shook her head.

Lucinda sat down on the floor of the carriage while Oyster jumped into her lap. She started giggling helplessly as the dog licked her face. Villiers watched with some interest as the shape of her face emerged from all the dirt.

But he didn't see what she really looked like until he

pulled Oyster outside, bringing Lucinda with him. And then he almost dropped to his knees in surprise.

Her eyes were a gorgeous dark lilac, the color of larkspur in late summer.

"My grandmother's eyes—" he started to say to Eleanor, then realized that she was still inside the carriage. He poked a head in to find that she had coaxed Phyllinda out of the box.

"He's not a bad dog," Eleanor was saying. "If you just peek out the door, you'll see your sister playing with him. Oyster is just a puppy."

But Villiers took one look at Phyllinda's terrified, obstinate face and knew that it was all too much for her. She was five years old, and she'd spent the night in a pigsty, presumably terrified of being eaten; she'd escaped the sty only to find her way—God knows how—into their carriage; and now she was risking being chewed by a wild dog. Her instincts for self-preservation had clearly been honed inside the orphanage.

"Here," he said, plucking her off the seat.

Her body went rigid, but he scooped her against his shoulder and backed out of the carriage.

It was only when he turned around that he realized what an audience they had drawn. By now, most of the Duke of Gilner's household had emerged from the house and were watching transfixed.

Eleanor bent over Lucinda, now sitting on the ground with Oyster in her lap. "If you stand up and come with us, Oyster will come as well," he heard her say.

The coachman was staring straight ahead, as was proper, but Villiers could see his ears practically wiggle as he listened.

"This is Lucinda, and this is Phyllinda," he said. "Lucinda, stand up." She scrambled to her feet. There was a little rustle among the servants, as if wind blew through a pile of straw.

"Does anyone know where my son is?" Villiers inquired.

They all looked around, as if someone else was sure to know. "He left for the orphanage this morning," Villiers continued. "Did anyone see him go or return?"

No one said a word.

"Is he in the nursery?"

Popper gestured and a footman dashed up the stairs.

"What would Tobias be doing at the orphanage?" Eleanor asked, knitting her brow. "He—"

"He said he was going home," Lucinda put in, looking up from the dog.

*This* was unexpected. All eyes turned to the little girl.

"You know Tobias?" Eleanor asked.

Lucinda grinned, and Villiers looked past the streaked dirt and dog spit and who knows what to discover that his daughter was an extraordinarily beautiful girl. "He got us outta the sty this morning," she said. "We heard a banging."

"We thought it was Mrs. Minchem coming again," Phyllinda said, her voice high and thready.

He tightened his hold on her. "Mrs. Minchem is incarcerated."

"Where's that?" Lucinda asked.

"The Clink," Eleanor explained. "And she's not coming out either."

"Tobias unlocked the sty and took you out," Villiers said, rather stunned. "And then he stowed you in the blanket box."

"He put the blanket down and said as we should just go to sleep and he'd walk home and then sneak us out of the box later."

"So you've been asleep?" Villiers asked, suddenly remembering talk of virginity in the carriage.

"We couldn't sleep last night because of that old sow," Lucinda said. "But I would have just *kicked* her good if she tried to bite us!"

"I was too scared," Phyllinda whimpered.

"We stayed awake all night instead," Lucinda said. "An' then we slept in that box until we heard this doggie barking."

"Don't let Oyster lick your mouth," Eleanor told Lucinda. "Your cheek is all right, but your mouth, no."

"Send someone out on horseback to look for Tobias," Villiers said to Popper. "It's quite a few miles, and he has to have stowed the girls after Lisette sent the carriage back."

"Why didn't he just climb in the carriage and wait for us?" Eleanor said. "He could have told any of the groomsmen and they would have fetched us."

"It's a surprise," Phyllinda whispered against Villiers's cheek. "We weren't supposed to move even after the carriage stopped."

"Why not?"

"We was going to have a bath first," Lucinda said. "We still needs to have that bath. He said our pa won't like us if we aren't clean." She gave Oyster a final pat. "If you don't mind, mister, we'd better have that bath because our pa might be along at any moment."

The entire household went utterly quiet, every eye fixed on Villiers.

He looked down at Lucinda. She stood almost as high as his waist. She had one hand on her hip, and she looked five going on forty. Phyllinda was staring at him expectantly.

"What on earth is going on out here?" Lisette cried,

bouncing down the front steps and waving at her maid. "Beatrice, I've been looking for you everywhere! Please fetch my painting materials; I had a fancy to paint a portrait of young children." She smiled at Eleanor. "How could one not want to paint youth, after seeing those beaming faces this morning?"

"Yes, well," Eleanor said, "they did beam after we dispatched with Mrs. Minchem, of course."

"Their joy was wonderful," Lisette said, sighing.

Eleanor turned away and Villiers noticed that she had a remarkably jaundiced look on her face, which wasn't quite fair. Lisette had no way of knowing the particular conversation she was interrupting.

He pulled himself together. "I am your father," he stated, looking first at Lucinda and then at Phyllinda.

Lucinda's eyes narrowed, and Phyllinda's eyes grew round, and Villiers thought he learned quite a lot about each of his daughters in that moment.

He learned even more just seconds later when Tobias appeared around the edge of the carriage, limping slightly. Lucinda dashed over and threw her arms around him, and Phyllinda began struggling and gave Villiers a solid kick before he realized that she wanted to get down.

From a safe position behind Tobias, Lucinda shook her head. "You're not our pa," she said. "We've got the same one as Tobias. He promised us, and so—"

"Sorry," Phyllinda said to Villiers, peeking around from behind Lucinda.

"He is your father," Tobias said cheerfully.

"*Is* he?" Lisette said, turning her large eyes on Villiers. "My goodness, but you're very virile, Leopold." There was a little snigger from one of the footmen, which died instantly.

Villiers tried to arrange his face into what he imagined

to be a nicely paternal expression. "I am your father. I accidentally lost you when you were quite small, and only found you today."

"You lost both of us," Lucinda said pointedly.

Phyllinda was hiding behind Lucinda, who was behind Tobias. "Yes," Villiers said, trying to meet Phyllinda's eyes. "I lost both of you at the same time, of course."

"Remarkably careless," Lisette put in, not helpfully.

"I'm sorry," he said. What else could he say? He held himself as stiffly as he always had, except it was only lately that he felt stiff. Before, he just felt ducal.

Tobias hauled Lucinda out from behind him. "He's not so bad," he said, so that every servant could hear him. Villiers was used to living out his life in front of the household, but this was ridiculous. The sting of humiliation was practically Dantesque.

He turned to Lisette. "Can you summon your housekeeper to take care of these children? They need baths."

"Nonsense, I'll bring them to the nursery myself," she said. With one look at her smiling blue eyes, both girls trotted away with Lisette, who was promising baths, hot soup, and Lord knew what else.

Villiers walked silently into the house, drawing back to allow Eleanor to climb the stairs before him. He occupied himself by noticing how small her waist was, and mocking himself for responding in an altogether physical way to the effect achieved by her corset.

At the very top she paused. "Do you know what I keep thinking?" A wildly mischievous smile spread across her face.

"Please don't feel that you have to share it with me."

*"Oh, Lucifer, angel of the morning, how art thou fallen,"* she said. And then whisked herself off, grinning.

Two could play at that game. He went straight to his room, out onto the balcony, and, after pausing at her window to make sure her maid wasn't in the room, walked into Eleanor's chamber.

She was washing her hands, and turned around with an undignified squeak.

Villiers wasted no time. Her maid might arrive at any moment. He pulled her into his arms and took that sweet hot mouth of hers, kissing her so hard that he expected a protest, or a shove, or even a curse.

Not from Eleanor.

Her arms went around his neck and one hand curled into his hair; his ribbon fell to the floor and her body came against his with joy. She squirmed against him, she sighed into his mouth, she gave a little moan when his hand stroked her back.

It wasn't that women hadn't done the same before. He knew how to turn a woman's body into molten liquid, to shape and mold her so she couldn't stop panting, so she couldn't remember her own name, let alone his.

But Eleanor's breathing was unsteady before he tried his practiced caresses. It didn't have to do with his title, because he'd already learned that she didn't care about it. It didn't have to do with his beauty, because he didn't have much. And it didn't have to do with his money, because the way she was rubbing herself against him, without shame, without guilt . . . that had nothing to do with money.

A thought occurred to him and he broke free even as her lips clung. "Are you thinking of *him*?" he demanded.

"Yes," she breathed. "What?"

His heart thudded and he pulled free of her hands.

She pulled him back. "Kiss me again." He looked at her half-open eyes and groaned. There was something about Eleanor—something about the contrast between her composed, snappy personality and the wildness she unleashed in him that made him unable to control himself.

Even if it meant kissing her while she fantasized about someone else.

He kissed her as if to convince both of them that he owned her, that he controlled her. Eleanor was too free to be controlled. And yet when she pressed against him and craved him, obviously craved him . . . he believed.

He couldn't not believe. He was only a man, after all. He couldn't stop his hand from stroking down her back, circling that small waist.

"Are you wearing a corset?" he murmured in her ear.

She chuckled and he grew even harder, if that were possible. "What do you think?"

His hands, practiced and sure, roamed her back. "I think you're wearing a gown of tobin silk, sometimes called Florentine," he said, nibbling her ear.

She shrugged. "I have no idea. My sister ordered it."

"This piece at your bodice is gauze, a very thin silk made at Paisley."

"But am I wearing a corset?" she demanded.

"That is the real question."

There was a scrabble at the door and Villiers sprang to her open window. He looked back for one more drink of her, to see the color in her cheeks, her tumbled hair, her desirous eyes.

"I'll discover the answer to that question tonight," he said, and it came out sounding like a vow.

# Chapter Sixteen

Eleanor bathed in silence, her mind whirling. She was playing a dangerous game with Villiers. But there was no reason not to play.

Flirting with him felt fresh . . . clean. It felt as if all the empty places inside her that had yearned for Gideon these many years were being filled, even if Villiers wasn't another Gideon, and even if she wasn't falling in love with him.

She was falling in lust with him, a thought that would make most of the maidens in the *ton* swoon from shock. Men were the only ones allowed to lust; women were allowed only an impassioned yet mysteriously platonic "love." Not to be consummated, naturally, until all the necessary papers and ceremonies were tidied up.

Gideon had been slender, young, and beautiful. Villiers was hard, masculine, and—not bitter, but sardonic. There was a dark core to him that she would never know.

Not that she needed or wanted to know it, she reminded herself.

She wanted his body. She couldn't bring herself to feel shame over that, though the world would think she ought to. But she'd never been able to feel particularly shameful when she loved Gideon either.

Villiers's very touch made her melt and shudder. It brought out the same side of her that had enticed Gideon into a haymow, the side of her that dared Villiers to wonder whether she was wearing a corset.

"I'll wear Anne's chemise dress," she told Willa after her bath. The gown was made of pale lilac taffeta, so delicate that the fabric flowed to the ground without pleats or folds. It fit very close on the bodice and buttoned from the bosom to the hem with small canary-yellow buttons.

"Are you sure, my lady? You said that you would never wear it, because we couldn't fit a corset under that bodice," Willa said.

"I have changed my mind." She would wear the gown for Villiers's sake. Willa knew the reason, but they preserved the fiction, the way polite women do. Willa buttoned her up and then went off to borrow Anne's face paints.

"Lady Anne will not be at supper," she reported, coming back with a small box in hand.

"Is she ill?"

"Marie says that she was up and about for a short time this morning, but she felt so poorly that she went back to bed and has been able to take nothing but chicken broth."

Eleanor grinned. "She overindulged last night." She picked up Anne's face paints and began experimenting. First she tried brushing dark lines around her eyes, the way Anne had the night before, but somehow she looked more badger-like than mysterious.

"You've overdone it," Willa said dubiously.

"I look like a badger, don't I?"

"More like someone with the Black Death. Not that I've ever seen the illness, but you look mortal with all that around your eyes."

Eleanor shuddered and rubbed some off. Then removed a little more. Drew some more back on. Put color on her lips and on her cheeks. Rubbed some of that off. Put a little flip of black at the outside edges of her eyes.

Rubbed some off.

Stood up for one final glance . . . and smiled.

Her gown was the opposite of the stiff satin gowns that had been in style so long. The French chemise had been introduced only last year, and she hadn't even thought of buying one. But her sister had.

Thank goodness for Anne and her predilection for fashion. Willa had piled her hair in waves of curls, with small sprays of violets tucked here and there. And after all that work, her eyes were perfect. Smudged, but not so much that she looked like a dying person. Or a badger.

Her lips were crimson. She made a kissing gesture to the mirror, and Willa burst into laughter.

"Do you think I'm too extravagant?" Eleanor asked, just before turning to leave.

"No. Not at all. It's as if—well, it's as if it's more *you*, if you see what I mean, my lady."

Apparently more of her meant dressing like a hussy, which was a disconcerting thought.

"It's just too bad that we're not in London," Willa went on happily. "Because those gentlemen would go absolutely mad. They would fall at your feet."

"I don't know that I want men at my feet. Would you?"

"That's not for me," Willa said.

"Why not?"

"Because that's for ladies and gentlemen. You should have four or five beaux at least, my lady. I want just one."

"I think," said Eleanor, "that I want just one as well."

"It would be a great waste," Willa said, shaking her head. "Look at your gown, and how beautiful you are, and all. And then there's your dowry. It's always better if a gentleman has to fight off other men."

"For his sake or for mine?"

"Oh, for both," Willa said, getting into the spirit of the conversation. "He feels better because he's had to fight off rivals."

"Well, I don't think that Villiers cares," Eleanor said, feeling a touch of wistfulness. "He just wants a mother to his children."

"That's not what he wants from *you*," Willa said with a chuckle.


Villiers inspected himself one last time in the glass while Finchley waited, another cravat close at hand in case he decided to redo the knot. He was wearing one of his favorite coats, made of a pale green silk, the color of the very first leaves in spring. It was embroidered with mulberry-colored flowers, a fantasy of climbing trumpet vines. His hair was tied back with a ribbon of the same green.

He looked like what he indeed was: an idiosyncratic and powerful duke. He did not look like a man who was prey to unaccustomed and unwelcome emotions. Shame, for one. And fear. When Tobias couldn't be found . . . when the daughters he had never met couldn't be found . . . he had felt sick.

That was unacceptable.

And what he felt for Eleanor was, frankly, unacceptable as well.

He had to make a dreadfully important decision that

would determine his children's future happiness. He didn't need a wife or a lover. The important thing was that they needed a mother. And Lord knows, they deserved whatever he could give them.

His jaw tightened as he pictured the fusty, filthy sty again. And Tobias, wading through the bitterly cold mud of the Thames.

"Your Grace?" Finchley prompted. "Would you like your gloves?"

"No," he said, turning to go. "I think I'll stop by the nursery before going downstairs for dinner."

"Very well, Your Grace. I will wait in the downstairs entry with your gloves."

Villiers pushed open the door to the nursery with some trepidation. He and Tobias seemed to be able to rub along together. But he had another son and a daughter at home with whom he had hardly exchanged a word. And now two more daughters. It was overwhelming.

The first thing he saw when he entered was Lisette. She was sitting in a rocker by the fire, singing. She had a beautiful voice, as clear as a bell and yet surprisingly low. *"Hush-a-bye baby, on the treetop,"* she sang. Lucinda or Phyllinda was curled in her lap, wearing a white nightie. Villiers looked around for the other girl, and found her in one of the beds, sucking her thumb in her sleep.

> *"When the wind blows, the cradle will rock.*
> *When the bough breaks, the cradle will fall,*
> *Down will come baby, cradle and all."*

The moment Lisette stopped singing, the little head on her shoulder popped up. "Don't stop, lady, don't stop . . ."

That had to be Lucinda, given her exhausted but stubborn tone. Lisette stroked the little girl on the shoulder, then bent her bright head over the girl again and sang.

*"Mama will catch you, give you a squeeze.*
*Send you back up to play in the trees . . ."*

Villiers smiled. He didn't remember ever being sung to. His nanny was greatly taken with the young duke's consequence and treated him as a small prince from the moment he could remember.

No one sang to princes.

*"When twilight falls, and birds seek their nest.*
*Come home to the one who loves you the best."*

Lisette's voice was so beautifully soothing that it wasn't in the least surprising to find Lucinda had succumbed. A maid tiptoed over to take the little girl, but Villiers waved her away and picked up the child himself.

She was utterly beautiful, from her curls to the long eyelashes hiding those lavender eyes she inherited from his grandmother. In sleep, her mouth was a rosebud rather than the defensive, obstinate grimace that she had worn downstairs.

"Put her down carefully," Lisette said softly, at his shoulder. "You don't want to wake her."

He started toward one of the other little beds lining the wall of the nursery, but her light touch on his arm stopped him. "With her sister."

Of course. He placed Lucinda on the bed next to Phyllinda. Their ringlets curled together on the pillow.

"You're going to have a fine time fending off suitors when they're old enough to be noticed," Lisette whispered.

"They may be rejected by the *ton*. I'll dower them, of course, but they're bastards." He had promised to himself that he wouldn't try to avoid what he had done to them, and that meant naming it.

"If they were mine, I would teach them not to care."

"Hard to do in the midst of London, and children to a duke," he said wryly.

"I don't agree." She gave a disdainful little wave. "I would teach them to ignore such foolishness. The *ton* is made up of unimportant, stupid persons. I care nothing for them; why should they?"

She meant it. He could see the truth in her eyes: she really believed the *ton* was unimportant.

"What do you think of my title?" he asked her.

"What do you mean, what do I think of it?" She smiled. "It has four letters. D-U-K-E."

"Do you revere it?"

"Should I?"

"No."

"My father does not revere his title in the least," she said.

Villiers hadn't even thought about her father. Gilner was an excellent man in Parliament, by all accounts. "Your mother died some time ago. Do you know if your father ever thought to marry again?"

"Oh no," Lisette said peacefully. "He says he would prefer that his direct bloodline die out. My second cousin will inherit."

"How extremely—"

But she slipped her delicate hand into his and put a finger to her mouth. As they watched, Phyllinda shifted to her side and threw an arm around her sister.

"We will be missed downstairs," Lisette whispered. "I only meant to stop by the nursery and see how they were doing."

Villiers said. "I've heard the first part of that lullaby, but never the second verse."

"Oh, I made it up," Lisette said. "I never liked the idea of the basket falling. Why, the babe would be hurt!" She tugged his hand gently. "Come on, Leopold. My aunt has returned home and she'll be vexed with me if I'm overly late."

She called him Leopold so easily, as if they had been intimates forever.

# Chapter Seventeen

Eleanor entered the drawing room and was greeted by a tall, thin woman wearing a towering, snowy white wig. "Darling, it's been *years*! I haven't seen you since you were in pinafores, and look at you now. Utterly gorgeous."

"Lady Marguerite," Eleanor said, dropping into a curtsy. "It's such a pleasure to see you again. *I* may have changed, but you have not."

Marguerite laughed at that, but it was true. She was not only beautiful, but stylish, with arching dark eyebrows that sharply contrasted with her white wig. She had to be in her forties or even her early fifties, but she dressed with the éclat of a young woman.

"It's such a pleasure having visitors, even though several of them are confined to their chambers. Apparently your mother has a toothache," she said, leading Eleanor into the room, "and dear Anne refuses to leave her bed. So we're very thin company tonight, with Lisette, Villiers, and myself. But I must introduce you to my good friend, the Honorable Lawrence Frederick Bentley the Third."

Bentley was from Yorkshire, with stiff white whiskers and very bright eyes. He looked as if he enjoyed galloping the moors shouting *Tally-Ho!* "How do you do?" he said with a flourishing bow.

"We've been discussing the endlessly fascinating subject of matrimony," Marguerite said, seating herself. "I myself have never been married, as you know, and I shall never choose to be at this point in life. I prefer to have devoted friends."

"But what of love?" Lisette said, cocking her head to one side and regarding her aunt as if she'd never seen her before.

"Love is all very well in its way—Eleanor, dearest, do have one of these small tarts; they are delicious—as I was saying, love is fine, but friendship is much more important." Marguerite shot an amused smile at Bentley. "Which is not to say that there can't be love in friendship . . . at least *devoted* friendship."

"Without marriage no one would have children," Bentley said. "Family, what? Important, that sort of thing."

"Bentley has two children, though of course they're grown now," Marguerite informed the rest of them, speaking for him in a comfortable way that made it clear that while she may have declined to marry Bentley, the contours of their relationship weren't unfamiliar.

"One can certainly have children without marriage," Lisette said, with her unerring gift for saying what most people think, but never utter. "Just look at Villiers's children. Your girls have startlingly beautiful eyes," she said, turning to him.

"Children? Didn't know you were—what, ho!" Bentley said, stopping in some confusion.

"I'm not married," Villiers said calmly. "But I do have children. Three of whom are upstairs, and about whom Lady Lisette has kindly expressed some admiration."

"Do you have any children born outside your marriage?" Lisette asked, turning to Bentley. "You must have had a wife earlier in life, before you met Marguerite, I mean."

Bentley was clearly used to Lisette; he didn't even flinch. "My wife died many years ago. I don't have any children other than those Marguerite mentioned, but a brother has one. Nice lad; we set him up as a cartwright and he's as fine as fivepence. A sturdy fellow too, not at all like my nephew."

Marguerite laughed. "Poor Erskine! Bentley's nephew is in love with the daughter of a colonel, and all he does is mope and carry on for the love of her."

"They are *both* your nephews," Lisette pointed out.

Eleanor felt very glad that her mother felt a toothache; this was not a conversation that she would enjoy. What's more, the Honorable Lawrence and Marguerite were holding hands now, and the duchess wouldn't approve of that either.

And Villiers was smiling at Lisette, likely because of her defense of the illegitimate cartwright. Eleanor felt a stab of jealousy. He was *hers*—except he wasn't. "Did Sir Roland happen to stop by while we were at the orphanage?" she asked Marguerite.

"Of course he did," Marguerite said with a wicked twinkle. "I gather you have captivated the attention of our local bard. I invited him to join us after supper for a musical interlude. Which reminds me, we really should go to supper now. Popper seems to be quite unnerved. I think it'd be best if we do exactly as he requests tonight."

"Did you bring back any interesting stories from

London?" Lisette implored, after they were seated around the table.

"Your papa sends his best wishes and said to tell you that he'll be coming home in a week or so."

"Not that sort of news," Lisette said impatiently. "Interesting news. As when you told us about Mrs. Cavil eating a bushel of cherries."

"That was a sad story," Marguerite said, "given what happened to Mrs. Cavil the next day."

"Exactly," Lisette said, grinning.

"Well, along the same lines, but Popper just told me that Gyfford's brew house burned down. It's a village over," Marguerite explained to Villiers and Eleanor. "Half the village is insisting that it was Gyfford's dead wife, come back for revenge. The other half of the village is much less poetic, and feels that Gyfford was smoking his pipe in bed."

"What does Gyfford say about it?" Lisette inquired.

"Unfortunately, he's cinders," Marguerite said.

Lisette blinked. "He was our neighbor." Her lower lip started to tremble.

"Stow it," Marguerite said, rapping Lisette sharply on the hand with her spoon. "You didn't know him, and by all accounts he was a hoary old bastard."

"Now, now, Marguerite," Bentley said. "Lady Eleanor is not used to your lively ways. You'll shock the poor lass."

"I've never seen that particular lass shocked," Villiers drawled. "Do go ahead and see if you can do so, Lady Marguerite."

"I am rarely shocked or frightened," Lisette announced. "Except by dogs, of course. Fierce dogs." She threw a meaningful look at Eleanor.

"Oh, don't go on about that puppy again," Marguerite

said, earning Eleanor's gratitude. "Let's see, what else can I tell you. The dowager Lady Faber has had a horrible accident." She paused dramatically.

"Do tell," Lisette said, clapping her hands together.

"She saw an advertisement in the *London Gazette* for a depilatory."

"Any story beginning on that note will end badly," Villiers said.

"What's a depilatory?" Lisette asked.

"A medicine to remove hair," Marguerite told her. "Lady Faber rubbed it all around her mouth, and unfortunately everywhere it touched turned bright garter blue."

Lisette went off in a peal of laughter.

"And while it is *not* funny, did you hear about the Duchess of Astley?" Marguerite added. "Yes, thank you, Popper, I will have just a trifle more. Please tell Cook that the baked carrots are extremely good."

Villiers's head swung up and he met Eleanor's eyes. "What on earth has happened to the duchess?" he inquired.

"I do hope you weren't close to the poor dear," Marguerite said. "Yes, Popper, I think we could move on to the next course now."

"The duchess?" Villiers repeated.

"You appear quite dismayed," Lisette observed. "Was she a friend of yours, Leopold?"

"You are addressing the duke by his first name," Marguerite said, narrowing her eyes and looking from Villiers to Lisette. "That is inappropriate. You are a betrothed woman."

Villiers blinked, and Eleanor felt a perverse satisfaction. Not that a betrothal would stop Villiers, if he decided he wanted to marry Lisette.

Lisette gave her a lazy smile. "Leopold is a *devoted* friend. And since my fiancé hasn't set foot in England for six years, I hardly feel he deserves the title."

"Please, Lady Marguerite, how is Ada?" Eleanor asked.

"I am so sorry if she was a friend of yours, darling. Why, I'm afraid she's dead. She couldn't breathe . . . what day was that now? Oh, it must have been last Friday. I suppose they just put her in the ground, the poor dear. Not that I knew her, but by all accounts she was a kindly person. And so young. What a loss."

"She was kindly," Eleanor said. She felt sick. She had never wished ill of Ada. Never.

"The duke was at the Beaumonts' benefit for the Roman baths when it happened," Marguerite said with a kind of grinding cheerfulness that made Eleanor's nausea increase. "Apparently his wife didn't suffer. She just coughed once or twice and then collapsed. The doctor said he wouldn't be surprised if something in her brain had simply burst."

"Lady Eleanor is not feeling well," Villiers said, sounding to Eleanor as if his words came from far away and underwater. She gripped the edge of the table hard because the roaring in her ears made her dizzy. It was stupid to feel responsible, even the slightest bit responsible. She had *never* wished ill of Ada. She had . . . she was sure of it.

"I'm a beast! I'm a bear!" Marguerite was lamenting. "Of course I should have known that the young duchess would have friends. I never met her about London, so I'm afraid I didn't think . . . Popper, Popper! Get a footman—"

"I'll escort her upstairs," Villiers said, cutting her off.

Eleanor let go of the table and rose from her chair. "I'm

perfectly all right. It must have just been the shock. I do believe I shall retire, however."

"Please forgive me!" Marguerite called imploringly after her.

Eleanor's heart was beating a guilty rhythm.

"Don't be a fool," Villiers said harshly, behind her on the stairs.

She waited until they reached the landing. "I never wished her ill. But I—I wished to be her."

"Well, be grateful that you didn't get your wish," Villiers said, as unemotional as ever. "You'd be measuring a plot of ground right now." But she was learning to read those gray eyes, and they said something. Not that she was sure what.

The image of Gideon standing over Ada's body was so heartbreaking that Eleanor actually swayed and caught hold of the railing.

Villiers swore and plucked her up as if she weighed no more than one of his daughters.

"You needn't," she said feebly.

"Be quiet," he ordered.

So she was quiet and stopped thinking about how she felt about Ada when she was alive, and just remembered her quiet smile, the sweetness in it, and the happiness with which Ada would show her newest embroidery project. Tears began to roll down her face.

Willa pulled open the door to her bedchamber and left immediately when Villiers jerked his head. He sat down in the chair and tucked her head against his shoulder, and Eleanor sobbed as if she were no older than one of his little girls. He handed her a white handkerchief but he didn't say a word.

After a while she stopped crying, sat up, and blew her nose. "I'm sorry she's dead."

"I know you are."

"I must look awful," Eleanor said, remembering all her makeup.

"It's interesting," Villiers said. "The shoe black around your eyes has run in little streaks down your cheeks. You look like the sister to a zebra."

"It's not shoe black," she protested, wiping it off with his handkerchief.

"I should return to the supper table," he said, not moving, staring at her with his curiously beautiful gray eyes.

"Tobias has exactly the same eyes you do, have you noticed?" she asked.

"The same temperament as well. And the same brute nose."

"He doesn't have a brute nose."

Villiers leaned closer, so slowly that it seemed an eternity before their noses touched. "Yours is quite patrician," he said. "Slender, straight, narrow. Like the pathway to heaven, now that I think of it."

"Then yours is as short and wide as the path to another place," she whispered.

"Nothing about me is short."

"Nothing about you is humble."

"False humility is one of the seven deadly sins."

He snatched a kiss, the kind that made Eleanor realize just how much she loved kisses. How much she wanted more. How—How *desperate* she felt. And if that wasn't humiliating, what was? She had to regain her composure.

"We shouldn't be kissing like this when Ada is just buried," she said.

"I expect at least four women around the world died during the time I kissed you. If not more." He was frighteningly good at speaking in an utterly unemotional voice.

"It's not the same."

"Why not? Are you telling me that you were genuinely fond of Ada?"

That question was a mistake, because she thought again of how critical she had been, thinking that she herself would have been a more affectionate wife, and tears welled in her eyes again. "If I wasn't fond of her, it was my own shortcoming and my own stupidity," she said, getting off his lap rather clumsily. She walked over to the black window and looked blindly out. "She was a very kind person."

"Why do her virtues mean that I can't kiss you?" Villiers said, rising from his chair.

"It doesn't seem respectful."

"Or do you think we shouldn't kiss because Ada's death leaves an opening for a new duchess?"

It took a moment for that to sink in, and then she spun about, took one step and slapped him. They stared at each other for a moment.

"I apologize," Villiers said finally. "I should not have implied that you wept for any reason other than the obvious. I met the duchess only once, but I cannot imagine her uttering an ill-natured comment."

"That was her greatest accomplishment," Eleanor said. "She must have known . . ."

Villiers's eyes didn't even flicker. "Must have known what?"

She was tired of all the lies she had told her mother, all the lies she had told everyone. "That Gideon and I were devoted friends," she said. "Before."

"*Devoted*. And yet—he married Ada."

"She had every accomplishment," Eleanor pointed out.

"And as I told you, his father's will dictated his choice."

"She had every accomplishment, except that of making people love her," Villiers stated.

"Of course people loved her." But she knew what he was saying. Ada was so acquiescent and sweet that one easily turned a shoulder to her, walked away, forgot she was in the room. "I'm sure that Gideon loved his wife," she added, giving it emphasis.

"Perhaps," Villiers said, without a smile. "More to the point, now that she has passed away, I believe that you have two dukes to consider as potential husbands."

"Of course not!"

"He may be a fool, but not that much of a fool. I saw the way he looked at you." Villiers pulled her into his arms again, which was just what she wanted him to do. "It was damnably close to the way I look at you," he whispered. His mouth silenced her before she could utter her deepest fear: that Gideon had chosen sweet Ada *because* she was so sweet.

She had loved Gideon, but she also wanted him, and her desire disturbed Gideon. It made him uneasy. That certainly wasn't the case for Villiers.

Villiers kissed her with the sort of passion that demanded that she respond, forced her to respond. Even now his breathing was ragged, and yet his hands were shaping her, teasing her, caressing her—trying to make her mad with desire.

What had frightened Gideon about her pleased Villiers. Though she really ought to call him Leopold, given the fact that he was rapidly becoming her closest . . . friend. If not quite devoted, yet.

As if he read her mind, he broke away and said, "Say my name."

"Villiers."

He pulled her against him so hard that she could feel every button in his coat, and below that, lower still . . .

He was hard, and he was big, and he made sure she knew it.

"Leonard," she whispered.

He nipped her lip.

"Leander."

He really bit her this time, on the lobe of her ear. She shivered and felt a wash of heat over her body. Their eyes met and there was a slow smile in his. He bent his head and she didn't move, held her breath as he pushed aside the soft silk of her chemise dress. Of course . . . there was no corset. His lips closed over her nipple and he suckled her until she sagged against his arm.

"Say my name," he growled.

She was the master of herself. "I know!" she said, voice shaky. "Lloyd!"

"You're a danger to yourself." Her chemise gown gave way easily on the other side, and she leaned against his shoulder again, trembling, eyes closed. He scraped his teeth across her breast and she gave a little scream.

"Say it."

"Leo," she said, and her voice broke into a throaty cry. "Leopold!"

His hand replaced his mouth, gave her a rough caress that made the blood race from her head.

"Why won't you call me Leopold except when I kiss you into submission?" He was kissing the corners of her mouth, the line of her jaw, and all the time, his hand . . . She arched forward in case he wanted more of her.

"It's not proper," she gasped. "You heard Lady Marguerite."

"Perhaps not in London, but in this house . . . with Marguerite and her devoted Lawrence? One of Lisette's most charming virtues is her utter disregard of etiquette."

"Propriety is important." She pushed away his hand, remembering. "You should go downstairs. They might be wondering where you are."

"Too late for that," he said with a lopsided smile. "They know exactly where we both are."

"But they don't know what we're doing. You must return; I shall retire for the evening."

"Risqué Roland will be heartbroken if you miss the scintillating musical interval that awaits us."

"He will have to suffer," Eleanor said, pulling her bodice back into its crisscross shape. Her whole body was pulsing a little, as if her very blood was dancing.

Villiers was adjusting his cravat in front of the glass. "You've crushed my neckcloth. I'll have to stop by my chamber to fetch another."

"Why bother?"

He raised an eyebrow. "Go downstairs with a crushed cravat?"

She mimicked him. "Call you by your first name in public?"

He took one step toward her and the light in his eyes made her knees weaken. "I can make you do it."

"I can crush all your cravats," she said loftily.

"For the right cause," he said, turning toward the door, "a man might discard any number of cravats. There are two armchairs in my chamber."

"I would *never* visit your chamber," Eleanor said. "How can you even ask?"

"I didn't ask," Villiers pointed out.

"Oh."

"I merely commented that there are two such chairs, and then I was about to add that I intend to instruct Finchley to place those chairs on the balcony. That way, should anyone desire to join me, it would be possible to have a glass of brandy while looking at the stars."

"That sounds monstrously improper," Eleanor observed.

"My favorite kind of activity."

# Chapter Eighteen

She should probably stop by her mother's room and inquire about her toothache. And she ought to write a note of condolence to Gideon. Instead Eleanor called for a bath, added essence of jasmine, and climbed in holding Shakespeare's *Sonnets*.

Willa took down her curls and brushed out all the wilting violets. Then she poured a bit more hot water from the jug into the bath.

"Would you mind if I went down to the kitchens to finish ironing your linens, my lady?" she inquired.

"Absolutely not," Eleanor said. "This bath is deliciously warm. Just leave me a towel and I'll get out when I wish."

"It's right there," Willa said, "but your wrapper is downstairs to be mended, I'm afraid. Oyster dragged it from the bed and snagged the fabric."

"Oyster!" Eleanor said. He raised his head groggily

and gave her a little woof before subsiding again. "Has he been outside lately?"

Willa frowned. "Perhaps I should take him for a walk as well, my lady."

"I can put myself to bed, Willa, if you would just bring him up later."

Willa let herself out and Eleanor returned to Shakespeare's sonnets, which probably everyone in the world had read except for her. That fact made it all the more disconcerting to discover that she couldn't make head or tail of most of them.

*Let me not to the marriage of true minds admit impediments,* she read. And then read it again. An impediment was an obstacle. It made her feel a little sad, really. She and Gideon had been a marriage of true minds until an impediment came along.

She and Villiers spent their time jousting with each other, whereas she and Gideon had thought as one. They had talked for countless hours and agreed on everything, though all these years later, she couldn't remember what those discussions were about.

He belived dueling was a terrible sin, she remembered that. Of course she agreed. There was no point to dueling. It was dangerous.

She dragged herself back to the sonnet. *Let me not to the marriage of true minds admit impediments. Love is not love which alters when it alteration finds.*

This line was even harder. Alteration? Could Shakespeare be talking about getting older? So love is not love if a man stops loving his wife because her hair turns gray. Her love for Gideon would never have faltered if he lost his beauty. *Or bends with the remover to remove.*

Again, unreasonably difficult, she thought. Just who was the remover?

The thing that made her uneasy, though, was that first

line. She kept reading it over and over. *Let me not to the marriage of true minds admit impediments.* True love doesn't admit *impediments.* Gideon's father's will had been an impediment. And Gideon obviously admitted the impediment.

Had he not loved her?

The water was growing cold. She climbed out and grabbed the towel Willa had left. Why was she going over all this old ground? But she knew why. She had to put Gideon out of her mind, fold away her memories of feverish love.

Ada was gone. But that didn't mean Gideon wanted to marry her, that he loved her the way she had loved him.

She couldn't delude herself any longer. Love was *not* love when it admitted impediments. When it *bent with the remover to remove.* Gideon had bent to his father's will.

It would be far better to marry Villiers. Their relationship was not as heady, not as romantic—but what emotion they had was real.

She and Villiers would never fool themselves into thinking they had a marriage of *true minds.* It would be a different kind of marriage. That of true bodies.

Willa brought Oyster back; after an energetic tail-wagging wiggle, the better to show how much he missed her, he collapsed back on the floor and Willa left for the night. A moment later Oyster shot up and launched himself at the curtains covering the door leading to the balcony.

Eleanor found herself smiling. Villiers must have returned from dinner. He was likely sitting in one of those armchairs, looking at the stars. She looked down at herself. Her towel didn't cover much more of her legs than Villiers's had his.

But then, she liked her legs. They were shapely. And

she and Villiers were getting married, after all. She tucked the towel more securely around her breasts, loving the feeling that she was playing with fire, and walked to the door, hushing Oyster.

It was pitch-dark outside. Oyster started barking again, so she scooped him up, almost losing her towel, and stepped outside.

"Is anyone out here?" she called cautiously.

"Ah, my princess!" came a response.

Eleanor fell back a step.

*"She appears before me like the shadow of a white rose in a mirror of silver."* Roland's head came into view at the top of the balcony railing.

Oyster gave an aggressive little woof. Apparently he didn't care for poetry.

She had to admit that Roland spoke verse beautifully. "Oh, hello," she said, taking another step backwards toward the door to her room and wishing desperately that she had her wrapper. "Are you quite—"

He interrupted her. *"She has the beauty of a virgin! She has never defiled herself. She has never abandoned herself to men, like the other goddesses."*

Oyster barked again, and Eleanor felt like joining him. "That's—ahem—very kind of you," she managed. Never mind the fact it wasn't true. "Are you on a ladder, Sir Roland?"

"Certainly," Roland said, making no effort to climb onto the balcony. "I am acting out my play for you."

"Don't tell me you're standing on a silk ladder!" she exclaimed. "Please do come onto the balcony, Sir Roland. I'm worried for your safety."

"It's made of wood," he said. "Now if you'll allow me to gather my thoughts . . ." There was silence for a moment and then he intoned in such a booming voice that she jumped, *"The night is fair in the garden, and my princess has eyes like amber."* He flung out a hand and gestured to the sky. *"How strange the moon looks! Like the hand of a dead woman seeking to cover herself with a shroud."*

Eleanor looked up, but the moon looked pretty much the same as usual to her, and it had never included dead women or shrouds. In fact, that comment was in fairly poor taste, given the news about Ada . . . but then Roland hadn't been there during dinner. But surely he was told when he arrived for the musicale why she had retired early.

He ascended another rung. Now she could see him from the waist up. His eyes were burning with excitement. Or desire.

That made her feel rather pleased, but unfortunately not at all as if she'd like to pull him to her, the way she felt when Villiers issued one of his sardonic jibes.

And yet Roland really was beautiful. In the light that fell from the windows behind her, he looked like the prince from an old fairy tale, climbing the tower to rescue a princess.

*"Thy body is white like the snows that lie on the mountains of Judea, and come down into the valleys,"* he said. Eleanor could feel her cheeks getting a little warm. She refused to glance down at her bare legs, but of course her body was white. Why wouldn't it be?

*"The roses in the garden of the Queen of Arabia are not so white as thy body,"* Roland said feverishly. *"Nor the feet of the dawn when they light on the leaves, nor the breast of the moon when she lies on the breast of the sea . . ."*

"Too many breasts," came a deadpan voice at her left shoulder.

Eleanor jumped and uttered a little scream. "Villiers!" Then she looked back at the poet. "Don't mind him, Sir Roland."

But Roland wasn't there any longer. "Oh, no!" she cried, dropping Oyster and running forward. Sure enough, the ladder was slowly swinging away from the house, the poet clinging to the top of it.

"He'll be all right," Villiers said.

"No, he won't! He might—he might—"

The ladder gained speed as it went down and finally crashed. There was a sound of splintering wood. Eleanor peered into the dark, trying to figure out where Roland had landed.

"Help, someone!" she shrieked. "Go see what happened! Go get help. Don't just stand there—are you *laughing*?"

"Of course not, princess. Just wait a moment. Your swain liveth."

She couldn't see exactly what was happening, but someone was cursing and it sounded like Roland.

"I estimate that he landed in the raspberry bushes," Villiers said. "He probably hit them dead on. Not good for his clothing. Or," he added thoughtfully, "delicate parts of his anatomy. But the good news is that he landed rump down rather than the other way around."

"Sir Roland!" Eleanor called, ignoring the jaundiced commentary at her shoulder. "Are you all right?"

There were thrashing noises.

"Do you want help? Shall I call someone?"

A door had opened onto the gardens now, and a couple of servants were cautiously emerging.

"Go help Sir Roland out of the raspberry bushes," she called over the balcony.

They peered up at her and then set out across the lawn.

"Why don't you go help?" she asked crossly, turning to Leopold.

"I'm holding up your towel," he said. She could just barely see his smile in the light from the doorway. If Roland looked like a troubadour, Villiers looked like Lucifer himself, all dark shadows and pure lust.

He dropped the grip he had on the back of her towel and fell back a step. All of a sudden she could feel the place where his hand had touched her skin, burning as if he had branded her.

Below them, Roland was being hauled out of the raspberry bushes. Eleanor tore her eyes away from Villiers and tucked her towel more securely around her. "Sir Roland, are you quite all right?" she called, turning to lean out over the balcony.

He was limping across the lawn, supported by one of the footmen. A lock of hair had fallen over his face, making him look like a beautiful, fallen warrior.

"Your poetry is sublime," Eleanor called, hoping Villiers would keep himself out of sight. "I'm so sorry that you were startled and the ladder slipped."

"I was pushed," he said.

Eleanor blinked. "Oh, no, I assure you—"

"Pushed by words!"

"Words?" she repeated.

She couldn't see Villiers. She couldn't hear him or feel him. But she knew that he was shaking with laughter.

"The force of sarcasm pushed me from the perch of love."

"Ah. Well . . ."

*"They jest at scars that never felt a wound."* He limped past and into the house without another word. She was still bent over the balcony, looking down, when a large male body encircled hers from behind.

He was warm, burning . . . hard . . . strong. She sud-

denly felt, as if through his body, the provocative tilt of
her bottom as she leaned over the balustrade. Where his
body touched hers, she felt the impress of his desire, as if
she were experiencing her curves through his skin.

"You could drive a man insane," Leopold said. His lips
were on her neck, but it wasn't his lips that she felt most
acutely. She wriggled against him. "Don't move." His
voice grated in her ear but she moved anyway, straightening.

He allowed her, of course. She turned around, hitching
up her towel once again. "Now I know why women wear
such large panniers," she said.

"To repel their admirers?"

"Precisely. Now if you'll forgive me, I shall retire for
the night."

He caught her hand. "Are you marrying me?"

"I thought—"

"What?"

"I thought," she said, picking her words carefully, "that
you were rather admiring of Lisette, and might wish to
make her your duchess. And I say that without prejudice,
Leopold, as one intelligent person to another. I hope
we can speak to each other without tempests of emotion."

His smile was all the more welcome for being so rare.
"You are an unusual woman, Eleanor. Though I don't
think I like that name."

"Tell me it's *heavy* and I'll push you directly off the
balcony."

"Maybe I'll take a leaf from the poor poet's book and
call you *princess*."

"I'm no princess," she said, laughing. "Though my
mother tells me that you live in a castle."

"Since I never go to that particular estate, you'd have to
settle for my other houses."

She laughed as if he'd made a joke, because there was something odd about his voice that didn't welcome any further questions.

"I will admit, then, that I'm torn between the two of you," he said abruptly.

Something in her heart, in her chest, in her stomach—somewhere—fell with a resounding thump. She managed to keep her voice light and even. "Between myself and Lisette?"

"I am persuaded that she would be a truly superb mother for my children. She seems to have no regard whatsoever for the circumstances of their birth, either in the way she treats them here, in her house, or in her daily work with orphans."

"I have never known Lisette to display the least prejudice toward any sort of person," Eleanor said, adding, "Though she is quite unreasonable toward dogs."

Villiers smiled. "Poor Oyster has not made an admirer there, it's true."

Eleanor thought that the way people acted toward dogs, especially innocent puppies, said a great deal about them, but she held her tongue.

"But then when I think about marrying you," Villiers said, his voice deepening, "well . . ."

"You think about bedding me," Eleanor said.

He didn't move toward her, but the flame that was always between them suddenly leaped higher. "It's impossible not to do so," he said. "I think about you first thing in the morning when I wake, and last thing at night. And," he added thoughtfully, "a good deal in between as well."

All Eleanor could think of was dropping the towel and moving toward him. But she had succumbed to pleasure before, and it had ended in heartbreak. Not that she could ever love Villiers the way she had loved Gideon, but she must have learned something from her mistakes. Hadn't she?

She should return to her room. She didn't move.

"There's something about the way you move, the way you laugh, the way you snap at me that I find—appealing," Villiers said.

He was making her sound like a warmed-over apple tart.

"Yet I swore to myself that I would find the best mother possible for my children. This evening, Lisette was wonderful in the nursery. The girls adore her already. I asked her how she would handle the *ton* when the children grew up."

"What did she say?" Eleanor asked, feeling that she ought to make some contribution, or else she might give voice to a scream: *Are you as cracked as Lisette?*

"She snapped her fingers and said that she would teach them to care nothing for such foolishness. Of course, she herself doesn't care. She lives here so happily, without being caught in the absurd farce that makes up our social life."

Several things came to mind, but they all seemed too severe, so Eleanor said merely, "Lisette truly does not care for societal conventions."

"It's as if she's designed to mother these particular children," Villiers said.

"You are not bound to me in any fashion," Eleanor pointed out. "I announced our betrothal merely to placate my mother, as I'm sure you realized. Or perhaps I meant to irritate her. I'm quite certain that one would do better not to initiate a marriage on such flimsy grounds."

"Probably not," he agreed.

His smile twisted something inside her, so she said, rather quickly, "Well, now that we've settled that, I really should retire. It's growing chilly and I'm not properly dressed."

But he didn't move, and neither did she.

"Damn it," he said finally, very quietly.

And when he crossed those two steps between them, she wound her arms around his neck as if it were the most natural thing in the world. Neither of them moved for a moment. She could feel the heat and hardness of his body.

Finally she leaned in and simply touched her tongue to his lips. "Hello," she whispered.

"What's my name?" he whispered back.

"Lucifer!"

The lines by his eyes crinkled and she knew he was smiling at her, but it didn't matter because he bent his head and kissed her. It was slow, it was possessive, it was voluptuous. He was a master of the kiss . . . and the master of her.

With one slow movement, he brought his palm down over her hair and hooked a finger under the edge of her towel.

"Leopold!" she said, breaking away from his kiss.

"Ah, you remembered my name." He looked so much younger, grinning at her in the moonlight. His teeth were very white; his hair was out of its ribbon and he looked free.

She suddenly realized that the way he loved to play with her, to provoke her to call him by other names so he would kiss her harder, was dangerous—not only to her reputation, but also to her heart.

Even now his finger was tracing a little flower on her back, inside the dip of her towel.

"I must go inside," she said. "I really must."

"Say my name one more time."

"Villiers." She met his eyes. "Let go of my towel, if you please."

With a rueful smile in his eyes, he left one final touch on her back, a touch that burned like fire, and stepped back.

"I'll inform my mother tomorrow morning," she said.

She could tell that he'd forgotten the subject, and it gave her a queer spasm of female pride. "I'll tell my mother that we shall not marry," she clarified. "So that you can speak to Lisette. Unless . . . you already have?"

His eyes cooled. "I have many faults, but bigamy has never been one of them."

"We're not married," she protested.

He bowed and turned away, but she wasn't going to allow that.

"Leopold!" she snapped, reaching out for his arm. "We are not children, and I won't tolerate your silent reproach merely because I queried you."

He opened his mouth, shut it, said finally: "I would never speak to another woman about marriage while betrothed to you."

"I didn't know if you considered yourself betrothed. After all, I simply announced the fact."

"Oh, I considered myself betrothed," he said, the chill in his eyes easing. "In fact, I'm still betrothed."

"No, you're not."

"Until you leave the balcony, and I leave the balcony."

She laughed, but something in his face made the laughter fade.

"I'm a man, princess, nothing more, nothing less." With one movement, so swift that she didn't even see it, he plucked her towel away and dropped it to the ground. She was so startled that she didn't even squeak. Didn't try to cover herself or run for the door.

Their eyes caught and he didn't lower his. "May I?" he asked.

They weren't marrying, after all. He was going to marry Lisette, who had children following her like the Pied Piper. This was merely . . .

This was merely a dalliance in the moonlight.

She felt a surge of womanly power, a force as seductive as the shape of his body. "You may look," she instructed. "But you may not touch."

"You don't belong to me. I have no right to touch."

True enough. He'd chosen Lisette. And some small, mean part of her mind thought that—well, to be truthful, it wasn't a *small* part of her mind. With her whole mind she thought he was even more blind than Lisette was crazy, which was to say: completely.

He deserved what he got. And just like Gideon, he deserved to lose what he was about to lose. So she stepped back and smiled, releasing his eyes from their voluntary bondage.

Of course, being Leopold, he surprised her. His eyes moved so slowly.

If he were naked, she wouldn't even know where to look first . . . Perhaps his chest. She knew it was muscled, but . . . and his stomach. Lower. The way his thighs felt when pressed against hers, hard and potent.

Her imagination made her own body change, feel liquid and powerful. She opened her legs slightly, not even glancing at the discarded towel, and leaned back against the balustrade.

Leopold was inspecting her as slowly as if she were a sovereign he suspected of being copper rather than true gold. She arched her back a little. She liked the way her breasts curved, and her delicate pink nipples, and the way those nipples didn't point downwards, like some women's did.

His breath was ragged but he was taking too long in his inspection, so she bent over to pick up the towel, taking her time.

When she straightened, she met his eyes again. The look in them was smoky and seductive, and made her feel as if she might do something foolish. It was time to leave.

She blew him a kiss.

He groaned as if he was in pain.

Good.

She left.

# Chapter Nineteen

*Knole House, country residence of the Duke of Gilner
June 19, 1784*

The next morning, Eleanor walked over to the other wing of the house, trailed by Oyster and a footman with a tea service. Anne was sitting up in bed, reading. "How are you feeling?" Eleanor asked.

"Tea!" Anne cried rapturously. "You are my favorite of all sisters."

"You are the most easily bribed of mine," Eleanor said, sitting down with her cup of tea.

"Marie, will you come back in two minutes?" Anne asked her maid. And then: "She told me about Ada. I'm so sorry, Eleanor."

"There's no reason to give me particular condolences."

"Yes, there is," her younger sister said, smiling ruefully.

"I've known you for years, after all. I would guess that you stayed up half the night weeping into your pillow."

"Ada deserved tears. She had a terribly short life."

"I agree. I do agree. But it's not your fault, my dear. And I would guess yours were guilty tears."

Eleanor nodded. But what was there to be said about it, after all? She had liked Ada, but Ada was gone, and there was no changing that. "Villiers has decided to marry Lisette."

"I'm not sure that's a bad thing for you," Anne said. "Though it certainly is for him. Lisette really is eccentric, the poor thing. She's not made for marriage. She is best here, in the place where everyone knows her and makes allowances for her behavior. Does Villiers still fancy himself as a rescuer of fair maidens?"

"I believe he fancies her as an excellent mother."

Anne snorted. "This is the most wonderful book," she said, waving it at Eleanor. "It's called *The Castle of Otranto*. I scared myself silly last night when the son of the lord was crushed to death by a monstrous helmet that falls out of the sky just before he was supposed to be married. Have you read it?"

"I'm still trying to read Shakespeare's sonnets," Eleanor said.

"So boring," Anne said. "Sonnets all just talk about one thing, really. But this book has portraits that sigh mysteriously, and bits of armor falling out of the clouds. And now Lord Manfred is trying to divorce his wife to marry his son's fiancée . . . I believe I shall just stay in bed and read the whole thing today. I can't possibly survive another night unless I've found out how it ends. This house creaks terribly in the dark."

There was a knock on the door and Anne's maid reentered. "Do you happen to know how the duchess is feeling?" Eleanor asked her.

"Her Grace had a poor night," Marie reported. "But the surgeon comes today and he'll pull out the tooth. Meanwhile Lady Marguerite gave a great bottle of laudanum to Her Grace's maid, and so Her Grace is fast asleep. Lady Marguerite told the maid to keep her that way so that the tooth can just be pulled before she wakes up."

"Oh dear," Eleanor said. "But I'm sure Mother would much rather be asleep. She is not fond of pain."

"Who is?" Anne said. "I gather you are clambering up on a horse this morning, Eleanor? I must say, that habit is just lovely, and I didn't even pick it out myself."

Eleanor glanced down at herself. For almost the first time since arriving, she was wearing a costume that she herself had ordered. The habit was made of blue ribbed silk with a deep turned-down collar behind.

"I particularly like your coattails," Anne added.

"Why should men be able to wear coattails and not women?" Eleanor agreed, tipping her tall hat a little farther forward over her eyes. It was blue as well, and had two jaunty tassels that hung to her shoulder.

"May I offer my felicitations on your betrothal to the Duke of Villiers, my lady?" Marie asked.

"You may not," Anne said promptly. "My sister has decided not to marry the duke."

"Those children!" Marie cried immediately, clasping her hands. "I absolutely understand, my lady. The household is convulsed."

"*Convulsed?*" Eleanor repeated. "That seems an odd word choice."

"Popper is a very pious man, you understand. He has all of the maids praying three times a day. Then the duke brings these children in the house and of course they're—" She broke off.

"They're bastards," Anne put in cheerfully.

"Popper was distraught enough when the first one arrived, thinking the boy was a limb of Satan and so on. But Lady Lisette just told him not to be tiresome, and the Duke of Villiers pays no heed to Popper, of course."

"I'm sure he just waved his fingers disdainfully," Eleanor said.

"The first day wasn't too bad, but then when the two little girls arrived . . . well, there's been a terrible commotion belowstairs. Popper isn't anything compared to Mrs. Busy, the cook. She told the upstairs maid that her immortal soul might be in danger if she cleared the grate in the nursery. And she keeps sending up gruel because she says that meat does something to flesh and causes carnal provocations . . . I think I have that right."

"That's purely cruel," Eleanor said sharply. "Those are innocent children and they ought to be treated well. Did you say the cook's name is Mrs. Busy?"

"Mrs. Zeal-of-the-Land Busy," Marie said.

"Zeal of the what?"

"Zeal-of-the-Land Busy," Marie repeated. "Her husband was a famous preacher in London—a Puritan, of course—until he died from a surfeit of boiled pig and she was forced to go into service."

"Absolute rubbish," Eleanor said. "Are you telling me that Popper agrees with this extraordinary behavior?"

"Well, he does and he doesn't. He did tell Lady Lisette about the gruel, and she said that some gruel wouldn't hurt them, and that Popper should just make peace in the household. From what they say, Lady Lisette does not like to involve herself in household matters. And I'm afraid that Lady Marguerite travels a great deal of the time."

"Well, she's here now, and she ought to be boxing Mrs. Zeal-of-the-Land's ears," Eleanor said.

"Actually Lady Marguerite is not here," Marie said. "She rose early this morning and she and Mr. Bentley went on a trip to Royal Tunbridge Wells. She left you a note."

"What an interesting life Lady Marguerite leads!" Anne said with delight. "I expect I shall be just the same, if I find myself widowed. Not that I would wish to be."

"I shall go to the kitchens myself," Eleanor said. She was experiencing a nice burst of pure rage, which had swept away the melancholy. She *hated* melancholy. "I shall bring Oyster," she added. If Lisette was going to allow children in her house to be fed nothing but gruel, she would simply have to tolerate the presence of a fat, cheerful puppy.

"Go forth and conquer!" Anne said, settling back into bed. "Perhaps I shall see you at supper, and perhaps not. It all depends on whether a whole suite of armor smashes the castle."

Eleanor walked down the front stairs, planning to sweep up Popper and take him along with her. Clearly he was a weak link in the household, but at the least he could back her up when it came to children's need for more than gruel to eat.

Oyster started barking energetically the moment they rounded the curve of the stair, so she peered down and saw Villiers standing in the entrance hall.

For a moment her heart bounded—it had been so much fun toying with him and thinking of marrying him but then she remembered that he had chosen Lisette over her. So she said, "Oyster, be quiet," not loudly, but there must have been something in her tone because he actually obeyed.

The duke was as polite as ever, which was to say not very. He had a way of bowing that implied he was above such observances.

That being the case, she didn't curtsy to him, just pulled

on her gloves. She wasn't going to touch anything in Mrs.
Zeal-of-the-Gut's kitchen with her bare hands.

He raised an eyebrow.

"When you bow as if you give a damn, I'll bother to
bend my knee to you again." She gave him a sweet smile.
Then she turned to Popper. "I'll thank you to show me
the kitchens."

"What, my lady?" he said, starting to stammer because
he was that sort of man.

Eleanor was her mother's daughter, even though she
didn't choose to act as such most of the time. She pinned
the butler to the wall with one look and then said, softly,
"The kitchens, Popper."

Oyster gave a little whine by her leg. At least someone
knew when she meant business.

"Of course, my lady," Popper cried, pulling open
the green baize door at the back of the entrance hall so
quickly that it banged against the wall.

"Eleanor?" she heard Villiers say behind her.

She looked at him over her shoulder. "Housekeeping
matters," she said coolly. "You continue on with whatever
you were doing. Play some chess or something."

She heard him snort. He followed her through the door,
but she paid him no mind.

"Tell me about Mrs. Zeal-of-the-Land, Popper."

"I do hope that breakfast was to your satisfaction, my
lady?" Popper trotted backwards down the servants' corridor, at imminent risk of bouncing into a wall. His round
face was creased with anxiety.

"Perfectly acceptable," Eleanor said dryly. "No prayers
delivered with my eggs."

"Prayers?" Villiers echoed.

They reached the kitchen. Popper thrust open the door
and then flattened himself against the wall to allow her
to pass.

"Prayers?" Villiers asked again, from a few paces behind Eleanor. But she had turned into a woman intent on battle, a species he recognized, so he wasn't surprised when she ignored him.

The kitchen was enormous and appeared to have changed little since medieval times. One wall was taken up by a fireplace with five spits rotating before it, thanks to a half-asleep boy operating some sort of a treadmill with his feet. Every last inch of the other walls was covered with shelves holding china, held upright by small wooden dowels. There were rows of teapots fenced in and adorned with strings of onions and garlic. Up above hung strings of sausages and cuts of other meats that Villiers couldn't identify.

There had to be ten people at work, carrying food about, stirring things on a big iron stove, washing crockery, or in the case of an elderly gentleman, sleeping in the corner.

"Lady Eleanor. His Grace the Duke of Villiers," bellowed Popper.

A large woman turned about from the stove and squinted at them. "I don't hold with visits to my kitchen." She turned her head. "Witless, if you don't keep them spits turning I'll put you on one of them!"

"Sister Busy," Popper said, wringing his hands. "Make the duke and lady welcome. Be charitable, Mrs. Busy, be charitable!"

Eleanor advanced to the center of the kitchen. The cook had scarlet cheeks and small eyes, not to mention a huge, dripping ladle.

"I would like some bacon for breakfast," she said, walking forward as if the ladle were no threat.

The cook's small eyes narrowed. "I don't hold with pork," she said shrilly. "The spice of idolatry, I call it! And what are you doing, bringing a mongrel into my kitchen!"

"Bacon is meat, and it is nourishing meat," Eleanor said coldly. Villiers had never heard quite that tone in her voice before, and he was glad of it. "I want bacon and eggs sent up to the nursery immediately."

The cook slammed her ladle back into the large pot so hard that boiling soup splashed out on the stove and the floor. "So this is what you're about!"

"Indeed," Eleanor stated.

Why on earth was she fussing over the children's breakfast? Villiers could have told her that Tobias had it all in hand, what with his bribes to the footman, but there wasn't time to interrupt.

"Food is not meant to be gorged with gluttony or greediness," the cook said shrilly. "Nor to be eaten by those who are an abomination under the Lord!"

For the first time Villiers noticed that Eleanor held a riding crop, and he grew a little concerned. She was running her fingers over it as if it were a delicate ribbon. Mrs. Busy didn't look like the type of woman to be intimidated.

"I would hesitate to categorize anyone as indulging in gluttony," Eleanor said, her eyes lingering unpleasantly on the cook's admittedly abundant curves. "But I do know that those children cannot thrive on a diet of gruel."

Villiers froze.

Mrs. Busy's small mean eyes darted to him and then back to Eleanor. "Meat breeds foul temptations! Carnal provocations! Those children are the seed of the devil and their appetites will be strong."

"*You* are the foul face of the devil," Eleanor said, taking another step forward.

She didn't do anything with the whip, but the cook flinched.

"If you do not send up a nourishing meal, including at least two kinds of meat, within the hour, I will have you turned out on the road, Mrs. Zeal-of-the-Land Busy. You will no longer be so *busy.* Do you understand me?"

Mrs. Busy didn't answer. A drop of sweat ran down her forehead.

"She understands," Popper said, popping up between them. "She does, don't you, Sister Busy? She knows that the children are innocent creatures who aren't to blame for the circumstances of their wicked conception. Children, Sister Busy," he implored. "Just children."

"Aye," the cook said slowly.

Villiers stood behind Eleanor, the truth of it slowly sinking in. Apparently the gruel Tobias complained of wasn't just Mrs. Busy's idea of a child's diet, but something of a purgative. Thank God, Tobias had taken care of himself.

Eleanor's face looked as if it were carved of the finest marble, as if the goddess Athena had come to life.

Mrs. Busy was no match for her. "I'll send them breakfast," she said, wilting.

"And every meal, as long as those children are here. If I hear that there is the least inadequacy, if you misplace an herb or forget an ingredient, I shall return."

"I shall not. I sought merely to curb the—the—"

Something in Eleanor's gaze warned against an explanation.

"I'll send excellent meals," Mrs. Busy said hastily.

"Good," Eleanor said. "Then I'll bid you good day, Mrs. Zeal-of-the-Land Busy. Oyster, come."

Villiers waited until she left the kitchen, because he didn't want Eleanor to feel that he didn't trust her success. Mrs. Busy didn't stir, just waited, with her eyes fixed on him. "My children are not an abomination," he stated, hearing his own cold voice and knowing there were few brave enough to endure the sound without flinching.

"That they are not," Mrs. Busy readily agreed, showing that she wasn't one of the brave.

Villiers turned to go.

"But you are!" she burst out. "Verily, I must say the truth and that is that thou dwellest in the tents of the wicked and feedest the vanity of the eye."

Apparently she didn't care for his coat. Or perhaps it was the embroidery that was spurring her censure.

"I am moved by the spirit to say so!" Mrs. Busy insisted.

"As long as the tents of the wicked are replete with the smiles of beautiful women," Villiers said, "I shall be happy."

"I shall daunt the profaneness of mine enemies," Mrs. Busy stated. "When sin provokes me, I shall not be silent."

"Sister Busy," implored Popper. "Cry you mercy, Sister Busy, consider your place in life."

"And while you are contemplating that, Mrs. Busy, you might include the thought that I may well marry your mistress, Lady Lisette," Villiers said. "In which case this house will become one vast tent for my wicked self. And then you, Mrs. Busy, will need to thrust yourself onto the sanctified highway because I may well bring all *six* of my children to live under this roof. In case you are wondering, none of the six was conceived with the benefit of matrimony."

"Six!" she gasped, falling back and regarding him as if he were the very devil himself. "Thou tellest untruths. No man is so rank in the face of the Lord."

Against all odds, Villiers was beginning to enjoy himself. "Are you gnashing your teeth, Mrs. Busy? That's an odd sound you're making."

"Thou art a Nebuchadnezzar, a very Nebuchadnezzar, come to mock me!" Mrs. Busy said.

One of the pot boys giggled.

"Sister Busy," Popper implored.

"I must take my leave," Villiers said with a flourishing bow. "Thank you for this charming conversation."

Popper ran after him down the corridor. "I beg your pardon, Your Grace," he said, panting.

Villiers stopped. "What relation is she to you?"

Popper rang his hands. "She's my sister, Your Grace. We were raised Puritan, you see, but she took to it fiercely, and then she married Zeal-of-the-Land, and I'm afraid that she became rather rigid. She needs this position. She has nowhere else to go, and Zeal-of-the-Land left all his possessions to the church."

"He left *everything* to the church?"

Popper nodded. "With a request that they say prayers for his soul four times a day for a year. Which they will, because it transpired that Brother Busy had acquired quite a large estate. But unfortunately his will left my sister destitute and in need of a position. Please, Your Grace, I know that she's a fierce woman. But Brother Busy's death left her soured."

"I can imagine," Villiers said, pushing open the baize door that led back to the foyer.

They emerged into chaos. Oyster was barking hysterically and running in circles, Eleanor was shouting, one of the footmen was chasing the dog, and Lisette was standing on the second or third step of the staircase, screaming. Into all of this rushed Popper, uttering useless admonitions in a shrill voice.

"Quiet!" Villiers bellowed.

Everyone obeyed him except, characteristically, Eleanor. She whipped around, hands on her hips, and said through clenched teeth, "Escort Lisette elsewhere before I do something I may—or may *not*—regret."

Oyster had dropped onto his haunches and was gazing

at him in a rather charmingly attentive position, so Villiers raised a finger to the footman, who scooped up the dog. "Take him outside," he commanded before turning to Lisette.

She was clinging to the banister, her face absolutely drained of color. Although she had stopped screaming, she was obviously paralyzed with fright.

"Lisette," he said, coming to the bottom of the stairs.

She looked at him, her face pathetically wan, her blue eyes huge.

"Poor scrap," he said, and held out his arms. She fell into them and he scooped her up. She put her head against his shoulder, as trustingly as if she were a child.

"Take her into the drawing room," Eleanor said. "I'll go outside and make sure that Oyster is out of sight and sound." She said it flatly, without an edge, but Villiers could read her voice easily enough.

He looked down at Lisette's spun-gold hair. She wasn't the bravest of creatures, but there was no point in defending her at the moment. Besides, Eleanor had already stamped out the door after Oyster.

So he walked into the drawing room and sat down on a sofa. After a moment Lisette eased off his lap and onto the bench beside him. "I'm quite irrational when it comes to dogs." Big tears made her eyes glisten. "I hate being such a coward."

"Many people are afraid of dogs," he said, trying to sound consoling, although sympathy wasn't exactly his forte. "There's no need to apologize."

"Oyster is likely a quite nice dog." She was twisting her fingers around and around each other. "It's just that I had such a terrible experience last year in the village. A feral dog was threatening everyone, and there were children in the square. I had to protect them."

"Terrible," Villiers said, only half listening.

"If we marry," Lisette said, "you must promise me that we will have no hounds on the premises."

"If we marry?" he echoed, snapping to attention.

It was the second time in as many days that a woman had announced their imminent marriage without bothering to wait for his proposal. In this case, he hadn't even broached the idea of marriage, which made her announcement seem truly presumptuous.

"Yes," Lisette said, apparently unmoved by the surprise in his voice. "I am truly considering it, Leopold. I like your children *so* much."

Of course, that was why he was considering it too: because she would be a bighearted, wonderful mother to his motley brood.

She smiled up at him. "I think we should suit, especially because you don't own a dog."

No dog but six children. Most women would run screaming in the opposite direction, so it seemed he had found the perfect woman.

At least from that particular point of view.

"Why don't you kiss me now?" Lisette asked. Her eyes were the exact color of sky outside the window. Of course he wanted to kiss her.

He leaned over and placed a gentle kiss on her lips. They were pale pink, very soft.

"I like kissing," she said, sighing a bit. She put a hand on his chest. "Do you like kissing, Leopold?"

"Of course," he said, wondering what the hell he'd gotten himself into. It was her fresh sweetness that made her such a perfect choice for a wife. He would have to be slow and kind, and hope that he didn't wilt from pure boredom during the act.

"Of course, I like other things about bedding men," she said.

He blinked.

"Kiss me again," she cooed, pursing her lips. He obliged, settling his lips over her soft ones. She couldn't have meant that comment the way it sounded.

"What do you like about bedding men?" he inquired.

She looked up through her lashes modestly. "I'm certain that you can teach me a great deal."

Lisette was the very model of a respectable virgin. Not like infuriating Eleanor, who had clearly slept with Godless Gideon before he ran off to marry Ada. And not like her in other ways too, because Eleanor had that trick of setting a man's blood on fire just by looking at him.

Whereas Lisette's sweet blue eyes were restful.

"Kiss me again," she said, placing a slender arm around his neck.

He bent his head again and this time ran his tongue along the seam of her lips. He was a little afraid that she might be prudish in her approach—weren't virgins always nonplussed by their first real kisses?

But she opened her mouth readily enough. They played with their tongues for a while, and she even stroked his shoulders.

They'd be fine in bed.

The fact that he kept thinking about Eleanor, and the way she uttered those absurd little noises when she kissed him . . . that was unacceptable.

He had made his bed the moment he allowed Tobias to be conceived. He couldn't undo those wrongs after all these years, but he could make a level-headed choice for wife, rather than choosing someone based on lust.

Because damn it, he felt lust for Eleanor. Even thinking about her made him harden. Remembering the way he bent over her on the balcony, and her bottom tucked—

He woke to himself to find that Lisette was protesting

the strength of his mouth. "Really, Leopold," she said a bit querulously. "I know that you have a man's desires, but there's no need to be immoderate."

Never, in the length of his misspent life, had he kissed one woman while arousing himself with thoughts of another. He had horrified himself—not an easy task. "I will never do that again," he stated. "I apologize."

Lisette dimpled at him. "Actually, I'm quite happy to see the strength of your—" She coughed delicately. "—desire. I have seen you looking at Eleanor and I thought perhaps you had feelings for her."

"The decision not to marry was mutual," he said, his voice coming out more sharply than he intended.

"I'm glad to hear that!" Lisette said, her dimples appearing again. "Not that I would normally worry about competition, but Eleanor is so witty. And she has a kind of *je ne sais quoi* that makes her very attractive to men."

"I know."

"And," Lisette continued, "she's truly intelligent. When we were all children here we used to have chess tournaments and she always won. She would beat her brother and my father as well."

"Chess?" Villiers said. "She plays chess?"

"Didn't you know? I thought Marguerite told me once that you have quite a *penchant* for it yourself, don't you?"

"You could say that," he said. Since he was one of the three top players in the kingdom.

"You see, one of my other aunts is a quite good chess player. So she taught everyone chess in the summer, and she would organize us into tournaments."

"What is her name?" Villiers said, squinting through the window. A carriage had just drawn up, but he couldn't see if it had a crest on the door.

"Rosamund Patton," Lisette said. "Have you ever met her?"

"I've played Mrs. Patton at the Chess Club," Villiers said. "She was the only woman who had won entrance to the club until very recently, when the Duchess of Beaumont won a place."

"Well, if that's the case, I'm sure that Eleanor could do the same. She used to beat Rosamund all the time. I think Eleanor is probably the most intelligent woman I know."

"I think that *you* are one of the nicest women I know," Villiers said, dropping a kiss on her mouth. "There aren't many ladies who would praise another woman the way you do."

Lisette's whole face lit up when she smiled. "Women can be so silly to each other! Men are easy to come by, but female friends are not. Goodness, look at that! We have another visitor." She clapped her hands, jumping to her feet. "What fun this is! I haven't had visitors for a month of Sundays, and now it's positively raining people."

"There's a crest on the carriage door," Villiers said.

"Oh well, then I expect it's Astley," Lisette said.

*"What?"*

She turned to look at him. "The Duke of Astley, of course. Didn't you hear at dinner last night? His wife has died. He will have come for Eleanor."

Villiers grabbed her arm. "What do you mean?"

She frowned until he loosed his grip and then she bestowed a smile on him. "I said, it's the Duke of Astley, come to fetch Eleanor, of course."

"But—"

"Oh, I forgot. You probably don't know. They were in love as children. And then he was forced to marry a woman named Ada. That was so sad."

"How on earth do you know all this?"

"I told you! We used to play together as children, and

we still correspond occasionally. At any rate, Astley—I think his name is Gideon, though I haven't met him—loves Eleanor. And she loves him. So I expect he's come for her."

"He's come for her?"

Lisette looked up at him. "Eleanor is not the sort of woman whom any man would forget," she pointed out.

"Of course it's not Astley," Villiers stated. "His wife is barely in the ground." He held out his arm.

"I shall go outside to see," Lisette said, and she actually dashed off without waiting for his escort.

Villiers decided that the code of gentlemanly behavior did not insist one had to trot after a fleeing woman, so he walked into the entrance hallway at a measured pace.

Never mind the fact that he was fighting an impulse to walk faster and faster. Of course it wasn't Astley. Though it wouldn't matter to him if it were. He had no wish to marry Eleanor; he was to marry Lisette. The only thing that bothered him was the fact that there would be a tremendous scandal if Eleanor bolted with the Duke of Astley a few days after his duchess died.

Impossible. He knew Astley. The man defined the word *conventional*. Astley would think as prudently as he himself had when choosing Lisette as a wife. Astley was a rational man.

Dukes had to be rational men. They couldn't simply dash off and do whatever they pleased. He quickened his pace. The carriage likely held Lisette's father, which was all to the good, because he should extend a formal request for Lisette's hand in marriage. Not to mention the fact that someone had mentioned a purported betrothal between Lisette and the next-door squire Thestle's son. Not Roland, but another one. That would have to be dealt with, he supposed.

There was always the chance that Gilner would refuse

him, based on his bastard children, or Lisette's existing engagement. But now that he'd had a close look at the Gilner estate, he doubted it. Gilner was clearly not a stickler for propriety. His daughter was chaperoned by a woman who brazenly lived with her devoted friend.

Moreover, from what he could see, Lady Marguerite spent a good deal of her time traveling. No severe elderly relative was part of the household, assigned to serve as a damper so that a suitor couldn't court Lisette whenever and wherever he wished. In fact, if he wanted, he could probably waltz right into Lisette's bedroom and deflower her.

No one would even notice, most likely.

Not that he would do it, because—

He walked down the front steps feeling like a fool. The carriage did not have the Gilner crest. A small group was standing in front of the steps, and Lisette turned around, waving.

"Leopold! Do come!"

He walked over, knowing the truth of it in his gut.

"You see?" she said happily, slipping her fingers into his. "I told you so!"

Eleanor was locked in the arms of a man.

Not just any man either. Gideon, Duke of Astley, was a particularly beautiful man. Not terribly tall, but who needed height when he had that profile?

Villiers took a deep breath.

Gideon was kissing Eleanor in front of her sister Anne, Lisette, the butler, three footmen, assorted groomsmen— and Eleanor's own mother, the duchess. Who was smiling, Villiers realized with another jolt. Not with the kind of barbed acceptance with which she greeted the news that he, the Duke of Villiers, was marrying her daughter, but with a kind of wild, surprised joy.

And Eleanor? He could see only the back of her head,

but Gideon's hand was rumpling her hair, holding her with such tenderness that even he, coldhearted bastard that he was, felt . . . something.

"Isn't it romantic?" Lisette said, squeezing his hand.

It took everything he had not to pull away from her.

"They love each other so much. She waited for him. And he came to her the very first moment he could. I suppose he's been thinking of her every day for years."

He could just imagine that.

Unfortunately.

# Chapter Twenty

The Duchess of Montague was smiling with a fierce happiness that Eleanor hadn't seen since her brother gained his majority. "Just wait until your father learns of this," she said to Eleanor, more or less under her breath. "He'll be so pleased."

They were leading Gideon to the drawing room, since her mother had graciously allowed that her daughter might have a short unchaperoned conversation with the duke.

"It's utterly mad, of course," she continued. "We'll have to deny all rumors. The duke should be mourning Ada; of course, he *is* mourning Ada. We won't announce anything. We'll keep it entirely secret. You'll have to drop Villiers. But no one knows of your engagement to him; it will be a seven-day wonder."

"Villiers is going to marry Lisette," Eleanor said flatly. She glanced back to find that Gideon had been caught by Anne. She felt a qualm, given Anne's express dislike for Gideon, but her sister seemed to be behaving politely enough.

"Lisette's father won't be happy with that. Gilner will have to come home now. I can't imagine that he wants his daughter to marry Villiers, not with those children of his in the picture."

"Villiers is a good man," Eleanor said. "And a duke."

"What's more, there's the question of Lisette herself," her mother continued, not even listening. "The other night the squire rattled on about his elder son being engaged to Lisette, but it was clear to me that the man was desperate to save his son. The poor boy has been living abroad for years, ducking the marriage."

The conversation felt both morbid and ill-bred, so Eleanor moved to a sofa and sat down, hands folded.

"I'll allow you fifteen minutes together," her mother said. "No more than that, if you please. I can't have the servants gossiping more than they're already likely to do. I suppose Astley will spend the night, but I'll instruct him to leave tomorrow morning. This really is a most disgraceful visit." She looked entirely happy.

Gideon appeared, and the duchess slipped out, closing the door firmly behind her.

Eleanor felt as if she were having one of those odd experiences described in the papers by people who claimed to have encountered a ghost. Surely this Gideon could not be the living, real Gideon? But there he was, standing in the door frame, apparently solid and real.

Yet the Gideon she had known for the past few years, ever since his eighteenth birthday, was polite, unfailingly mannered, and distant. Entirely correct behavior for a married acquaintance.

*This* Gideon had feverish eyes, so fervent that her own dropped, which meant that she saw he was holding a sparkling object in his right hand.

A few weeks ago she would have flown to him. Now she sat primly on the sofa. She could feel the weight of her panniers on either side of her legs, holding her down.

Gideon didn't move either. "You're so beautiful," he said finally. All she felt was a wave of embarrassment because his voice was thick with emotion.

She opened her mouth and said just the wrong thing. "I'm terribly sorry about Ada's death." His face went slack, as if the only thing holding him together had been the fire in his eyes. "I apologize!" she cried, jumping to her feet. "I didn't mean to bring up such a painful subject."

Grief was much easier to sympathize with than love, or whatever emotion he had been displaying before she mentioned Ada. So she fetched him from the doorway and brought him over to the sofa and patted his hand, just as the sister of a good friend would do. Like any acquaintance with a warm affection for a newly widowed man.

"You should know that I concluded all ceremonies for Ada before travelling here," he said.

Eleanor managed a weak smile.

"She was Quaker. Did you know that?"

And, when Eleanor shook her head, "Her father permitted it. She was quite devout. I wasn't . . . I'm Church of England, of course. But I liked her rector, Mr. Cumberwell. He buried her immediately at St. John's in Westminster. Quakers have a very simple ceremony."

Eleanor curled her fingers around his. "I'm glad that she found solace."

"I told Cumberwell to take her portion and endow a chapel in her memory. He refused because he said she wouldn't have liked that. So we're giving the money to a Foundling Hospital instead. *I* don't want it."

"Ada loved children," Eleanor said soothingly.

"I shouldn't be here with you," he said, "but I couldn't stop myself."

She resisted the impulse to shrink back on the sofa, to stop the conversation before it could start. There was something indecent about all the emotion in his eyes, as if she were seeing something she had no right to.

"I feel shame," he said, hardly pausing for breath. "But shame is something a man can learn to live with. I felt shame years ago because of our love, because of the way we—we were together. The shame I feel now is nothing compared to that."

Eleanor was starting to feel ill. In some remote part of her mind she wondered whether she could stage a faint, in order to force him into silence. He was still turning that sparkling thing, a ring of course, a diamond, in his fingers. They were long and too slim, she thought. Almost prehensile. Grasping.

And then she caught her own thought, as if someone else had said it, with an echo of shock. She was thinking about Gideon. *Gideon*. The man she loved. The most beautiful man in the world.

But when she looked at him now, she saw little to admire. The sharp planes of his cheekbones seemed too thin, almost hollowed. His chin didn't have even the shadow of a beard; he hadn't had facial hair at eighteen, and perhaps he simply never developed it.

Some part of her mind insistently compared that to the line of another jaw, another man's jaw . . .

"I shouldn't be here," he said miserably, "but I had to come. Because of Villiers."

Eleanor started. It was as if he had read her mind.

"You can't marry Villiers; it's absurd. It's disgusting," Gideon said. "I couldn't allow such a thing to happen, couldn't allow such an abomination, not when I knew you were really waiting for me. I felt as if I would be turning my back on God Himself if I did not save you from that marriage."

Eleanor fruitlessly tried to think of a comment. Was she supposed to agree that she'd been waiting for him for years? She would sound like the worst sort of wet hen.

But Gideon didn't seem to require an interlocutor anyway. "Ada died without pain," he said.

"Wonderful," Eleanor managed. Though that didn't seem quite the right response either.

"She was walking across the floor of the library, they told me, and she started to cough. I know people thought she was malingering," Gideon said, "but she wasn't. A coughing attack was a terrible thing, once it started. She would bend over and hack so violently that I felt as if her lungs must be injured."

"I saw it once," Eleanor said, putting her hand over his again. The one that wasn't holding the ring. "I was terrified for her."

He shuddered. "You couldn't not be. Sometimes I wouldn't go home at night, simply because I couldn't bear it. It looked so painful, though she said it wasn't. She was *appallingly* brave."

Eleanor murmured something.

"I used to wish that she would just scream at me, or at fate, or someone. But she never did." His hands clenched and then he opened his right hand and looked down at the ring as if surprised to find it there.

"No," Eleanor said quickly. "No."

"It's the only solution," he said. "I love you, and you love me. I always loved you, even before you noticed me."

"You did?"

"You can't have been more than thirteen when I came home with your brother the first time. But you were already yourself." He ran a finger along her eyebrow. "You were already laughing in that way you have."

Eleanor couldn't stop herself. "What do you mean?"

"Other women smile. Or when they laugh, it comes out a pinched sound. Your mouth is so wide."

He fell silent, to Eleanor's relief. She'd never thought of her mouth as *wide*, and it wasn't an image she particularly cared to dwell on.

But then he started talking again. "I brought this ring with me because it's the ring I should have given you years ago. It was my mother's. I never gave it to Ada."

"I don't think we should have this conversation now," Eleanor said.

His eyes were burning again. His skin seemed drawn too tightly over his bones, and yet he was still Gideon. The same dear Gideon whom she had watched so hungrily at fourteen, had smiled at shyly—and then not so shyly—at fifteen, the boy she had lured to kiss her at sixteen . . .

"You miss her," she said.

"No!" he said, almost violently. "I hardly knew her. We lived in the house like a brother and sister."

She touched him on the shoulder and it was the way it used to be, finally. She met his eyes and she knew what he was feeling, just the way she used to, when she thought they were two hearts beating as one. She held out her arms. "It's all right to miss her," she said.

He fell forward, head on her shoulder, still protesting that he didn't miss his wife at all. That he hardly knew her.

Until he began weeping.

# Chapter Twenty-one

*E*leanor didn't manage to escape to her bedchamber until very late that night. By then her nerves felt like the strings of a violin, pulled too tight and vibrating helplessly. She had a bath, dismissed Willa, put on her nightgown, and wrapped herself in a dressing gown.

But she couldn't settle down. She tried lying on the bed. She tried sitting before the fire. She tried writing a letter to a friend, and tore up three different drafts.

Finally she remembered that there were armchairs on the balcony. Villiers wouldn't be there, waiting to see if he had a companion in stargazing. He had hardly met her eyes all day, just smiled at her coolly and offered his felicitations. She had done the same, of course.

Lisette had swanned around the house talking about her marriage to *dearest Leopold*. He was probably in his betrothed's bedchamber that very moment. God knows, Lisette wouldn't bar the door.

She pushed open the tall doors and walked into the

velvety darkness. The chairs were positioned on Villiers's side of the balcony, so she walked forward until she bumped into one. Then she rounded the arm and dropped straight down.

Only to land on a pair of muscular legs.

"Oof," said a male voice. "You look like a feather-weight, but you're not."

"I should bounce on you for that," she snapped.

There was a moment of silence while they both contemplated the possibilities that comment brought to mind.

"Don't let me stop you," he said finally.

She rose as he spoke. "I shall leave you to the stars, Your Grace."

"You—"

Eleanor waited, though she knew she shouldn't.

"You turn me into a lecher," he stated.

She smiled, although she knew he couldn't see her expression. "I feel quite certain that I'm not the first woman to have succeeded in that respect."

"Oddly enough, I think that you are."

"Says the father of six children."

"Oh, I have felt lust. And I've indulged lust. But no other woman has turned me into another person. It's unreasonable."

She kept her voice light. "I thought that men enjoyed lechery."

With one swift, savage moment he stood before her. "Enjoyment has little to do with the way I feel about you." His voice was low and dark. "I could—I could eat you, drink you. I want to lick you, suck you, *own* you."

For a moment she sank into the mesmerizing sound of his voice, and then she shook free. "You can't own me, Leopold. You are marrying Lisette."

"And you—"

"Gideon came back for me, after all."

"Very romantic," Villiers said flatly.

She heard a faint sound from her bedchamber.

"Someone is knocking on your door," Villiers said. "I suspect it is not your maid."

She looked up at him in the dim light, a well of desperation in her heart. "Leopold—"

"You'll have to go," he said, composed as ever. "Obviously I am not the only man turned lecher by your beauty, Eleanor."

"I'm not beautiful," she whispered.

He said something but she couldn't hear it. The knocking sounded again.

"What did you say?" she asked.

His lips slid down her forehead, her nose, and he said it against her mouth. "Only the most beautiful woman I've ever met."

# Chapter Twenty-two

"Gideon," Eleanor said, opening the door.

He wasn't so young anymore. His eyes were tired and little lines flared from the corners. And yet he had the same bone-deep beauty he'd had as a boy. "I had to apologize for my behavior this afternoon."

"You need not excuse yourself," she said, holding out her hand. The day had passed in such a fury of emotion that she hadn't taken a breath, hadn't thought. Everything that she'd ever dreamed of—no, not Ada's death, but the rest—had come true in one moment.

Gideon walked in, and they sat by the fireplace as if they'd been married for over a decade, as if young love had faded and turned to something stronger.

"I shouldn't be here," he said after a moment.

"In my bedchamber, or in Kent?" She smiled, trying to ease the tension in his face.

"In Kent," he said, not smiling. "I must leave at dawn

tomorrow; all my people think I merely stopped here on the way to visit Ada's great-aunt. She had no other relatives."

The *ton* would certainly discover where he was, given the kiss with which he'd greeted her. But she didn't say anything. She kept searching his face, looking for that indescribable thing that had made him the man she loved above everyone and everything else.

"There will be gossip," he added. His mouth tightened. He was acquiring little marks by the edges of his mouth, likely from making that silent rebuke. Making it over and over.

"I expect that's the case," she said, realizing that the room had fallen silent again.

"I don't care."

Eleanor blinked. "You don't?"

"I have cared too much what other people thought. You never really understood why I married Ada, did you?"

"Likely not."

"But you must have suspected that I could have ignored or overturned my father's will."

Eleanor took a deep breath. It was absurd to think that she wasn't interested in hearing his reasoning. Of course she was interested. She *loved* Gideon. He was her true passion. "I thought perhaps . . ." But she stopped. He wasn't the sort of man with whom one could talk about lechery.

He was waiting, so she tried again. "We abandoned propriety . . ."

"It wasn't that, though I acted like a rakeshame when I took your virginity," he said, leaning forward. His eyes were the blue of the Aegean Sea. "And even worse, when I turned my back on you. I know you must have considered taking your own life, Eleanor."

Eleanor coughed. "Well, I—"

"It took me a year, even longer, to realize that a love like ours comes once in a lifetime. Only once, and never again."

"You didn't seem to feel as passionately as I did," Eleanor said bluntly. "If I felt we shared the love of a lifetime, you did not agree."

"That's because I was a fool." He captured her hand and wove his fingers through hers. "I had no idea what it meant—how much it meant—to have a woman's desire. To know that I *mattered* to you."

He stopped, so Eleanor said, almost reluctantly, "You were everything to me, Gideon." And he had been. That fact didn't explain why her heart didn't catch now with that familiar agony, the joy of seeing him. She thought love like hers would last forever.

Of course it would. Shakespeare said that love didn't alter with days or weeks. And she truly loved Gideon. Then.

He didn't seem to catch the silent *but* that followed her *You were everything to me*. His grip tightened on her hand and he leaned forward again. "That's why I breached every rule of society in order to come to your side, if only for a night. I can't see you again for a year, of course. I must honor Ada and mourn her properly. But I can't let you marry Villiers. Not with the way you feel about me!"

"What about the way you feel about *me*?" Eleanor asked, pulling her fingers free. She was conscious of a strangely bleak feeling around her heart.

"I feel just the same way," he said without hesitation. "I survived my marriage, after the first year or so, by remembering how you—how you trembled when I kissed you, Eleanor. How you used to ask me for another kiss, and another. How you . . . how you invited me to . . ."

"I understand." She folded her hands in her lap.

"I shouldn't even voice such emotions," he said, looking at her earnestly. "Not a word shall pass my lips until my mourning period is over. Servants may gossip, but there will be no consequences."

He rose to his feet and held out his hand for her.

Her fingers didn't burn at his touch. Her heart didn't flutter in her chest.

She felt as if a shadow Eleanor were in the room with them, the Eleanor of old, who would have been laughing, and crying, and throwing herself onto Gideon's chest. Who would have been unable to stop kissing him, her hands flying about his shoulders, touching him as he so clearly longed for her to do.

"Do you understand now why I left you for Ada?" he said, scooping up her hands and putting the palms against his mouth.

"No," Eleanor said. "No."

The shadow Eleanor would have kissed his palm. She might even have done something mad, like pull off his neck scarf, laughing at his protests, her fingers trailing over the strong column of his throat.

The real Eleanor just closed her lips tightly.

"I didn't understand that you were like food and drink. I never imagined that the attentions I—I silently chided you for would become the only thing I longed for. That without your desire I would shrivel into a man I scarcely recognize, a man without blood."

"You never revealed anything to me," she whispered. "Nothing. I saw you so many times after you married."

"Ada knew."

"I thought—I feared—"

"She understood. I used to talk of you sometimes."

"You didn't!"

"She had no interest in marital relations," he said. "None. If I was trapped by my father's will, she was equally trapped."

"You never made love?"

"A few times, in the first year. It made her cough. It made her uncomfortable and unhappy. She didn't enjoy it in the least." His hands tightened convulsively on hers. "After a while all I could think about was you, and the way you welcomed me, desired me. Of you, and what I threw away."

Eleanor took a deep breath. "I'm honored by your feelings—"

"There aren't many women like you," he interrupted. "Do you know that, Eleanor? Do you understand how life-giving, how important, you are to a man? I would kiss you now," he said, his eyes fierce, intent. "I would sweep you into my arms and carry you to that bed, if it were honorable, Eleanor. You know that, don't you?"

"Well—" she said, startled.

"In fact, the more I look at you, the more I feel my grip on honor slipping from my grasp," he said hoarsely. "Ada knew, after all. What's a scandal between you and me? We—"

"No," she said firmly. "Gideon, you have to leave at dawn and continue your journey to Ada's great-aunt."

"But I'll return to you," he said, his voice full of longing. "You can't stay here, with Villiers."

"I'm visiting Lisette, not the duke."

"I saw the way he looked at you."

"Villiers is marrying Lisette."

Gideon snorted.

Eleanor blinked. "Did you say something?"

"The Duke of Villiers has finally found the one woman he can't have." There was something bold and prideful in his voice that froze the words in her mouth. "He will have to live without you."

"As I said, he plans to marry Lisette," she said, moving toward the door. "Now I really must go to sleep, Gideon. It's been a long day."

"I would kiss you," he said, moving after her. "But I wouldn't be able to stop. And I know *you* couldn't. So I'm being good for both of us."

Eleanor swallowed. "I'm glad," she said faintly, opening the door.

It was all she'd dreamed of for years. He leaned toward her, his beautifully-shaped mouth hovering near hers. "Ask me, Eleanor," he whispered. "Beg me to stay. I can't say no to you. I never could say no to you."

The shadow Eleanor would have pleaded with him to stay. She would be a flame by now, intent on driving him to the same luxurious agony.

The real Eleanor felt strangely calm. Gideon seemed too beautiful, and too passive. Why did he want her to do all the kissing? Why did she have to—

She cleared her throat. "Not tonight," she said. "You're right. It wouldn't be appropriate."

She had the door almost closed when it opened again under the pressure of his hand. "I don't feel comfortable leaving you here with Villiers and those bastards of his."

"I'm visiting Lisette," she said patiently.

"How long?"

"How long what?"

"How long will your visit be?"

"Oh, a few more days," she said, not having given it much thought.

"I'll come back," he said. "I'll escort you and your mother back to London."

"But then everyone will know—"

"I *love* you," he said, his voice shaking a bit. "I love you and the world can know. I am willing to accept censure in order to have you."

"Wonderful," Eleanor said weakly. She closed the door, leaned against it, her forehead against the cool wood. "Wonderful."

# Chapter Twenty-three

*Knole House, country residence of the Duke of Gilner*
*June 20, 1784*

"Someone must find places to which we can send the children for the treasure hunt," Lisette said briskly. "Eleanor, why don't you do that? It's outdoors and you can take that dog with you. I need you to find four appropriate places from which a child might bring something back. An egg from the henhouse: that sort of thing. I'll write the clues tonight."

"It looks like rain," Villiers said, peering outside.

"Then you go with her and hold an umbrella," Lisette said. She turned to Eleanor's mother. "May I ask you . . ."

Eleanor rose and walked out of the room without a word, so Villiers followed. She had all the signs of a woman about to explode, whether from anger or grief, or something else, he didn't know.

Grief would be a bit much, given that the Duke of Astley had swooped in and declared his love. True, he was already gone when the household rose, but that was just his moralistic way.

"Are you feeling cross because your prince has left?" he asked, catching up with Eleanor just as she sent a footman to fetch Oyster.

She gave him a cool look over one shoulder. "He'll be back."

"No one could believe otherwise, given his ardor yesterday."

Eleanor had an odd look on her face, but just then the footman rushed up with Oyster, who was celebrating the happy prospect of a walk by barking.

"Hush," Eleanor said.

Naturally he paid no heed to that, so Villiers unbelted his sword stick, gave it to a footman, and took the leash instead. The dog was so ugly that he was an abomination. Nothing could be done about his jaw, but his manners were another story.

"Quiet," he said.

Oyster stopped in mid-yap.

They walked out of the house and around a path to the right, Eleanor leading the way as if she knew precisely where to go. Villiers took one look at her rigid back and decided that cheerful conversation was overrated. He occupied himself instead with refusing to walk every time Oyster pulled on the leash.

It didn't take long at all before the puppy was doing a reasonable imitation of a well-mannered creature. They headed out of the gardens as Eleanor took a small winding path that led into the woods stretching down the hill.

Villiers had lost sight of her by the time Oyster and

he had come to an amicable agreement about the proper pace for a walk.

He should have brought Tobias along, he realized. And perhaps even the two little girls. Then he could have marched down the walk like a damned middle-aged family man, with children and dog. Following an irate wife down the path. The shocking thing was that the picture didn't even feel aberrant—until he realized that of course he wouldn't be following Eleanor anywhere.

He would follow Lisette. Sweet golden Lisette.

He had to stop and apologize to Oyster because the poor beast didn't deserve to have his leash tugged so hard.

The path turned a hard right and then dumped into a rocky stream. It looked as if a giant had tossed white boulders and rocks the way children toss marbles. They lay in scrambled heaps, some as large as carriages, others the size of chamber pots. A weak stream trickled around them. On the far side of the stream was a great bramble hedge that climbed up a small hill.

"Eleanor!" Villiers called out.

"Yes?" Her head popped up from behind a huge rock.

He felt foolish. "Oyster and I are here."

"I see that."

"What are you doing?"

"Wandering about. We used to come here as children. Look how good Oyster is being. I would have thought he would be a water dog. Perhaps he's becoming sick."

Villiers raised an eyebrow at the dog quietly sitting on the ground, only his tail betraying excitement. "I doubt it," he said. "I believe I'll let him off the leash."

"Really?" Eleanor said dubiously. "I never—"

Oyster was off the leash and joyously dashing onto the rocks. He squealed like a piglet when his paw slid into the water, so Villiers judged him unlikely to drown.

"Come on, then," Eleanor said impatiently. "Don't you want to see?" Her head disappeared.

He sighed. It didn't suit him to clamber about on the rocks. It didn't suit his clothes, either. It was very tiresome, growing to be self-aware. He preferred life when he used to stride around London paying no mind to anyone except the occasional chess opponent.

He managed to get over the rocks without scuffing his boots. Notwithstanding the earlier look of the skies, the sun was out and pouring over the rocks, throwing shadows into high relief. The river wandered into tiny eddies and pools, but most of the rocks were dry and hot. They were bleached as white as the cliffs of Dover.

"What are you— Oh."

Eleanor had found a small pool. Scandalously, deliciously, she had taken off her slippers and her stockings. Her ankles were delicate, not white, but the color of sweet cream. Her toes wiggled like small fish in the clear water.

She looked up at him and smiled. Her bad mood seemed to have evaporated. "My brother and I used to spend hours here when we were children visiting the estate."

He sat down and pulled off his boots. He didn't like cold water. He didn't like undressing in the outdoors. But he had ceased to pay much attention to his own likes and dislikes, not while his body was driven by this hunger. "Did Lisette like putting her toes in the water?"

Eleanor's face stilled and he cursed himself silently for bringing up his fiancée's name. "Oh, no," she said after a second. "Lisette . . . no. But those are her favorite roses." She jerked her head over her shoulder.

He glanced up and saw that an apricot rosebush had scrambled partway up the bramble hedge on the far side of the stream. The blossoms hung in heavy clusters, their petals the color of orange liqueur in the sunlight.

"If you want to make her happy, you'll fetch her some," Eleanor said, pulling her skirts up a little higher so she could reach the bottom of the stream with her toes.

"You must be joking," he said, dragging his eyes away from her legs. They were elegant and slim. "They're over my head, not to mention the fact that I'd fall into the water. It looks much deeper on that side."

"It is."

"You can't be thinking of sending children *here* on the treasure hunt," he said.

"Why not?"

"It's not safe," he said. "They could easily fall and break a limb."

"You're not going to be one of those wildly protective papas, are you? We spent all our time here when we were children."

"Climbing for roses?" He squinted at the rocks. The water on this side ran in tiny rivulets and pooled in small hollows. But on the opposite side, there was a three- or four-foot climb straight up the rocks before one could cut a rose.

"The footmen used to fetch those roses for Lisette all the time," Eleanor said. She pulled her skirts a little higher. "This water feels so good." She swirled her hand beneath the surface and then let drops fly from her fingers. "Where's Oyster?"

"He found a patch of sunshine and went to sleep."

"Do you think all dogs are as lazy as Oyster?"

"I don't like dogs," he observed.

"Well, he likes you," she said, grinning at him. "Aren't you going to put your feet in the water?"

"I suppose," he said dubiously.

"Didn't you play in a river when you were a child?"

"Of course, my brother—" He said it without thinking and shut the sentence off halfway through.

She was dipping her fingers in the water and then drawing patterns on the rock. They were ridiculously slender fingers. Beautiful. They gave him a strange aching sensation.

"I didn't know you had a brother," she said. "Look, Villiers, I'm drawing a horse. Could you tell?"

He looked at the blobby wet spot on the rock. "No."

She shrugged and started over. "Tell me about your brother." Then her fingers stilled on the rock and she turned her head. "Now that I think of it, I've never heard about your brother."

"He died."

"I'm sorry. I'm so sorry. Was he very young?"

"Eleven." He cleared his throat. "He was just eleven."

"What happened?"

"He caught diphtheria," Villiers said. He heard the lack of expression in his own voice but was powerless to stop it.

"That's awful," Eleanor said. "Did many people get it?"

"No. My mother acted quickly. She isolated him."

"What do you mean, she isolated him?"

"She put him in a wing of our house and wouldn't allow anyone in or out."

Eleanor had forgotten about the new horse she was painting. Her fingers curled on the rock. He watched them because he couldn't bear to meet her eyes.

"Not—by himself?"

He cleared his throat. "No, his manservant was with him, of course. Though the man got diphtheria as well."

"Then who took care of them?"

"One of the footmen, a man named Ashmole. He was a cantankerous bastard even back then, when he was only a second footman. He slammed his way into that part of the house and brought them food and cared for them, and my mother didn't say a word."

Eleanor reached over and put her hand on his cheek. He could feel the chill of her wet fingers to the back of his teeth. "That's horrible."

He jerked and her fingers fell away. "I wasn't there. I was off at school."

"Or you would have gone to your brother, and probably died of the illness as well," she said, nodding.

"Not necessarily. Ashmole, the cantankerous footman, didn't get ill. He's now my butler."

She liked that. Her expression eased the clamp that always settled on his heart if he thought about his brother. Or his mother. Or the country estate where he grew up.

"That's why you never go to the castle that my mother talked of."

He grimaced. "We closed off that wing, but even my mother stopped going home after a time. We lived with it."

"Surely you will go home someday?"

"It's falling apart."

"The castle?"

"I'll let every stone in Castle Cary fall to the ground before I enter that place again."

"I can understand that," she said after a time. She had gone back to dabbling in the stream, flicking water onto the rocks opposite.

He didn't want to think about his brother anymore, or the castle. Everything he wanted sat opposite him, flicking water and humming under her breath. Her lashes curled in the sunlight and the bodice of her gown strained a little over her breasts. He guessed it had been originally made for her sister.

He'd never wanted anyone like this in his life, not with this ravening hunger, the kind that made him tell her secrets he had told no one, that threatened to bring him to his knees . . . though now that he thought of it, his knees would be a very good place to be, given the part of her body that position would make available to him.

"Villiers," Eleanor said, "what do you think I drew this time?"

"Leopold," he corrected her. He peered at the patch of wet she'd traced on the rock next to her. "Why did you paint a pizzle on that rock?" he inquired, pulling off his stockings at last.

"It's not a pizzle!" she said, giggling. Her laughter ran along his skin and raised the hair on the back of his neck.

He put his feet down into the little puddle she'd chosen. They were huge next to hers, and they both stared for a moment. Then he moved in one smooth motion to *her* rock.

"What are you doing?" she gasped, just like the heroine in a bad play.

"I could ask the same of you," he said.

"Why?"

"Good point. Why ask? You're seducing me, and I don't care why." He looked down at her wide eyes. She'd forgotten to put on the black makeup this morning. He wouldn't want to tell her, but she looked even better without it. Eyes like hers didn't need cosmetics.

"I am not!" she said, but he could tell her heart wasn't in the protest.

"I'm not married," he said, pulling her to her feet and pushing her gently back onto the large, gratifyingly flat rock that stood at her back. "Neither are you. You can hardly have made serious vows to Master Gideon, since he informed everyone in the drawing room last night that he fully intends to mourn his wife for the next year. Apparently he feels you will simply wait for him."

"He didn't!" Eleanor said. But she didn't try to move away, just leaned against the rock, trapped by his arms braced on either side of her.

"Oh, yes he did," Villiers said. "Unless you managed to change his mind later?"

"Actually, I did," she said. "He's coming back to escort us to London."

Even given the urgent hunger coursing through his body, he felt that like a blow. He froze for a moment, looking down at her almond-shaped eyes, the way her bottom lip curved out, plump and full, and then shook his head. "Don't try and get out of it now, princess. It's too late."

"What—" she began.

He bent his head and nipped her lip. He was going to say something else, but she sighed into his mouth and all of a sudden he could smell her, the faint perfume of jasmine and something indescribably better, more sensual. Something that took him from normal to rock hard every time he came close to her.

"Essence of Eleanor," he whispered. "If I could bottle it, I would become famous."

Her lips curved into a smile and he kissed her again. He emerged from that kiss dazed, his body on fire, heart pounding.

"I am not trying to seduce you," Eleanor stated.

All the higher parts of his brain were considering the logistics of making love in the midst of a river, and he barely understood her.

"You aren't?"

"No."

"It doesn't matter because I'm seducing you. Would that be all right with you?"

"You're seducing me?"

"Yes," he said calmly. As calmly as he could, given that

he felt like a ravening animal. "Don't pick this moment to become chaste, Eleanor."

"What if I did?" she said, and there was something in her eyes, some sort of confused hurt.

He kissed her hard, the kind of kiss that stole his breath and made his fingers curl with the wish to touch her. But he didn't. "I'd seduce you anyway," he told her, honestly enough. "God, Eleanor, I've never felt this way. Ever."

And then he stood up and wrenched off his neck cloth. Threw his heavy silk jacket over one rock and his fine linen shirt over another.

The woman he meant to seduce laughed at him while sunbeams danced in her hair, turning individual hairs into spun gold and glossy bronze and darker hues, like brewed tea. He didn't care how she laughed as long as she didn't leave.

And she didn't, falling silent when he eased his breeches down over that aching, hot part of himself. He didn't see fear in her eyes, thank God. Or reluctance, either.

Naked, he walked back through the pool, not even feeling the chilly water on his ankles. She kept her hands at her sides.

"You can't mean . . ." she whispered.

Her eyes were very wide and very dark. But not reluctant.

"Yes." Her body was curves and shadows, pink here, cream there. He wanted to tear her gown off, taste all of her. She had buttons all the way down her dress. It was the work of mere moments to unbutton some two hundred buttons, not counting those that flew off, sinking into the pool with tiny splashes.

"We can't do this," she whispered.

He glanced over his shoulder. They were far from the house, and even if someone did come down the path, they were around the curve of the stream, well out of sight.

"No one will come." He had dispensed with her corset and was inching up her chemise. "We are alone, Eleanor. Do you realize that we are almost never alone? Finchley is always hanging around my bedchamber, and there's your maid—"

"We can't make love in the open air. I've never heard of anything so scandalous. We are, both of us, promised to others."

"I am marrying for the sake of my children." He said it flatly. "I have every expectation that Lisette and I will be quite comfortable together. And I will be faithful to her. But I am not yet married. In fact, I haven't even proposed."

"She announced your engagement," Eleanor pointed out, keeping a tight grip on her chemise so he couldn't pull it up her legs.

"That surprised me, but not as much as when you announced the same," he said, giving her a little kiss at the edge of her mouth. He had a hand under the edge of her chemise now, running circles on her smooth skin.

"I should have made you go on one knee," she said. "Gideon didn't either; at this rate, I'll never have a proper proposal."

Villiers didn't want to think about Gideon. He didn't even want to hear the man's name. He slid his hand higher and then ran his lips over her eyebrow. "You're beautiful, Eleanor," he whispered. "At first I thought your eyes were black, but they're actually blue, the color of the sky just before the sun sets."

"We can't do this! Oyster is watching," she said, pulling the hem of her chemise back down.

Villiers had been alive a few years more than thirty. He knew perfectly well when a woman was truly protesting and when she was offering excuses for the mere sake of it.

The pug was sprawled out on a sunny rock, paws in the air, snoring. In his estimation, Oyster was a pathetic excuse for a dog, so he didn't even bother answering that protest, just wrestled the fabric out of her hand and swept the whole garment up and over her hair.

And then, there they were. Naked.

Her hair had started to fall from its pins, locks sliding over her breasts. Her stomach was gently rounded and curved into a beautiful shadow, dusted with hair the color of brandy.

He was never at a loss for words. Never. Until now. "You're so—" He stopped. He'd been wanting to explore her with his mouth for hours, days. And she wanted a man to kneel before her.

So he did, pushing her legs apart slightly so he could run his tongue up a beautiful slender thigh.

"Oh—" she cried, her voice far away and thin.

Her skin was sweet and smooth, and he painted designs on her with his tongue, sliding higher and higher, as if she too were a smooth rock in the sunshine. Her fingers were playing with his hair, twisting, caressing.

"You're not going to—" Her breathing was growing ragged.

"I am."

"You can't do that!" She sounded truly shocked, so he stood up and let his fingers drift over the rounded curve of her inner thigh that he had just kissed.

She had a flush high in her cheeks that made his whole body thrum with pleasure, so much so that he didn't even realize for a moment how odd it was that *her* pleasure would be causing *his*. He didn't think of that until they were kissing again and he was sipping the sweet darkness of her mouth, one arm around her back to protect her from the hard stone, the other still caressing her thigh, sliding closer, farther away, closer again.

"You aren't going to touch me *there*, are you?" she whispered tremulously.

He pulled back and frowned at her. "He didn't even *touch* you?"

"I— No. Is that always part of lovemaking?"

The struggle with his conscience took a split second, and his conscience lost, as always. "Absolutely," he said firmly. "One wouldn't want to criticize a former lover, but . . ." He had her trembling, so he slid his fingers just to the edge of the soft curls between her legs. "A man always touches a woman here. Because—" He pulled her closer so he could feel her soft breasts against his chest. "—because that is where a woman is most luscious and most delicate, which in itself sets a man on fire." He let a finger drop deep, stroke and glide.

Her head dropped back against his arm, so he bent to kiss her throat.

"He touches her like this," he said, licking her shoulder and letting his fingers wander.

"That's—lovely," Eleanor said, the break in her voice sending another jolt down to Villiers's groin.

"Surely he kissed you here?" He kissed his way down the slope of her breast, ran his teeth gently over her nipple.

"Of—Of course," she said, her back arching toward him. "That feels so good!" He didn't think she was talking only about the fact he was suckling her, so he increased the pressure of his fingers a little bit.

Her little cries were an aphrodisiac like no other, so he knelt again before she had a chance to protest and pulled her legs apart even farther.

She was so exquisite that he was shaking like a lad experiencing his first woman.

"I'm not sure," she cried. "Oh Leo, you can't—"

"Of course I can."

"It's not proper," Eleanor cried desperately. "I can't think that it is. I've never heard of such a thing." She looked around wildly, apparently remembering again that they were outside. "And we're—"

Her voice broke off because he had dipped his fingers into the chilly water and stroked them over the hottest part of her body. Her mouth fell open and she made a choked noise. He smiled against her leg and let his fingers dance.

"I'm going to kiss you now," he said, when he had her trembling.

She managed to say "Leo," but it was a weak protest and he knew it. He put his mouth on her, delicately, in the sweetest kiss of all. It took only a moment. Her hands twisted in his hair, her hips arched, and she broke in a cry, a quaking, muffled cry that was the most beautiful thing he'd ever heard.

He straightened slowly, knowing he was just barely in control. "You look like a virgin sacrifice, waiting on the rock for a dragon to sweep by," he said, hearing the growling tone in his own voice.

She opened her eyes. "I'm no virgin," she whispered, pulling him closer.

"And I'm so grateful for that," he whispered back. "I just need to find my breeches."

"Now," she cried, pulling him to her. "Oh God, Leo, please, please . . . I want you."

"Not as much as I want you," he growled. He couldn't even let his body touch hers. If he allowed himself even a touch, he would lose control, plunge into her sweetness, take her right there under God's sky and with no shame.

Eleanor couldn't think lucidly. She was leaning against a rock in the sunshine. She was naked. She was about to make love with a man to whom she had no formal attachment. She was . . .

All the considerations that should have made her run shrieking into the woods seemed inconsequential, when she could instead watch Leopold's beautiful haunch as he leaned over and pulled a French letter from the pocket of his breeches, throwing them toward the riverbank.

"Do you carry those with you at all times?" she asked.

He straightened and turned around. His body almost took her breath away: it was so powerful, muscled and beautiful . . . so very different from hers. She wasn't prone to feeling dainty and feminine, though she felt just that as she stood there in the sunshine, waiting. But she didn't move, afraid that she would break the spell if she moved. That one of them would regain some common sense and reach for clothing.

"Are we going to make love standing up?" she asked shyly a few moments later. "Oh!" Because they clearly *were* going to do just that. His big hands cupped her bottom and he pulled her up a bit and then . . .

And then she opened her thighs and he was sliding in, and it was different—so different—than she remembered. His hands were curled around her bottom but her entire being was focused somewhere else. He was slow and she needed it. She could feel every inch.

It was enthralling—a bit painful—exquisite. Her nails dug into his shoulders.

"Too much?" he whispered, his voice a growl. "You're so tight, Eleanor."

"Just go slow," she said in a gasp. He took another inch and the pleasure of it streaked like fire down her legs. She bit his lip.

He growled at her and took another inch.

She meant to tell him something else, but what she said was, "Don't stop, don't stop, please don't stop."

"I'm not planning to," he said, and nipped her ear.

Stole another inch. Waited, let her feel him, adjust to the invasion, his thickness, his possession.

"I'm sorry," she said, gasping again.

"Princess, you have nothing to apologize for." There was a kind of raw truth in his voice that made her feel so ecstatic that she arched, and he came home. All the way. His groan ripped from his lungs, and she would have done the same but she couldn't breathe; it felt that good.

And then he was sliding back, and it was like silk, easier the second time, better the third, dizzying the fourth . . . she lost track. He was braced against the rock on either side of her, kissing her deep and sweet, and all the time his hips were pumping back and forth.

Little thoughts floated through her mind and then were lost in a sea of pleasure. This was what it was like making love to a man, rather than a boy. It was all different: the heat, the strength, the—

She couldn't even count the ways it was different.

They were both sweaty now, and flames were licking at her legs, her stomach. She was arching against him, feeling every time he pushed back, but it wasn't quite happening.

Not quite.

And yet she couldn't—she didn't want to say anything. To direct him. To be—to be what Gideon thought she was.

But then he said, "Eleanor," and his voice was harsh and pleading at once, and she suddenly realized how ridiculous she was being.

"Here," she said in a gasp, and hooked one leg around his hip so she was just a bit higher, so that when he pumped it wasn't just pleasurable but pure, unadulterated paradise. "This way," she said, flinching because she was doing what she swore to herself she would never do again.

But it was Leopold, and he didn't look scandalized, or insulted; he just thrust. She actually cried out.

She heard him grunt with satisfaction but she couldn't think, couldn't speak, because he was hard and fast now, and a tidal wave of pleasure curled her toes and swept up her legs and threw her back onto the rock.

Her cries floated into the high blue sky and disappeared. His growl probably frightened some sleeping forest animal.

And then . . .

And then she found herself standing in his arms, her knees weak, her breath harsh in the quiet air.

"God damn," he said quietly. He had his arms around her but his forehead against the rock.

After she and Gideon had made love, all ten times, they had both been riddled by guilt afterwards. He would swear that they would never do it again, not until he was of age and they were married. And she would know that she had lured him to it, and feel guilty and slightly sick.

With Leopold there was none of that.

He finally lifted his head off the rock, and the look on his face had to approximate the grin on hers. "We're good," he said. Then, "*You're* good."

She felt the smile fall from her face. "No," she said, "I'm not good at this. It's not a skill that I've developed. I just—"

"Hush," he said, putting his lips against hers. "I wasn't implying you were the Whore of Babylon. I was just saying that it was the best sex I ever had in my life."

It was a flat statement.

"Really?" she asked, hearing the incredulity in her voice. "Isn't this what—" She waved her hand.

"What I have all the time?" It was his turn to grin at her. Had she ever thought his eyes cold? They were full of laughter now, laughter and something else, the echo of desire.

No, the presence of desire. He wanted her.

Still.

It was something to think about. Gideon had always panicked after they made love, growing snappy and anxious.

Of course, he'd been just a boy, and it was years ago.

"You're thinking about him, aren't you?" He bit her ear, and not nicely either.

"It was so different," she said.

The nip turned into a kiss. "Yes."

She remembered suddenly. "Oyster?"

He didn't need to look so he must have already checked. "He's still asleep. How much does that dog sleep?"

"Most of the day. Every moment that he's not running in circles."

They should return to the house. People might be wondering whether they were. Lisette might notice . . . No, Lisette wouldn't notice. But someone else might.

"We should move," she whispered. His cheek was just beside hers, and he smelled potent and male, so she ran her tongue carefully over his skin. He tasted wonderful.

"You're right," Leopold said.

Some tiny part of her heart registered disappointment. Of course he was right. Gideon had always been right, too.

But standing straight just meant that she was in full contact with his body. And at least part of him was interested in . . .

"Moving is my favorite activity," Leopold said, low and easy. "Are you going to look at me any time soon, princess?"

She had barely met his eyes since they made love. It

was too embarrassing. And too frightening, if she admitted it to herself. She didn't want to see awe in his eyes, didn't want to see acknowledgment that she was some sort of amazing courtesanlike woman.

Even though somehow she was. Apparently.

She was starting to feel a little sick. Who knew it would be so depressing to make men happy?

"Hey." There was a soft growl in her ear and a strong hand pulled her face around. Leopold was frowning down at her. "What are you thinking about?"

"Nothing," she said quickly.

He kissed her, quick and fierce. "Tell me."

"No." She couldn't tell him. He would think she was mad. He might even laugh at her.

"Stubborn wench." With one swift movement he swung her into his arms and started walking over the rocks.

"Where are you going?" she gasped, holding onto his arm. "I'd prefer to walk. I'd like to put my clothes back on now. My clothes!" She looked back. "We left my chemise on the rock."

"We don't need it," he said, climbing out of the river.

"*I* need it!" she said indignantly. "Will you please put me down now? I must collect my clothing."

He laid her flat on her back in the soft grass, and followed her down so quickly that she could hardly twitch before his body was covering hers.

"You said we should move," he reminded her. It was now clear what kind of moving he had in mind.

"No, thank you," Eleanor said, smiling but determined. She'd had enough of being everybody's favorite doxy for the moment.

He almost let her up, but then suddenly pushed her down again. "No."

"No?"

"You're going to have to tell me what went wrong in that head of yours, or I'll never let you go back to the house. I'll have to keep you here."

She giggled. "Keep me *here*? On the riverbank?"

"Exactly." He wasn't the sort of man who changed his mind. And it didn't really matter, after all.

So she just blurted it out. "I know that I'm different from other ladies. And in some ways I'm grateful, but in other ways it all seems rather tiresome."

"Different in what way?" He let her go and rolled to the side, grabbing his breeches off a rock. His gray eyes weren't even sympathetic. He wasn't a sympathetic sort of man.

"You said I wasn't the Whore of Babylon, but sometimes I feel as if I am."

"Really?" That interested him. But she could see amusement too, in the gleam of his eyes under his eyelashes. It wasn't fair that a man should have such thick, dark lashes when she had to put black stuff on hers.

"I can't describe it," she said dispiritedly, sitting up. "I really must put my clothing back on, Villiers."

His scowl was so potent that she actually recoiled. He threw his breeches back down again.

"I'm sorry," she said after a second's pause. "Leopold."

"Leopold all the time, Eleanor. Never Villiers, to you."

"Leopold," she said gently, "you're marrying another woman. And I'm marrying Gideon."

He lay down and pulled her over, onto his body. He was so hot that she involuntarily shivered. "Then tell me what the hell you're thinking about," he growled. "Tell me and then we'll go off and live our perfect lives with our perfect spouses. Have you realized that we're both marrying extraordinarily beautiful people?"

She gave him a lopsided smile. "I hadn't thought of it that way."

"We are. Golden girls and boys, as Shakespeare has it."

"Is that one of the sonnets? I'm just reading them for the first time."

"No, it's from a play. *Golden girls and boys all must, like chimney sweepers, come to dust.* I've always thought it was a good motto for a duke to keep in mind."

"So you count yourself among the golden boys?"

"Not when it comes to beauty."

"But dukes are golden," she said. "I see that."

"Strip away the title and I'm as brutish as a chimney sweep. People like Astley carry their nobility on their face."

"Is that why you dress so extravagantly?" Eleanor asked. She was oddly balanced on his body, her breasts squished into his chest, her elbows on either side of him. But she was comfortable.

"No," he said slowly. And then: "Perhaps. But you were going to confess your dark fear that you're really the ducal version of a palace whore. And I have to admit that I'm really curious."

He was laughing again, if only with his eyes, so she leaned down to give him a reproving nip, but they started kissing and somehow she lost track of her chastisement. She only slowly came back to herself, from that heated, tender place his kisses took her.

"I feel like a doxy," she said to him, not even whispering. "I lured Gideon into making love all those years ago, you know. I made him do it."

"You would have had to, given that he takes himself so seriously. Too much attention to manners turns a man into a judicious bore," Leopold said, pushing her so she was sitting on his stomach. "I'm listening breathlessly, but meanwhile, if you felt like edging back just a tad?"

She grasped what he was getting at and could feel her cheeks flaming. "Have you no shame?" she asked, curious, not reprimanding.

"Shame has nothing to do with it," he said promptly. "Warn me some more about your seductive self, and meanwhile I'll show you what I have in mind."

"You make me sound so foolish," Eleanor said, covering her face with her hands.

He pulled them down. "I shouldn't make fun. You slept with the inestimably tedious Gideon, who doubtless credited you with every spark of passion that ignited between you. Because that way he could stop himself from feeling any blame."

"Well . . ." Eleanor said.

"And by blaming *you* for every rule the two of you broke, he could walk away from you and marry someone else. Because you made him uncomfortable, Eleanor. All that passion, and he's nothing more than a dry husk after all."

"You mustn't say that," she protested. "You're talking about my fiancé."

He made a rude gesture. "And then I came along, and we're like tinder and spark, the two of us. But you measured me by his ashes and thought I was crediting you with being the courtesan of my dreams."

"You did say . . ." Eleanor whispered, feeling herself turn even pinker.

"I said that it was the best sex I ever had. I didn't say you were the best lover I ever had."

She scowled at him.

"You're getting the hang of it," he said, drawing his hands slowly over her breasts. She looked down at his hands. They were large, and darker than her skin. They shaped her breasts, played with them with exactly the right mix of tenderness and strength.

"What should I have done?" she asked.

"Are you genuinely curious, or are you going to fall into a pit of despair and decide that you are the *worst* courtesan in all of England?"

"I'm not a courtesan," she pointed out.

"No. You're an utterly delectable woman, with the most gorgeous breasts in Christendom."

His voice was darker, lower. "What should I have done?" she persisted.

"Touch *me*," he said. "You kept your hands on my shoulders, more or less."

"Oh." She colored. "I didn't think . . ."

"You didn't think I'd like to be touched, because that fool Astley had a poker up his arse about it. But I don't. I want you to touch me everywhere." Suddenly his hands were around her waist, picking her up, easing her back down.

She squeaked, but it was so much easier this time. She felt soft and wet. He thrust into her with a groan that sent a bird flying from the bushes beside them.

Neither of them moved for a moment. Their breath was harsh.

"Would you like me to touch you like this?" she said, circling his nipple with one finger.

"Hmm. That's not terrible but it's not great either," he said. "What *else* might you do with that finger?"

He was teasing her again, so she pinched him as a rebuke, and his breath caught—and she learned something.

He recovered fast, though, and pulled her tighter, whispering, "Any more of that and this will be a very short encounter, princess." She didn't want that, and neither did he. So he gave her one of the kisses that made her feel as if she were both drowning and catching on fire, all at once.

"I want you to lick me all over," he said, hoarse in her ear. And he started to move.

It took a minute for what he was saying to sink into her mind, and then she suddenly imagined herself on her knees before him, as he had been before her, making him groan and cry out, as he had to her.

"I'd like that," she whispered.

His fingers were gripping her hips, but she could feel the fire clamping down so soon, too soon. "Oh, Leopold," she said helplessly, running her fingers through his hair. "I can't touch you now, I can't because . . ." But whatever she was going to say was lost in a wave of pure, violent pleasure.

She came back to herself slowly to find that he was still there, still . . . with her.

"A courtesan would never come before her client," Leopold said in her ear. "And if she did, she'd have to come again, just to make up for it."

She would have laughed but she was too tired.

"There are other things I'd like you to do," Leopold said, his voice like a velvet whip. And he started to tell her. In detail.

She came twice more before he finally conceded that perhaps she might, just might, achieve some modicum of skill such as a real courtesan had.

But she didn't care what he said, because he cried out when he came, cried her name in such a way that she threw away all those fears.

She was no Whore of Babylon.

"Eleanor," he said again, afterwards. And held her very tightly. Just that: "Eleanor."

It was enough.

# Chapter Twenty-four

That night at supper Lisette talked of nothing but the treasure hunt to take place two days hence. Her plate looked like a small boat adrift in a sea of foolscap, on which were scrawled notes and lists. For the most part Villiers, Eleanor, Anne, and the duchess simply allowed the monologue to burble forth. There was unspoken agreement in the room that Lisette's enthusiasm was like a fever, and should be treated with extreme caution.

"Everyone in the county will be here, of course. *You* will have a particularly enjoyable time, Eleanor," Lisette said, beaming. "Not only will Sir Roland and his parents attend, but I invited the Duke of Astley to return and he said that he may well do it. His late wife's great-aunt is only an hour's ride from here, and he thought to return for the treasure hunt."

Eleanor's mother frowned. "That is a remarkably inappropriate idea. It has been barely a week since his wife died."

"It's for charity," Lisette said blithely. "No one expects him to stay in the house weeping."

"They may not expect tears, but they expect a modicum of observance," the duchess said acidly. But her comment didn't have the usual force to which she normally gave even the smallest impropriety. The surgeon had pulled her tooth, but the pain lingered, and she was treating it with laudanum. Which had the pleasant effect of making her lose about half of what made her a duchess, as Eleanor saw it.

Her Grace was a far more agreeable companion in her current state.

Lisette ignored her, simply plucking a paper from the mess in front of her. "I wrote all the clues for the treasure hunt last night. Shall I read them aloud to you?"

"Absolutely not," Anne said without particular inflection. "Are the children meant to read the clues to themselves? I very much doubt that they are literate."

"Of course they can read," Lisette said. "They receive classes in reading, writing, and deportment every day except Sunday."

"How do you know?" Eleanor asked.

"I'm on the Ladies' Committee of the orphanage," Lisette said, glancing at her with a trace of irritation. "I've been reading the schedule of their activities for years. The Committee insists that all the girls learn to read. I myself have urged the acquisition of a musical education, though to this point they do little more than sing."

"Mrs. Minchem may have claimed the children were being taught reading, but did they learn, or did they spend all their time making buttons?" Eleanor asked.

"Please," Lisette said with a little shudder. "I can't bear such disagreeable subjects. Mrs. Minchem is gone, and I hope we can simply forget these unpleasant events."

Eleanor found herself looking at Lisette with real dislike, and bit her tongue. Certainly Lisette should have made those tours of the orphanage. But likely, Mrs. Minchem would have kept the disturbing truth out of sight anyway.

"How are the orphans doing now?" Villiers asked, breaking into the cool little silence that followed Lisette's speech. Not that Lisette had even noticed; she kept scribbling on the pieces of paper spread around her plate.

"Oh, very well!" Lisette replied. "The baker's wife from the village has moved in temporarily. The Ladies' Committee is going to hire a new headmistress. In the meantime, I'm arranging everything myself. It will be just fine, I'm sure."

Eleanor hated to be such a doubting Thomas. But it seemed to her that someone energetic and truly directed was needed to head up the orphanage. Whereas Lisette was energetic in bursts, generally only when she became obsessed with a project, as she was now. The treasure hunt was all she could speak of.

"Do you think that fifty pounds is enough?" Lisette was asking.

"Fifty pounds?" the duchess asked. "What for?"

"The first child to bring back all four items will win fifty pounds," Lisette explained. "It's enough to set her up in an apprenticeship."

"That's a very generous thought," Villiers said.

Lisette beamed at him. "I would love to fund all of the orphans, but I don't have enough pin money. Luckily, I rarely spend it, so I have enough for one orphan this time."

The worst of it was that she meant it. Lisette would readily give all her money to the orphans. Eleanor found herself picking at her food and letting the discussion whirl around her. Villiers threw in fifty pounds for another prize. She was rather surprised when her mother offered a third prize, but put it down to the effect of laudanum together with the general air of virtue around the table.

"I spend all my pin money on gowns," Anne said. "Though I hate to lower the altruistic tone by admitting it."

"I must ask Aunt Marguerite if she would sponsor an orphan as well," Lisette was saying.

"Lady Marguerite is an eccentric," the duchess murmured. She was starting to look rather more befuddled than at the start of the evening.

"Mother," Eleanor said, "I'm not sure that wine and laudanum are a good mix."

"But I feel better. So—So much better. Really, so much better."

"You're three sheets to the wind," Lisette commented.

"What did you say?" the duchess asked, peering at her.

"You're totty," Lisette said, louder. "Top-heavy. Sluiced over."

"That's enough," Her Grace said, standing up with just a mild waver. "You always were a rude little girl, and you've only become worse. I can't abide you." And with that, she left.

Anne was grinning behind her napkin, but Villiers's face was utterly expressionless. "I'm sorry, Lisette," Eleanor said into the silence that greeted the slam of the door. "I think the laudanum and wine are influencing my mother's temperament."

"My mother always said that your mother was small-minded," Lisette said cheerfully.

Eleanor wasn't sure how to speak to that assessment, so she returned to her *sole à la venitienne*.

"Did you know that your children plan to participate in the treasure hunt, Leopold?" Lisette asked.

He looked up, rather startled. "Will they indeed?"

"Tobias at least." She returned to her list.

"How exactly will the hunt work?" Villiers asked.

"Each clue leads you to a location, and tells you to bring back an object. We'll give out all four clues at once; that way the children won't end up just trooping around after each other."

"Won't Tobias have an advantage over the other children, since he has been living here for several days?" Eleanor asked.

"Perhaps," Lisette said. "But I'm sure that he will be a fine candidate for an apprenticeship."

"Tobias does not need an apprenticeship," Villiers stated.

"Of course he does," Lisette said, not really listening. "He's a clever boy. You could apprentice him to a violin maker, for instance. He might create wonderful instruments. He has lovely fingers."

"I plan to give him an estate worth ten thousand pounds a year."

Eleanor took a sip of her wine. Apparently, Leopold had forgotten to share a few details of his anticipated home life with his fiancée. But Lisette merely shrugged. She was always easygoing—unless you crossed her.

"Tobias will not participate in the treasure hunt," Villiers stated.

Lisette's brows drew together. "Of course he will. He's just the right age to win, and he's already excited about it. You can't disappoint the boy. I was in the nursery this morning and he talked of nothing but the hunt."

"Tobias talked of nothing else?"

Eleanor knew what Villiers meant. Tobias was eminently his father's son: he would never babble.

"In his own particular fashion," Lisette said airily.

"It's not appropriate for him to compete against orphans to win fifty pounds," Villiers pointed out.

"I know!" Lisette exclaimed, clapping her hands. "If he wins, you can simply tell Tobias that he can't keep the money."

"You might want to inform him of that salient fact ahead of time," Anne noted. It seemed to Eleanor that her sister was enjoying the dinner a good deal more than she herself was.

"I will instruct him that it would be improper for him to participate," Villiers said, accepting a partridge served on a *croustade* from the footman.

Lisette huffed but went back to her list.

"What sort of things are the children supposed to fetch?" Anne inquired.

"I told you. An egg from the henhouse, that sort of thing." Impish pleasure lit up Lisette's face. "But they have to bring the egg home without breaking it!"

"And when will the treasure hunt begin?"

"As soon as Aunt Marguerite arrives," Lisette said. "And my father, of course."

Eleanor resolutely turned up the corners of her mouth into something approximating a smile.

"I won't say a word to Marguerite about the Duke of Astley's clandestine visit," Lisette said, turning to her. "Though of course you'll want to tell everyone, I'm sure."

"Actually, no," Eleanor said. Villiers's head swung up and she avoided his eyes. "His Grace's whereabouts are his own business."

"You'll disappoint the gossip lovers," Lisette said, looking back and forth between two pieces of foolscap. "Do you think that the winning orphan should be crowned in gold or with laurel leaves?"

"Gold?" Eleanor asked, still avoiding Villiers's eyes.

"How on earth would you manage that, Lisette?"

"Well, there is an old crown in the west wing," she said. "It's locked up, but of course I could get it out. I think Queen Elizabeth left it here when she was on progress years ago. Something like that."

"Your family never returned it?" Anne asked. "You'd think that Queen Elizabeth would have missed the crown."

"Apparently there is some sort of letter she wrote in the library, asking for the crown back, but my ancestor pretended he'd never seen it. I'm due in the nursery to say good-night to your little girls, Leopold. Do come with me."

He looked down at his half-eaten partridge. "I'm still eating."

"You can finish later," Lisette said cheerfully, holding out her hand.

"Anne and I don't mind if you both leave," Eleanor put in, without being asked. "I'll just finish my plate and retire upstairs."

"Well, I do mind," Villiers said coolly. "If you must leave the table, Lisette, you might ask Lady Eleanor or Mrs. Bouchon to act as hostess in your place."

Lisette laughed, but there was a dangerous edge there, an edge that Eleanor remembered from tantrums of years ago. "Why on earth would I adhere to such stuffy rules? I don't run my household that way! It's time to say good-night to the girls, so I shall go. And I know that you want to come with me."

"I don't," he said flatly, looking up at her.

Her hand dropped.

"I wish to finish my fowl, and then I plan to have some of that excellent lamb that Popper has on the side table," Villiers said. "And after that I shall likely have some sugared plums, since I see them waiting as well."

There was a dangerous, trembling moment when peace hung in the balance. But then Lisette's face cleared and she burst out laughing. "You men!" she said, half shrieking with laughter. "You're completely worthless if you haven't finished your meal. I know that." She shook her head. "My papa is exactly the same. Cross as a bear until he's had his morning tea and toast."

"Exactly," Villiers said, taking a bite of fowl. "Do give the children my best."

"I'll tell them you'll be upstairs in ten minutes," she said blithely, trotting out the door.

"I won't—" he said. But she was gone.

"Popper," Villiers said to the butler, "wait until Lady Lisette has left the nursery, and then inform the children that I will visit them in the morning, just as I told them a short while ago, would you?"

"Of course, Your Grace," Popper said.

Eleanor allowed a footman to take away her sole, since it was rather salty to her taste, and accepted a slice of Milanese flan in its place.

"That was awkward," Villiers said after a time.

"Lisette has never cared much for eating," Eleanor said.

"Yes," Villiers said thoughtfully. "I, on the other hand, care a great deal for eating. You seem to share my preference."

Eleanor was instantly conscious that she was far more curvy than Lisette, and likely could stand to lose some weight.

"Do you suppose that the Duke of Astley will really return for the treasure hunt?" Anne asked.

Eleanor felt a deep certainty that he would. In her opinion, Gideon had gone slightly mad. He had always been so prudent and principled . . . but no longer.

"Of course he will," Villiers said. "He's in love."

"In love," Anne said, as if tasting the words. "What an extraordinary concept for such a tiresome man. You know," she said, turning to Eleanor, "I really do owe both you and him an apology."

"I can't think why," Eleanor said, endeavoring to end the conversation the way their mother surely would have.

"I told you that the man never loved you enough, that he was a weak-chinned milksop. I was obviously wrong."

"Did you indeed?" Villiers said. "Interesting."

"As I said, I was wrong," Anne said, ignoring him. "The fact that Astley snapped back to your side shows that he does love you—is *in* love with you, in fact. How romantic."

"Yes, very," Villiers chimed in.

Eleanor just concentrated on eating her flan. She had wished, years ago, that Gideon was brave enough to risk his reputation in order to marry her rather than Ada. She couldn't have asked for more than what he was doing now. If he appeared at that treasure hunt, and particularly if he showed a marked preference for her, the scandal would ricochet across the *ton*.

"At this rate, everyone will be discussing the treasure hunt for the next month," Anne said, confirming Eleanor's anxiety. "I am very happy that I accompanied you. I shall be *so* popular."

"Perhaps we should give Mother an extra laudanum dose that morning," Eleanor said. And she was half-serious.

"If Astley has decided that you are worth more than the world's opinion," Villiers said, his voice very even, "your mother will simply have to get used to that fact. I don't expect he will wait for a full year of mourning before marrying you."

"He must," Eleanor said firmly. "He's Ada's only close family member, since her father passed away last year."

"He won't."

"Why not?" Anne put in. "My sense is that he is making sure Eleanor doesn't end up married to you while his back is turned. But he seemed genuinely fond of his wife, in a lukewarm kind of way."

"Astley is in the grip of passion," Villiers said. "Yes, I will take some of that lamb now, Popper. Thank you."

"Passion needn't last more than a week," Anne said with her usual cynicism.

Villiers glanced at Eleanor. "It will in this case."

"A tiresome subject of conversation," Eleanor said. "How are your daughters settling in, Villiers?"

But Anne wasn't diverted. "Why do you think Astley won't settle down and wait once he is certain that Eleanor won't marry you?"

"Because he's had a few years to realize what he threw away."

Back to the immeasurable charms of the Whore of Babylon, Eleanor thought dismally.

Anne was relentless. "What exactly do you think he's realized?"

"He thinks that there's no reason to eat breakfast unless Eleanor is there to give him that silly wide grin of hers. He wants to have an argument with her just so he can kiss her into a good mood again. He wants to sleep with her every night, see her holding a baby with brandy-colored hair like hers."

Eleanor's mouth fell open.

"He wants her forever," Villiers continued. Their eyes met and his were as cool as ever. "He can't bear the idea that she might ever love another man. I'd bet my entire estate that he will arrive tomorrow."

Anne sighed. "If I wasn't so prodigiously fond of my husband, I'd probably fall in love with you just for that description, Villiers."

Eleanor's mind was whirling. If his face hadn't been so impassive, so composed, she would have thought . . .

"Since you inquired about my daughters," he said, turning to Eleanor, "Lisette spent several hours with them today. I expect they will be very sad when we return to London."

"You ought to leave soon, before she tires of them," Anne said, proving her voice could be just as emotionless as Villiers's.

"That seems an unnecessarily unkind assessment," Villiers said. "I believe that Lisette genuinely enjoys the girls. And she is looking forward to being their mother."

Eleanor shot Anne her most ferocious look, the one copied from their mother. Anne twitched an eyebrow but said in a sweetly musical voice, "Of course it will all be different this time, Villiers. I quite forgot that the two of you are to be married."

"Don't try for a life on the stage," Villiers said flatly.

"I think we should go back to discussing Astley," Anne said. "That's a far more fascinating subject than your marital mishaps."

"There is no marriage yet," he snapped.

"Then we can save the discussion of your unhappiness for the next time we meet," she said brightly.

Eleanor rose. "If you'll excuse me."

"Do tell me that you're going to succor some orphans," Anne said, fluttering her eyelashes. "Or perhaps you plan to distribute food among the starving villagers?"

"I am retiring to my chamber," Eleanor said, with what she considered a masterful control of her temper. "I plan a tedious night with a bath and my book."

"Ah, Shakespeare's sonnets," Villiers said. "Love that lasts ages, into which category we must now place the Duke of Astley. A good choice."

Eleanor managed to get herself out of the room without saying something she might later regret.

The two people remaining at the dining table stared at each other.

Then Villiers looked at Popper and jerked his head, so the butler and his footmen quickly left.

"A touch of the bourgeois," Eleanor's sister said mockingly. "I didn't know you cared about servants' talk, Duke."

He ignored that. "I was under the impression that you were not in favor of my suit."

"What suit?" Anne said. "You're marrying Lisette. And, in case I haven't said it already, congratulations. Your life is certainly going to be interesting."

He narrowed his eyes.

"All those children," she said innocently. "What a responsibility. It'd be one thing if you were planning to bundle them all off to the country with fifty pounds and a package of bread and cheese, but to bring them up as nobility? To pitch them onto the civilized world as if birth and illegitimacy didn't matter?"

"I know they matter."

"Well, of course, they don't matter to Lisette."

He didn't know why he was defending himself to Anne, whom he hardly even knew. He had a flash of nostalgia for the old Villiers, the one who tolerated no insolence of any kind. The duke who was coolly uninterested in anyone's opinion except his own.

What had happened to him? He had given Mrs. Bouchon a look that would have silenced anyone from the queen to a scullery maid, and she paid him no heed.

"That is precisely why Lisette will be a perfect mother

for them," he said, wading into the sort of explanations he never would have made a mere year ago. "She cares nothing for the formalities of the *ton*, for its strictures and rules."

"She can't *afford* to care for them," Anne said. "She is considered mad."

"She's not mad," Villiers said sharply. "She seems eminently sane to me."

"I agree," Anne said, rather surprisingly. "I've known Lisette for years, and I've never considered her to be cracked. Not in the way that Barnabe Reeve went mad. Did you ever know him? You must be about the same age."

"Yes," Villiers said, placing his fork and knife precisely on his plate. "Reeve told me when we were both at Eton that he thought he might be able to fly someday. At the time, I considered it a boyish ambition that I rather shared. His later conviction that he was growing wings was a surprise."

"So, there's madness like Reeve's, and then there's Lisette."

"There is no comparison," Villiers said. "None."

"Reeve doesn't listen to the people who tell him repeatedly that people rarely, if ever, grow wings. Lisette doesn't listen to people who tell her anything that she doesn't want to hear."

"The difference between will and wings is the difference between madness and its opposite," Villiers pointed out.

"Exactly." She beamed at him. "Reeve thinks he can grow wings and he can't. Lisette thinks she can spend her life doing exactly as she wishes, no matter the amount of human wreckage she leaves behind her—and she can. *That* is the difference, my dear Villiers."

One had to say that Eleanor's sister understood a good exit line. She hopped to her feet and dropped into a deep curtsy. "Your Grace."

Villiers stood, but only because the rules of society were drilled into him. They were second nature at this point.

He remained standing even after she left the room.

Until it occurred to him that Eleanor was in her bedchamber. And she was likely taking a bath. That ridiculous excuse for a man, Astley, was returning for the treasure hunt, and that was—

That was very soon.

# Chapter Twenty-five

Eleanor lay in the bath once again staring at her book of sonnets, but only because that's what she had told everyone she was going to do. She hated Shakespeare. What did he know about real human relationships? About how complicated they were?

*Love alters not with his brief hours and weeks . . .* Perhaps he was right about that, but it was all so much more complex than that simple sentence promised. Gideon still loved her. He did. Shakespeare said that love *looked on tempests and was never shaken.*

Yet hers was shaken. There was no other way to describe it. Her love had altered. All these years she'd been loving Gideon, and not allowing herself to be angry at him for his cowardice, for not loving her as deeply as she loved him.

But it came down to it, *she* was the one lacking in true depth of feeling.

After a while, tired of trying to sort it all out, she

dropped the book to the floor by the bath. Then she realized it might get wet, and shoved it so hard that it spun under the bed and disappeared.

She wasn't even surprised when the door to the balcony silently opened. It was a relief, really.

Villiers—*Leopold*—wasn't in love with her, so she didn't have to align her feelings for him with the claims made in a love sonnet. She could just enjoy being indecent. Shameful. Outrageous.

When she didn't hear anything more after the soft click of the door, she pulled one leg slowly out of the water and pointed her toe. She had nice legs, if she said so herself. She was particularly fond of the roundness of her kneecap.

After discovering one had a shallow soul, it was very reassuring to be able to retreat to the solid reality of a kneecap.

Though she'd heard nothing, a pair of burning lips suddenly pressed the left side of her neck. She obligingly bent her head to the right to give him more access, and two hands slid around her from behind and cupped her breasts.

"Look what I found." His voice was a low rumble at her ear. "A brassy baggage, waiting in her bath for a man to wander by so she can entice him with her skills." The odd thing was that the sound of his voice sent heat to her legs even faster than the sight of his hands caressing her breasts, even faster than *feeling* him caress her.

"Villiers," she said, dropping her head back against his shoulder and ignoring his foolish comment.

He bit her ear, and growled. "What did you call me?"

It was a command, a brand, a thrilling display of domination and authority. She felt her mouth curve. "Leslie."

One hand slid over her stomach.

"Try again."

"Landry."

He snorted and his hand slid down another few inches, hovering. Eleanor just stopped her hips from arching toward him. Inside, she kept thinking, *Please, please, please . . .*

"Leopold," she whispered. "Leo."

He turned his head and caught her in a kiss, an erotic, dizzying kiss that was so absorbingly like a conversation that she didn't even realize at first that his hand was between her legs. Then it all blended together into the taste of his tooth powder, flavored with something—cinnamon, perhaps—and the smell of him, and the dancing, sleek power of those wicked fingers.

It wasn't until after he made her arch so high that water rolled off her body, until she cried his name aloud, until her body flared into brief, blazing perfection, that she remembered Gideon.

Gideon was back. He was in love with her. Why was she lying in a bath waiting for a different duke to prowl illicitly through the door?

What sort of woman did that make her?

Obviously Leopold was wasting no time thinking about Gideon, or his own fiancée, for that matter. Before her knees had regained strength, he bundled her out of the bath, wrapping her in a towel. She swayed on her feet, her body still singing with pleasure, her mind confusedly trying to sort through her moral iniquities.

"No going to sleep," he muttered at her.

"That felt so good. I could do it all night."

He laughed. "Just what a man most wants to hear."

"Untrue," she said, opening her eyes. He had put her on the bed and was rubbing her hair dry with a towel.

"I assure you that it is."

"Men don't want their wives to be too desirous," she said flatly. "I believe it makes them nervous."

"Never having been married, I couldn't say. But just in case you're right, I'm glad we're not married," Villiers said, throwing aside the towel and standing back as if he were a pirate about to ravish a fainting maiden.

"Don't be like Lisette, and pretend that rules don't matter," she said, raising her head and then letting it flop back down because he wasn't looking at her face. "They matter. We're not supposed to make love like this without marriage, because marriage matters."

"I agree. It does."

She studied him for a moment, but he had bent over so he could run his lips over her ribs, and tease the curve of her breast. He wasn't following the conversation very closely.

"Immoral, illegal—and yet so—beautiful." She sighed.

"Come on, princess." Villiers pulled her upright.

She hadn't realized that he was wearing a wrapper. It was deep black velvet, embroidered with pearl arabesques.

"I don't like this garment," she said, tracing an embroidered design with her finger.

"I didn't buy it for you."

She eased the thick velvet apart in the front. Suddenly she wasn't in the least sleepy. Leopold's chest was broad and ribbed with muscle. He didn't say a word, so she put her face against him and just inhaled.

He smelled wonderful. Faintly of starched linen. But also of decadence, and privacy, and plain dealings.

Even better, of private sin.

She slid her hands inside the robe and the fabric fell over her arms, too thick, too luxurious. "I don't like this wrapper," she murmured. She found his nipple and licked it. The tiniest shiver passed through his frame.

"I didn't ask for sartorial advice," he said. He managed

to sound indifferent, but she wasn't fooled by him any longer. Leopold had perfected a blasé, ducal manner. But he wasn't indifferent.

"You care," she said, nipping him with her teeth because he had done the same to her. And, she discovered, he liked it as much as she had.

So she slid her hand down to his bottom. It was firm and muscled and about as different from her rear as it could possibly be. She kept kissing him, exploring all the curves and angles of his body, the places that made him suddenly draw in breath, or sway toward her.

A brutal-looking white scar marked his right side. "Your duel?" she asked, tracing it with her fingers.

"It doesn't seem large enough, does it?"

"For what?"

"For death."

She reached out and pressed her lips to the mark. "I'm so glad you didn't die."

"At this moment," he said, and the fervency in his voice couldn't be mistaken, "so am I."

She sipped and nipped and experimented until he was muttering something that sounded like a prayer or a curse, but with her name tangled in . . . and then with a quick twist, she rose and pushed him back on the bed.

"I need to—" he gasped.

"Not yet," she said, grinning.

"Enough practice for you," he said, grabbing her wrists.

"I—" He seemed intent on getting up, so she cut him off. "There may not be a tomorrow, Leo. You know that."

He shook his head as if to clear it. "What are you talking about?"

"My mother, Anne, and I will leave for London in two or three days at the most."

His grip tightened. "You can't."

She waited a split second and realized he wasn't going to say more. "I must," she said, pulling out of his grip. He let her go, of course.

But she wouldn't drown in the sudden bleakness that threatened to engulf her. It wasn't as if they were in love, that unshakable, unalterable thing. She could alter, and she would alter. Once she had slaked herself with him.

His brow was drawn, and he looked as if he were trying to coerce his foolish male brain into figuring out what she was thinking. So she slid down to her knees, which put her right where she needed to be.

He tasted hot, and male, and faintly like soap. Even putting her lips on him made heat shoot to her groin. It wasn't because of his taste, or the fact that he felt like heated honey against her lips.

It was the power of it, if she were honest. Leopold obviously stopped thinking, was unable to think. Every time she tightened her lips, he let out a groan. In just a few minutes he seemed to be struggling for breath. Every time he groaned, a scalding wave of desire washed down her legs.

Suddenly his strong hands caught her and he pulled her up to face him. All the cool self-possession was gone from his face, from his eyes. He kissed her urgently, desperately, falling back on the bed and pulling her on top of him. The French letter took a moment and then she slid down, taking him as if they had always belonged together, as if the rhythm they forged was the rhythm of life.

She braced her arms on either side of his head and looked down through the screen of her hair. "I know why you wear such elaborate clothing," she told him.

He wasn't listening. Instead he thrust up, his fingers biting into her shoulders. She fell for a moment into voluptuous, toe-curling pleasure, and then recovered. "It's because you're hiding your eyes," she whispered.

"What?"

"You don't want anyone to see your eyes, so you dress like a peacock."

He grunted and thrust up again, sending a shock of white heat through her body. "I suppose you think you're very clever?"

"I *am* very clever," she said. "For example, it takes a clever woman to figure *this* out . . ."

What she did then made the Duke of Villiers actually cry out.

And those eyes, the eyes he hid from the world behind a screen of ice and a mask of gold thread . . . they were almost black with desire and yet he never closed them.

He kept looking at her, and she kept looking down at him.

"I know what is dangerous about you," he said suddenly, a few shuddering moments later.

"What?" she gasped.

"You see me too clearly." He flipped her over in one smooth motion, pinned her down, bit her lip. "You're damned dangerous, Eleanor, Lady Eleanor."

It made her feel shy . . . to be dangerous for other reasons than her own desire.

"My Eleanor," he whispered.

And she didn't correct him because her heart was singing the same tune, and there was no need to speak about it.

# Chapter Twenty-six

*Knole House, country residence of the Duke of Gilner*
*June 21, 1784*

By the next morning Lisette had lost interest in the treasure hunt. The piles of paper had disappeared. At luncheon she airily announced that the housekeeper would be handling all the rest of the details, from the children's whereabouts, to the refreshments, to the—

"All of it," she said, with a wave of her hand. "I shall spend the day in the nursery with Phyllinda and Lucinda."

"Those are not their names," Villiers said with a distinct chill in his voice. "Mrs. Minchem assigned those names."

"I must call them something," Lisette said, reasonably enough. "The girls do not seem to know other names."

"Villiers, you can perform a truly paternal action," Anne put in. "You can name your children."

In answer, the duke got up and left the room.

"I positively detest such bad manners," Lisette said.

Eleanor detested the pain she'd seen in Leopold's eyes.

"I have half a mind not to marry him after all," Lisette continued fretfully. "Marguerite returns this afternoon and I doubt she will be pleased."

"What will your father say?" Eleanor asked.

Lisette hunched a shoulder. "He won't be pleased either."

"Don't they wish for you to marry?"

"No." Lisette pushed her potatoes to the side. "They don't."

"Because . . . because of what happened years ago?" Eleanor thought back to the scandal that had ended her mother's visits to the estate, and coincided with the *ton*'s perception of Lisette's madness.

"I can't have children," Lisette said, darting off on a tangent, as she was wont to do.

"I'm sorry," Eleanor said.

"Leopold has a family already, so he won't care. If only that boy Tobias wasn't part of it. I don't like him. He thinks he's clever but in fact he's only rude. I can quite see bringing the girls up as ladies, but that boy will never be a gentleman."

"The fact that Tobias doesn't care for others' opinions makes him only more akin to a gentleman," Eleanor suggested.

"I shall marry Leopold, but I'll tell him that the boys have to be apprenticed. That's reasonable. There are three girls, or perhaps four. More than enough children for one household, given the number of maids they need and such."

"I don't think that Villiers will be happy with that bargain," Eleanor said.

Lisette suddenly laughed, but the sound was jarring, like bells falling to the ground. "Must you keep to such affectations?"

"Such as?"

"Calling him Villiers! Remember, I've seen the way he looks at you!"

She was in a dangerous state that Eleanor remembered from years ago. It would take only one unwary remark to send her off into a towering rage followed by a passionate fit of crying.

"I shall do my best to please you," Eleanor said. And she whisked out of the room.

# Chapter Twenty-seven

*Knole House, country residence of the Duke of Gilner*
*June 22, 1784*

The morning of the treasure hunt dawned bright and clear. Eleanor had gone to sleep puzzling over love, and woken up, thinking about the shape of Leopold's hands, and from the two constructed an understanding that made her sit up straight in bed.

Gideon was an exquisite male animal, a finely drawn, beautifully painted specimen with whom any healthy young woman would be hard put not to fall in love. Villiers—or Leopold, as she had taken to thinking of him in the inner recesses of her mind—had beautifully shaped thighs and a large nose and even larger parts that she ought to know nothing of . . . And he was infuriating, fiercely intelligent, and, in his own way, as ethical as Gideon.

Gideon followed rules with precision—at least until he discarded them in his pursuit of her. To him, life was properly lived if one followed the behest of an ethical watchman who combined the precepts of the Anglican church with the dictates of society.

But Leopold was doing something far more difficult: forging rules from the mistakes he had made. He was building an ethical life from the consequences of his not-always-ethical choices, and consciously pursuing a course designed to ameliorate the wrongs he had committed.

It was causing him no end of trouble, of course, given those six children. And it had to be said that his mistakes seemed to be more grossly evident in the world than those of other men: *six* children, after all. Though the sum total was, in fact, five, if one deducted Lady Caroline's contribution, Eleanor reminded herself.

Her own ethical standing was just as confused. She had flagrantly broken the most important precepts of church and society that pertained to women when she slept with Gideon the first time, though in her own defense, she scarcely remembered those rules in the tumult of first love.

She thought for a moment about the implications of the phrase *first* love. No matter: the point was that her youthful shame was compounded by her extraordinary folly in making love to the Duke of Villiers. One could not be more shameless than to do so in the out-of-doors.

The problem—the real problem—was that the rules governing women's behavior explicitly structured things so that women protected themselves from men. Because women were supposed to be designed along the lines of Ada: submitting to their husbands from a sense of duty, angelic in their desire to please.

She was out of bed and drawing back the drapes covering the door to the balcony, just so she could see the two chairs Leopold had placed there, before she realized that there should be no shame.

She had hurt no one. Gideon was none the worse for her seduction—indeed, she had the distinct feeling that he would consider himself the better for it. She had not injured Leopold by seducing him—or yielding to his seduction, however one wished to put it. And Leopold had not injured her, either.

She knew instinctively that Gideon was already in his coach on the way to the house, having said a hasty farewell to Ada's great-aunt. And Leopold was in the chamber next to hers, and she had a shrewd suspicion that he had felt as hungry and aching as she had the previous evening, when she'd crawled into her bed and found it woefully empty.

And she was sure of another thing too: that a life in which there was no reevaluation of beliefs and behavior was a life not worth living.

Both men, both dukes, were doing just that. Gideon was laying his reputation and his fortune at her feet, to make up for the error of having turned his back on her years earlier. And Leopold was marrying Lisette because he believed that she would be the better mother for the children he had carelessly brought into the world, without love or even great affection. With women whose names he seemed hardly to remember.

*That* was the problem, to Eleanor's mind. He would marry a woman without love, to nurture the children he had created without love.

It seemed wrong to her, deeply wrong, as surely as the way her own erotic impulses had never seemed wrong. It was almost a relief to feel something so strongly. At least she had *some* sort of moral compass, though it wasn't one of which the church or her mother might approve. Leopold did not love Lisette, so he should not marry her.

With a scratch on the door, Willa entered, full of household news. "Lady Lisette is tired of the very idea of the treasure hunt," she reported. "And she's not interested in the orphans anymore either, though her maid, Jane, says she will regain interest when it's time for the Ladies' Committee to meet. But right now she doesn't want to hear a word of them *or* Mrs. Minchem."

There was nothing surprising in that. "Has she a new passion, then?" Eleanor inquired.

"Why, it's those two little girls of the duke's," Willa said. "She was in the nursery with them for hours yesterday, playing as if she were a little one herself, so Jane says. She took breakfast with them today, and has started teaching the quieter one the lute. Phyllinda, I think her name is."

"How nice," Eleanor said.

"She's dressed them up as beautiful as if they were little daughters of the manor," Willa continued. "She had three seamstresses working at their costumes all night long."

"I'll wear that blue gown that Madame Gasquet had time to alter," Eleanor said, not wanting to think about Lisette's appropriation of the twins. "The one ordered by another customer."

Willa brought out the gown. "Lady Lisette insisted that each girl must have her own maid, which upset the housekeeper because she has only two downstairs maids now. Their hair is piled *that* high; the maids were given special wool pads to give height."

"Wool?" Eleanor exclaimed. "But that's so hot and the sun is already shining!"

"It's a bit strange because Lady Lisette herself doesn't ever wear such things, but she ordered the maids to dress the girls' hair with them. I hear the children aren't that pleased."

"Wait until the sun heats up that wool," Eleanor said.

"Master Tobias wants to know if he may take Oyster with him on the treasure hunt," Willa said.

"I suppose he may," Eleanor replied. "As long as he keeps Oyster out of Lisette's sight."

"Oh, he will. There's no love lost there, apparently. The little girls just dote on her, or so the nursery maid told me, but Master Tobias was quite snappish with her when she wanted the girls to sleep in her room for the night."

"Why on earth would she wish to do that?"

"She planned to tell them stories of fairies and goblins," Willa said. "Would you like this blue ribbon, my lady, or this dark green one?"

"The blue, please," Eleanor said. "Fairies and goblins?"

"Jane says that Lady Lisette often stays up all night long singing and playing her lute and such, and then she sleeps during the day."

"That must be difficult for the household."

"Everyone receives a generous gift on Boxing Day from the duke. Apparently he makes a joke of the fact that his household is better-paid that any other in the county: he says it's the 'Lisette Toll,' as if she were a toll road, you see."

"Has her father arrived yet?"

"Not yet. Lady Marguerite is here, though. She arrived just before breakfast. The squire's family will be coming for the day, and all the ladies on the orphanage committee. It's a proper fête! The house will be bursting at the seams."

"I believe my mother wishes us to leave after the treasure hunt," Eleanor said.

"Not now that the Duke of Astley has returned," Willa said with a knowing look in her eye. "He arrived two hours ago, practically at the crack of dawn, and Her Grace told her maid that we'd stay as long as he does. Mrs. Busy is cooking so you wouldn't believe, as it'll be a grand dinner tonight with Lisette's father here. He's almost never home, you know. They say he can't bear to see Lisette as she is. He never broke off that betrothal with the squire's son because he keeps hoping she'll change."

Eleanor digested that in silence. It was only when Willa had declared her to be quite ready that she asked, "What did Tobias say to Lisette, do you know?"

"He told her to stubble it because she'd give the girls nightmares," Willa said, laughing. "And the whole household is saying how Lisette has met her match at last, because she didn't have a word to say back to him. She knew that a spasm would just make him laugh at her, so she didn't bother, just left the room, and that was the end of her plan."

"I would guess that he will have no problem controlling Oyster during the treasure hunt," Eleanor said. "If he can manage Lisette, he can manage a naughty puppy."

She cast a look out the balcony door before going downstairs. The lawn was already dotted with the white gowns of the committee ladies, their lacy parasols making them look like daisies. The orphans in their blue pinafores were darting and running about, and Eleanor didn't think it was her imagination that they already looked heartier.

She didn't want to go downstairs. She wanted to avoid Gideon, and avoid her mother as well. She wanted to avoid Lisette, because she might be tempted into unkindness, if not violence. She wanted to avoid Roland, because she wasn't in a poetic mood, and she didn't particularly wish to meet his father's hopeful eyes, either.

But she couldn't hide. So she wandered downstairs just in time to see Lisette formally begin the hunt by ringing a little silver bell. A stage had been built in the back garden, and she was prancing about like the Queen of May, handing out flowers to all the children. Apparently the winning child wasn't to wear a gold crown, unless Lisette was planning to take it off her own head. She was wearing a small but unmistakably genuine crown; Eleanor couldn't believe that there were two such crowns in all of Kent.

"Titania, Queen of the Fairies," Roland said, appearing at her shoulder.

"I always pictured Titania clad in gauzy leaves with her hair loose," Eleanor said, giving him a smile.

"Titania was a termagant," Roland said, "and that's the crucial distinction. Remember how Shakespeare says that she fought with her husband so violently that all the corn rotted in the field?"

"You *are* unkind," Eleanor said, frowning at him.

"I will admit that I hadn't conceived of Titania's fairies as bastard children of a duke."

Phyllinda and Lucinda were standing on either side of Lisette, looking like small attendants, if not fairy ones. Their hair was piled so high that they appeared to be wearing airy beehives. They were both dressed in cloth of gold, which seemed utterly inappropriate for such a hot day, but their dresses did match Lisette's crown.

Still, what did she know about children? Perhaps they loved Lisette's reflected glory. Certainly the ladies from the orphanage committee were agog over the girls' beauty. And Lisette was rather carefully not identifying their lineage. Eleanor had a strong feeling that the good Christian members of the Ladies' Committee might not be quite so rapturous over Phyllinda's lovely eyes if they knew her parentage.

"No child is going to win the prize," Roland said disgustedly, looking up from the page of clues. "I wouldn't be able to solve them. Listen to this: *In marble walls as white as milk, lined with a skin as soft as silk, within a fountain crystal clear, a golden apple doth appear.*"

"What?"

"Wait, I'm not done. *No doors there are to this strong-hold, yet thieves break in and steal the gold. What am I?*"

"I haven't the faintest idea."

"I know that one, but only because my nanny used to tell it to me. The answer is, an egg. Lisette apparently expects the children to figure the riddle and then be able to find the henhouse and bring back an egg."

Eleanor shrugged. "I suppose she'll just give the prizes to whichever children solve one or two riddles, then."

"That will be Villiers's bastards," Roland said with a sneer.

"Why do you say so?"

"Because Lisette isn't playing fair, of course." He nodded.

Sure enough, Lisette was whispering in Lucinda's ear. The little girl dimpled up at her and patted her hand, and then ran off.

Eleanor discovered that she was smiling. The expression on Lucinda's face didn't display adoration, the way Willa had described. She would describe it as something altogether more knowing—and more manipulative. Well, what would she have expected? They were Villiers's daughters, after all.

She looked around again, trying to ignore the way Roland was standing too close to her. Gideon was basking in her mother's smiles. Lucinda had run directly from Lisette over to Tobias, who was lounging by the raspberry bushes. There was no sign of Oyster, to her relief. A great flock of orphans in blue pinafores were clustered together, puzzling over the clues; they seemed to be having as much trouble reading them as solving them.

Villiers was nowhere to be seen. It was ridiculous to find that the day lost its flavor simply because an errant duke had chosen not to participate in the frolic.

Just then a soft voice said, "Lady Eleanor." She looked down to find Phyllinda smiling up at her.

With precisely the same smile her twin had just used on Lisette.

"I don't know the answers," Eleanor said bluntly. "I can't help you."

Phyllinda's smile just broadened and she held up her hand. "Will you help me with something in the house, Lady Eleanor? Please?" The last *please* was tacked on with pitiful emphasis.

Eleanor could hardly say no, even given the fact that the child was clearly up to something. "What?" she asked.

Phyllinda leaned close and whispered, "It's private. To do with my petticoats."

Since, in her better moments, she was a lady, Eleanor didn't roll her eyes. Instead she took the hand Phyllinda was offering and followed her into the house. They passed Gideon, who cast a look at their linked hands and grew a little stiff.

"It's up here," Phyllinda said, lisping a bit.

Having a naturally suspicious mind, Eleanor thought back to the way Phyllinda spoke when she and her sister were first uncovered in the carriage. No lisp. One had to suppose that the lisp had been proven effective in outwitting adults susceptible to mindless sentiment.

"This is your bedchamber, isn't it?" Phyllinda lisped, stepping to the side. She was overacting terribly.

"Yes," Eleanor said, pushing open the door to her room and walking in. "What do you—"

It was with no great feeling of surprise that she heard the door shut behind her and a key turn in the lock. It seemed she had been given a reprieve from the spectacle, just as she wished. She pulled off her blue slippers and wiggled her toes, then strolled over and reached for the bell to ring for Willa, only to find that it had been cut off. Intrepid of them. One might even call it diabolical.

The only thing that made her remotely curious was *why*. She didn't present any particular threat to the children's desire to win the prizes donated by her mother, Lisette, and the Duke of Villiers. Of course she could go onto her balcony and call down to the crowd below. But it seemed ungracious, somehow.

So, taking advantage of the unscheduled opportunity, she lay down on her bed and listened to the hubbub of polite voices drifting from the garden. She didn't wake up until the door opened.

"I wondered where you were," she asked in a drowsy voice. "Did they just lock the door behind you, too?"

"Yes." Villiers sounded a bit testy.

"Perhaps the adults are being removed to allow more time for answering riddles," Eleanor offered, turning on her side and tucking a hand under her cheek. "In that case, we should expect Lisette to join us any moment."

He snorted and threw himself into an armchair. She was trying to remember her dream, because he had been in it. Oyster had thrown himself at her in his usual frenzied display of love, and—

"You were wearing a pinafore," she exclaimed. To a raised eyebrow, she explained, "In my dream. And," she added thoughtfully, "nothing else."

"I would like to have that dream about you, but I don't care for the thought of myself in a frock. You look tiresomely beautiful," Villiers observed. He stretched out his legs. "It's not that I mind being locked up with you, but what the devil are we doing in here?"

"I have no idea."

"I told Tobias that I would not allow him to win the prize."

"Well, that explains why you're here, then. I fail to see why I should suffer the same fate. Nor why we have to be together."

"You think that my son locked me in a room so that he could win fifty pounds, after I expressly forbade him to do so?" Villiers's voice was cold, so cold, but she knew him now. She knew to look past the utterly dazzling costume he was wearing, and past his chilly look, straight into his eyes. He was angry . . . he was a little hurt.

"He's just like you," she pointed out. "What he wants, he intends to get."

"I'm not like that. Well, I might be like that, but I don't lock people in rooms."

"Then you've learned something useful about your son. And I must say, if you didn't already know that he believes in shortcuts to winning, you haven't played knucklebones with him."

"You're the one who cheated," he pointed out.

"Only after prying the bones out from under his leg and then again from his sleeve. He's got those little girls of yours begging the answers from Lisette. Cheating, in other words."

He was silent a moment. And then, very un-ducally: "Devil take it!"

"That's parenthood," she said cheerfully. "If you don't lay down the rules the right way, the child simply slips the leash and does as she wishes. Just look at me. My poor mother has no idea what a hussy I am. She would be not only astonished, but affronted."

"I don't see why it's her fault that you succumbed to Gideon's blue eyes. Though may I add that I am astonished by the vapid shallowness with which he is basking in your mother's attentions?"

"Gideon does adore my mother. When his mother died, she became something of a substitute."

Villiers snorted. "Now what are we supposed to do?"

"I think we should probably prevent them from winning," Eleanor said, standing up and stretching. "That was a very nice nap."

"And just how do you suggest— Oh."

Eleanor went to the balcony door, pulled the key from the keyhole, and paused, looking over her shoulder. "You know, I think it might be best if you allow me to handle this."

Villiers got up, frowning. "Of course I will not—"

She didn't hear the rest, because she had closed the balcony door behind her and turned the key. Then she walked through Villiers's bedchamber, pausing for a moment to look at his silver-backed brushes, and went down the stairs.

It didn't take her long to find the three children; she just had to call for Oyster and then listen for his bark. They were inside the half-ruined folly, another of Lisette's abandoned projects.

"What are you three doing?" she asked, going down on one knee to greet Oyster.

Phyllinda's eyes grew very round. "How did you get out?"

"The balcony."

Tobias gave a quick look around.

"Your father is still locked in my room," she told him, answering his unspoken question.

His mouth fell open too, so she was faced with three astounded little faces. Inheritance was a truly amazing thing: they could not be anyone else's children. Not even given the fact that Tobias had cool gray eyes and the girls had lavender ones . . . it was the turn of their chins, the shape of their eyes, and some sort of shrewd, fierce intelligence.

"So why don't you tell me exactly what you're doing?"

"We're planning to win, of course," Lucinda said. Eleanor could see a dawning respect in her eyes. "Why did you lock the duke in?"

"I thought he might create more trouble than your plan merits," she said, giving Oyster a last pat and standing up. "So you want to win all three prizes."

"Fifty pounds each!" Phyllinda said with a little gasp.

"A lot of money," Eleanor agreed.

Tobias just waited, his eyes narrowed. He knew her reappearance meant trouble.

"How are you doing with the clues so far?" she asked.

Lucinda stepped back so Eleanor could see their collection. Tobias's velvet coat was crumpled into a nest that included, among other things, three rather dirty eggs. "We have all but one," she said, giving her the syrupy sweet smile that Lisette so favored.

"Stop that," Eleanor said sharply.

The smile froze.

"If you want to smile, smile. But spare me the acting. You don't do it very well. Now which riddle haven't you solved?"

"It doesn't make any sense," Tobias said reluctantly. "It's only two lines. *Little girl, little girl, where have you been?*" And then, *Gathering apricots to give to the queen*. We were about to go back to Lisette again because we don't know where to find an apricot. I don't think they even grow here. I've only seen one once."

"It's a nursery rhyme," Eleanor said. They all blinked at her. "A rhyme for children," she explained. Of course they hadn't learned any frivolous rhymes, given their childhoods. "Next line is, *Gathering roses to give to the queen.* The girl gives the roses to the queen, who gives her a big diamond as a reward. I suppose that Lady Lisette is the queen—she is wearing a crown—and you need to give her an apricot-colored rose."

"That's easy!" Lucinda said. "There's a load of roses around the side of the house."

"They're not the right color. She wants the ones by the river. Come on," Eleanor said.

They walked out of the folly and around the back of the house, Tobias carrying his precious cargo wrapped in his coat.

"Oh, there you are!" Gideon called, walking toward her. He didn't bother to acknowledge the children, just took her arm and brought her to a halt. "I've been looking for you everywhere. You missed the strawberries and cream."

"I'm sorry," she said, pleasantly enough, "I'm engaged at the moment. But I should be back in five minutes."

He didn't like it, but she gently pulled free and walked on. As they left the gardens and started down the path to the river, a small hand slipped into hers. Phyllinda was looking up at her, her eyes clear and her mouth unsmiling. "I don't like him."

"That's because he doesn't like you," Lucinda put in.

"He's a molly," Tobias said. "There's something ratty about him. Just stay away."

"Why ratty?" Eleanor inquired.

"He has big front teeth. You know how the duke looks a proper fright in those coats he wears?"

"I suppose you mean Villiers?"

"Yes, him. He's got awful taste, but all the same, when he looks at you, you know what he's thinking. Whereas that one looks a bit unhinged. Maybe he'll marry Lisette. She's the same."

Eleanor thought about it for a moment and then said,

"Your father is marrying Lisette, Tobias. So you mustn't say slighting things about her, particularly in front of Phyllinda and Lucinda."

"They're not *stupid*," he said.

They rounded the curve and arrived at the stream. "The roses grow over there," Eleanor said, pointing.

Lucinda started forward, of course, so she grabbed her arm. "That's straight up the rocks, and you can't do it in those clothes. Your hair alone would disbalance you. Tobias, you fetch three roses."

He was up the slope in a moment, and barring a bit of colorful language when he was introduced to the roses' vicious thorns, he was successful. "We've got everything!" he said triumphantly, pulling open his crumpled coat to add the roses. By some miracle the three eggs were intact.

"So you're going to claim the three prizes," Eleanor said genially.

"Yes." Tobias sounded guarded.

"And those other orphans, the ones Lucinda and Phyllinda lived with . . . they won't win."

"Not everyone can win," Tobias pointed out.

"There are those who would say that you *have* won. After all, your father intends to give you each ten thousands pounds when you reach eighteen years. Whereas the Janes and Marys and the other girls will go off to be ladies' maids."

Phyllinda had her hand in Eleanor's again. "At least they don't have to make buttons any longer."

"That's true. But they will never live in a grand house with their brothers and sisters. You do know that you have three more siblings, don't you?" And when Phyllinda and Lucinda nodded, "The Marys will go out to work because there is no one to take care of them. Whereas you have a father, and while he may have lost you for a while, he will *always* take care of you from now on, you know that."

"Bloody hell!" Tobias said.

"Not in front of your little sisters," she said, giving him a look.

"Sorry," he muttered.

"Jane-Melinda didn't solve a single clue because she can't read," Lucinda said. "She's awfully nice. I'll give her my egg and rose and stuff."

"A girl named Sarah-Susan told me where to find you in the sty," Tobias said. His tone was begrudging but accepting.

"We could give mine to Mary-Bertha," Phyllinda said. "Because once when Mrs. Minchem said that Lucinda couldn't have any breakfast *or* lunch, she kept some bread and gave it to us. Do you remember that, Lucinda?"

Her sister nodded, but Eleanor was having trouble speaking around the anger in her throat, so they just went up to the lawn in silence and found the girls in question.

Eleanor stood watching the excitement as the three little girls claimed their prizes, until she remembered that she had a duke locked in her room. Tobias seemed reconciled to losing; he was trying to train Oyster to walk on his hind legs, which was an anatomical impossibility, as anyone could have told him.

"I know why you locked your father up," she asked him, "but why did you lock me in as well? And why in my bedchamber?"

He looked up with an odd twist to his mouth. "I don't like Lisette."

She nodded. "I see."

"The old nanny told me that if a lady and gentleman are locked in a room together, they have to get married. Which doesn't make sense," he said frankly, "because if they want to be shaking the sheets, they don't need sheets to be doing it, if you know what I mean."

Clearly Tobias had seen more than he should have in his short life, but he didn't seem particularly scandalized.

"So you thought . . ."

"I'd rather you than her," he said. It wasn't much of an endorsement, but it felt good. "How'd you get out, anyway?"

"The balcony door was unlocked and no one had the faintest idea we were together, so your plan came to naught. And I do think that people do better to choose their own spouses. Your father wants to marry Lisette."

"And you want to marry that ratty duke?" His tone was indescribably scornful.

"Yes," she said rather faintly. "He's an old friend." She looked up and saw Gideon determinedly making his way across the lawn toward her, followed by her mother. "I had better let your father out now. Take care of Oyster."

She dashed into the house, pretending she didn't hear her mother calling.

Leopold was asleep. He had stripped off his coat and was lying sprawled out on her bed. She tiptoed across the carpet and stood next to him. He would never be beautiful, like Gideon. He was blunt and complicated, and still grieving for his brother.

She was in love with him.

Horribly, truly in love. The kind of love that wouldn't alter, ever, and wouldn't admit impediments.

Lisette was an impediment.

Gideon was another.

And frankly, Leopold was the third obstacle, given his professed intention to marry Lisette. Her love may not alter, but it wasn't going to succeed either.

She kicked off her slippers and then reached under her skirts to unhook her panniers and her petticoat. Unfortunately, she couldn't unlace her gown without help, so once she'd taken off her stockings, and left a heap of petticoats on the floor, she pulled up her skirts and climbed onto the bed.

Well, to be exact, she climbed on top of Leopold.

He grunted and pulled her down to him, and in that moment she realized that he hadn't been asleep, not all the time she stood watching him, and certainly not while she was undressing.

"Did you dream about me wearing nothing but a pinafore?" she asked. He was kissing her neck and seemed to be—from all signs—very happy to see her.

"No pinafore," he said. His voice had already taken on the wildness that was so opposite to his immaculately polished appearance as a duke. Her entire heart, her body, welcomed it. His fingers were . . . everywhere.

"Eleanor?" he asked, pulling his shirt over his head.

She didn't respond, just waited for him to throw off his breeches, grab a French letter, and then greedily took all of him.

"I didn't get to kiss you," he said, arching up with a look of fierce bliss that belied his complaint.

"Next time," she said, gasping. "I have decided not to marry Gideon."

His eyes were closed, but at that they opened. She put a hand over his mouth and rode him hard, but she couldn't divert him. His eyes stayed on her face, even as his body rose to meet hers.

"I know you want to marry Lisette," she told him, keeping her hand over his lips even though he was nipping her fingers. "And I honor your decision. I am not saying this because I want you to marry me."

Though she did, she did.

He managed to pull away her hand and she froze. "Say a word and I'll leave," she said. He shoved upwards and she easily evaded him. "Right now. I'll leave this room."

"It's *your* room!"

She took him with a wave of heat and pleasure, and lost track of her thoughts for a bit, but then remembered.

"I'm not trying to make you marry me," she said, gasping a little because he had picked up the pace.

"Why not?"

That couldn't be hurt in his eyes.

"Because you're doing something honorable," she said. "You feel that Lisette will make a better mother to your children. We're not children, Leopold. We can speak the truth aloud to each other."

"I just—"

"I know," she said, leaning over to give him a kiss. It was almost too tender, though, and she had to sit up again fast, before she kissed him again. "It's easier for me, because I don't have children." She gave him a lopsided grin. "I've decided to marry for love."

This time he froze.

"I don't love Gideon, so I won't marry *him*. I used to love him, but somehow it all changed."

A moment later she found herself flat on her back, and they weren't making love any more.

"Leo," she whispered.

He was braced over her, frowning down through a lock of hair that had fallen over his eyes. He was delicious . . . heartbreaking.

She nipped his lip. She'd be damned if he'd ever find out how she felt. She didn't ever want yet another man to know that she loved him more than he loved her. Never again.

"You're so calm about my marriage to Lisette," he said, scowling. "I want to kill Astley, every time I see him. Hell, every time he even looks at you I feel like wringing his scraggy neck."

"That's because you're a man," she said, ignoring the

little voice in her head that reminded her just how murderous she felt every time Lisette trilled out her excitement over becoming half of Leopold and Lisette, as she kept referring to them. "Do you suppose that you could make love to me now, Leopold?" She reached up and ran her fingers along his cheeks. And then she said it, because it had to be said. "We'll be leaving first thing in the morning."

He looked down at her, and then he pulled away.

"Leopold?" She looked down at herself. Her blue gown was rucked around her waist, and her bare legs were trembling.

But he got up and walked away from the bed, raking his fingers through his hair.

The words going through her head were not words that a lady was supposed to know, let alone think. She pulled her gown down over her knees and sat on the edge of the bed.

"I can't make love to you knowing it's the last time," he said finally, his voice tight.

She didn't know what to say. She couldn't fight for him. If she were to voice what she thought about Lisette . . . she might convince him. But it would always be her opinion against his. He had to either see it himself, or—or marry Lisette. That was all there was to it.

He turned around. "I've never felt this way about another woman. But I don't have the freedom to choose whom I wish."

"I understand," she said. "I have—" She stopped.

"You've heard this before," he said, his voice flat. "There's no will constraining me, Eleanor. But I honestly think that Lisette is unique in her attitude toward the children's illegitimacy. She doesn't even see it as a problem. She can teach them to live without shame. She already adores the girls, and they adore her. I can't—"

He turned away again.

There was a long moment of silence. Sunshine came in through the balcony door and slashed across his broad shoulders. She didn't let herself feel . . . anything.

Finally he said, "I can't choose whom I would, because I made this bed, as the saying goes. And I must lie in it." He turned back to her.

"I understand," she said, quite peaceably. After all, as he said, she'd been through this exact scene before. She had a precedent; she understood the undertow of anguish that would follow, the sense of regret and loss, the bewilderment of loving someone more than he loved her.

The next time around, she thought, it's going to be different.

But it *was* different. She knew that. There wouldn't be any next time around for her when it came to love . . . but that was all right, too.

If she couldn't have the complicated duke in front of her, she didn't want to love anyone. He was still staring at the empty fireplace, so she just drank in the sight of him, his muscled legs and lean powerful rear, the way his shoulders flared, the exact color of his hair—

And that was when the door burst open.

# Chapter Twenty-eight

$\mathcal{I}$t happened so fast that afterward Leopold was never quite able to describe it. One moment he was trying to figure out why his heart felt as if it were splitting in two, and the next moment he was faced by an utterly enraged, out-of-control Duke of Astley who was screaming— literally screaming—about the fact that he had dishonored Eleanor.

Which he had.

No one could argue otherwise, given the fact that he was stark naked in her bedchamber. He pulled on his breeches, but could think of only one thing to say. "Do you want everyone in this house to know?" His voice cut across Astley's hysteria like a knife.

The man choked.

"You will give me satisfaction," Astley said, his eyes bright as a lunatic's. "Immediately."

"You must be out of your mind," Leopold said, unwisely. "You don't believe in duels."

Astley went for his throat, forcing Leopold to throw him across the room, which was ridiculous and made him feel even more foolish.

"I know why you want to keep quiet!" Astley hissed, lurching back on his feet. "I will marry Eleanor no matter whether you've debauched her or not. She is not in control of her own impulses. She needs a man, and I left her. This is all my fault."

"I will not marry either of you," Eleanor cried, intervening. "So Gideon, if you wish to save my reputation, I would beg you to stop speaking so loudly."

Astley stared at her. "Of course you're marrying me. I have forgiven you, Eleanor."

She shook her head. "I will not marry either of you."

"I *forgive* you," he persisted.

"She doesn't need your forgiveness," Leopold found himself saying through clenched teeth. "You should be groveling at her feet, begging for *her* forgiveness."

"I already have," he said, with an odd sort of punctured dignity. "And now I shall defend her honor, just as I should have defended her years ago." The sound of his slap was shockingly loud in the quiet room. "Name your seconds."

"Oh, for Christ's sake," Leopold said. He turned away and walked toward the balcony window. He had won four duels and lost one, badly. And he had sworn never to fight with a sword again. He was too good—and it was only after almost losing his own to a dueling wound that he realized how much he prized life.

His successful duels had ended with him wounding his opponents, none mortally. It was only by the grace of God that he hadn't killed someone. He had no desire to alter that record.

"I don't want to kill you," he said, turning around.

"You won't. Virtue—truth—*God* are on my side."

"Astley, you're one of the House of Lords's most vocal opponents of dueling, and you have been for the last few years at least. Tell me that you even know how to handle a rapier."

"Of course I do. I was trained as is any gentleman's son. Do I need to slap you again, Your Grace?" Astley was maddened by rage. His face was completely white.

"No," Leopold said slowly. "But I won't fight you with seconds. If you want to fight, you'll have to do it privately."

"Why?"

"Because if you involve another, the world will know. And if Eleanor then refuses to marry you, as she has a perfect right to do, she will be ruined."

"You wouldn't marry him instead of me!" Astley swung around.

"He hasn't asked me," Eleanor said, head high.

Leopold actually sympathized with Astley this time. He could have ducked; he certainly knew what was coming. But he took a hard right to his chin.

Eleanor grabbed Astley's arm. "He's marrying Lisette! For pity's sake, Gideon. He can hardly marry me when he's promised to her."

"Then why are you in her bedchamber?" Astley said, panting.

Although it hurt like the devil, Leopold refused to give his opponent the satisfaction of seeing him feel his chin. "Because I'm a bastard," he said heavily.

"You are that," Astley said. "Look me in the eye and tell me that you'd rather marry Lisette than Eleanor."

It hurt to open his mouth, and not only because of the blow. He didn't manage to open it before Eleanor intervened once more.

"He does!" she said, her voice tight. "What are you trying to prove, Gideon? Leopold has decided that Lisette will be a better mother to his children. He bedded me, but that gave him precisely as much desire to marry me as it gave you. In short: not much."

Astley started to speak, but she held up her hand. Her eyes were flaming. "Neither of you seem to care, but I'll tell you this: I deserve better than either of you. I deserve a man who will love *me*, who will believe to the bottom of his heart that I'm exactly the woman he wants to raise his children. Who won't think of me as just a woman to bed."

Leopold felt her words as if a blow had shuddered down his spine. He had never meant to hurt her. And yet there were tears standing in her eyes.

"I deserve more," she repeated savagely.

"I think you'll be a wonderful mother," Astley said, like an eager puppy dog.

"No, you don't."

"I do!"

"You want to marry me because you realize you made a mistake. But that's not the same as loving me now, Gideon. We lost each other, somehow. And frankly, you loved Ada, for all you are disparaging your time together. You *loved* her."

Astley swallowed. "I—"

"You loved her and the sooner you realize that, the sooner you can mourn her properly."

"But if you won't marry either of us—"

"Don't tell me that you're afraid I'll end up a spinster! I'll tell you exactly who I am going to marry: a common man, not a duke. Both of you are so steeped in privilege that you never really thought I was good enough for you. I am going to find an ordinary man who will court me. And he won't be a duke. Now if you don't mind, I'll leave you."

She left.

Leopold pulled on his shirt. "I'll leave for London immediately," he said, tired to the bone. He felt as if a clamp were tightening around his heart, as if he'd— He couldn't let himself think about what he had done.

"No, you won't."

"For God's sake, Astley. She doesn't want either one of us."

"You *fool*," Astley said. "You utter blithering *fool*."

Leopold laughed, shortly. "Are you trying to get me to slap you this time? Because believe it or not, I don't believe in duels anymore."

The slap made his head fall back and his teeth rattle.

"What in God's name was that for? That's the third time you've struck me in five minutes."

"Because I love her," Astley said. "I behaved like a young ass when I left her. And maybe she's right when she says it's too late for us. But you—you *used* her. You made her fall in love with you, and you rejected her. I'm going to kill you."

For the first time, Leopold felt a stir of alarm. Faint, but real. "You can't kill me."

"Yes, I can," Astley stated clearly. "I dishonored Eleanor. This will atone for what I did to her. I'll revenge her. I'll take you down because it's the right thing to do. You broke her heart. I've never seen her look like that, not when I left her, and not thereafter. By God, I never understood the point of dueling before but I understand it now."

Leopold knew when a man had irrevocably made up his mind. He pulled on his boots. "Tomorrow at dawn."

"Where?"

"There's a stretch of green down by the river. It will do." He felt inexpressibly weary. A man wanted to kill him because he had broken the heart of—

It was impossible.

She was so logical, so cool, when she agreed with him that he should marry Lisette. Women had moaned and murmured and shouted their love for him before, not that he ever believed them. Hell, Lisette had patted his cheek and told him that she loved him earlier that morning.

Eleanor never said a word.

"She doesn't love me," he said, just as Astley was leaving the room.

"You fool," Astley said savagely. "You utter ass."

"You're hardly an uninterested bystander," Leopold said.

"I do love her. But what I see in her eyes when she looks at you . . . I never saw that before. She used to desire me. She *loves* you. But that doesn't matter, does it?" He turned around, his eyes bright with scorn. "You've made your choice."

"I can't marry whom I wish—"

"Just what I told her all those years ago," Astley said, stepping into the corridor. "Precisely those words."

And he was gone.

# Chapter Twenty-nine

Eleanor thought she had lived through nightmares before, but the torment of dinner that night surpassed any anguish she had felt when Gideon left her. Lisette's father, the Duke of Gilner, had returned, and contrary to Lisette's prediction was enchanted to give his daughter's hand to the Duke of Villiers.

He didn't turn a hair over the question of the duke's illegitimate children, just said cheerfully—and in front of the entire table, "I'm sure my little girl has told you that she can't bear young of her own, so this is perfect."

Eleanor had been looking everywhere except at Villiers, who was sitting across from her, but at this she peeked from under her lashes, just enough to see that Lisette had not bothered to inform her future husband of this fact. But of course he nodded as if the news were of no account.

Perhaps it wasn't. After all, he wanted a mother for the children he already had. Surely an heir was less important. That thought led to bitterness, so she took a deep breath and pushed the question of Villiers's children aside.

"It seems we both have reason to celebrate," her mother said archly, from her position at Gilner's right hand. "Our dear children are matched—and so suitably too!"

For all his liberal notions, the duke didn't seem quite as pleased with her mother's announcement, once he realized that Gideon's wife was barely in the grave. He was a nice man, Eleanor thought. Too nice, perhaps. If he'd placed more of a curb on Lisette . . . She sighed. There was no use thinking about it.

Anne squeezed her hand under the table. "Almost through," her sister whispered. "One more course."

Eleanor gave her a lopsided smile. "I'm so glad you're with me."

Anne leaned over and said in her ear. "You'll see. We'll get revenge—on both of them. I have plans."

Eleanor didn't care.

At that moment she heard the scribble-scrabble of sharp claws on the parquet. Her heart stopped. It couldn't be. It—

Oyster tore around the corner into the dining room, going so quickly that she heard his claws scrape the wood.

"Oh, no!" she yelped, as loud as Oyster himself.

Lisette was sitting to the left of her father. She leaped up, jumped on her chair and screamed. Of course.

Eleanor was running around the table, trying to catch her puppy, and only learned afterwards what happened. Apparently Oyster bounded onto Lisette's chair as if he'd grown wings.

"He's trying to bite me!" Lisette screamed.

Anne said later that it looked as if he was planning to lick her slipper.

Whatever Oyster's intention, he had only a second before Lisette, without breaking her scream, scooped him up and threw him with all her might across the table and through the air. He didn't even have time to bark as he sailed over Gideon's head and slammed into the wall.

Time became slow, like honey pouring from a spoon. The puppy slid down the paneling and collapsed in a boneless heap of too-large paws.

"Daughter!" Gilner roared.

Still Lisette screamed.

Eleanor found herself on her knees by Oyster, tears streaming down her face. She was afraid to move him. Not that it mattered. He didn't appear to be breathing. Then Villiers was there, sliding one huge hand under the puppy's neck and the other under his body. "We'll take him into the library," he said, straightening.

He must have caught Lisette's eye.

"Don't look at me like that!" she screamed. "You have no right to look at me like that!"

"I'm not—" Villiers said.

"You are, you are! You look at me the same way that bastard son of yours looks at me!"

There was a curious silence in the room, and a feeling that Eleanor suddenly remembered from Lisette's tantrums all those years ago. It felt as if the air in the room was in short supply.

Villiers didn't say a word, just shifted Oyster closer into his arms. His paw flapped lifelessly and Eleanor's tears came harder. Her sister's arms went around her, pressing a handkerchief to her cheek.

"It's your fault!" Lisette shrieked, turning to her father.

He was on his feet as well, looking miserable and

exhausted. "Be quiet, Lisette," he said, his voice heavy.

"It's all your fault—all of it. Everything!" She looked around the table, her eyes as bright and hard as cannonballs. "He took away my baby. He took him away and since then nothing has been right." She turned to her father. "You are a horrible man! You are a despicable, child-stealing—"

Lady Marguerite's voice cut through the tirade with barely controlled rage. "You will not speak to your father that way, Lisette. You sent away your own child because you said he smelled and cried too much."

"That's a falsehood!" Lisette shouted. "A lie because you're all liars!"

Marguerite's hand shot out and she pulled Lisette down from her perch on the chair and then grabbed her chin. "Look at me! *You* told your mother to get rid of that child. You did that to my poor sister, who never recovered. She was never the same from the moment she gave that child to his father. She did it because she knew you would ruin that boy's life. But don't you ever, ever, blame another soul for that."

"I *will* blame him," Lisette said, her voice a horrible sobbing half shriek. "I will blame him because it is his fault. And *his*, as well." She pointed at Villiers. "He brought that boy here, that horrible boy, who made me think about my own child, the one you took from me. The one my own mother stole from me."

Eleanor couldn't bear another moment. She reached out and plucked Oyster from Villiers's arms before he could stop her. Then she began to walk away.

"And you!" she heard on a rising shriek. "You think I don't know what—"

There was a sound, of the slap of water, and Lisette's voice broke off.

Eleanor glanced over her shoulder. Anne had apparently snatched a pitcher of water from the sideboard and thrown it directly into Lisette's face.

Eleanor just kept going, down the hall to the library. The footman threw open the door, such an appalled expression on his face that she realized everything must have been audible in the entry.

"My lady," Popper said, hurrying to her as she sat down on a sofa. "I'll bring a cold cloth."

"There's no need," Eleanor said, icily calm in her grief. "It won't help." Oyster's head had fallen over the crook of her arm and she couldn't see his eyes. She closed her own for a moment, and opened them to find Tobias standing before her. All color had drained from his face.

"It was me," he said hoarsely. "I did it."

"You didn't do it. Lisette threw him against a wall."

"I did it," he repeated, his shoulders back as if he faced a magistrate. "I rubbed a beef steak on the bottom of her slippers, and then I took Oyster out of your room and let him go."

Eleanor swallowed. "Why?"

"Because I wanted the duke to see what she was like. I never thought she'd kill him. I never thought that!"

He looked like a boy who had never cried in his life. His skin was drawn tightly over the bones of his face.

Tears slipped down Eleanor's cheeks again. She slipped one arm out from under Oyster and held it out to him. "I know you didn't. And Oyster knows you didn't."

He stood there, frozen, and she thought, My God, he's never been hugged. But then suddenly his wiry body was pressed against hers, and a not very clean hand fell on Oyster's fur, and they were both crying.

Someone handed her a large handkerchief of such fine quality that it could belong only to one person. He slipped a hand under Oyster's body.

"Don't," she said. "Not yet."

His eyes met hers over the head of his weeping child. "But I think he's breathing," Leopold said softly. "Tobias, he's breathing. Oyster isn't dead."

Popper trotted up with a wet cloth. They turned Oyster over. His legs seemed boneless, so limp that Eleanor secretly lost hope again. Tobias began gently rubbing the cloth around Oyster's closed eyes and around his muzzle, crooning, "Come on, boy. Come on, old boy. Open your eyes, boy."

Oyster didn't stir. Eleanor pressed her lips together.

"Smelling salts!" Popper said, and left the room again.

"I can feel his heart," Leopold said, his deep voice steady. "Just keep doing it, son. Oyster will wake up."

"We'll go running as soon as you wake up," Tobias said, his voice hoarse from crying. "I'll take you out to the raspberry bushes and you can look for a rat. Remember when we looked for a rat? Remember that, Oyster? Come on, old boy, wake up!"

Tears were running down his face again, so Eleanor pulled him a little closer.

"Shit," he muttered, reasserting his masculinity.

"I agree," she said.

"He's not waking up." Despair cracked his voice. He said an even worse curse word, one that Eleanor had only heard once before.

"Give him a moment," Leopold said.

Popper reappeared, waving a vial of smelling salts. The duke twisted the cork, putting the bitter smell directly under the puppy's nose.

"Ew!" Tobias said, turning his head away.

In so doing, he missed the moment when Oyster opened his eyes and looked blearily around. But he didn't miss Oyster's weak lick.

"He—He—He—"

"He's alive," his father said in his measured way. But Eleanor knew to look past the magnificent ruby velvet coat, past the thick eyelashes. The Duke of Villiers was watching his boy bury his face in Oyster's fur, and she saw love in his eyes.

"Tobias," Eleanor said softly, "Oyster is yours now."

Tobias raised his head. "What?"

"I'm giving you Oyster." She smiled at him. "He loves you, and you love him."

"But he loves you best!"

"I don't take him looking for rats." She ran her fingers through Oyster's short hair. The puppy suddenly trembled all over, as if a stiff wind had ruffled through his fur. "He's pretty bored with me. And when I thought he was dead—well, I think he's going to live to a good old age now. But just in case, I want him to do all the ratting he can."

"You don't have to," Tobias said. "We could share him. Maybe he could sleep with me sometimes. I know you like him in your bedchamber at night."

"I'm afraid that wouldn't really work."

Oyster tumbled off her lap. He seemed a bit wobbly, but gave himself a vigorous shake.

"He'll love living in the nursery with you. You have to let all the other children play with him, though."

Tobias nodded. Oyster put his paws onto Tobias's knees, and he hoisted the dog into his lap.

"He would really be your dog, even if the other children can play with him," Eleanor said, watching Oyster lick Tobias's teary face.

"But you'll be right there," he burst out. "Won't she?" He looked at his father. "Won't she? You said you were going to choose between them, and now you have to admit that the one out there is cracked. That Lisette, she's a bleeding nightmare!"

"I would be honored," Leopold said, looking up and meeting her eyes.

Eleanor's throat ached. She'd seen his eyes rest on her arm, encircling Tobias. And he finally understood what Lisette was like.

But she wanted more. She wanted someone who loved her for herself. Who didn't think she was good enough to bed but not good enough to mother—and who changed his mind only when she proved herself maternal enough. She wanted to be married for herself.

"Come on," Tobias said, sounding as if he were pleading with Oyster again. "You'll marry him, won't you? He's not so bad. That way, Oyster can stay with both of us."

She shook her head, taking a deep breath. "I can't, Tobias."

"Please!" The word sounded wrung from his chest.

"It will be all right," she said, oddly touched. "I promise you can keep Oyster."

"But I—I like you," he said, the words dropping into the silent room. "An' the girls do too. You'll see, we'll be good. You'll like Violet. She's not real pretty, like Lucinda and Phyllinda, but she's—she's nice. And—"

"I can't," she said, standing up. "I just can't, Tobias. I'm sorry."

Leopold made a sharp movement, but said nothing.

Oyster jumped down and started frolicking around her ankles. Obviously his little brain had completely forgotten what had just happened to him. "Stay, Oyster," she said.

Wonder of wonders, he actually sat down and wagged his tail.

"Good dog."

It seemed a very long way to the door, but that was probably because of the silence behind her.

# Chapter Thirty

*Knole House, country residence of the Duke of Gilner*
*June 23, 1784*

"I can't fight with you," Leopold said flatly. The sun was barely over the horizon and the air was surprisingly chilly.

"I didn't give you a choice," Astley said. He was pacing out the wet grass, his rapier unsheathed and ready.

"I'm a father."

"You should have thought of that before you debauched Eleanor. Before you made her fall in love with you and then chose a raving lunatic over her."

"I might well kill you. I rarely lose."

Astley started pacing in the other direction, measuring the ground. "Ada's dead. Death doesn't frighten me."

"I thought you were in love with Eleanor."

Astley's face crumpled for a moment. "I am. But I loved Ada too. Eleanor was right about that. It's all so complicated . . ." He shook himself and kept pacing.

"If I kill you, I'll have to leave the country. But the children—"

"Cart them away with you. You can't tell me that anyone will care if *you* leave, let alone them. You? The Duke of Villiers? You have no family, other than your clutch of bastards. Everyone will be glad to see you take them away from decent society."

"Are you ready to fight?" Villiers said, a wave of ice filling his veins. Astley was right. Well, almost. Elijah and Jemma would care if he had to leave England permanently. But no one else would.

It would probably be better for Eleanor, actually. She wouldn't even have to see him. He hadn't been able to sleep, slowly taking himself though an understanding of his catastrophic idiocy. He had spurned Eleanor because he thought Lisette would be a better mother for his children. But Lisette, he now understood, looked upon children as if they were playmates—or worse, playthings.

All the time, Eleanor was just the mother they needed: a woman who looked problems straight on, who didn't ever lie or pretend. Tobias had known that. Hell, even Oyster knew how perfect she was.

So why was he such an idiot? Why was he the only one who didn't know what motherhood looked like?

But even that was just a digression: the real question was why he was the only one who didn't know what *love* looked like. Who didn't realize that his heart, that stubborn organ that he'd always ignored, would be seared with agony by the idea of never seeing Eleanor again?

Why couldn't he have known that was—that was love. Real love. The kind of love that never goes away.

*"En garde!"* Astley cried.

Leopold raised his rapier, still thinking.

"I fully plan to kill you," Astley said pleasantly. "Perhaps you should pay attention."

Leopold met Astley's eyes and saw his determination. "In which event, you'll be the one to leave the country."

"No one cares what I do," Astley said. "My mother's dead. My father's dead. Eleanor doesn't love me anymore. I don't want to sound like a sniveling schoolboy, but I no longer have the faintest interest in seeing tomorrow. And if I happen to be around for it, it won't matter whether I'm in England or India."

"Hell," Leopold muttered. The man was mad with grief. He'd seen that look once before, on his aunt's face—at the funeral for his five-year-old nephew.

He assumed his stance.

Obviously, Astley wasn't practiced. And he didn't even fight that well. In less fraught circumstances, Leopold could have chosen a spot to insert his blade and injured the duke within a minute. But passion, it seemed, changed everything.

He found himself fighting defensively, parrying Astley's inexperienced lunges. It was surprisingly difficult, perhaps because Astley didn't respond like a trained fencer. He simply slashed away as if Leopold were a hedge he had decided to prune.

Within ten minutes they were both sweating in the still-cool air. But Leopold couldn't keep his mind on the duel, no matter how he tried. He just kept thinking what a fool he was. He didn't seem to be able to trust his instincts.

His heart.

He took a step back. Astley bounded toward him, sword raised like some sort of avenging angel.

Leopold threw down his rapier.

Astley tried to stop, but slid on the wet grass and ended

up on his back, sword in the air. Leopold offered him a hand. Astley ignored it and came to his feet, breathing hard. "What in the holy hell are you doing?" he demanded.

"I refuse to fight," Leopold said, certain of the absolute rightness of that decision.

"Do I have to slap you *again*?"

"You can try. But I will not fight you. A duel is for protecting one's honor," he said painstakingly.

"You don't think you need to protect your honor, after what you did?"

"I don't think I have any." He picked up his sword and untucked his shirt from his breeches in order to wipe the dew from the blade.

There was an odd little silence in the meadow, broken only by the song of a lark over the river.

"You can kill me if you want," Leopold added.

"Oh, for Christ's sake." Astley sat down on a large rock at the side of the stream, then observed, "My arms ache."

"You should get a fencing master," Leopold said. "You're not bad."

"Why? In case I find some honor of my own somewhere?"

Their eyes held the same rueful acknowledgment. They were the two luckiest, and two most brainless, men in the kingdom.

"She loves you. You can get her back," Astley offered.

Leopold shook his head. "She'll never believe that I love her now. She thinks that she's nothing more than a second-best mother, that I never wanted to marry her until I saw how much Tobias cared for her."

"Even worse, she likely thinks that you want her now only because Lisette proved herself stark raving mad."

"I don't know what to do."

Astley stood up with a little groan. "My back!"

"Find an instructor," Leopold said, looking up. "Not for defending your honor, but because it's fine exercise."

"I see that," Astley said, moving slowly toward the house.

He stopped and looked back. "If I were you, Duke, I would fight for her."

Leopold's eyes fell on his rapier.

"Not that way," Astley said with disgust.

And he was gone.

# Chapter Thirty-one

*London residence of the Duke of Montague*
*August 6, 1784*

It took almost six weeks for the Duchess of Montague to plummet from the heights of maternal bliss to utter despair. At first she didn't believe Eleanor's declaration that she had refused Gideon's proposal, even if he followed the strict protocol of a year of mourning. After finally grasping and accepting that, she leapt on the idea of her daughter marrying Villiers, bastard children or no. Resigning herself to the finality of Eleanor's edict regarding the second duke led to wailing and gnashing of teeth. Literally.

Melancholy hung over the house like a shroud. The duchess took to drifting from room to room, her face a combination of dejection and rage.

"Don't imagine that you can live with your brother for life!" she said shrilly one morning at breakfast. "I won't have his life destroyed by having to live with a spinster sister. It would have ruined my marriage had your aunt lived with us."

"I mean to marry," Eleanor said steadily, repeating what she had said a few hundred times in the past weeks. "Just not a duke."

"Two dukes! Two dukes asking for your hand in marriage and you refused them both!" The lament sounded like a lullaby to Eleanor now, so familiar that she didn't even distinguish the words in the general flow. "The only good thing to emerge from this disaster is that you've got rid of that horrid dog, though I vow the Aubusson in the morning room still has an odor."

Then the letter arrived.

*Dear Lady Eleanor Lindel,*

*I hope you will excuse the audacity of this missive. We danced together once in the past, although I am quite certain that you hardly noticed my presence. For my part, I was unable to express my admiration as I was engaged abroad on His Majesty's behalf. I am now returned to England, and thus I am bold enough to inquire, as I would have three years ago, if you would be so kind as to accompany me on a drive to Kensington Gardens.*

*Hon. Josiah Ormston*

"You might as well go," Anne said, reading over her shoulder. "He's obviously been nursing a tendre for you all this time. It will cheer you up. Do you have any idea who he is?"

"No, I don't. And it won't cheer me up," Eleanor said evenly.

*Dear Mr. Ormston,*

*No lady can consider it an affront to learn that a gentleman has remembered her name over the span of three years. However, I must beg you to excuse me. Since I do not have the same memory of you, it would feel odd indeed to join you for a drive. Perhaps we shall renew our acquaintance when the season begins again.*

*Lady Eleanor*

"Never mind the fact that you'll be a burden on the family for life!" the duchess wailed, upon learning of the letter. "The least you could do would be to marry someone above the merchant class. Though if your father ever returns from Russia, I shall direct him to inquire amongst that sort. Beggars can't be choosers."

Anne, who was kindly sharing most of her meals with them, doing her best to blunt the flow of recriminations, said, "Mother, you can't mean to say that you intend to sell Eleanor to the highest bidder."

"Why not?" the duchess demanded. "No one can tell me that she isn't a serpent's tooth, gnawing on my bosom! Her dowry should be sufficient to buy us a merchant. Perhaps one of the Wedgwoods. I vow their crockery has grown so expensive that they must be worth a fortune."

"Mo-*ther*," Anne said, grinning.

Eleanor said nothing. Her father would never agree to such a scheme. And her mother didn't really mean it. By refusing two dukes, she had struck at the roots of her mother's strongest belief: that a title is God's own way of marking his blessed few. Marrying her daughter to a cit would likely kill her.

"The least you could do is devote an afternoon to this—this Ermster fellow," the duchess continued. "He's a gentleman. He might marry you."

"I don't know who he is," Eleanor objected.

"He's not in *Debrett's*," Anne added.

"*Debrett's, Debrett's*," the duchess said fretfully. "It can be terribly inaccurate, you know. They completely neglected to note that your great-aunt was related, on her mother's side, to a Russian prince."

Eleanor sighed. "If you wish me to accompany Mr. Ormston to the park, I shall, if he asks me again."

"It's the least you could do," her mother said. "The very least. You'll have to make a true effort now, Eleanor. Everyone will think that Villiers rejected *you*. They'll be scrutinizing you to see what he found lacking."

Despite herself, the back of Eleanor's throat tightened.

"Mother," Anne interceded, leaning forward and waving a copy of the *Morning Post*, "did you read about this extraordinary robbery?"

"There are so many," the duchess said. "Who can keep account?"

"Yes, but this one happened in our own street!"

"Here?"

"It says that an old gentleman, residing in Arlington Street, was sitting in his front parlor when he was extremely alarmed by the sudden appearance of a man with black crepe over his face."

"A cape on his face? How extraordinary."

"No, black *crepe*. He must have worn it . . ."

Eleanor stopped listening. She had beaten back the tears, again. Perhaps she should go for a drive with Mr. Ormston. She had made up her mind to marry a mere gentleman, and any man who didn't even appear in *Debrett's Peerage* certainly qualified.

There was no real point in waiting for the new season. She suspected—nay, she *knew*—that her heart would never be whole. Yet she would marry, and she would have children, and she would feel joy again.

But she would never love with that kind of ravening, blissful hunger that she felt for Leopold—the kind of hunger that made her want to touch his arm when they were at supper, meet his eyes at breakfast, sleep next to him every night.

Mr. Ormston's next letter provided something of a relief from these gloomy thoughts.

*Dear Lady Eleanor Lindel,*

*I entirely concur with your dismay at the idea of a tête-à-tête with an unknown man, though I should assure you that I am indeed a gentleman. As the younger son of Baron Plumptre, I took my uncle's surname in honor of his leaving me a snug fortune. I hope that I do not offend you by speaking so directly of these matters. Though I have little hope of refreshing your memory, as I recall, you wore a gown of some sort of blue stuff, and we talked of Miss Burney's play,* The Witlings. *You did not care for the actress who played Mrs. Voluble.*

> *With deep respect,*
> *Hon. Josiah Ormston*

"Well, now you *must* remember him," Anne said with triumph, waving the letter. "You didn't like Mrs. Voluble."

"No one did," Eleanor said. "I barely recall the play,

but every review said that Mrs. Voluble was shrill and unpleasant."

"What I like about this man is that he remembers everything about dancing with you," Anne said, dropping the letter and turning to her mother's *Debrett's*, always handy on the parlor table. "It would be very nice for you to experience some adoration. Yes, he's here, listed not under Ormston, but as a second son to Plumptre. Josiah is not a wonderful name, but a sturdy one, don't you think?"

"I suppose."

"You must go," Anne said. "Mother will never let you hear the end of it otherwise."

*Dear Mr. Ormston,*

*I would be pleased to accompany you to the park tomorrow.*

*Lady Eleanor*

"You should wear the blue gown you took to Kent," Anne said. "It might remind him of whatever it was you were wearing three years ago."

"I'll wear one of my old gowns," Eleanor said. "It did me no good to put on a wanton appearance, Anne. You have to admit that."

"No lip color?" Anne asked, horrified.

"None. And a modest dress."

"Perhaps you weren't aware of this, but I instructed Willa to give away most of the gowns you used to own," her sister pointed out.

"You didn't!"

"I certainly did," she retorted. "Just because you've been thwarted in love . . ." She paused, and added, "*again,* doesn't mean that you should turn yourself into a pattern card of domestic dreariness. You've had very bad luck, Eleanor. Now you need to be prudent."

"I am being prudent."

"No. You are going to dress like the desirable young lady that you are. You are going to act in a proper manner. Don't tell me that Villiers didn't get a good look at your silver combs, Eleanor, because I know perfectly well that he did."

"You're saying I'm a fool."

"I'm saying that perhaps you should just follow the path that the rest of us have taken successfully," her sister said gently. "Flirt with the gentleman, be enticing and yet modest. It's a game, Eleanor, but it's a most rewarding one."

"Very well," Eleanor said, inexpressibly depressed.

"Remember, that was your first season, and your head was full of Gideon. Any number of respectable gentlemen might have fallen in love with you, and you wouldn't have noticed. I would suggest the sprigged muslin, because the gauze around the bodice makes it practically prudish."

Eleanor nodded, acquiescing.

"And I suppose that you might eschew the black around your eyes," Anne said. "But you simply must have a bit of cheek color. You look as pale as a ghost. Poor Mr. Ormston will think you suffered from a bout of consumption while he was abroad."

At precisely two of the clock, Eleanor was ready. In truth, the muslin was so delectable that it was hard to feel miserable while wearing it. It had a cream background, sprigged with tiny cherries. The skirts were puckered around the bottom with cherry-colored gauze; the same gauze was tucked into the bosom, which would have been indecently low without it. The ensemble was completed by a supremely fashionable cabriolet bonnet with gauze ribbons that fluttered behind.

"You look quite good," her mother said grudgingly. And then, rather surprisingly, "You needn't feel that Mr. Ormston is your only resort, Eleanor. Your beauty means that you can certainly marry where you wish. Witness the two dukes begging for your hand. I know I have been snappish on the subject, but I have no doubt but that you'll take at some point."

Eleanor brushed her mother's cheek with a kiss. "Thank you, Mama."

Anne was standing at the window, most improperly peering through the drapes. "He's got a perfectly lovely landau," she reported. "It looks to be painted on the sides with cupids, or something like that. I can't quite see. And he has a footman. Really, Mr. Ormston was not jesting when he said his uncle left him a living."

"That is vastly unseemly of you," the duchess scolded. "You look like a housemaid at the window. What do you see of the man himself?"

"The footman is coming to our door and blocking my view. Oh! Mr. Ormston is wearing a wig *à Grecque*. Very fashionable of him! His coat is black. Quite plain. I don't see any large buttons."

"*À Grecque*?" Eleanor asked, pulling on her gloves.

"You know . . . two curls on each side, and a long tail behind. It's quite smart." She turned around, smiling. "He looks to have broad shoulders as well. I expect you'll remember him the moment you enter the carriage." She danced over and gave Eleanor a kiss.

Eleanor followed Mr. Ormston's footman to the landau, lecturing herself the whole way about second, nay, third chances.

Mr. Ormston had descended from the carriage to meet

her, of course. She raised her eyes just enough to see that he was wearing a coat of black cloth. Very respectable and sober. He bowed, taking her gloved hand and kissing it before handing her into the landau.

Eleanor sat down and looked up, prepared to smile.

# Chapter Thirty-two

*London residence of the Duke of Montague*
*August 8, 1784*

"*I* am honored that you accepted my invitation," Mr. Ormston said quietly. "It is a true pleasure to meet you again."

Eleanor could feel heat rising in her cheeks. "Indeed?"

"You are not the sort of woman whom any man could forget," he said.

"And what have you been doing in the intervening three years since we last met?" Eleanor inquired. "Unless it is a matter of great national import that you cannot share with me? A delicate matter, perhaps?"

"Oh, this and that," Mr. Ormston said. "I do a great deal of work with orphans."

His dark eyebrows were quite dramatic beneath his snowy wig. His shoulders were remarkably broad, but something about his unadorned black coat made them look even broader. "Indeed," Eleanor said. "And how are your orphans, Mr. Ormston?"

"Quite well. We have occasional problems, as I'm sure you can imagine."

"I don't have children," she said pleasantly. "I know nothing of raising children."

He cleared his throat and said, very low, "You know more than I do."

Eleanor looked down at her hands, clenched together in her lap. "I think I should like to return to my house now." By some miracle her voice was quite steady.

"But we are here, at Kensington Gardens," Mr. Ormston said. The carriage glided to a halt and he leapt out and stood, holding up his gloved hand.

Eleanor sat for a moment. She felt as empty as a vase without flowers or water. She had no emotion, not anger, grief, or even longing. So there could be no harm in taking a brief stroll, she thought.

She numbly put her hand in his, and dropped it the moment she descended. Then she opened her parasol at such an angle that it entirely shielded her face from that of her companion. "How lovely," she said. "The fuchsias are in bloom."

"Yes," he said. "Shall we rest for a moment, Lady Eleanor? There seems to be a suitable bench overlooking the Round Pond. I thought you might like to feed the swans."

She glanced to the side. He was holding a cotton bag, presumably filled with bread crusts. *That* was rather interesting. Mr. Ormston, alias Leopold Dautry, alias the Duke of Villiers, did not appear to be the sort of man whom she imagined carrying bread around.

They sat down next to each other and in total silence threw crusts at the swans. There were seven of them, counting a mated pair and five cygnets. The parents curled and bobbed their long necks, pushing their offspring out of the way in order to gobble bread.

"So why have you disguised yourself as Mr. Ormston?" she asked after a time.

"It is more than a mere disguise. I want to be everything that you wish me to be. If you don't want a duke, then I don't want to be a duke."

She closed her parasol and took a deep breath before replying. "You will forgive me if I impute your motives to an entirely commendable paternal instinct rather than a wish to please me."

"I can find a mother for my children anywhere."

"I am quite certain that is true," she said. She pulled out a large crust and threw it unerringly at the male swan, hitting him in the beak. The cob took no affront and gobbled it up.

"That being the case, my motives are purely selfish."

"As surprising as it may seem to those who know you—or know of you," she corrected herself, "I doubt that very much. Your attention to your children's well-being is commendable. I am sure that you will be successful with the daughter of a marquis. Though one should not discount the distressful possibility that you will have to lower yourself to the level of earl."

"I'm not here because of the children. I have hired an excellent tutor and two more nannies. They are fine."

"Marvelous," Eleanor said tonelessly. "Who would have thought it was so easy to be a parent?" This time she tried to hit the female swan, but missed.

"Will you look at me before you brain those hapless birds?"

She drew a deep breath. Of course she would look at

him. She raised her eyes reluctantly. Mr. Ormston's coat did not clamor for attention; neither did his discreet, if fashionable, wig. Instead, those accoutrements framed his face.

What they really framed were his eyes.

Without the distraction of his famous hair, the gleaming embroidery of his coats . . . when she looked at Leopold, she saw his eyes.

"Oh . . ." she said quietly.

"I love you. I will always love you, until the day I die." His voice was sure and deep, the voice of a man who knew himself. "The kind of love I feel has nothing to do with the children I have, or children we might have together."

"But you said—" She reached out to take his hand without even realizing what she was doing.

"I went about things the wrong way. I didn't know how to recognize a *mother*, Eleanor. I never really had one."

"I see."

"I recognized motherhood in Lisette, because she reminded me of my mother. She liked my brother and me to behave like little dukes, and she dressed us like royalty, almost as if we were dolls. When my brother became ill, she cut him out of her life. And though he didn't die for eight days, as far as I know, she never faltered in her resolution."

Eleanor's hand tightened. "I'm so sorry," she whispered.

"I don't believe Lisette's accusation that her mother was the one to bring her son to the Earl of Gryffyn. I would guess that she dispensed with the child herself. Did you realize Gryffyn was the father of her son?"

"My mother told me everything on the journey home," she admitted.

"Lisette and my mother are quite similar. That is not

an excuse, but an explanation for why I so foolishly chose the one woman likely to wound my children to the core. And worse, I didn't see *you*; I threw away what you offered." His voice was lashed with self-hatred. "But I never, ever, thought of you as only good enough to bed, Eleanor. Never. I wanted you—more than I could even let myself know. More than I've ever wanted to be with a woman in my life."

Eleanor felt the corner of her mouth curl up.

"I—" He broke off, rose and held out his hand. "Lady Eleanor, would you care to continue our stroll?"

She took one more look at those beautiful gray eyes, drank deep of the emotion in them, stood up and opened her parasol again. She tucked her hand through her companion's arm.

"Do tell me, Lady Eleanor, why you have stayed in London now that the season is almost over?"

"I dislike the artificial boundary created by the season," she said, tilting her parasol so its pale silk lining cast its shadow over her face. "During the season people are all chasing after each other with matrimony on their minds. The grouse season starts in August, but I believe it is truly all the same."

"Although people do not always engage in a matrimonial pursuit," he added gravely, "but often in something less respectable. After all, many a wife seeks to avoid her husband. And gentlemen often pursue matrimony out of season."

"So you would say that when ladies are not hunting down gentlemen, they are engaged in hiding from them? Yes, that sounds reasonable."

"On occasion the gentleman must, like a hunter, employ subterfuge."

"Hiding in a blind built from willow?"

"A black coat and wig, or even a distant cousin's identity. There is a chess exhibition tomorrow in Hyde Park. As I understand it, you are a fine player in your own right. May I escort you?"

"What on earth is a chess exhibition?" Eleanor inquired.

"A demonstration," he said. "I gather that a number of England's best chess players will be pitted against each other for the edification and pleasure of the public."

"I have heard that the Duke of Villiers is the best player in England," she said, twirling her parasol. They were almost back at the carriage.

"Not so. The top two players are the Duke and Duchess of Beaumont."

"Will they participate in the exhibition?"

"I have no idea," he said. "I'm afraid that the doings of such elevated beings is quite outside the purview of Mr. Ormston."

"In that case," Eleanor said, "I shall be very pleased to accompany you, Mr. Ormston."


"How was it?" Anne demanded the moment Eleanor entered the house. "Oh, I can see from your face that it went well! You look happy again!" She pulled her into her arms. "You see? Men really are quite interchangeable. A woman merely needs to find the one who promises to adore her without being too irritating."

Eleanor smiled at her. "He asked me to accompany him to a chess exhibition tomorrow."

"Well, better you than me," Anne said. "How utterly tedious. You didn't talk about chess with Mr. Ormston, did you, Eleanor? He won't like it when he finds out how good you are. Men never like being beaten at games. If you play, you'll have to fudge it."

"I can do that," Eleanor said, and disappeared, rather dreamily, up the stairs.

Mr. Ormston's landau appeared the next afternoon, promptly at two. "I'm really not sure about this person," her mother said fretfully. "Anne, if you don't get away from the window, I shall bar you from this house. You'll have to ask him to tea, Eleanor. You can't continue to see this gentleman whom we haven't met."

"Oh, but you have met him, Mother," Eleanor said.

"I'm quite sure I have *not*!" the duchess retorted.

"It was some years ago . . . but of course one must make allowances for one's memory as the years pass."

The duchess threw her a glance of total revulsion. "I suppose I met the man. Ormston . . . it sounds vaguely familiar."

"I assure you that you did," Eleanor said, smiling widely.

Mr. Ormston was waiting by the landau, of course, and handed her up with the utmost courtesy. For a moment Eleanor thought that perhaps he was even courteous to a fault, but then she decided to simply enjoy it.

Hyde Park was crowded with open carriages and gentlefolk; every person in the *ton* seemed to be promenading, or waving from a carriage.

Mr. Ormston didn't appear to have that many acquaintances—though he did receive a few puzzled glances—but she, of course, saw many friends.

"The chess exhibition is on Buck Hill Walk," he said as his landau came to a halt.

Eleanor climbed down, dropping his hand the moment her toes touched the ground, as was proper.

A few moments later they found themselves watching a chess match between a Russian gentleman and an elegantly-clad young courtier. The courtier looked up and gave a little start. "Dashed if I didn't think for a moment that I recognized you, sir!" he said, laughing.

Mr. Ormston bowed without speaking, which was a

good idea because his voice was altogether too recognizable.

The Russian gentleman looked up for a moment and then back at the board with a faint smile.

"I'm demned if I haven't lost to you again, Potemkin," the courtier said discontentedly.

"Surely not," Eleanor said sweetly.

The young man took a good look at her extremely fetching walking dress, with particular attention to the low bodice, and quite visibly made up his mind to smile. He would have been surprised to learn that the exquisite lady before him considered his gesture condescending.

He rose and bowed, and even brought her gloved hand to his lips. "Alas, I am already despairing," he said, giving a charming little shrug.

Eleanor leaned forward and said, "Queen to Rook Four, then he'll move pawn to King's Rook Three. You take his pawn with your bishop, he will recapture. Then you play Queen takes pawn. His King is laid open and your attack is invulnerable."

The man blinked.

"Dear me," Mr. Ormston said with a glance at the sun, "it's looking alarmingly cloudy."

The courtier sat down.

"You are a formidable opponent," Leopold said as they walked on.

"He might still lose," Eleanor said.

"If he misplays the attack."

"My dear Mr. Ormston," Eleanor cried. "Surely you jest. The moves are devious. White simply brings his pieces to bear on the denuded King, one by one."

"I must be distracted," he said.

Eleanor threw him a teasing glance. "My sister gave me firm instructions not to play chess with you, for I may frighten you. Are you afraid, Mr. Ormston?"

"Yes."

They walked a pace or two and then she took his hand. "Leopold?"

He spun her off the path and behind a thick lilac hedge so quickly that she didn't breathe. "I'm afraid, Eleanor. I'm afraid that you don't love me as much as I love you. I'm afraid that you won't believe me, that you'll think I want you merely for the benefit of my children. And oh God, Eleanor, I'm afraid I can't live without you."

She reached out and slowly, very slowly, undid the pearl buttons on his very proper right glove. Then she peeled back the heavy gray silk—far too fine, really, for a plain Mr. Ormston—and gently pulled it off his hand.

She raised his hand, still without meeting his eyes, and kissed each finger. They trembled slightly in hers. She turned over his hand and pressed her lips to his palm. Only then did she meet his eyes. "I am not afraid, because I love you. And I will always love you. Always. Your love stands between me and fear."

His face transformed itself—without a smile, of course. Then before she realized what was happening, he went down on one knee.

"Leopold—"

"Will you do me the inexpressible honor, Lady Eleanor, of becoming my wife?"

"Yes," she whispered. "Oh yes, I will, I will."

Then he was on his feet again and holding her tightly, and kissing her with that sort of passionate force that made Leopold . . . Leopold.

"I have a ring in honor of our betrothal," he said some time later.

Eleanor was nestled against his chest, his arm around her.

"You may not feel it is fit for a duchess," he said, just a touch of doubt in his voice.

She opened her eyes to find that he had pulled the glove from her left hand and was sliding a ring over her finger. It was made of pale gold, shaped into the petals of a lily, with a beautiful diamond in the center. It was neither ostentatious nor lavishly ornamental. It was the kind of ring that delicately heralded true love. It was elegant; it was subtle. It was everything the Duke of Villiers wasn't, and Mr. Ormston was.

Tears welled in her eyes. She put her arms around his neck. "Oh, Leo," she said, "it's absolutely perfect."

Had she ever thought his eyes were cold? "I could get you a marquise-cut diamond as big as—as a mouse," he said. "If you would prefer?"

"So I could impress everyone with my glittering rodent?" She managed to smile even though tears were slipping down her cheeks. "This is utterly perfect."

"May I speak to your father?"

She couldn't help laughing a little. "He returns on the *Saint Esprit,* due to dock tomorrow, if it's on course."

He wiped away her tears and replaced her glove. Then they stepped out from behind the hedge and decorously made their way back to the carriage.

When Eleanor walked through her front door, she almost felt as if the past hour had not happened. Her hair was unmussed. Apparently Mr. Ormston did not believe in twisting his hands into a lady's coiffure when he kissed her. He had kissed her . . . but only on the lips.

Anne looked up. "Why—Why—"

Eleanor smiled and took off her glove.

"But you've seen him only twice!" Anne shrieked. "Oh, what an utterly darling ring!" She froze. "Eleanor, I've seen this ring." Her voice was hushed. "Your Mr. Ormston is—is quite extravagant."

"What do you mean?" Eleanor said, looking lovingly down at the ring. "I have certainly seen bigger diamonds."

"It has been on display at Stedman and Vardan, the jewelers on New Bond Street for over a month—because it belonged to Queen Elizabeth, until she threw it to Sir Walter Raleigh after a jousting tournament. The diamond in the middle is one of the finest examples of a European cut that Mr. Stedman has ever seen . . ." Her eyes grew round. "Eleanor, what sort of fortune could Mr. Ormston have inherited?"

She couldn't stop laughing. It was so like her own, darling Leopold. He had found the one ring in England that would suit both of them. "Would you say that this ring cost more than a marquise-cut diamond?" she asked Anne.

"Why . . . why this ring probably cost more than ten such rings, Eleanor! He must love you so much." She peered at the ring, awed. "He must have thought of nothing but you for the last three years."

"Not exactly," Eleanor said, beaming. "Not exactly."

# Chapter Thirty-three

*London residence of the Duke of Montague*
*September 14, 1784*

"**Y**our Grace," the Duchess of Montague said, bestowing a measured smile on the man who, in a matter of two days, would become her son-in-law. "I suppose you would like to see Eleanor. She is in the morning room, and I shall allow you to go there on your own."

The duchess's visitors, Lady Festle and Mrs. Quinkhardt, smiled at the duke and then sighed at the look in his eye.

He was almost out the door when the duchess called after him. "My daughter tells me that you plan to bring her yet another betrothal gift."

The Duke of Villiers bowed, with a great deal of address. "I did promise. And I have it with me this morning, Your Grace."

The duchess must be forgiven if her smile was a trifle gloating. For, as she explained to her bosom companions, the Duke of Villiers was courting her daughter in a manner that was truly above reproach. "He never engages in the slightest indiscretion," she told them. "They say there's nothing as prudish as a reformed rake, and though I wouldn't have believed it myself, I believe it now! He doesn't even dance with her more than twice or at most three times." She lowered her voice. "One can sense if a young couple engages in inappropriate behavior, and I can assure you . . . they never do!"

All of London was discussing the ring, naturally, and the duchess's chest swelled with pride as she confirmed to Lady Festle that her dearest daughter Eleanor was indeed wearing a diamond ring that had previously been worn by Queen Elizabeth. "I am most curious about that betrothal gift," she told them. "I'll give them ten minutes . . . more than enough. Perhaps there is a diadem to match the ring!"

Eleanor looked up from a note she was writing to Lisette, commiserating over the fact the orphanage was being moved to Hampshire, when Villiers entered the room and closed the door behind him.

Since their betrothal, he had settled on a style somewhere between himself and Mr. Ormston. "You needn't," she had said, laughing, when he first appeared without a wig—but still clad in subdued black velvet. Magnificent black velvet, but without even a touch of embroidery, and certainly no gold buttons.

"I don't do it for you," he had said, imperturbable as ever. "It's the children. They are so wildly disrespectful when I appear in full court dress that I have adopted the path of least resistance."

Now he walked forward with that little secret smile of his.

"Leopold," she said, dancing into his arms and then, because he was so very well-behaved, pulling his head down and demanding a kiss. One of his kisses. One of those that sent them both into a spin of heat and pleasure and desire.

"I have brought you a betrothal present," he said, catching his breath and starting to unbutton his very proper coat.

"You mustn't! My—" But her voice broke off.

For Leopold had pulled back his coat and there . . . there . . .

Eleanor reached out her hands. "How beautiful!"

With the kind of smile that she never saw on his face— let alone in his eyes—before their betrothal, he pulled a very small, sleeping puppy from his inside pocket. It was a pug . . . probably. It didn't even open its eyes, just gave a little sleeping snore.

Eleanor took the puppy in her arms, whispering so she didn't wake it. "I've never seen anything so wonderful! Look at its little round tummy." She lifted the tiny dog up to her cheek. "Its fur feels like black velvet. And it smells just like milky puppy . . . Oh Leopold, you couldn't have given me a present that I would love more."

"Her name is Lettuce," her betrothed observed. "A number of different names were bandied about, but Lucinda's choice won. Of course you may prefer a more elegant name."

"Lettuce," Eleanor breathed. "It's perfect for her."

"You see, Lucinda said that her little ears are as soft as pieces of lettuce," Leopold said, holding up the tiniest scrap of velvet Eleanor had ever seen.

"One can hardly call that an ear," she said, giggling. "She's such a darling."

"I'm afraid her nap will give you a false impression of that puppy," Leo said, curling his hand around Eleanor's cheek. Lettuce yawned, showing needle-sharp little teeth, and opened her eyes. "My personal name of choice was Cassandra."

"Cassandra?" Eleanor held a suddenly wiggling bundle of fur up to her face so she could look into Lettuce's bright eyes. "Why such a long name for a tiny dog? You don't have bad news to tell us, do you, Lettuce?"

"Yap!" Lettuce said, struggling to lick Eleanor's chin. "Yap, yap, yap, yap, yap!"

"Oh my goodness," Eleanor said. "You *do* have a lot to say."

"Yap!" Lettuce repeated.

Many times.

Eleanor put her down and discovered that Lettuce had mastered the art of running in circles and barking at the same time, something Oyster never managed. "She's so intelligent," she said, turning in Leo's arms so she could see his face.

"She certainly is expressive," Leo murmured, looking down at her. She knew the expression burning in his eyes. And if she hadn't known what it meant, she could feel it thrumming throughout her body. "I can't last another two days," he said conversationally. "These have been the longest weeks of my life."

Eleanor put a kiss on his chin and another on the very edge of his mouth. "You want to make love to me in my mother's sitting room?"

He groaned.

He really had been very, very good.

"Now that I have a new puppy, I shall have to take her for walks in the back gardens, even during the night," she informed him. "Thank goodness, the nights are so unseasonably warm."

Leopold froze.

"I shall walk her at two o'clock in the morning. All the way out to the little summerhouse at the end of the gardens . . . and back."

"Ah," he said, and for just one moment pulled her hard against his body. Then he backed up and bowed. When her mother entered, he was kissing the very tips of her fingers.

"Why, Duke," the duchess called gaily. "May I see your betrothal gift? I confess I am all agog."

"Certainly, Duchess," he said, bowing to her as well. "Here it is."

Truly, his manners are beyond reproach, the duchess thought happily—until she turned her eyes in the direction of the duke's pointing finger.

At the little dog, squatting on the Aubusson rug.

It was fortunate for the duchess's heart that she didn't happen to glance out of her bedchamber window in the middle of the night. If she had added to the horror of seeing her beloved rug serving, once again, as an impromptu chamber pot, the anguish of seeing her eldest daughter dash stark naked out of the summerhouse, chased by her oh-so-proper fiancé (in a similar state of undress), well . . . it might have been too much for her.

But as it was, the household slumbered peacefully, while the two happiest people in it danced in the rain until Leo managed to catch his wife-to-be and hold her still long enough to kiss her . . . and kiss her . . . and kiss her again.

# Epilogue

*Seven years later*

It was the Duchess of Villiers's birthday.

When Eleanor was growing up, her mother had, by all indications, no birthday. When one makes the decision not to age, birthdays are a necessary sacrifice. When Leopold was growing up, for all he knew his mother might well have celebrated all night long, but she had certainly never invited her children to participate.

Eleanor's thirtieth birthday was of a different sort. The South Parlor of the Duke of Villiers's country house in Essex—as opposed to his houses in Norfolk, Wiltshire, and Devon, not to mention Castle Cary, which had presumably tumbled into an elegant heap—was exploding with excitement. Tobias was in one corner, doing last minute work on the parts for their game of charades, an annual tradition since 1785.

A knot of dogs was frolicking in another corner. A naughty puppy named Muffin was being watched over by his mother. "Yap!" she warned him as he tugged on the curtains. "Yap, Yap!" Muffin shook his head back and forth, pretending he couldn't hear her. *"Woof,"* his father added, waking up, and Muffin let go of the curtain altogether. His father went back to sleep while his mother launched into a loving, high-pitched diatribe that covered everything from curtains to grooming. Not that Muffin paid much attention.

In a third corner, the duchess was sitting on a snug sofa, nursing a baby. In her delightfully full, chaotic, and joyful seven years of marriage, no babies had joined the household until Theodore came along.

Which explained why Phoebe (who used to be called Phyllinda) and Lucinda (who liked her name just fine) were sitting closely on either side of their mother. Not that the girls had generally been far from their mother's vicinity in the last year. At age twelve, they could sense the slight chill wind that signaled the end of childhood. This last month in particular they had hardly stirred from Eleanor's side, so fascinated by gummy smiles and plump toes that the twins, who never fought, found themselves squabbling over the privilege of holding their brother.

"May I hold Theodore now?" Lucinda asked. "Please? It looks like he's *finally* done eating. I never thought anyone could drink milk for so long! I don't even like milk."

"It's different for babies," Eleanor said, lifting roly-poly Theo over her shoulder. He let out a satisfied burp.

"But it's my turn," Phoebe said, intervening in her quiet way.

"No, it's *my* turn," her father said, scooping the baby off his wife's shoulder and swinging him into the air.

Theodore burst into a storm of giggles. He was adorable in the way that deeply loved babies are: bald, fat, and altogether scrumptious.

"You girls need to start planning for charades," the duke said, looking down at his daughters. "Tobias has finished writing all of the parts and he's handing them out."

"Last year he made me be Lucifer, from *Paradise Lost*," Lucinda said resentfully.

"Your fault," Phoebe said, laughing. "You shouldn't have played that trick on him when he came home from Oxford for the summer. You know he's particular about his clothing."

"I just wish he'd let *me* pick out parts some time," Lucinda said. "I'd make him play an old beggar woman. Or *Puss in Boots*! He would have to put on paper ears and a tail, or he would never win. Can you imagine? Tobias would rather die than be so undignified!"

"Come on," Phoebe said, grabbing her hand. "Let's go, because if we get a wish from Mama for winning, we can say that we want Theo all tomorrow afternoon."

Lucinda's eyes brightened and they trotted off.

The duke slipped into the place next to his wife, holding Theo's hands so the bowlegged babe could practice sitting upright in his lap.

"He's the best birthday present you ever gave me," Eleanor said, leaning her head against his shoulder.

"It's true that he's three months old," Leopold said, grinning at Theodore. "But I think of him more as your present to me."

"Oh no," Eleanor said. "I have very, very clear memories of my birthday last year. And naturally, I expect that you plan to top your performance. Practice," she said demurely, "makes perfect."

Her husband shot her a wicked glance, full of laughter— and desire. "After the charades or before?"

"Before," she whispered, leaning over and brushing a kiss on his jaw.

"Tobias!" Leo shouted, leaping to his feet.

His eldest son, a sleek, brilliant version of himself, strolled over.

"Take this scrap," Leo said, dumping Theo unceremoniously into Tobias's arms. "Whatever you do, don't let Phoebe and Lucinda start fighting over him."

Theodore reached up and grabbed at his big brother's chin, giving him his best toothless smile.

"Did he burp?" Tobias asked sternly. He had quickly learned that sartorial standards can be severely threatened by leaky babies.

"Yes," Eleanor said, taking her husband's hand. "Thank you, sweetheart."

"The charades begin in one hour," Tobias said, not letting on with even the tiniest smile that he might have some idea what his beautiful stepmother and adoring father meant to do in the interim.

"We should be fine with that," Leo said, grinning down at Eleanor. Unlike his son, he'd lost his ability to appear emotionless.

But he did wait until he was out of the parlor to pick up the duchess in his arms and carry her up the stairs.

# Historical Note

My literary debts in this book are numerous. Shakespeare makes several appearances, with particular reference to Sonnet 116. But the unnamed hero of *A Duke of Her Own* is Lord Byron, who lent the English version of his French play, *Salomé*, to Sir Roland. I feel quite certain that he would have resented my gift of his sensual lines to such a young and foolish man. In my defense, Byron himself was not yet forty when *Salomé* was written.

The inspiration for—and some of the invective in—the scene featuring Mrs. Zeal-of-the-Land Busy sprang from a play written by Shakespeare's contemporary, Ben Jonson. *Bartholomew Fair* puts Zeal-of-the-Land Busy in the stocks; I gave him both a funeral and a wife, and in this case I would venture to say that Ben Jonson would not disapprove.

And finally, Lisette sings a version of an old lullaby, "Hush-a-bye Baby," that has mixed ancestry. When my son Luca was born, fourteen years ago, he liked to be sung to sleep. One night I was singing that lullaby when my stepmother peeked in. I confessed to her that I didn't really like the song because it ends with the baby plummeting from the treetop.

She sang two lines of a second verse for me, but couldn't remember any more. So during those long evenings of singing to a fretful baby, I wrote another two lines. I'm including the whole lullaby below, in the hopes that perhaps some of you are still lucky enough to be singing small, delicious-smelling scraps to sleep.

> *Hush-a-bye Baby, on the treetop,*
> *When the wind blows, the cradle will rock.*
> *When the bough breaks, the cradle will fall,*
> *Down will come Baby, cradle and all.*
> *Mama will catch you, give you a squeeze.*
> *Send you back up, to play in the trees.*
> *When twilight falls, and birds seek their nests,*
> *Come home to the one who loves you the best.*

*At Avon Books, we know your passion for romance—once you finish one of our novels, you find yourself wanting more.*

May we tempt you with . . .

- **Excerpts** from our upcoming releases.

- Entertaining **extras,** including authors' personal photo albums and book lists.

- Behind-the-scenes **scoop** on your favorite characters and series.

- **Sweepstakes** for the chance to win free books, romantic getaways, and other fun prizes.

- Writing **tips** from our authors and editors.

- **Blog** with our authors and find out why they love to write romance.

- **Exclusive content** that's not contained within the pages of our novels.

Join us at
**www.avonbooks.com**